Praise for *Deacon King Kong*

'*eacon King Kong* is deeply felt, beautifully written and profoundly humane; McBride's ability to inhabit his characters' foibled, all-too-human interiority helps transform a fine book into a great one.'

New York Times Book Review

'A hilarious, pitch-perfect comedy set in the Brooklyn projects of the late 1960s. This alone may qualify it as one of the year's best novels.'

Washington Post

'The sheer volume of invention in *Deacon King Kong* commands awe . . . And the sentences! The prose radiates a kind of chain-reaction energy.'

New Yorker

'James McBride's *Deacon King Kong* is a feverish love letter to New York City, people, and writing . . . full of heart, humor, and compassion . . . I say we give him another National Book Award for this one. It's that good.'

NPR

'*Deacon King Kong* reaffirms James McBride's position among the greatest American storytellers of our time.'

BookPage

'Dazzling, spiritually rich.'

Oprah Magazine

'McBride's hilarious dialogue and an attention to detail reveals a complex local history. Capturing humanity through satire and witticisms, McBride draws everyday heroes.'

Time

'McBride is operating in the realm of social allegory, a lineage that extends back through generations of writers: Ralph Ellison, Terry Southern, Darius James.'

Los Angeles Times

'*Deacon King Kong* cements McBride as a master storyteller.'

Shelf Awareness

www.penguin.co.uk

James McBride is the author of the award-winning *New York Times* bestsellers *The Color of Water* and *The Good Lord Bird*, which is currently being made into a television series starring Ethan Hawke. His other publications include *Miracle at St. Anna, Song Yet Sung, Kill 'Em and Leave* and *Five-Carat Soul*. A former reporter for the *Washington Post* and *People* magazine, McBride holds a master's degree in journalism from Columbia University and a BA from Oberlin College. In 2015 he was awarded the National Humanities Medal by President Barack Obama.

DEACON
KING KONG

JAMES McBRIDE

doubleday

TRANSWORLD PUBLISHERS
Penguin Random House, One Embassy Gardens,
8 Viaduct Gardens, London SW11 7BW
www.penguin.co.uk

Transworld is part of the Penguin Random House group of companies
whose addresses can be found at global.penguinrandomhouse.com

Penguin
Random House
UK

· First published in the United States of America by Riverhead Books
an imprint of Penguin Random House LLC

First published in Great Britain in 2020 by Doubleday
an imprint of Transworld Publishers

A CIP catalogue record for this book
is available from the British Library.

ISBNs
9780857527653 (hb)
9780857527660 (tpb)

Printed and bound in Great Britain by Clays Ltd, Elcograf S.p.A.

Penguin Random House is committed to a sustainable
future for our business, our readers and our planet. This book
is made from Forest Stewardship Council® certified paper.

MIX
Paper from
responsible sources
FSC® C018179

1 3 5 7 9 10 8 6 4 2

For God's people—all of 'em

CONTENTS

DEACON
KING KONG

1

JESUS'S CHEESE

DEACON CUFFY LAMBKIN OF FIVE ENDS BAPTIST CHURCH became a walking dead man on a cloudy September afternoon in 1969. That's the day the old deacon, known as Sportcoat to his friends, marched out to the plaza of the Causeway Housing Projects in South Brooklyn, stuck an ancient .38 Colt in the face of a nineteen-year-old drug dealer named Deems Clemens, and pulled the trigger.

There were a lot of theories floating around the projects as to why old Sportcoat—a wiry, laughing brown-skinned man who had coughed, wheezed, hacked, guffawed, and drank his way through the Cause Houses for a good part of his seventy-one years—shot the most ruthless drug dealer the projects had ever seen. He had no enemies. He had coached the projects baseball team for fourteen years. His late wife, Hettie, had been the Christmas Club treasurer of his church. He was a peaceful man beloved by all. So what happened?

The morning after the shooting, the daily gathering of retired city workers, flophouse bums, bored housewives, and ex-convicts who congregated in the middle of the projects at the park bench near the flagpole to sip free coffee and salute Old Glory as it was raised to the sky had all kinds of theories about why old Sportcoat did it.

"Sportcoat had rheumatic fever," declared Sister Veronica Gee, the president of the Cause Houses Tenant Association and wife of the minister at Five Ends Baptist Church, where Sportcoat had served for fifteen years. She told the gathering that Sportcoat was planning to preach his first-ever sermon that upcoming Friends and Family Day at Five Ends Baptist, titled "Don't Eat the Dressing Without Confessing." She also threw in that the church's Christmas Club money was missing, "but if Sportcoat took it, it was on account of that fever," she noted.

Sister T. J. Billings, known affectionately as "Bum-Bum," head usher at Five Ends, whose ex-husband was the only soul in that church's storied history to leave his wife for a man and live to tell about it (he moved to Alaska), had her own theory. She said Sportcoat shot Deems because the mysterious ants had returned to Building 9. "Sportcoat," she said grimly, "is under an evil spell. There's a mojo about."

Miss Izi Cordero, vice president of the Puerto Rican Statehood Society of the Cause Houses, who had actually been standing just thirty feet away when Sportcoat pointed his ancient peashooter at Deems's skull and cut loose, said the whole ruckus started because Sportcoat was blackmailed by a certain "evil Spanish gangster," and she knew exactly who that gangster was and planned to tell the cops all about him. Of course everybody knew she was talking about her Dominican ex-husband, Joaquin, who was the only honest numbers runner in the projects, and that she and her Joaquin hated each other's guts and each had worked to get the other arrested for the last twenty years. So there was that.

Hot Sausage, the Cause Houses janitor and Sportcoat's best friend, who raised the flag each morning and doled out free coffee care of the Cause Houses Senior Center, told the gathering that Sportcoat shot

Deems on account of the annual baseball game between the Cause Houses and their rival, the Watch Houses, being canceled two years before. "Sportcoat," he said proudly, "is the only umpire both teams allowed."

But it was Dominic Lefleur, the Haitian Cooking Sensation, who lived in Sportcoat's building, who best summed up everybody's feelings. Dominic had just returned from a nine-day visit to see his mother in Port-au-Prince, where he contracted and then passed around the usual strange Third World virus that floored half his building, sending residents crapping and puking and avoiding him for days—though the virus never seemed to affect him. Dominic saw the whole stupid travesty through his bathroom window as he was shaving. He walked into his kitchen, sat down to eat lunch with his teenage daughter, who was quaking with a temperature of 103, and said, "I always knew old Sportcoat would do one great thing in life."

The fact is, no one in the projects really knew why Sportcoat shot Deems—not even Sportcoat himself. The old deacon could no more explain why he shot Deems than he could explain why the moon looked like it was made of cheese, or why fruit flies come and go, or how the city dyed the waters of the nearby Causeway Harbor green every St. Paddy's Day. The night before, he'd dreamed of his wife, Hettie, who had vanished during the great snowstorm of 1967. Sportcoat loved to tell that story to his friends.

"It was a beautiful day," he said. "The snow came down like ashes from the sky. It was just a big, white blanket. The projects was so peaceful and clean. Me and Hettie ate some crabs that night, then stood by the window and watched the Statue of Liberty in the harbor. Then we went to sleep.

"In the middle of the night, she shook me woke. I opened my eyes and seen a light floating 'round the room. It was like a little candlelight.

'Round and 'round it went, then out the door. Hettie said, 'That's God's light. I got to fetch some moonflowers out the harbor.' She put on her coat and followed it outside."

When asked why he didn't go to the nearby Causeway Harbor after her, Sportcoat was incredulous. "She was following God's light," he said. "Plus, the Elephant was out there."

He had a point. Tommy Elefante, the Elephant, was a heavyset, brooding Italian who favored ill-fitting suits and ran his construction and trucking businesses out of an old railroad boxcar at the harbor pier two blocks from the Cause Houses and just a block from Sportcoat's church. The Elephant and his silent, grim Italians, who worked in the dead of night hauling God knows what in and out of that boxcar, were a mystery. They scared the shit out of everybody. Not even Deems, evil as he was, fooled with them.

So Sportcoat waited till the next morning to look for Hettie. It was Sunday. He rose early. The project residents were still asleep and the freshly fallen snow was largely untouched. He followed her tracks to the pier, where they ended at the water's edge. Sportcoat stared out over the water and saw a raven flying high overhead. "It was beautiful," he told his friends. "It circled a few times, then flew high up and was gone." He watched the bird till it was out of sight, then trudged back through the snow to the tiny cinder-block structure that was Five Ends Baptist Church, whose small congregation was gathering for its eight a.m. service. He walked in just as Reverend Gee, standing at his pulpit in front of the church's sole source of heat, an old woodstove, was reading off the Sick and Shut-in Prayer List.

Sportcoat took a seat in a pew amid a few sleepy worshippers, picked up a tiny one-sheet church program, and scrawled in a shaky hand, "Hettie," then handed it to the usher, Sister Gee, who was dressed in white. She walked it up to her husband and handed it to him just as Pastor Gee began reading the list out loud. The list was always long, and it usually bore the same names anyway: this one sick in Dallas, that one dying out in Queens someplace, and of course Sister Paul, an original founder of Five Ends. She was 102, and had been living in an old folks' home way out in Bensonhurst so long that only two people in the congregation actually remembered her. In fact there was some question as to whether Sister Paul was still alive, and there was some general noise in the congregation that maybe somebody—like the pastor—ought to ride out there and check. "I would go," Pastor Gee said, "but I like my teeth." Everybody knew the white folks in Bensonhurst weren't fond of the Negro. Besides, the pastor noted cheerfully, Sister Paul's tithes of $4.13 came by mail faithfully every month, and that was a good sign.

Standing at his pulpit mumbling down the Sick and Shut-in Prayer List, Pastor Gee received the paper bearing Hettie's name without a blink. When he read out her name he smiled and quipped, "Git in your soul, brother. A working wife is good for life!" It was a funny dig at Sportcoat, who hadn't held a steady job in years, while Hettie raised their only child and still worked a job. Reverend Gee was a handsome, good-natured man who liked a joke, though at the time he was fresh off scandal himself, having recently been spotted over at Silky's Bar on Van Marl Street trying to convert a female subway conductor with boobs the size of Milwaukee. He was on thin ice with the congregation because of it, so when no one laughed, his face grew stern and he read Hettie's name aloud, then sang "Somebody's Calling My Name." The congregation joined in and they all sang and prayed and Sportcoat felt better. So did Reverend Gee.

That night Hettie still didn't come home. Two days later, the Elephant's men discovered Hettie floating near the shore at the pier, her face gently draped with a scarf she'd worn around her neck when she left the apartment. They pulled her out of the bay, wrapped her in a wool blanket, laid her gently on a large tuft of clean, white snow near the boxcar, then sent for Sportcoat. When he got there, they handed him a fifth of scotch without a word, called the cops, and then vanished. The Elephant wanted no confusion. Hettie was not one of his. Sportcoat understood.

Hettie's funeral was the usual death extravaganza at Five Ends Baptist. Pastor Gee was an hour late to the service because gout had swollen his feet so badly he couldn't get his church shoes on. The funeral director, old white-haired Morris Hurly, whom everybody called Hurly Girly behind his back because, well . . . everybody knew Morris was . . . well, he was cheap and talented and always two hours late with the body, but everybody knew Hettie would look like a million bucks, which she did. The delay gave Pastor Gee a chance to preside over a hank between the ushers about the flower arrangements. No one knew where to put them. Hettie had been the one who always figured out where the flowers went, placing the geraniums in this corner, and the roses near this pew, and the azaleas by the stained-glass window to comfort this or that family. But today Hettie was the guest of honor, which meant the flowers were scattered helter-skelter, just where the deliverymen dropped them, so it took Sister Gee, stepping in as usual, to figure that out. Meanwhile Sister Bibb, the voluptuous church organist, who at fifty-five years old was thick-bodied, smooth and brown as a chocolate candy bar, arrived in terrible shape. She was coming off her once-a-year sin jamboree, an all-night, two-fisted, booze-guzzling, swig-faced affair of delicious tongue-in-groove-licking and love-smacking with her sometimes boyfriend, Hot Sausage, until Sausage withdrew from the festivities for lack of endurance. "Sister Bibb," he once complained to Sportcoat, "is a grinder, and I don't mean organ." She arrived with a pounding headache and a sore shoulder from some kind of tugging from last night's howling bliss. She sat at her organ in a stupor, her head resting on the keys, as the congregation wandered in. After a few minutes, she left the sanctuary and headed for the basement ladies' room, hoping it was empty. But she stumbled down the stairs on the way and twisted her ankle badly. She suffered the injury without blasphemy or complaint, vomited last night's revelry into the toilet of the empty bathroom, refreshed her lipstick and checked her hair, then returned to the sanctuary, where she played the whole service with her ankle swollen to the size of a cantaloupe. She limped back to her apartment afterward, furious and repentant, spitting venom at Hot Sausage, who had gotten his breath back from the previous night's tumble and now wanted more. He followed her home like a puppy, lingering half a block behind her, crouching behind the mulberry bushes that lined the projects' walkways. Every time Sister Bibb looked over her shoulder and saw Hot Sausage's porkpie hat protruding over the bushes, she flew into a rage.

"Git gone, varmint," she snapped. "I'm done merryin' with you!"

Sportcoat, however, arrived at the church in great shape, having spent the previous night celebrating Hettie's life with his buddy Rufus Harley, who was from his hometown and was his second-best friend in Brooklyn after Hot Sausage. Rufus was janitor at the nearby Watch Houses just a few blocks off, and while he and Hot Sausage didn't get along—Rufus was from South Carolina, while Sausage hailed from Alabama—Rufus made a special blend of white lightning known as King Kong that everyone, even Hot Sausage, enjoyed.

Sportcoat didn't like the name of Rufus's specialty and over the years had proposed several names for it. "You could sell this stuff like hoecakes if it weren't named after a gorilla," he said once. "Why not call it Nellie's Nightcap, or Gideon's Sauce?" But Rufus always scoffed at the notions. "I used to call it Sonny Liston," he said, referring to the feared Negro heavyweight champ whose hammer-like fists knocked opponents out cold, "till Muhammad Ali come along." Sportcoat had to agree that by whatever name, Rufus's white lightning was the best in Brooklyn.

The night had been long and merry with talk of their hometown of Possum Point, and the next morning Sportcoat was in fine shape, seated in the first pew of Five Ends Baptist, smiling as the ladies in white fussed over him and the two best singers in the choir got into a fight over the church's sole microphone. Church fights are normally hushed, hissy affairs, full of quiet backstabbing, intrigue, and whispered gossip about bad rice and beans. But this spat was public, the best kind. The two choir members involved, Nanette and Sweet Corn, known as the Cousins, were both thirty-three, beautiful, and wonderful singers. They had been raised as sisters, still lived together, and had recently had a terrible spat about a worthless young man from the projects named Pudding. The results were fantastic. The two took their rage at each other out on the music, each trying to outdo the other, hollering with glorious savagery about the coming redemption of our mighty King and Savior, Jesus the Christ of Nazareth.

Reverend Gee, inspired by the sight of the Cousins' lovely breasts swelling beneath their robes as they roared, followed with a thunderous eulogy to make up for his joke about Hettie when she was already dead in the harbor, which made the whole thing the best home-going service Five Ends Baptist had seen in years.

Sportcoat watched it all in awe, reveling in the spectacle with delight, marveling at the Willing Workers in their white dresses and fancy hats who scurried about and fussed over him and his son, Pudgy Fingers, who sat next to him. Pudgy Fingers, twenty-six, blind, and said to be half a loaf short in his mind, had evolved from childhood fat to sweet slimness, his etched chocolate features hidden by expensive dark glasses donated by some long-forgotten social service agency worker. He ignored everything as usual, though he didn't eat afterward at the church meal, which wasn't normal for Pudgy Fingers. But Sportcoat loved it. "It was wonderful," he told his friends after the service. "Hettie would have loved it."

That night he dreamed of Hettie, and like he often did in the evenings when she was alive, he told her the titles of sermons he planned to preach one day, which usually amused her, since he always had the titles but never the content: "God Bless the Cow," and "I Thank Him for the

Corn," and "'Boo!' Said the Chicken." But that night she seemed irritated, sitting in a chair in a purple dress, her legs crossed, listening with a frown as he talked, so he brought her up to date on the cheery news of her funeral. He told her how beautiful her service was, the flowers, the food, the speeches, and the music, and how happy he was that she had received her wings and gone on to her reward, though she could have left him a little advice about how he could get hold of her Social Security. Didn't she know it was a pain to stand in line downtown at the Social Security office all day? And what about the Christmas Club money she collected, where the members of Five Ends put away money every week so they could buy Christmas gifts in December for their kids? Hettie was the treasurer, but she had never said where she hid the money.

"Everybody asking about their jack," he said. "You shoulda told where you hid it."

Hettie ignored the question as she fluffed at a wrinkled spot in her bodice. "Stop talking to the child in me," she said. "You been talking to the child in me fifty-one years."

"Where's the money?"

"Check your poop hole, you drinking dog!"

"We got some chips in there, too, y'know!"

"We?" She smirked. "You ain't throwed a dime in there in twenty years, you joy-juice-swillin', lazy, no-good bum!" She stood up, and just like that they were off, arguing like the old days, a catfight that developed into the usual roaring, fire-breathing, ass-out brawl that continued after he awoke, with her following him around as usual, with her hands on her hips, tossing zingers while he tried to walk away, snapping back responses over his shoulder. They argued that day and the next, fussing right through breakfast, lunch, and into the next day. To an outsider, Sportcoat appeared to be talking to walls as he went about his usual duties: down into the projects boiler room for a quick snort with Hot Sausage, back up the stairs to apartment 4G, out again to take Pudgy

Fingers to where the bus picked him up to take him to the blind people's social center, then out to work his usual odd jobs, and then back home again. Wherever he went, the two of them fussed. Or at least Sportcoat did. The neighbors could not see Hettie, of course: they just stared at him talking to someone nobody could see. Sportcoat paid them no mind when they stared. Fussing with Hettie was the most natural thing in the world to do. He'd done it for forty years.

He couldn't believe it. Gone was the tender, shy, sweet little thing that giggled back in Possum Point when they slipped into the high corn of her daddy's garden and he poured wine down her shirt and thumbed her boobs. Now she was all New York: insolent, mouthy, and fresh, appearing out of nowhere at the oddest times of the day, and each time wearing a new damn wig on her head, which, he suspected, was something she'd received from the Lord as a gift for her life struggles. The morning he shot Deems she'd appeared as a redhead, which startled him, and worse, she flew into a rage when he asked, for the umpteenth time, about the Christmas Club money.

"Woman, where's them dollars? I got to come up with them people's chips."

"I ain't got to tell it."

"That's stealing!"

"Look who's talking. The cheese thief!"

That last crack stung him. For years, the New York City Housing Authority, a mega-mass of bloated bureaucracy, a hotbed of grift, graft, games, payola bums, deadbeat dads, payoff racketeers, and old-time political appointees who lorded over the Cause Houses and every other one of New York's forty-five housing projects with arrogant inefficiency, had inexplicably belched forth a phenomenal gem of a gift to the Cause Houses: free cheese. Who pushed the button, who filled out the paperwork, who made the cheese magically appear, no one knew—not even Bum-Bum, who made it her *cause d'être* for years to find out the origin of the cheese. The assumption was it came from Housing, but nobody was stupid enough to awaken that beast by calling downtown to ask. Why bother? The cheese was free. It came like clockwork for years, every first Saturday of the month, arriving like magic in the wee hours in Hot Sausage's boiler room in the basement of Building 17. Ten crates of it, freshly chilled in five-pound hunks. This wasn't plain old housing-projects "cheese food"; nor was it some smelly, curdled, reluctant Swiss cheese material snatched from a godforsaken bodega someplace, gathering mold in some dirty display case while mice gnawed at it nightly, to be sold to some sucker fresh from Santo Domingo. This was fresh, rich, heavenly, succulent, soft, creamy, kiss-my-ass, cows-gotta-die-for-this, delightfully salty, moo-ass, good old white folks cheese, cheese to die for, cheese to make you happy, cheese to beat the cheese boss, cheese for the big cheese, cheese to end the world, cheese so good it inspired a line every first Saturday of the month: mothers, daughters, fathers, grand-parents, disabled in wheelchairs, kids, relatives from out of town, white folks from nearby Brooklyn Heights, and even South American workers from the garbage-processing plant on Concord Avenue, all patiently standing in a line that stretched from the interior of Hot Sausage's boiler room to Building 17's outer doorway, up the ramp to the sidewalk, curling around the side of the building and to the plaza near the flagpole. The unlucky ones at the end of the line were forced to constantly watch over their shoulders for the cops—free or not, something this good had to have an angle—while the ones near the front of the line salivated and edged forward anxiously, hoping the supply would last, knowing that to get within sight of the cheese and then witness the supply run out was akin to experiencing sudden coitus interruptus.

Naturally, Sportcoat's affinity with the very important distributor of that item, Hot Sausage, guaranteed him a hunk no matter what the demand, which was always good news for him and Hettie. Hettie especially loved that cheese. So her crack about it infuriated him.

"You ate that cheese, didn't you?" Sportcoat said. "You ate it like a butcher's dog every time. Stolen or not. You liked it."

"It was from Jesus."

That drove him wild, and he harangued her till she disappeared. Their fights, in the weeks previous to the shooting, had become so heated he had begun to rehearse his arguments to himself before she appeared, drinking booze in her absence to clarify his thoughts and wipe the cobwebs out his mind so he could lay out his reasoning clearly and show her who was boss once she showed up, which made him seem even more bizarre to the residents of the Cause Houses, seeing Sportcoat in the hall holding a bottle of Rufus's homemade King Kong in the air and saying to no one in particular, "Who's bringing the cheese? Jesus or me? If I'm the one standing in line for the cheese . . . And I'm the one fetching the cheese. And I'm the one hauling the cheese home in the rain and snow. Who's bringing the cheese? Jesus or me?"

His friends excused it. His neighbors ignored it. His church family at Five Ends shrugged. Big deal. So Sport was a little crazy. Everybody in the Cause had a reason to be a little left-handed. Take Neva Ramos, the Dominican beauty in Building 5 who poured a glass of water on the head of any man stupid enough to stand beneath her window. Or Dub Washington from Building 7, who slept in an old factory at Vitali Pier and got busted every winter for shoplifting at the same Park Slope grocery store. Or Bum-Bum, who stopped in front of the picture of the black Jesus painted on the back wall of Five Ends each morning before work to pray aloud for the destruction of her ex-husband, that the Lord might set his balls on fire and they might sizzle on a frying pan like two tiny, flattened potato pancakes. It was all explainable. Neva got wronged on her job by her boss. Dub Washington wanted a warm jail. Sister Bum-Bum's husband left her for a man. So what? Everyone had a reason to be crazy in the Cause. There was mostly a good reason behind everything.

Until Sportcoat shot Deems. That was different. Trying to find reason in that was like trying to explain how Deems went from being a cute pain in the ass and the best baseball player the projects had ever seen to a dreadful, poison-selling, murderous meathead with all the appeal of a cyclops. It was impossible.

"If there's no time limit on fortune-cookie predictions, Sportcoat might make it," Bum-Bum said. "But outside of that, I reckon he's on the short list." She was right. Everyone agreed. Sportcoat was a dead man.

2

A DEAD MAN

OF COURSE THE FOLKS IN THE CAUSE HOUSES HAD PRE-
dicted Sportcoat's death for years. Every year in the spring, when the
project residents would emerge from their apartments like burrowed
groundhogs to walk along the plaza and sample whatever good air was
left in the Causeway—much of it polluted from the nearby wastewater-
treatment plant—some resident would spy Sportcoat staggering through
the plaza after a night of bingeing on King Kong rotgut at Rufus's or
playing bid whist at Silky's Bar over on Van Marl Street and say, "He's
done." When he caught the flu back in '58, which floored half of Building 9 and gave Deacon Erskine of Mighty Hand Gospel Tabernacle his
Final Wings, Sister Bum-Bum declared, "He's going up yonder." When
the ambulance came to get him after his third stroke in '62, Ginny Rodri-
guez of Building 19 grumbled, "He's finished." That was the same year
that Miss Izi of the Puerto Rican Statehood Society won raffle tickets to
see the New York Mets at the Polo Grounds. She predicted the Mets,
who had lost 120 games that year, would win and they did, which encouraged her to announce Sportcoat's death two weeks later, explaining

that Dominic Lefleur, the Haitian Sensation, had just arrived back from Port-au-Prince after visiting his mother, and she actually saw Sportcoat drop in his tracks, right in front of his apartment on the fourth floor, from the strange virus Dominic brought back that year. "He went 'fatty boom bang'!" she exclaimed. Gone. Quit. Outta here. She even pointed to the black van from the city morgue that showed up that night and hauled out a body as proof, only to recant the whole bit the next morning when it turned out the body they'd claimed belonged to the Haitian Sensation's brother El Haji, who had converted to Islam and broken his mother's heart, then collapsed of a heart attack after his first day on the job driving a city bus—after trying to get on at Transit for three years, too, imagine that.

Still, Sportcoat seemed earmarked for death. In fact, even the cheerful souls at Five Ends Baptist—where Sportcoat served as a deacon and president of the Five Ends chapter of the Grand Brotherhood of the Brooklyn Elks Lodge #47, which for the grand sum of $16.75 (paid annually, money order only please) had a standing guarantee from the head honchos at Five Ends Baptist to "funeralize any and all Brooklyn Elks Lodge members who need final servicing, at cost of course," with Sportcoat serving as honorary pallbearer—had predicted his death. "Sportcoat," Sister Veronica Gee of Five Ends said soberly, "is a sick man."

She was right. At seventy-one, Sportcoat had contracted almost every disease known to man. He had gout. He had the piles. He had rheumatoid arthritis, which crippled his back so bad he limped like a hunchback on overcast days. He had a cyst on his left arm the size of a lemon, and a hernia in his groin the size of an orange. When the hernia grew to the size of a grapefruit, doctors recommended surgery. Sportcoat ignored them, so a kind social worker at the local health clinic signed him up for every alternative therapy known to man: acupuncture, magnet therapy, herbal remedies, holistic healing, applying leeches, gait analysis, and plant remedies with genetic variations. None of them worked.

With each failure his health declined further and the death predictions grew more frequent and ominous. But not one of them came true. The fact is, unbeknownst to the residents of the Cause, the death of Cuffy Jasper Lambkin—which was Sportcoat's real name—had been predicted long before he arrived at the Cause Houses. When he was slapped to life back in Possum Point, South Carolina, seventy-one years before, the midwife who delivered him watched in horror as a bird flew through an open window and fluttered over the baby's head, then flew out again, a bad sign. She announced, "He's gonna be an idiot," handed him to his mother, and vanished, moving to Washington, DC, where she married a plumber and never delivered another baby again.

Bad luck seemed to follow the baby wherever he went. Baby Cuffy got colic, typhoid fever, the measles, the mumps, and scarlet fever. At age two, he swallowed everything: marbles, rocks, dirt, spoons, and once got a kitchen ladle caught in his ear, which had to be extracted by a doctor over at the university hospital in Columbia. At age three, when a young local pastor came by to bless the baby, the child barfed green matter all over the pastor's clean white shirt. The pastor announced, "He's got the devil's understanding," and departed for Chicago, where he quit the gospel and became a blues singer named Tampa Red and recorded the monster hit song "Devil's Understanding," before dying in anonymity flat broke and crawling into history, immortalized in music studies and rock-and-roll college courses the world over, idolized by white writers and music intellectuals for his classic blues hit that was the bedrock of the forty-million-dollar Gospel Stam Music Publishing empire, from which neither he nor Sportcoat ever received a dime.

At age five, Baby Sportcoat crawled to a mirror and spit at his reflection, a call sign to the devil, and as a result didn't grow back teeth until he was nine. His mother tried everything to make his back teeth grow. She dug up a mole, cut off its feet, and hung the feet on a necklace around the baby's neck. She rubbed fresh rabbit brains on his gums. She stuffed snake rattles, hog tails, and finally alligator teeth in his pockets, to no avail. She let a dog tread on him, a sure remedy, but the dog bit him and ran off. Finally she called an old medicine woman from the Sea Islands who cut a sprig of green bush, talked Cuffy's real name to it, and hung the bag upside down in the corner of the room. When she departed she said, "Don't say his true name again for eight months." The mother complied, calling him "Sportcoat," a term she'd overheard while pulling cotton at the farm of J. C. Yancy of Barnwell County, where she worked shares, one of her white bosses uttering it to refer to his shiny new green-and-white-plaid sport coat, which he proudly wore the very afternoon he bought it, cutting a dazzling figure atop his horse in the harsh Southern sun, his shotgun across his lap, dozing up on his mount at the end of the cotton row while the colored workers laughed up their sleeves and the other overseers snickered. Eight months later she woke up and found the mouth of ten-year-old Sportcoat full of back teeth. She sought out the medicine woman excitedly, who came over, examined Cuffy's mouth, and said, "He's gonna have more teeth than an alligator," whereupon the mother happily patted the boy on the head, lay down for a nap, and expired.

The boy never recovered from his mother's death. The ache in his heart grew to the size of a watermelon. But the medicine woman was right. He grew enough teeth for two people. They sprouted like wildflowers. Bicuspids, molars, liners, fat long double chompers, wide teeth in the front, narrow teeth in the back. But there were too many of them, and they crowded his gums and had to be pulled out, the extractions dutifully done by delighted white dental students at the University of South Carolina, who desperately needed patients to work on to obtain their degrees and thus held Sportcoat dear, extracting his teeth and giving him sweet muffins and little bottles of whiskey as payment, for he'd discovered the magic of alcohol by then, in part to celebrate his father's marriage to his stepmother, who often recommended he go play at

Sassafras Mountain, 258 miles distant, and jump off the top naked. At age fourteen, he was a drunk and a dental student's dream. By age fifteen, the medical school had discovered him, as the first of many ailments gathered forces to attack him. At eighteen, blood poisoning blew up his lymph nodes to the size of marbles. Measles reappeared, along with a number of other diseases, which smelled the red meat of a sucker marked for death and dropped by his body for a go-round: scarlet fever, hematoid illness, acute viral infection, pulmonary embolism. At twenty, lupus had a throw and quit. When he was twenty-nine, a mule kicked him and broke his right eye socket, which sent him stumbling around for months. At thirty-one, a crosscut saw cut his left thumb off. The delighted medical students at the university sewed it back on with seventy-four stitches, chipped in, and bought him a used chain saw as a gift, which he used to cut off his right big toe. They reattached that with thirty-seven stitches, and as a result two of the students won major medical internships at hospitals in the Northeast, and they sent him enough money to buy a second mule and a hunting knife, which he used to slice into his aorta by accident while skinning a rabbit. He fell unconscious that time and nearly died, but he was rushed to the hospital, where he lay dead on the operating table for three minutes but came back again after a surgeon intern stuck a probe in his big toe, which sent him sitting up, cursing and swearing. At fifty-one, measles came back for one last fling and quit. And thereupon Cuffy Jasper Lambkin, rechristened "Sportcoat" by his mother and loved and admired by all whom he knew in Possum Point save the two people responsible for his well-being in the world, his stepmother and father, left the entreaties of the grateful medical students of the state of South Carolina and ventured to New York City to join his wife, Hettie Purvis, his childhood sweetheart who had moved there and set things up nicely for him, having gotten a job as a domestic for a good white family in Brooklyn.

He arrived at the Cause Houses in 1949 spitting blood, coughing gruesome black phlegm, and drinking homemade Everclear, later switching to Rufus's beloved King Kong, which preserved him nicely until his sixties, at which point the operations began. Doctors removed him piece by piece. First a lung. Then a toe, then a second toe, followed by the usual tonsils, bladder, spleen, and two kidney operations. All the while he drank till his balls hurt and he worked like a slave, for Sportcoat was a handyman. He could fix anything that walked or moved or grew. There was not a furnace, a TV, a window, or a car that he could not fix. What's more, Sportcoat, a child of the country, had the greatest green thumb of anyone in the Cause Houses. He was friends with anything that grew: tomatoes, herbs, butter beans, dandelions, beggar's-lice, wild spur, bracken, wild geranium. There was not a plant that he could not coax out of its hiding place, nor a seed he could not force to the sun, nor an animal he could not summon or sic into action with an easy smile and affable strong hands. Sportcoat was a walking genius, a human disaster, a sod, a medical miracle, and the greatest baseball umpire that the Cause Houses had ever seen, in addition to serving as coach and founder of the All-Cause Boys Baseball Team. He was a wondrous handyman to the residents of the Cause Houses, the guy you called when your cat took a dump and left a little piece of poop hooked in his duff, because Sportcoat was an old country man and nothing would turn him away from God's good purpose. Similarly, if your visiting preacher had diabetes and weighed 450 pounds and gorged himself with too much fatback and chicken thighs at the church repast and your congregation needed a man strong enough to help that tractor-trailer-sized wide-body off the toilet seat and out onto the bus back to the Bronx so somebody could lock up the dang church and go home—why, Sportcoat was your man. There was no job too small, no miracle too wondrous, no smell too noxious. Thus the sight of him staggering through the plaza each afternoon drunk, headed to some odd job, caused the residents to murmur to one another, "That fool's a wonder," while secretly saying to themselves, "All's right in the world."

But all that, everyone agreed, changed the day he shot Deems Clemens.

Clemens was the New Breed of colored in the Cause. Deems wasn't some poor colored boy from down south or Puerto Rico or Barbados who arrived in New York with empty pockets and a Bible and a dream. He wasn't humbled by a life of slinging cotton in North Carolina, or hauling sugarcane in San Juan. He didn't arrive in New York City from some poor place where kids ran around with no shoes and ate chicken bones and turtle soup, limping to New York with a dime in their pockets, overjoyed at the prospect of coming to New York to clean houses and empty toilets and dump garbage, hoping for a warm city job or maybe even an education care of good white people. Deems didn't give a shit about white people, or education, or sugarcane, or cotton, or even baseball, which he had once been a whiz at. None of the old ways meant a penny to him. He was a child of Cause, young, smart, and making money hand over fist slinging dope at a level never before seen in the Cause Houses. He had high friends and high connections from East New York all the way to Far Rockaway, Queens, and any fool in the Cause stupid enough to open their mouth in his direction ended up hurt bad or buried in an urn in an alley someplace.

Sportcoat, all agreed, had finally run out of luck. He was, truly, a dead man.

3

JET

THERE WERE SIXTEEN WITNESSES AT THE CAUSE HOUSES plaza when Sportcoat signed his death warrant. One of them was a Jehovah's Witness stopping passersby, three were mothers with babies in carriages, one was Miss Izi of the Puerto Rican Statehood Society, one was an undercover cop, seven were dope customers, and three were Five Ends congregation members who were passing out flyers announcing the church's upcoming annual Friends and Family Day service—which would feature Deacon Sportcoat himself preaching his first-ever sermon. Not one of them breathed a word to the cops about the shooting, not even the undercover cop, a twenty-two-year-old detective from the Seventy-Sixth Precinct named Jethro "Jet" Hardman, the first-ever black detective in the Cause Houses.

Jet had been working on Deems Clemens for seven months. It was his first undercover assignment, and what he found made him nervous. Clemens, he'd learned, was the low-hanging fruit on a drug network that led up the food chain to Joe Peck, a major Italian crime figure in

Brooklyn whose violent syndicate gave every patrolman in Jet's Seventy-Sixth Precinct who valued his life the straight-out jitters. Peck had connections—inside the precinct, down at Brooklyn's city hall, and with the Gorvino crime family, guys who would stake out a claim on a cop's guts for a quarter and get away with it. Jet had been warned about Peck from his old partner, an elderly Irish sergeant named Kevin "Potts" Mullen, an honest cop recently returned to the precinct after being banished to Queens for the dreadful habit of actually wanting to lock up bad guys. A former detective busted back to swing sergeant, Potts had dropped by the precinct one afternoon to check on his former charge after discovering Jet had volunteered to work undercover in the Cause Houses.

"Why risk your skin?" Potts asked him.

"I'm kicking doors down, Potts," Jet said proudly. "I like being first. I was the first Negro to play trombone in my elementary school, PS 29. Then first Negro in Junior High School 219 to join the Math Club. Now I'm the first black detective in the Cause. It's a new world, Potts. I'm a groundbreaker."

"You're an idiot," Potts said. They were standing outside the Seven-Six as they talked. Potts, clad in his sergeant's uniform, leaned on the bumper of his squad car and shook his head. "Get out," he said. "You're outta your league."

"I just got in, Potts. I'm cool."

"You're in over your head."

"It's just small-time stuff, Potts. Grift. Jewelry. Burglary. A little narcotics."

"A little? What's your cover?"

"I'll be a janitor with a drug habit. First black janitor in the projects under the age of twenty-three!"

Potts shook his head. "This is drugs," he said.

"So what?"

"Think of a horse," Potts said. "Now think of a fly on the horse's back. That's you."

"It's an opportunity, Potts. The force needs Negro undercovers."

"Is that how the lieutenant sold it to you?"

"His exact words. Why you dogging me, man? You worked undercover yourself."

"That was twenty years ago." Potts sighed, feeling hungry. It was nearly lunchtime, and he was thinking of mutton stew and bacon stew with potatoes, the latter of which he loved. That's how he got his nickname—Potts—from his grandmother, because as a toddler he couldn't say "potato."

"Undercover work was mostly memos back then," he said. "Horse racing. Burglaries. Now it's heroin. Cocaine. There's a load of money in it. Thank God the Italians around here in my day didn't like drugs."

"You mean like Joe Peck? Or the Elephant?" Jet tried to keep the excitement out of his voice.

Potts frowned, then glanced over his shoulder at the precinct building to make sure nobody he knew was within earshot. "Those two got ears in this precinct. Leave 'em alone. Peck's crazy. He's probably gonna get burnt by his own people. The Elephant . . ." He shrugged. "He's old-fashioned. Trucking, construction, storage—he's a smuggler. He moves stuff out of the harbor. Cigarettes, tires, that kind of stuff. He doesn't work in drugs. He's a hell of a gardener."

Jet squinted at Potts, who seemed distracted.

"He's a weird bird, the Elephant. You'd think he'd favor Lionel trains or toy boats, or something. His yard looks like a flower show."

"Maybe he's growing flowers to hide marijuana plants," Jet said. "That's illegal, by the way."

Potts sucked his teeth and shot an irritated glance at him. "I thought you liked to draw comic books."

"I do, man. I draw them all the time."

"Then get back in the blues and draw your comics at night. You wanna be the first at something? Be the first Negro cop smart enough to forget the Dick Tracy crap and retire with your head in one piece."

"Who's Dick Tracy?" Jet asked.

"Don't you read the funny papers?"

Jet shrugged.

Potts snickered. "Get out. Don't be an idiot."

Jet tried to get out. He actually broached the subject with his lieutenant, who ignored him. The Seventy-Sixth Precinct, which Jet had only recently joined as a detective, was a demoralized mess. The captain spent most of his time at meetings in Manhattan. The white cops didn't trust him. The few black cops, smelling his ambition and terrified about being transferred to East New York—considered hell on earth—avoided him. Most wanted to talk about nothing more than fishing upstate on weekends. The paperwork was overwhelming: twelve copies for a shoplifting arrest. The bomb squad sat around and played cards all day. Potts was the only one Jet trusted, and Potts, at fifty-nine, was biding his time to retirement with one foot out the door, having been demoted to sergeant for reasons he never discussed. Potts planned to retire in less than a year.

"I'll get out," Jet said, "after I've done it a year. Then I can say I'm a pioneer."

"All right, Custer. If it goes bad, I'll call your mom."

"C'mon, Potts, I'm a man."

"So was Custer."

The day of the shooting, Jet, clad in the blue Housing Authority janitor's uniform and leaning on his broom, was standing in the plaza daydreaming about taking a job in his cousin's cleaners and being the first Negro to invent a new shirt steamer, when he saw Sportcoat in his ragged sports jacket and beaten slacks teetering out of the dim hallway of Building 9 and drifting toward the crowd of boys around Clemens, who sat at the plaza flagpole surrounded by his crew and customers, not ten feet from where Jet was standing.

Jet noticed Sportcoat smiling, which was not unusual. He'd seen the ancient coot around, grinning and talking to himself. He watched as Sportcoat stopped for a moment in the crowded plaza, did a batter's pose, swung at an imaginary pitch, then straightened, stretched, and teetered forward. He chuckled and was about to turn away when he saw— or thought he saw—the old man pull out a large, rusted pistol from his left jacket pocket and place it in his right-hand pocket.

Jet looked around helplessly. This was what Potts called "a situation." Most of his work up until this point had been smooth. Make a few buys. Take mental notes. ID this one. Figure out that one. Get the lay of the land. Figure out where the spiderweb goes, which was to a supplier in Bed-Stuy called "Bunch" and through a dreaded enforcer on Bunch's crew named Earl, who came around to distribute and collect. That was as far as Jet had gotten. There was a killer, he heard, a hit man named Harold who was apparently so horrible that everyone seemed afraid to mention his name, including Deems himself. Jet hoped not to meet him. As it was, he wasn't feeling skippy about matters. Every time he briefed his lieutenant on his progress, the man seemed nonchalant. "Doing good, doing good" was all he said. The lieutenant, Jet knew, was angling for a promotion and had one foot out the door, too, like most of the commanders at the Seven-Six. With the exception of Potts and a couple of kind older detectives, Jet was on his own, with no guidance and no direction, so he cooled it and did the job easy as Potts had instructed. No busts. No collars. No comments. Do nothing. Just watch. That's what Potts said.

But this . . . this was something different. The old man was approaching with a gun. If Potts were in his shoes, what would he do?

Jet glanced around. There were people everywhere. It was nearly noon, and the assortment of neighborhood gossips who met at the flagpole bench every morning to sip coffee and salute the flag had not quite departed. An odd truce had developed, Jet noticed, between Deems and his drug-slinging crew and the old-timers who came here every morning to gossip and insult one another with jokes. For a short period, between eleven thirty and noon, the two groups actually shared the flagpole space. Deems worked a bench on one side of the flagpole, and the morning residents gathered on the other, mumbling about the declining state of the world, which included, Jet noticed, Deems himself.

"I'd put a baseball bat to that little wormhead if he was my son," Jet had heard Sister Veronica Gee grumble once. Added Bum-Bum, "I'd send him hobbling, but why interrupt my prayers?" Threw in Hot Sausage, "I'm gonna warm his two little toasters one of these days—when I'm not under the influence."

Deems, Jet noticed, ignored them, always keeping his foot traffic to a minimum until the old-timers departed, leaving the squabblings, the posturing, the cursing, the harsh arguments, even the fights, for later. Before noon the plaza was safe.

Until now, Jet thought.

Jet checked his watch. It was 11:55. Some of the old-timers were starting to rise up from the bench, with the old man and his gun still coming, now fifty feet away, his hand thrust into his gun pocket. Jet felt his mouth go dry watching the old drunk teeter forward five feet at a time, stopping to swing an imaginary baseball bat, then swaying forward once more, taking his time, talking, apparently having a two-way conversation with himself: "Ain't got time for you, woman . . . Not today I don't! You're not yourself today anyway. And that's an improvement!"

Jet watched, unbelieving, as Sportcoat closed to forty feet. Then thirty. Then twenty-five, still talking to himself as he moved toward Deems.

At twenty feet, the old man stopped muttering, but still he came on.

Jet couldn't help himself. His training kicked in. He dropped to a crouch to grab the snub-nosed .38 strapped to his ankle, then stopped himself. A gun strapped to the ankle was a dead giveaway. It screamed cop. Instead, he stood up and drifted away as the old man circled the crowd surrounding Deems. As casually as he could, Jet walked to the wide, circular concrete flag base, placing his broom against the base, stretched his arms, and feigned a tired yawn. He glanced at the bench where the old-timers sat, and he saw with alarm that a few of them were still there.

They were laughing, saying a last word as they stood up, joking, taking their time. A couple of them glanced at Deems and his crew, who were gathering, happily ignoring the old folks on the opposite bench, the young troops surrounding their king. One of the boys handed his leader Deems a paper bag. Deems opened it and removed a large hero sandwich, unwrapping it. From where he was standing, Jet could smell it was tuna. He glanced at the old-timers.

Hurry up.

Finally, the last of them stood up. He watched with relief as Hot Sausage grabbed the giant coffee thermos and Bum-Bum picked up the cardboard cups and they were off, leaving only two: Miss Izi and Sister Gee. Sister Gee got up first, her arms full of flyers, and wandered off. That left only Miss Izi, a heavyset, light-skinned Puerto Rican with shiny black hair whose laughter followed Sister Gee, her cackles sounding like chalk screeching across a blackboard.

Get gone, Jet thought. *Go, go!*

The elderly Puerto Rican woman watched Sister Gee drift off, rubbed her nose, scratched her armpit, glared at the gathering of drug users now circling Deems, said something in Spanish toward Deems, which Jet guessed was an oath, and finally began to amble away.

Still, the old man came on. Ten feet. He smiled at Jet as he slipped past, smelling strongly of booze, then eased into the circle of heroin heads surrounding Clemens, disappearing from Jet's view behind the shoulders of the anxious users clamoring for their first hit of the day.

Jet's fear amped into panic. What the fuck was the old fool thinking? He was gonna get blasted.

He waited for the bang, terrified, his heart racing.

Nothing. The circle didn't move. The boys stood around Deems, bustling as usual, ribbing one another and joking.

Jet snatched his broom off the flagpole and, pushing it toward the circle of boys, tried to appear nonchalant, absentmindedly sweeping, picking up pieces of trash as he went, knowing that the normally careful Deems wouldn't bother noticing him, since he too was a customer. As he swept close to the group, he paused to tie his shoe this time, placing his broom on the ground. From this vantage point, low to the ground and less than ten feet away, he could see through the angle of bodies straight into the circle surrounding Deems and the old man. Deems was seated on the back arm of the bench working on his hoagie, talking to another boy, the two of them laughing. Neither noticed Sportcoat standing over them.

"Deems?" The old man spoke up.

Clemens looked up. He seemed surprised to see the old drunk swaying before him.

"Sportcoat! My man." He bit into his sandwich, the tuna hero dripping with mayonnaise and tomatoes. Sportcoat always made him a little uncomfortable. It wasn't the old man's drinking, or his bravado, or his stern lectures about drugs that bothered him. Rather it was the memory, not long ago, of Sportcoat shagging fly balls with him at the baseball field on warm spring afternoons; it was Sportcoat who taught him how to pivot and zing a throw to home plate from 350 feet out. It was Sportcoat who taught him how to pitch, to throw his weight on his back foot when he wound up, to extend his arm as he powered the ball home, to grip the ball properly to throw a curveball, and follow through with his legs so all his weight and power was on the ball, not on his shoulder. Sportcoat made him a star in baseball. He was the envy of the white boys on the John Jay High School baseball team, who marveled at the college scouts who risked life and limb to venture to the funky, dirty Cause Houses baseball field to watch him pitch. But that was another time, when he was a boy and his grandpa was living. He was a man now, nineteen, a man who needed money. And Sportcoat was a pain in the ass.

"How come you ain't playing ball no more, Deems?" Sportcoat asked.

"Ball?" Deems said, chewing.

"That's right. Baseball," Sportcoat said, swaying.

"Got bigger ball to play, Sportcoat," Deems said, winking at his cohorts as he took a second big bite of his sandwich. The boys laughed. Deems wolfed another bite, barely looking at Sportcoat, his attention focused on the dripping sandwich, while Sportcoat stared, blinking dully.

"Ain't nothing bigger than ball, Deems. I ought to know. I'm the big cheese when it come to ball 'round this projects."

"You right, Sportcoat. You the man."

"Best umpire this projects ever had," Sportcoat said proudly as he swayed. "I brings the cheese. Not Peter. Not Paul. Not Jesus. Me. *I* brings the cheese, see. And I has not excused you, Deems Clemens, from playing ball, y'understand? For that is what you do best. So how come you is not playing ball?"

Clemens, his hands clasped around the giant sandwich, chuckled and said, "G'wan, Sportcoat."

"You ain't answered me. I trained you to God's way, son. I taught you Sunday school. I teached you the game."

Deems's smile disappeared. The warm glow in his brown eyes vanished; a dark, vacant look replaced it. He was not in a mood for the old man's bullshit. His long, dark fingers clasping the hero tightened down on it tensely, squeezing out the white mayonnaise and tomato juice, which ran into his hands. "Git gone, Sportcoat," he said. He licked his fingers, bit into the sandwich again, and whispered a joke to a boy seated on the bench next to him, which sent the two of them chortling.

At that moment, Sportcoat stepped back and calmly reached into his pocket.

Jet, four steps away, still crouched, his hands on his shoelaces, saw the move and uttered the words that would ultimately save Deems's life. He howled out, "He's got a burner!"

Clemens, with a mouthful of tuna sandwich, instinctively turned his head in the direction of Jet's shout.

At that moment, Sportcoat fired.

The blast, aimed at Deems's forehead, missed, and the bullet struck his ear instead, severing it, the spent bullet clanging off the pavement behind him. But the force of the blast felt like it took Deems's head off. It tossed him backward over the bench and threw the bite of tuna sandwich against the back of his throat and down his windpipe, choking him.

He landed on his back on the concrete, coughed a few times, then rolled onto his stomach and began choking, desperately trying to rise to his hands and knees as the stunned boys around him scattered and the plaza collapsed into chaos, flyers dropping to the ground, mothers pushing baby carriages at a sprint, a man in a wheelchair spinning past, people running with shopping carts and dropping their grocery bags in panic, a mob of pedestrians fleeing in terror through the fluttering flyers that seemed to be everywhere.

Sportcoat squared his old pistol on Deems again, but when he saw Deems on his hands and knees choking, he had a change of heart. He was suddenly confused. He had dreamed of Hettie the night before wearing her red wig hollering at him about the cheese, and now he was standing over Deems, the dang thing in his hand had fired somehow, and Deems was on the ground in front of him, trying to breathe. Watching him, Sportcoat had an epiphany.

No man, Sportcoat thought, *should die on his hands and knees.*

As quick as he could, the old man climbed over the bench, mounted Deems, who was on all fours, and with the gun still in one fist, did the Heimlich maneuver on him. "I learnt this from a young pup in South Carolina," he grunted proudly. "A white fella. He growed up to be a doctor."

The overall effect, seen from across the square, the nearby street, and every window that faced the plaza, 350 in all, was not good. From a distance, it looked like the vicious drug lord Deems Clemens was on all fours being humped like a dog from the back by an old man, Sportcoat of all people, jouncing atop Deems in his old sports jacket and pork-pie hat.

"He fucked him hard," Miss Izi said later, when describing the incident to the fascinated members of the Puerto Rican Statehood Society of the Cause Houses. The society was only two other people, Eleanora Soto and Angela Negron, but they enjoyed the story immensely, especially the part about Deems's spitting up the leftover sandwich, which looked, Miss Izi said, like the two tiny white testicles of her ex-husband, Joaquin, after she poured warm olive oil on them when she found him snoring in the arms of her cousin Emelia, who was visiting from Aguadilla.

The humping didn't last long. Deems had lookouts everywhere, including from the rooftops of four buildings that looked down on the plaza, and they scrambled into action. The lookouts from the roofs of Buildings 9 and 34 bolted for the stairs, while two of Deems's dope slingers who had scurried away after the initial blast got their wits back and stepped toward Sportcoat. Even though he was still drunk, Sportcoat saw them coming. He released Deems and quickly swung the big barrel of the .38 toward them. The two boys fled again, this time for good, disappearing into the basement of nearby Building 34.

Sportcoat watched them run, suddenly confused again. With the gun still in his hand, he turned toward Jet, who was ten feet off, standing erect and frozen now, one hand on his broom.

Jet, terrified, stared at the old man, who squinted back at him in the afternoon sun, which had come up high now. Their eyes locked, and at that moment Jet felt as if he were looking into the ocean. The old man's gaze was deep-set, detached, calm, and Jet suddenly felt as if he were floating in a spot of placid sea while giant waves roiled and swelled and lifted up the waters all around him. He had a sudden revelation. *We're the same*, Jet thought. *We're trapped*.

"I got the cheese," the old deacon said calmly as the moans of Deems wafted behind him. "Unnerstand? I got the cheese."

"You got the cheese," Jet said.

But the old man didn't hear. He had already turned on his heel, pocketed the gun, and limped quickly toward his building a hundred yards off. But instead of heading to the entrance, he veered off, teetering down the side ramp that led to the basement boiler room.

Jet, frozen with fear, watched him go, then out of the corner of his eye he saw the lights of a police cruiser fly by the street edge of the pedestrian plaza, a distance of about a city block. The car skidded to a stop, backed up, then plunged straight down the pedestrian walkway toward him. Relief washed over him as the squad car fought its way through the fleeing pedestrians, causing the driver to brake, swivel left, then right to avoid the panicked bystanders. Behind that car, Jet saw two more cruisers swing onto the walkway and follow. His relief was so enormous he felt like he'd just taken a great relieving piss, one that had drained him of every bit of life force.

He turned one last time to see the old man's head disappearing down the basement ramp of Building 9, then felt his guts unlock and found himself able to act. He dropped his broom and leaped over the bench toward Clemens, just as he heard the tires of a squad car slide to a stop behind him. As he crouched over Clemens he heard an officer shouting at him to freeze, stand up, and put up his hands.

As Jet did, he said to himself, *I'm no longer doing this. I am finished.*

"Don't move! Don't turn around!"

Two hands grabbed him from behind and pinned his arms. His face was slammed against the squad car hood. He felt cuffs slapped onto his wrists. From his view, with his ear flush against the hot hood of the car, he could see the plaza, busy as a train station minutes before, completely deserted, a few flyers fluttering in the wind, and the thick, white hand of the cop on the car hood near his face. The cop had put his hand there to brace his weight on it, while the other hand pinned Jet's head into place. Jet stared at the hand a foot from his eyeballs and noticed a wedding ring on it. *I know that hand*, he thought.

When his head was snatched from the hood, Jet found himself staring at his old partner Potts. Deems was on the ground, twenty feet off and surrounded by cops.

"I didn't do nothing," Jet shouted, loud enough for Clemens and anyone nearby to hear.

Potts spun him around, then patted him down, carefully avoiding the .38 strapped to his ankle. As he did, Jet muttered, "Arrest me, Potts. For God's sake."

Potts grabbed him by the collar and swung him toward the backseat of his squad car.

"You're an idiot," he murmured softly.

4

RUNNING OFF

SPORTCOAT WALKED INTO THE BASEMENT FURNACE ROOM
of Building 9 and sat on a foldout chair next to the giant coal furnace in
a huff. He heard the wail of a siren, then forgot all about it. He didn't
care about any siren. He was looking for something. His eyes scanned
the floor, then stopped as he suddenly remembered he was supposed to
memorize a Bible verse for his upcoming Friends and Family Day sermon. It was about righting wrongs. Was it the book of Romans or
Micah? He couldn't recall. Then his mind slid to the same old nagging
problem: Hettie and the Christmas Club money.

"We got along all right till you decided to fool with that damn Christmas Club," he snorted.

He looked around the basement for Hettie. She didn't appear.

"You hear me?"

Nothing.

"Well, that's all right too," he snapped. "The church ain't holding no
notes on me about that missing money. It's you who got to live with it,
not me."

He stood and began to search for a bottle of emergency King Kong that Sausage always kept hidden someplace, but was still pie-eyed and feeling addled and murky. He pushed around the discarded tools and bicycle parts on the floor with his foot, muttering. "Some people got to *stay* mad to keep from *getting* mad," he grumbled. "Some goes from preaching to meddlin' and meddlin' to preaching and can't hardly tell the difference. Well, it ain't my money, Hettie. It's the *church's* money." He stopped moving items with his foot for a moment and stilled, talking to the air. "It's all the same," he announced. "You got to have a principle or you ain't nothing. What you think of that?"

Silence.

"I thought so."

Calmer now, he started searching again, bending down and talking as he checked toolboxes and under bricks. "You never did think of my money, did you? Like with that old mule I had down home," he said. "The one old Mr. Tullus wanted to buy. He offered me a hundred dollars for her. I said, 'Mr. Tullus, it'll take a smooth two hundred to move her.' Old man wouldn't pay that much, remember? That mule up and died two weeks later. I coulda sold her. You shoulda told me to turn her loose."

Silence.

"Well, Hettie, if I weren't taking that white man's good hundred dollars on principle, I surely ain't gonna take no mess from you 'bout some fourteen dollars and nine pennies you done squirreled up in Christmas Club money and hid someplace."

He paused, looked out the corner of his eye, then said softly, "It *is* fourteen dollars, ain't it? It ain't, say, two or three hundred dollars, is it? I can't do three hundred dollars. Fourteen is sheep money. I can raise that sleeping. But three hundred, that's over my head, honey."

He stopped moving, frustrated, still looking around, unable to find what he was looking for. "That money . . . it ain't mine, Hettie!"

There was still no answer, and he sat down again in the folding chair, flummoxed.

Sitting in the cold seat, he had an unfamiliar, odd, nagging feeling that something terrible had occurred. The feeling wasn't unusual for him, especially since Hettie died. Normally he ignored it, but this time it felt bigger than usual. He couldn't place it, then suddenly spied the prize he was looking for and forgot about the problem instantly. He stood up, shuffled over to a hot-water heater, reached under it, and pulled out the bottle of Rufus's homemade King Kong.

He held the bottle up to the bare ceiling lightbulb. "I say a drink, I say a glass. I say *do you know me*? I say the note is due! I say bring the hens! I say a poke and a choke, Hettie. I say God only knows when! Brace!"

Sportcoat turned up the bottle, drank a deep swallow, and the nagging feeling bubbled away. He placed the bottle back in its hiding place and relaxed in his seat, satisfied. "G'wan, King Kong," he murmured. Then he wondered aloud, "What day is this, Hettie?"

He realized she wasn't speaking to him, so he said, "Hell, I don't need ya. I can read . . . ," which was actually not true. He could read a calendar. Words were another matter.

He rose, ambled over to a weathered wall calendar, peered at it through the haze of his drunken glow, then nodded. It was Thursday. Itkin's day. He had four jobs, one for every day but Sunday: Mondays he cleaned Five Ends church. Tuesdays he emptied the garbage at the nursing home. Wednesdays he helped an old white lady with the garden of her brownstone. Thursdays he unloaded crates at Itkin's liquor store, just four blocks from the Cause Houses. Fridays and Saturdays had once been baseball practice for the Cause Houses baseball team before it disbanded.

Sportcoat looked over at the wall clock. Almost one o'clock. He had to get to work.

"Gotta go, Hettie!" he said cheerily.

He pulled out the bottle again and took another quick nip of the Kong, slid it back to its hiding place, and walked out the back door of the basement, which exited a block away from the plaza flagpole. The street was clear and quiet. He wobbled easily, freely, the fresh air steadying him a bit and partially lifting the drunken haze. Within moments he was heading down the row of neat shops that lined Piselli Street and the nearby Italian neighborhood. He loved walking to Mr. Itkin's place, toward downtown Brooklyn, seeing the neat row homes and storefronts, the stores full of shopkeepers, some of whom waved at him as he walked past. Stacking booze and helping customers cart their wine to their cars was one of his favorite small jobs. Small jobs that didn't last more than a day and didn't require tools were perfect for him.

Ten minutes later, he ambled to a door under an awning that read *Itkin's Liquors*. As he reached it, a police car roared past. Then another. He paused at the door, hastily felt in his jacket vest pocket, where he stored booze or any empty or stray liquor bottles that might've been stuffed in there from some previous unremembered moment of elbow bending—forgetting his hip pockets altogether—then turned the door handle.

The doorbell tingled as he entered and closed it behind him, shutting off the howl of yet another police car and ambulance roaring past.

Mr. Itkin, the owner, a stout, easygoing Jew, was wiping the countertop, his paunch protruding over the edge. The store was silent. The airconditioning was blasting. It was still five minutes till opening time. Itkin nodded over Sportcoat's shoulder at the cop cars racing toward the Cause Houses. "What's going on out there?"

"Diabetes," Sportcoat said, plodding past Itkin's counter to the back stockroom, "killing 'em off one by one." He slipped into the back room, where stacks of newly arrived liquor boxes awaited opening. He sat down on a crate with a sigh. He didn't care about any sirens.

He removed his hat and wiped his brow. The counter where Itkin stood was a good twenty feet from the door to the back room, but Itkin, from his vantage point at the edge of the counter, could see Sportcoat clearly. He stopped wiping and called out, "You look a little peaked, Deacon."

Sportcoat dismissed the concern with a grin and an easy yawn, stretching his arms wide. "I'm feeling dandy and handy," he said. Itkin returned to wiping his counter, moving out of sight to work the other side of it, while Sportcoat, carefully keeping out of Itkin's sightline, grabbed a root beer from a crate, cracked it open, took a long drink of it, put it down on a nearby shelf, and began stacking boxes. He glanced to make sure Itkin was still at the far end of the counter and out of view, then, with the practiced smoothness of a cat burglar, he snatched a bottle of gin out of a nearby case, unscrewed its cap and poured half its contents into the root beer can, closed the bottle, stuffed it into his jacket hip pocket, removed the jacket, and placed it on a nearby shelf. The coat landed with an odd *clank*. For a moment Sportcoat thought he had a forgotten bottle stuffed in the pocket on the other side, since he'd only quickly rifled through his chest pockets before entering the store and not his hip pockets, so he snatched up the coat again, fished in the hip pockets, and yanked out the old .38.

"How'd my army gun get here?" he muttered.

Just then the jingle of the door sounded. He shoved the gun back into the jacket and glanced up to see several of the day's first customers entering, all of them white, followed by the familiar porkpie hat and brown worried face of Hot Sausage, still wearing his blue Housing Authority janitor uniform.

Sausage lingered at the door a moment, feigning interest in a nearby liquor display as the paying customers fanned out. Itkin, irritated, glanced at him.

Sausage blurted, "Deacon left something at home."

Itkin nodded curtly toward the back room, where Sportcoat could be seen, then was called down an aisle by one of the customers, which allowed Sausage to slip past the counter and into the back room. Sportcoat noticed he was sweating and breathing hard.

"Sausage, what you want?" he said. "Itkin don't like you back here."

Hot Sausage glanced over his shoulder, then hissed, "Goddamn fool!"

"What you so hot about?"

"You got to run! Now!"

"What you fussing at me for?" Sportcoat said. He offered the root beer can. "Have a sip-sot for your coal-top."

Sausage snatched the root beer soda can, sniffed it, then slammed it down on a crate so hard liquid popped out the opening.

"Nigger, you ain't got time to set around sipping essence. You gotta put your foot in the road!"

"What?"

"You got to go!"

"Go where? I just got here."

"Go anyplace, fool. Run off!"

"I ain't leaving my job, Sausage!"

"Clemens ain't dead," Sausage said.

"Who?" Sportcoat asked.

"Deems! He ain't dead."

"Who?"

Hot Sausage stepped back, blinking.

"What's the matter with you, Sport?"

Sportcoat sat down on a crate, wearily, shaking his head. "Don't know, Sausage. I been talking to Hettie 'bout my sermon for Friends and Family Day. She got to hollering about that cheese again, and the Christmas Club money. Then she throwed in my momma. She said my momma didn't—"

"Cut that mumbo jumbo, Sport. You in trouble!"

"With Hettie? What I done now?"

"Hettie's been dead two years, fool!"

Sportcoat puckered his face and said softly, "You ain't got to speak left-handed about my dear Hettie, Sausage. She never done you no wrong."

"She wasn't so dear last week, when you was bellowing like a calf about that Christmas Club money. Forget her a minute, Sport. Deems ain't dead!"

"Who?"

"Deems, fool. Louis's grandson. Remember Louis Clemens?"

"Louis Clemens?" Sportcoat tilted his head sideways, looking genuinely surprised. "Louis *been* dead, Sausage. He been dead five years this May. He been dead longer than my Hettie."

"I ain't talking about him. I'm talking about his grandson Deems."

Sportcoat brightened. "Deems Clemens! Greatest ballplayer this projects ever seen, Sausage. He's gonna be the next Bullet Rogan. I seen Rogan play once, back in forty-two. In Pittsburgh, just before I come up here. Hell of a ballplayer. He got to arguing with the umpire and got throwed out the game. Bob Motley was umping. Motley was something. Greatest Negro umpire ever. Jumped like a basketball player, Motley did."

Hot Sausage stared at him a moment, then said softly, "What's a matter with you, Sport?"

"Nothing. Hettie's just been a bear. She come to me said, 'I know your momma—'"

"Lissen to me. You shot Deems and he ain't dead and he's gonna come at you with his hooligans. So you gotta get moving . . ."

But Sportcoat was still talking and didn't hear him, "'—degraded you.' My momma did not degrade me. That was *not* my momma, Hettie," he said to no one in particular. "That was my *stepmomma*."

Hot Sausage whistled softly and sat down on another crate across from Sportcoat. He looked out into the store at Mr. Itkin, who was still busy with customers, then he picked up the root beer can full of gin and took a long swallow. "Maybe I can get a visitor's pass," he said.

"For what?"

"For when they put you in the penitentiary. If you live that long."

"Quit chunking at me 'bout nothing."

Hot Sausage sat thoughtfully a moment, sipped the gin, then tried one more time. "You know Deems, right? Louis's grandson?"

"Surely," Sportcoat said. "Coached him in baseball. Taught him in Sunday school. That boy got talent."

"He's shot. Near dead."

Sportcoat's brow furrowed. "Gosh almighty!" he said. "That's terrible."

"He's shot on account of you. Hand before God. You shot him."

Sportcoat chortled for a moment, thinking it was a joke. But Hot Sausage's serious face didn't waver, and Sportcoat's smile thinned. "You funning, right?" he said.

"I wish I was. You rolled up on him and throwed that old cannon of yours on him. The old one your cousin from the army gave you."

Sportcoat turned and reached into the pocket of his sports jacket lying on the shelf behind him and pulled out the Colt. "I wondered why I got this damn thing . . ." He hammered it against his hand to check. "See, it ain't been fired since I bought it. Ain't got but one bullet in it, and that's just for show." Then he noticed the empty cartridge and a pasty look crossed his face as he held the gun in front of him, staring at it.

Hot Sausage pushed the gun barrel toward the floor, glancing at the door. "Put that goddamn thing away!" he hissed, his voice low. "You already done caused a world of trouble with it!"

For the first time, seeping through Sportcoat's drunken stupor, the words began to have an effect. Sportcoat blinked in confusion, then laughed and snorted. "I disremember a lot of what I do these days, Sausage. After you and me got pixilated on the Kong last night, I went home and had a dream about Hettie and we got to fussing as usual. Then I woke up needing a breakfast of champions as they say so I had a taste of the Kong to keep the crease down, y'know. Then I went to see Deems about getting the baseball game against Watch Houses going again. We can't win without Deems, y'know. That boy got talent! Could throw seventy-eight miles per hour when he was thirteen." He smiled. "I always favored him."

"Well, you picked a poor way of showing it. You walked to the plaza and throwed that gun on him. Right in front of his gang of heathens."

Sportcoat looked stunned. His brow crinkled in disbelief. "But I hardly carry this thing, Sausage. I don't know how I . . ." He wet his lips. "I was drunk, I reckon. I didn't hurt him bad, did I?"

"He ain't dead. They say just his ear's shot off."

"That don't sound like me. It ain't smart to shoot a man's ear off. A man ain't got but two."

Hot Sausage couldn't help himself. He stifled a chortle. "You been home today?"

"Naw. I come straight to work after I . . ." Then Sportcoat paused a moment, his face etched with remembrance and concern. "Well, now that I think on it, I do remembers some boy with his head bleeding and choking for some reason. I remembers that. So I gived him that thing I seen a doctor do back home once. He was having trouble drawing air, poor fella. But I cleared him. I reckon that was Deems I cleared. He all right now?"

"He's well enough to pin a gold star on your chest before airing you out."

"Can't be!"

"You done it!"

"I disremember it! It couldn't have been me."

"You shot that boy, Sport. Understand?"

"Sausage, I reckon that running lie is a good one to truck about, being that a boy with that kinda talent that don't use it ought to be shot in this world for wasting it. But—hand before God—I didn't shoot him to my recollection. Even if I did it's only 'cause I wanted him to go back to pitching baseball. He'll forget all about it when his ear heals. I got only one good ear myself. A man can still pitch with one ear." He paused a moment, then added, "Anybody seen it?"

"No. Just everybody at the flagpole."

"Gee," Sportcoat said softly. "That's like being on TV." He took a swig of gin and felt better. He was having trouble deciding whether this was a dream.

Hot Sausage picked up Sportcoat's jacket and held it out for him. "Git down the road right now while you can," he said.

"Maybe I should call the police and explain it to 'em."

"Forget them." Sausage glanced at the door. "You still got people in South Carolina?"

"I ain't been to my home country since my daddy died."

"Go see Rufus over at the Watch Houses. Lay low over there. Maybe it'll blow over somehow . . . but I wouldn't buy no sweepstakes ticket on it."

"I ain't going over to no Rufus's place at no Watch Houses to sleep!" Sportcoat snorted. "That Negro ain't showered in two years. His body is dying of thirst. I got to be dead drunk to be around him. Plus, I got my own house!"

"Not no more."

"Where's Pudgy gonna go? I gotta take him to the school bus in the morning."

"The church'll see to that," Hot Sausage said, still holding out Sportcoat's jacket.

Sportcoat snatched his jacket from Sausage's hand and placed it back on the liquor rack, grumbling. "You lying! I didn't shoot Deems. I woke up this morning fussing with Hettie. I walked Pudgy to the blind folks' school bus. I maybe had a taste or three. Then I come here. Sometime in the middle there I had another swig of the erratic and took Deems's ear off. Maybe I done it. Maybe not. So what? He got another ear. What's an ear when you got an arm like Deems? I knowed a man back home who got his pecker cut off by a white man for stealing a lady's purse. He peed through a groin hole his whole life. He did all right. He's yet living, far as I know."

"The white man, or the man without a pecker?"

"They both yet living to my knowing. And they got to know each other good over time. So why you all hot and bothered about somebody's old ear for? Even Jesus didn't need but one sandal. The book of Psalms says you ain't desired my ears and you ain't opened 'em either."

"It says what now?"

"Something like that. What difference do it make? God'll straighten it out. He'll make Deems's one better'n two ears."

That business decided, Sportcoat began unpacking liquor bottles from a crate. "You wanna go fishing this weekend?" he said. "I'm getting paid tomorrow. I needs to reflect on my first-ever sermon at Five Ends. It's in three weeks."

"If it's about the hereafter, you ain't gonna be short on critters and believers, that's for sure. If I was a fly and wanted to get to heaven, I'd throw myself in your mouth."

"It ain't about no fly. It's about not eating the dressing without confessing. Book of Romans, fourteenth chapter, tenth verse. Or maybe it's Simon, seventh and ninth. It's one or the other. I got to look."

Hot Sausage stared, incredulous, as Sportcoat continued unloading liquor bottles. "Nigger, your cheese done slid off your cracker."

"Just 'cause you says I got a note due someplace don't mean I got one!"

"Is you listening, Sport?! You dropped Deems in his tracks! Then humped him like a dog. In front of everybody."

"You ought to test your lies someplace else other than your best friend, Sausage. I never humped a man in my life."

"You was drunk!"

"I don't swallow any more spirits than anybody else in these projects."

"Now who's lying? I ain't the one they calling Deacon King Kong."

"I don't get in a knot over the fibbing and twiddling things folks say about me, Sausage. I got my own thoughts about things."

Hot Sausage glanced out the door. Itkin's customers had left, and the store owner was peering into the back room where they were standing. Sausage reached into his pocket and pulled out a small clump of dollar bills. He held the crumpled bills out to Sportcoat, who had paused and was now standing before him, glaring, his arms full of liquor bottles.

"Thirty-one dollars. It's all I got, Sport. Take it and get a bus ticket home."

"I ain't going no place."

Hot Sausage sighed sadly, pocketed the money, and turned to leave. "All right. I guess I'll use it to buy a bus ticket to see you in the penitentiary upstate. If you live that long."

5

THE GOVERNOR

THOMAS ELEFANTE, THE ELEPHANT, HEARD ABOUT THE Deems Clemens shooting an hour after it happened. He was working on his mother's flower bed in his brownstone on Silver Street just three blocks from the Cause Houses, dreaming of meeting a plump, good-looking farm girl, when a uniformed cop from the Seventy-Sixth Precinct rolled up, called him over to his squad car, and relayed the news.

"They got a line on the shooter," the cop said.

Elefante leaned on the squad car door and listened in silence while the cop blabbed on about what the cops knew. They knew the victim. They were certain about the shooter too. Elefante didn't care about any shooter. That was Joe Peck's problem. If the coloreds wanted to kill each other over Peck's dope, that was Joe's headache, not his. Except, of course, killings brought cops like this one. Cops wrecked the economy—his economy anyway. Moving hot goods while cops were running an investigation in your backyard was like being the dumbest kid in class who always raises his hand anyway. No matter how stupid you are, it's only a matter of time before the teacher calls on you.

Elefante was forty, heavyset, and handsome; his dark eyes and gaunt jaw held a stony silence that cloaked a delightful, sarcastic sense of humor despite a childhood of bittersweet disappointment. His father had spent a good part of Elefante's childhood in jail. His opinionated, eccentric mother, who ran his father's dock at the harbor during his dad's imprisonment, spent her spare time collecting plants from every empty lot within five miles of the Cause, a hobby to which she increasingly dragged her reluctant bachelor son, who, she often noted, had worked himself well past the marrying age.

Elefante ignored those comments, though lately he'd conceded to himself she was probably right. All the good Italian women in the Causeway neighborhood were already married or had fled to the suburbs with their families, now that the coloreds were fully established. *The time to get married*, he thought, *was when I was young and stupid, like this cop.* Even this lumphead, he thought bitterly, was probably dating some hot young number. He could tell by the way the kid talked he wasn't from Brooklyn. He likely wasn't even from the Cause District. He looked barely twenty-one, and Elefante, staring at him, guessed the guy was clocking maybe seven grand a year—*And still, he's meeting women*, Elefante thought. *Me, I'm just a kickball. A blob. I might as well be a gardener.*

He listened with half an ear as the kid chatted, then stepped back and leaned on the fender of the parked car behind him to glance up and down the street while the cop yammered on. The kid was careless, and obviously inexperienced. He'd double-parked right in front of Elefante's house, in full view of every house on the block, which, like everything else around here, the Elephant thought ruefully, wasn't safe. It wasn't like the old days when everybody was Italian. The new neighbors were Russian, Jewish, Spanish, even colored—anything but Italian. He let the cop blab a little more, then, interrupting him, said, "The Cause ain't my business."

The cop seemed surprised. "You ain't got interests down there?" he said, pointing out the windshield of his patrol car toward the Cause Houses, which rose like a pyramid three blocks distant, glimmering in the hot afternoon sun that sent heat waves off the beaten streets, and the Statue of Liberty, which could be seen shimmering at a distance in the harbor.

"Interests?" Elefante said. "They used to have baseball games down there. I liked those."

The cop looked disappointed and a little afraid, and for the briefest of moments, Elefante felt sorry for him. It bothered him that people, even cops, feared him. But it was the only way. He had done a few terrible things over the years, but only to defend his interests. Of course he'd done some nice things, too, but got no credit for any of them. It was how the world worked. Anyway, this stupid kid seemed okay, so Elefante pulled a twenty out of his pocket, carefully folded it in his fingers in his left hand, leaned into the car window, and deftly let it slip to the floor of the patrol car before turning away and stepping back onto the sidewalk. "See ya, kid." The kid drove off fast. Elefante didn't bother watching his taillights disappear. Instead, he looked in the other direction. It was an old habit. If one cop goes this way, look for the second coming that way. When he was satisfied the street was clear, he stepped to his wrought-iron gate, opened it, and reentered the garden that fronted his modest brownstone, closing it carefully behind him. Still wearing his suit, he dropped to his knees and began digging at the plants, glumly consider-ing the shooting.

Drugs, he fumed silently as he dug. *Fucking drugs.*

He stopped digging to peer over his mother's flower garden. He scanned the different ones. He knew them all: sunflower, catchfly, Jeru-salem oak, bedfly, hawthorn, witch hazel, cinnamon fern, and what was the last, this one he was replanting right here? Lady fern, maybe? The ferns were not doing well. Neither were the hazels and hawthorn.

He bent over and began digging. *I'm the only forty-year-old bachelor in New York*, he thought ruefully, *whose mother collects flowers like junk—and then expects me to replant whatever crap she finds.* But the fact is, he didn't mind. The work relaxed him, and the garden was her pride and joy. She'd picked most of the plants out of the abandoned railroad tracks, ditches, and weeds that sprouted around the deserted lots and factories of the Cause District. Some, like this fern, were real treasures, arriving as near weeds and blossoming into full-grown plants. He scratched away at the fern, digging it out, pulling fresh earth out of a nearby wheelbarrow, pushing more earth aside, setting the new earth in place, and reanchoring the fern gently into place with the smooth efficiency born of experience and repetition. He stared at his work a moment before moving on to replant the next. Normally, his mother would check his work later on, but lately she'd been too sick to get out, and the garden was beginning to show small signs of neglect. Several plants were brown and dying. Others needed replanting. Several she wanted brought inside and potted. "There's something going around Brooklyn," she declared. "Some kind of disease." The Elephant agreed, but not the kind of disease she was worried about.

Greed, he thought wryly as he dug into the earth. *That's the disease. I got it myself.*

Two weeks before, in the dead of night, an elderly Irishman had wandered into his boxcar at the pier while he and his men were loading cigarettes onto a truck. Nighttime visitors and odd characters were not unusual given his line of work, which included moving hot goods off harbor boats, storing them, or moving them inland to wherever the customer wanted. But this visitor was odd even by his standards. He looked to be about seventy. He was clad in a tattered jacket and bow tie, with a full head of white hair. His face had so many lines and rivulets it reminded Elefante of an old subway map. One eye was swollen shut, apparently permanently. He was thin and sickly, and seemed to have trouble breathing. When he entered, Elefante motioned for him to sit. The visitor complied thankfully.

"I wonder if you could help a man in need," the old man said. His Irish brogue was so thick Elefante had trouble understanding him. Despite his physical frailness, his voice was clear and he spoke with an air of solidity and bearing, as if walking into the boxcar of one of Brooklyn's most unpredictable smugglers at three a.m. was as simple as walking into a bodega and ordering a pound of bologna.

"Depends on the need," Elefante said.

"Salvy Doyle sent me," the old fellow said. "He said you could help me out."

"Don't know a Salvy Doyle."

The old Irishman smirked and tugged at his bow tie. "He said you can move things."

Elefante shrugged. "I'm just a poor Italian who runs a trucking and storage company, mister. And we're running late."

"Construction?"

"A little construction. A little storage, some moving. Nothing heavy. Mostly I move peanuts and cigarettes." Elefante nodded at several nearby crates labeled "Cigarettes." "You wanna cigarette?"

"Naw. Bad for my throat. I'm a singer."

"What kind of singing?"

"The best kind," the old man said gaily.

Elefante stifled a smile. He couldn't help himself. The old bugger barely seemed capable of drawing air. "Sing me a song then," he said. He said it for amusement, and was surprised when the old man moved his head from side to side to stretch his neck muscles, cleared his throat, stood up, thrust his whiskered chin toward the ceiling, spread his thin arms, and burst into a gorgeous, clear tenor that filled the room with glorious, lilting song:

I remember the day, 'twas wild and drear
And night to the Hudson waves.
Our parson bore a corpse on a bier
To lie in the convict's grave.
Venus lay covered and taut
She was the beauty of Willendorf
She rests at the bottom of a shallow grav—

He broke off in a fit of coughing. "Okay, okay," Elefante said, before he could continue. Two of the Elephant's men who were trooping in a steady line hauling crates back and forth through the boxcar to a waiting box truck paused to smile.

"I ain't finished yet," the old man said.

"That's good enough," Elefante said. "Don't you know any Italian songs? Like a *trallalero*?"

"If I said I knew what that was, I'd be codding ya."

"It's a song from northern Italy. Only men sing it."

"Get your own bulldogs to sing that one, mister. I got something better," the Irishman said. He coughed again, a racking one this time, then regained himself and cleared his throat. "I take it you're in need of money?"

"I look that bad?"

"I have a small shipment that needs to go to Kennedy airport," he said.

Elefante glanced at the two men, who had stalled to watch. They quickly scurried back to work. This was business. Elefante motioned for the Irishman to sit in the chair next to his desk, out of the way of foot traffic.

"I don't haul stuff to the airport," Elefante said. "I do storage and light hauling. Mostly for grocery stores."

"Save that for the government," the Irishman said. "Salvy Doyle told me you could be trusted."

Elefante was silent for a moment, then said, "Salvy, last I heard, was pushing up worms in Staten Island someplace."

The Irishman chuckled. "Not when he knew me. Or your father. We were friends."

"My father didn't have friends."

"Back when we was guests of the state your father had many friends, may God bless him in his eternal resting place."

"If you want a wailing wall, use the desktop," Elefante said. "Get the show on the road."

"What?"

"What's your point, mister?" Elefante said impatiently. "What do you want?"

"I already said it. I need something moved to Kennedy."

"And past Kennedy?"

"That's my business."

"Is it a big shipment?"

"No. But it needs a trusted ride."

"Get a cab."

"Don't trust a cab. I trusted Salvy—who said you could be trusted."

"How did Salvy hear of me?"

"He knew your father. I told you."

"Nobody knew my father. He was hard to know."

The Irishman chuckled. "You're right. I don't think he said more than three words a day."

That was true. Elefante filed the fact that the Irishman knew this away for posterity. "So who do you work for?" he asked.

"Myself," the Irishman said.

"What's that mean?"

"It means I don't need a doctor's note when I call in sick," the Irishman said.

Elefante snorted and stood up. "I'll have one of my guys run you to the subway. It's dangerous around here at night. The junkies in the Cause will stick a pistol in your face for a quarter."

"Wait, friend," the old man said.

"I've known you two minutes and I'm tired of the friendship already, mister."

"The name's Driscoll Sturgess. I run a bagel shop in the Bronx."

"You oughta run a lying service. An Irishman running a bagel shop?"

"It's legal."

"You better head back to whatever packing crate you call home, mister. My pop had no Irish friends. The only Irish my father talked to were cops. And they were like a fungus. You want a ride to the subway or not?"

The old man's cheeriness emptied out of his face. "Guido Elefante knew plenty Irish in Sing Sing, sir. Lenny Belton, Peter Seamus, Salvy, myself. We were all friends. Gimme a minute, will ya?"

"I ain't got a minute," the Elephant said. He stood and moved to the doorway, expecting the old man to rise. Instead, Driscoll peered up at him and said, "You got a good company here. How's the health of it?"

Elefante snapped his glance down to the Irishman.

"Say that again," he said.

"How's the health of your trucking company?"

Elefante sat back down and frowned. "What's your name now?"

"Sturgess. Driscoll Sturgess."

"You got any other names?"

"Well . . . your father knew me as the Governor. And may your health always be fine, and the wind at your back. May the road rise up to meet you. And may God hold you in the palm of His hand. That's a poem, lad. I made up a ditty with the last line of it. Wanna hear it?" He stood up to sing, but Elefante reached a long arm out, grabbed the old man's jacket, and tugged him back into his chair.

"Sit a minute."

Elefante stared at him a long moment, feeling like his ears had just blown off his head, his mind buzzing the red alarm of an important, hazy memory. *The Governor.* He'd heard the name before, in a long-distant past. His father had mentioned it several times. But when? It had been years ago. It was near the end of his father's life, and he, Elefante, was nineteen then, at an age when teenagers didn't listen. The Governor? The governor of what? He dug deep in the recesses of his mind, trying to draw it out. The Governor . . . the Governor . . . It was something big . . . it had to do with money. But *what*?

"The Governor, you say?" Elefante said, stalling.

"That's right. Your poppa never mentioned me?"

Elefante sat a moment, blinking, and cleared his throat. "Maybe," he said. His father, Guido Elefante, had had a six-word vocabulary, spoken four times a day, but each word was a saber that cut through the dimly lit bedroom where he'd spent the last years of his life, crippled by a stroke suffered in prison, his grim, harsh commands cutting into the heart of his once happy-go-lucky boy, who had spent most of his growing years running wild with a mother unable to control him, raised by neighbors and cousins, while Guido had spent most of Elefante's childhood doing time in jail for a crime Guido never disclosed. Elefante was eighteen when his father came out of jail. The two were never close. Guido, felled by another stroke that got him for good just short of his son's twentieth birthday. By then, the son had spent a good part of his young life with-out a father. Other than a few occasions when he was five and the old man took him swimming at the Cause Houses pool, Elefante had few memories of leisure time with his pop. The old man who came home from jail that last time was silent as ever, a grim, suspicious, stone-faced

Italian, ruling his wife and son with iron efficiency, guided by the one motto that he forced into his son's consciousness, one that had led Guido safely from the poverty-stricken docks of Genoa to his dying moments in a handsome Cause brownstone bought and paid for, cash: Everything you are, everything you will be in this cruel world, depends on your word. A man who cannot keep his word, Guido said, is worthless. Only in his later years did Elefante truly appreciate his old man's power, his ability, even bedridden and debilitated, to manage his trucking, storage, and construction business with clever, assured firmness. The old man with an odd wife, working his business in a world of two-faced mobsters with no imagination, and always willing to break his long silences with the same warnings: *Keep a tight mouth. Never ask questions of customers. Remember, we're just a bunch of poor Genoans working for Sicilians who don't have our health in mind.* That and health. The old man was a fanatic about health. *Your health, your health is everything. Keep your health in mind.* Elefante heard that so much he grew sick of it. At first Elefante believed that credo came from the old man's own health misfortunes. But as the old man spiraled toward death, the admonition took on new meaning.

As he sat before the elderly Irishman in his boxcar, the moment of realization suddenly tumbled into Elefante's consciousness with startling efficiency, landing on his insides with a heaviness that felt like a blacksmith's hammer falling on an anvil.

They were in the old man's bedroom just days before he died. The old man had sent his mother to the store, claiming he needed fresh orange juice—something he disliked but occasionally drank for his wife's sake. They were in the bedroom, just the two of them, watching Bill Beutel, the longtime anchorman on Channel 7, giving the local news, Elefante in the room's only chair, the old man propped on the bed. His pop seemed distracted. He raised his head from his pillow and said, "Turn the TV sound up."

Elefante did as he was told, then moved his chair next to the bed. As he tried to sit, the old man reached up and grabbed his shirt and pulled him onto the bed, yanking his son's head close to his. "Keep your eyes open for someone."

"Who?"

"An old fella. Irishman. The Governor."

"The governor of New York?" Elefante asked.

"Not that crook," his father said. "The other Governor. The Irish one. That's his name: the Governor. If he shows—and he probably won't—he'll ask about your health. That's how you'll know it's him."

"What about my health?"

His father ignored him. "And he'll sing about the road rising up to meet you, and the wind being at your back and God being in the palm of your hand. All that Irish Catholic crap. If he's crowing that and asking about your health, that's him."

"What about him?"

"I'm holding something for him, and he's come to collect it. Give it to him. He'll treat you fair."

"What're you holding?"

But then they heard the door open and his mother return, so the old man shut down, saying they'd talk later. Later never came. The old man slipped into incomprehensibility a day later and died.

Elefante, seated before the Irishman, who was staring at him oddly, tried to keep his voice even. "Poppa did mention something about health. But that was a long time ago. Just before he died. I was twenty, so I don't remember so well."

"Ah, but a fair-play mate he was. He never forgot a friend. A better man I never knew. He looked out for me in prison."

"Look, get your blockers out the backfield, would ya?"

"What?"

"Put the show on the road, mister. What you selling?"

"I'll say it once again for Mother Mary. I need something moved to Kennedy."

"Is it too big for a car?"

"No. You can fit it in your hand."

"You wanna play blackjacks and spout riddles all day? What is it?"

The Governor smiled. "If I was light-headed enough to drag a barrel full of trouble to a friend's house, what kind of man would I be?"

"That's touching, but it sounds like a lie."

"I'd move it myself," the old Irishman said. "But it's in storage."

"Get it out then."

"That's just it. I can't. The header running the storage place don't know me."

"Who's the guy?"

The old man smirked and peered at Elefante out the side of his one good eye. "I'd tell you in installments, but at my age, how's that gonna work out? Whyn't you wind yer neck in and pay attention?" He smiled grimly, then from his chair sang softly:

> *Wars were shared and gay for each*
> *Until the Venus faced the breach*
> *The Venus, the Venus, so dear to me*
> *At Willendorf always her image be.*
> *The Venus oh beauty*
> *Now covered and taut*
> *Lost to me, but not for naught.*

When he stopped, he found Elefante glaring at him, his lips pursed. "If you wanna keep your teeth," Elefante said, "don't sing no more."

The old Irishman was nonplussed. "I got no tricks," he said. "Something fell in my lap many a year ago. I need your help getting it. And moving it."

"What is it?"

Again the old man ignored the question. "I'm on a short lease, lad. I'm on the way out. It won't do me no good. My lungs are going. I got a grown lass, a daughter. I'm giving her my bagel business. It's a good, clean business."

"What's an Irishman doing baking bagels?"

"Is that illegal? No worries about the cops, son. Come up and see it if you want. It's a good operation. We're in the Bronx. Right off the Bruckner Expressway. You'll see I'm square."

"If you're so square and tidy, give your daughter what you got and live happily ever after."

"I said I don't want my daughter mixed up in it. You can have it. You can keep it. Or sell it. Or sell it and give me a little piece if you want, and keep the rest for yourself. However you like. That'll be the end of it. At least it won't be wasted."

"You oughta be a wedding planner, mister. First you want me to move it. Then you want to give it to me. Then you want me to sell it and give you a piece. What is it, for Christ's sake?"

The old man looked at Elefante sideways. "Your old man told me a story once. He said you wanted a job working for the Five Families when he came out. You wanna know how the story ends?"

"I already know how it ends."

"No you don't," the Governor said. "Your poppa bragged on you in prison. Said you would run his business good someday. Said you could keep a secret."

"Sure can. Wanna hear one? My poppa's dead, and he ain't paying my bills now."

"What you getting hepped for, son? Your poppa gifted you. He put this thing up. Stored it for me years ago. And you got the key to it."

"How do you know I didn't use the key and sell the thing already, whatever it is?" Elefante asked.

"If you'd done that, you wouldn't be making a bag of it in this blessed boxcar in the wee hours, moving this shit you call goods, which, if I'm remembering right from the old days, let's see . . . twelve-foot box truck, thirty-four crates, at forty-eight dollars a crate, if it's cigarettes and maybe a few cases of booze, you're looking at . . . maybe five thousand gross and fifteen hundred clams in your pocket after everybody's paid, including Gorvino, who runs these docks—which if your father knew you were still working for him, he'd probably marmalade ya. He'd be shook, that's for sure."

Elefante blanched. The old guy had balls. And smarts. And maybe a point. "So you can add figures," he said. "Where's this thing that you can't name?"

"I just named it for you. It's in a storage box probably."

Elefante ignored that. He hadn't heard any name of anything. Instead he asked, "You got a slip?"

"A what?"

"A receipt? A storage slip. Showing the box is yours?"

The Irishman frowned. "Guido Elefante didn't give receipts. His word was good enough."

He was silent as Elefante took that in. Finally Elefante spoke. "I got fifty-nine storage lockers. All padlocked by whoever rents them. Only the owners got the keys."

The Irishman laughed. "Be a good lad. Maybe it's not in a storage box."

"Where is it then? Buried in a lot someplace?"

"If you want to relax with your slippers, I'm not your man. It's got to be clean, son. Clean as a bar of Palmolive soap. Your poppa would see to it."

"What's that supposed to mean?"

"Pull your socks up, lad. I just told you. Wherever it is, it's got to be clean. It might just *be* a bar of soap, or be *in* a bar of soap. That's how small it is. That'll keep it clean, I suppose, if you put it in a big bar of soap. It's about that size."

"Mister, you come in here singing riddles. You say this junk— whatever it is—needs a truck ride to the airport even though it's the size of a bar of soap. That it's got to be clean *like* soap, that it might even *be* soap. Do I look stupid enough to run around for a bar of soap?"

"You could buy three million dollars' worth of suds with it. Give or take a few dollars. If it's in good shape," the Irishman said.

Elefante watched the worker closest to him lug a crate from the door of the boxcar to the waiting truck outside. He watched him shove the crate into the truck without saying a word or changing his expression, and decided the man hadn't overheard.

"I'd let you talk pretty to me like that all night if I could," he said. "But I'd hate myself in the morning. I'll get one of my guys to take you back to the Bronx. The subway ain't what it used to be. I'll do that for my poppa's sake."

Sturgess held up an old, wrinkled hand. "I'm not having you on. I got no muscle to move this thing. I know somebody who might want to buy it in Europe. That's why I want to get it to Kennedy. But now, talking to you, you're a smart laddie, I think it's better if you take it. Sell it if you want, give me a small piece if you can. If you don't, that's okay. I got nothing except a lass at home. I don't want no trouble for her. She runs my business good. I just don't want to waste the thing, is all."

"What is it, Governor? Coins? Jewels? Gold? What's worth that much?"

The Irishman stood up. "It's worth a lot of crisps," he said.

"Crisps?"

"Chips. Money. Dollars. Guido said he'd keep it, so I know it's been kept. Where, I don't know. But your pop never went back on his word."

He dropped his card on the Elephant's desk. "Come see me in the Bronx. We'll talk about it. I can even tell you what to do with it. You can throw me a bone afterward if you want."

"What if I don't know where it is?"

"For three million biscuits, you'll know."

"For that kind of money, old man, anything but murder is a parlor trick. A guy can stop paying taxes for good, chasing that kind of money around," Elefante said.

"I ain't paid taxes in years," the old man said.

"Come on up to street level, would ya? How do I know you're square? What am I looking for?"

"Check your load. See what you got."

"How do I know you're not a bartender somebody floated out here just to mix drinks and box me in?"

"You think I'm some tosser who came all the way out here at this hour for exercise?" The Governor rose and stepped to the open back door, leaning on the door edge, looking out onto the dock, where two of Elefante's men could be seen several yards away, struggling to lift a huge, heavy box into the truck. He nodded at them. "You'd have ended up just like them if your father was like the rest of the gobshits we knew in prison, following the Five Families around. The thing is called the Venus, by the way. The Venus of Willendorf. She's in God's hands. That's what your poppa said to me. In a letter."

Elefante glanced at his father's old file cabinet, tucked in a corner of the boxcar. He'd been through it a dozen times. There was nothing in it. "Pop didn't write letters," he replied. But the old man had already stepped out the door, slipped into the dark empty lot across the street, and was gone.

6

BUNCH

FROM THE DIRTY WINDOW OF A WORN SECOND-FLOOR brownstone apartment, the great lights of Manhattan's skyscrapers danced in the far distance. Inside the dark parlor, a tall, slim brown man, wearing a colorful African kente kufi cap and dashiki, held a copy of the *Amsterdam News* newspaper in his hands and roared with delight. Bunch Moon was thirty-one, head of Moon Rental Cars and Moon Steak N Go, and codirector of the Bedford-Stuyvesant Development Corporation, and was seated at a polished dining room table, grinning as he held the latest edition of the city's major black newspaper and read the good news before him.

His laughter eased into a smile as he turned the page and finished the story he was reading. He folded the paper, fingered his goatee, then spoke softly to the twenty-year-old man seated across the table from him who was scratching at a crossword puzzle:

"Earl, Queens is burning, brother. The Jews are burning it up."

Earl Morris, Bunch's right-hand man, was clad in a leather jacket, the features of his smooth brown face etched in concentration as he worked his crossword. He had a pencil in his right hand and a lit cigarette in his left. He was having trouble negotiating both while trying to fill in the puzzle squares. Finally, he placed his cigarette in the ashtray and said without looking up, "Dig thaaaaaat."

"The city wants to build a housing project in Forest Hills," Moon said. "Them Jews out there are pissed, bro!"

"Dig thaaaaaat."

"So Mayor Lindsay goes out there and they give him hell. He gets mad and calls 'em 'fat Jewish broads.'" Bunch chuckled. "In front of the press and everything. Captain Marvel. You gotta love this guy."

"Dig that."

"Guess how many ran with it in their newspapers. Not one. Not the *Times*. Not the *Post*. Nobody. Just the *Amsterdam News*. He goes out there and insults the Jews and nobody says a drop about it. Except us. The Jews hate us, man! They don't want no projects out there in Forest Hills."

"Dig thaaat."

"And the whiteys hate the Jews, because the Jews run everything. You dig?"

"Dig thaaat."

"Dig thaaaat."

Bunch frowned.

"Can't you say anything else?" he asked.

"Dig thaaat."

"Earl!"

Earl, scratching at his crossword puzzle, snapped to and looked up. "Huh?"

"Can't you say anything else?"

"About what?"

"About what I just said. 'Bout the Jews running everything."

Earl pursed his lips in silence, looking puzzled. He took a quick puff of his cigarette, then said softly, "Which Jews now?"

Bunch smirked. *I'm surrounded by idiots*, he thought. "How's the kid from Cause Houses? The one who was shot yesterday."

Earl sat up straight now, recovering. He could tell the boss was heating up. "His ear's messed up," he said quickly. "But he's okay."

"What's his name again?"

"Deems Clemens."

"Sharp kid. How long till he's on his feet?"

"Maybe a week. Two at the outside."

"How's sales up there?"

"They fell off a little. But he got a man in place."

"Did he get arrested after he was shot?"

"Naw. He wasn't holding. He had a stash man. So the cops got nothing. Just the cash in his pockets."

"Okay. Pay him back his cash. Then get him off his ass and back on the street again. He gotta defend his plazas."

"He can't."

"Why not?"

"He ain't all the way well yet, Bunch."

"Shit, the nigger lost an ear, not his little Ray-Ray. He got a crew."

"Dig thaaat."

"Will you put a lid on the dig-that crap?" Bunch snapped. "Can he get back on his feet sooner? If his crew ain't tight, his sales are gonna fall off quick. Can he keep his crew selling at least?"

Earl shrugged. "Bunch, it's kinda hot over there. The cops are still looking for the shooter."

"Who was it?"

"An old man. Some bum."

"Narrow that down. They're a dime a dozen in the Cause."

"Dig th—" Earl coughed and cleared his throat as Bunch glared. Earl quickly hunched over the crossword puzzle, facedown, his chin inches from the page. "I'm using this here, Bunch," he said hastily, pointing at the crossword puzzle, "to get outta that habit. Finding new words every day."

Bunch sucked his teeth and turned away, heading to the window, his good humor gone now. He peered worriedly out to the street, first at the glistening Manhattan skyline in the distance, then at the tired, dilapidated brownstones lining the block. Piles of trash littered both sides of the street, along with several hulks of abandoned cars parked at the curbs in random fashion, hunched over like giant dead bugs, their motors missing and tires gone. He watched a group of kids playing atop one of the piles, vaulting like frogs from garbage bags to piles of refuse and ending at a broken fire hydrant. Amid the garbage and refuse along the bleak street, in front of the brownstone sat Bunch's gleaming black Buick Electra 225, which stood out in front of his place like a polished diamond.

"This fucking city," he said.

"Uh-huh," Earl said, not trusting himself to speak further.

Bunch ignored that, his mind churning. "The cops won't bother with Deems," he said. "There's not a peep about the shooting in the papers. Not even the *Amsterdam News*. The Jews in Queens is hot news now. And the riot in Brownsville."

"What riot?"

"Don't you read the papers? Last week a kid got shot out there."

"White kid or black kid?"

"Bro, is your head soundproof? It's Brownsville, nigger!"

"Oh yeah, yeah, that's old news," Earl said. "I read that. Wasn't he robbing an old man or something?"

"Who cares. The riots draw all the cop muscle from the Seventy-Sixth Precinct. That's good for us. We need the cops to stay there till we straighten out our business in the Cause. Tell you what: Call up my Steak N Go shop and tell Calvin and Justin to take the day off. Tell them to get flowers for the family, and cake and hot coffee. Have 'em take that stuff out to wherever the riot and protesters are meeting, wherever their headquarters is. Probably some church. Tell 'em to bring some chicken, too, now that I think on it." He chuckled bitterly. "No ideas flow through them Martin Luther King Cadillac types till they get some chicken. Call Willard Johnson to help set it up. He's still over there, ain't he?"

"Will called last night."

"About what?"

"Said he was a little short on money from that . . . whatever that thing is. The city thing we doing, the poverty program thing . . ."

"The Redevelopment Authority?"

"Yeah. He needs a little dough. For office rent and electric. Just to help him over the hump."

Bunch snorted. "Shit. The only hump that nigger is interested in got thighs like Calpurnia. He likes them big country girls."

Earl was silent as Bunch began to pace. "I gotta tie up that business at the Cause Houses. Tell me more about the guy who shot Deems."

"Ain't nothing to him. Some old guy got drunk and shot him. A deacon at one of them churches out there."

Bunch stopped pacing. "Why didn't you tell me that before?"

"You ain't ask."

"What kind of church? Big church or little church?"

"Bro, I don't know. They got fourteen churches for every man, woman, and child in the Cause. Some little nothing church, I heard."

Bunch seemed relieved. "All right. Find the guy. Find his church. First we deal with him. We gotta choke him hard or we'll have every dope slinger in South Brooklyn pushin' in on our corners. Make it look like a mugging. Steal his money if he got any. Cut him a little. But not too hard. We don't wanna get his church people in a snit. After that, we go to the church as the Redevelopment Authority and say how sorry we are about all this crime and horror in our community and so forth. We cool 'em out by buying 'em some choir books or Bibles and promise them some redevelopment city money. But we gotta straighten out that old guy first."

"Why don't we let the kid out there take care of him? He says he can."

"From his hospital bed?"

"He's home now."

"I can't run my business waiting for some kid to pull his Band-Aids off. Go over there and take care of the old man, before the Brownsville thing gets cold."

Earl frowned. "That ain't our territory, Bunch. I don't know all the players over there. Ain't that what we paying Joe Peck for, him being our supplier and all? He got the cops over there in his pocket. He knows everybody over there. Whyn't you call him?"

Bunch shrugged. "I did. I told him we'd take care of it ourselves."

Earl tried to hide his surprise. "Why?"

Bunch glanced at the window, then decided to take a chance. "I got a plan to get clear of him. Get our own supplier."

Earl was silent for a moment, contemplating. That was not the kind of information Bunch passed on lightly. It put him a little deeper into Bunch's thing. He wasn't sure if that was exactly good or safe—safe being the operative word. "Peck is Gorvino family, Bunch."

"I don't give a fuck if he's George Washington family. The Gorvinos ain't what they used to be. They don't like Peck no more anyway," Bunch said.

"Why not?"

"He's too wild."

"Dig thaaaat," Earl said, ignoring a hot glance from Bunch. He was distracted. He needed time to think this one through, because he didn't know what to say and he felt himself sliding into the hot seat. The Cause Houses made him nervous. Other than making money and dope drop-offs once a week, he was a stranger in those projects. He fingered his chin thoughtfully. "Even if the Gorvinos are souring on Peck, there's the

Elephant to deal with. A brother could end up in the harbor wearing cement shoes fucking with the Elephant. Remember Mark Bumpus? He
crossed the Elephant. What was left of him got tossed in the harbor
without instructions. I heard they picked him out the water in pieces."

"Bumpus was a hardhead. A smuggler. The Elephant don't traffic
in dope."

"Yeah, but he got the docks."

"Just his dock. There's other docks over there."

"The Elephant's funny about the Cause, Bunch. It's his turf."

"Who says?"

"Everybody. Even Peck and the Gorvinos don't monkey with the
Elephant."

"The Elephant ain't Gorvino family, Earl. Remember that. He works
with them, but he's mostly on his own. If it ain't cigarettes or tires or
refrigerators, he ain't interested."

"I hope so," Earl said, scratching his ear, his face etched in doubt. He
squashed his cigarette and fiddled with his pencil. "Bumpus ain't the only
one who ended up finding Negro freedom at the bottom of the harbor
care of the Elephant. That's some party I hear, when that wop gets mad."

"Get your subway tokens out and get rolling, would you? I told you,
we ain't gonna touch the Elephant. He ain't interested in our business.
Him and Peck ain't tight. So long as we take care of our business quiet,
we'll be all right. This is our chance to ease Peck out and make some big
dollars."

"How we gonna get our supply without Peck?" Earl asked.

"That's my business." Bunch sat down at the table, removed his kente
kufi African cap, and ran a hand over his thick, dark hair. "Go over to
the Cause Houses and clean up the old man. Bust his eye out. Break his
arm. Set fire to his clothes. But don't ice him. Just soften him up like it's
a mugging gone sour. Then we give his church a little donation from our
redevelopment fund, and that's it."

"Shit, Bunch, I'd rather Peck do it. Or Deems."

Bunch stared at him grimly. "Is you losing heart, bro?" he said softly. "If you are, I understand, because business is gonna get heavy soon."

"It ain't about heart. I ain't for beating up no old man, then paying his church."

"Since when did you grow a conscience?"

"It ain't that."

"Maybe I should call in Harold."

For the first time, Earl, who had been slouched in his chair at the table, sat straight up. "What you wanna let that nigger outta the cage for?"

"We might need an extra hand."

"You wanna tighten up the old man or you wanna nuke the projects?"

"Where's Harold living these days anyway?" Bunch asked.

Earl sulked silently for a good minute. "Virginia," he said finally. "It should be Alaska after that last job. Fucking firebug."

"That's the kind of talent we might need if Peck gets mad."

Earl rubbed his chin with the tips of his fingers, brooding. Bunch clapped the young man on the shoulders with both hands from behind, then massaged Earl's shoulders. Earl stared ahead, nervous now. He had seen what Bunch could do close up with a knife, and for a moment a fleeting panic gripped him, then passed as Bunch spoke: "I know how you are about them church folk. Your ma was church folk, wasn't she?"

"Don't mean nothing."

Bunch ignored that. "Mine was too. We was all church folk," he said. "Church is a good thing. A great thing, really. Building up our community. Thank God." He lowered his head to Earl's ear. "We ain't tearing down our community, brother. We're building it up. Look at all the businesses I got. The jobs we're providing. The help we give people. Is the white man opening car washes? Is he running car-rental places? Restaurants? Is he giving us jobs?" He pointed to the window, the filthy street, the abandoned cars, the dead brownstones. "What's the white man doing for us out here, Earl? Where's he at?"

Earl stared ahead, silent.

"We'll give the church a bunch of money," Bunch said. "It'll work out. You in or out, bro?"

It was an affirmation, not a question. "Course I'm in," Earl muttered.

Bunch sat down at the table again, leafing through the *Amsterdam News*, and then nodded Earl toward the door.

"Straighten out that old man. Clean him up good. Lop off one of his nuts if you have to. I don't care what you do. Send a clear message, and we'll leave Harold for another day."

"That assumes Harold knows the difference between day and night," Earl said.

"Just get it done," Bunch said.

7

THE MARCH OF
THE ANTS

JUST BEFORE FALL EACH YEAR, FOR AS LONG AS ANYONE could remember, the March of the Ants came to Building 17 of the Cause Houses. They came for Jesus's cheese, which came magically to Hot Sausage's basement boiler room once a month, with several one-pound hunks Sausage kept for himself, which he stored inside a tall stand-alone pendulum clock he'd found years ago in Park Slope and dragged into his basement to repair it. The repair never happened, of course, but the ants didn't mind. They happily headed for it every year, crawling through a slit in the building's outer door, marching through the labyrinth of discarded junk, bicycle parts, bricks, plumbing tools, and old sinks that crowded Hot Sausage's boiler room, moving in a curling line three inches wide that snaked its way around the discarded junk to the clock itself, which stood along a back wall. They climbed through the broken plate glass and across the clock's dead hour hand, then down into its guts and innards to the delicious, odorous white man's cheese wrapped in wax paper that lay inside. After demolishing the cheese, the line moved on, snaking its way out the back of the clock and along the wall, gobbling whatever was in its path—bits of old sandwiches, discarded Ring Dings, roaches, mice, rats, and of course their own dead. These ants were not normal city ants. They were big, red country ants with huge backsides and tiny heads. Where they came from no one knew, though it was rumored they might have wandered over from the nearby Preston Carter Arboretum in Park Slope; others said a graduate student from nearby Brooklyn College had dropped a beaker full of them and watched in horror as the beaker smashed to the floor and they scattered.

The real truth was that their long journey to Brooklyn began in 1951, care of a Colombian worker from the nearby Preston chicken-processing plant named Hector Maldonez. That was the year Hector slipped into New York on a Brazilian freighter, the *Andressa*. He spent the next six years living the good life in America, before he decided to divorce his wife and childhood sweetheart, who had dutifully remained back home with their four children in their village near Riohacha, in the northern Perijá mountains. Hector was a man with a conscience, and when he dutifully flew back home to explain to his wife that he'd found new love in America, a new Puerto Rican wife, he promised he would continue to support her and the children as always. His Colombian wife begged him to return to their once-blissful marriage, but Hector refused. "I'm an American now," he said proudly. He neglected to mention that as a big-shot American, he could not have a village wife, nor did he invite her to return with him.

Much angst and arguing followed, complete with swearing, hollering, and tearing out of hair, but at the end, after many assurances that he would continue to provide funds every month for her and their children, his Colombian wife tearfully agreed to a divorce. Before leaving she cooked him his favorite dish, a platter of *bandeja paisa*. She stuck the carefully wrapped blend of chicken, sausage, and rolls in a brand-new lunch box she had purchased and gave it to him as he left for the airport. He grabbed the whole business as he ran out the door, stuffed a few dollars in her hand, and left for America feeling light and easy, having gotten off scot-free. His plane landed back in New York just in time for him to make it to Brooklyn for his shift at the factory. After working his morning shift, he opened his lunch box to devour the delicious *bandeja paisa* and instead found the lunch box packed with *hormigas rojas asesinas*, the dreaded red ants from back home, along with a note that read more or less, in Spanish, "Adios motherfucker . . . we know you ain't sending no pesos!" Hector yelped and tossed the new lunch box into the long open trough that ran beneath the chicken factory, which sent chicken guts and sludge into a labyrinth of pipes that ran beneath the Cause Houses and out to the banks of the warm harbor. And there, in the agreeable coziness of the pipes and sludge, the ants lived in relative harmony, hatching, devouring each other, and happily indulging in the mice, rats, shad, crabs, leftover fish heads, and chicken guts, along with several other unfortunate live or half-live cats and mongrels from the nearby Cause Houses that wandered into the chicken factory for occasional munching, including a German shepherd named Donald, a favorite of the project's residents. Apparently the poor creature fell into the polluted Gowanus Canal and nearly drowned in the foul-smelling water. He emerged from the water a mess, his fur colored orange and barking like a cat. He staggered around the bank for a full hour before collapsing. The ants ate him of course, along with other unmentionable creatures that lurked in and around the sludge and waste pipes that ran beneath the chicken factory, the ants surviving fine until each fall, when their inner clocks denoted they make their pilgrimage to the surface to do what every God-worshipping creature from the tiniest cell-sized hatchling in Victoria Falls to the giant Gila monsters that wandered the Mexican countryside did, or should do, or should have done: they sought Jesus, or in this case, Jesus's cheese, which happened to be in Building 17 of the Cause Houses of the New York City Housing Authority, stored by Hot Sausage, a man who faithfully prayed every month

that the Lord would allow him to lay his own sausage beside the ten-
derloins of Sister Denise Bibb, the best church organist in Brooklyn, in
addition to faithfully laying aside several bars of Jesus's cheese every
week for a rainy day, which every year, in the fall, worked to the ants'
benefit.

Of course no one in the Cause paid much attention to the March of
the Ants. In a housing project where 3,500 black and Spanish residents
crammed their dreams, nightmares, dogs, cats, turtles, guinea pigs, Easter chicklets, children, parents, and double-chinned cousins from Puerto
Rico, Birmingham, and Barbados into 256 tiny apartments, all living
under the thumb of the wonderfully corrupt New York City Housing
Authority, which for $43-a-month rent didn't give a squirt whether they
lived, died, shat blood, or walked around barefoot so long as they didn't
call the downtown Brooklyn office to complain, ants were a minor
worry. And no resident in their right mind would go over their heads to
the mighty Housing Authority honchos in Manhattan, who did not like
their afternoon naps disturbed with minor complaints about ants, toilets, murders, child molestation, rape, heatless apartments, and lead
paint that shrunk children's brains to the size of a full-grown pea in one
of their Brooklyn locations, unless they wanted a new home sleeping on
a bench at the Port Authority Bus Terminal. But one year a lady in the
Cause got fed up with the ants and wrote a letter of complaint. The
Housing Authority ignored it, of course. But the letter somehow made
its way to the *Daily News*, which ran a story about the ants sight unseen.
The story triggered mild public interest, since anything about the Cause
Houses that didn't involve Negroes running around cockeyed screaming
for civil rights was seen as good news. NYU sent out a biologist to inves-
tigate, but he got mugged and fled. The City College of New York, desperate to clamber over NYU for public respectability, dispatched two
black female graduate students to take a look, but both had finals that
year and by the time they arrived the ants had departed. The city's proud

Environmental Action Department, which in those days consisted of hippies, yippies, draft dodgers, soothsayers, and peaceniks who smoked pot and argued about Abbie Hoffman, promised to take a look. But a week later a city commissioner, a first-generation Pole and a key mover in the New York Polish American Society's annual failed effort to get the City Council to honor that great Polish-Lithuanian general Andrew Thaddeus Bonaventure Kosciuszko by naming something after him other than that half-assed, pothole-filled, rust-bucket shit bomb of a bridge that yawned over Williamsburg, bearing the Brooklyn-Queens Expressway and whatever suicide jumper had the guts to wander up through the veering traffic before leaping off the crusty rails to crash into the poor souls below, wandered into the office, got a whiff of the freshly smoked Acapulco Gold being enjoyed by the hippie commie staffers who were busily engaged in arguing about the virtues of that esteemed early-twentieth-century union-organizing hell-raiser Emma Goldman, and left enraged. He cut the department's budget in half. The investigator assigned to look into the Cause ants was sent to the Parking Authority, where she collected dimes from parking meters for the next four years. Thus, to the wider city of New York, the ants remained a mystery. They were a myth, a wisp of annual horrible possibility, an urban legend, an addendum to the annals of New York City's poor, like the alligator Hercules who was said to live in the sewers below the Lower East Side and would leap out from manholes and gulp down children. Or the giant constrictor Sid from the Queensbridge Projects who strangled his owner, then slithered out the window to the nearby Fifty-Ninth Street Bridge, his ten-foot body camouflaged in the girders above traffic, occasionally reaching down at night to pluck an unlucky truck driver out of an open window. Or the monkey that escaped from the Ringling Bros. circus and was said to be living in the rafters of the old Madison Square Garden, eating popcorn and cheering as the New York Knicks got the shit kicked out of them for the umpteenth time. The ants were poor folks' foolishness, a forgotten story from a forgotten borough in a forgotten city that was going under.

And there they stayed, a sole phenomenon in the Republic of Brooklyn, where cats hollered like people, dogs ate their own feces, aunties chain-smoked and died at age 102, a kid named Spike Lee saw God, the ghosts of the departed Dodgers soaked up all possibility of new hope, and penniless desperation ruled the lives of the suckers too black or too poor to leave, while in Manhattan the buses ran on time, the lights never went out, the death of a single white child in a traffic accident was a page one story, while phony versions of black and Latino life ruled the Broadway roost, making white writers rich—*West Side Story*, *Porgy & Bess*, *Purlie Victorious*—and on it went, the whole business of the white man's reality lumping together like a giant, lopsided snowball, the Great American Myth, the Big Apple, the Big Kahuna, the City That Never Sleeps, while the blacks and Latinos who cleaned the apartments and dragged out the trash and made the music and filled the jails with sorrow slept the sleep of the invisible and functioned as local color. And all the while, the ants marched each fall, arriving at Building 17 kicking ass, a roaring tidal wave of tiny death, devouring Jesus's cheese, moving out of the clock and into the boiler room and into the trash can by the hall door, polishing off whatever leftover sandwiches and bits of cake from the wilted, soggy, uneaten lunches Hot Sausage left behind each afternoon as he and his buddy Sportcoat ignored food in favor of their favorite beverage, King Kong. From there they moved on to more plentiful goods in the halls and supply closets: rats and mice, which were in abundance, some dead, some alive, the mice still trapped in glue traps and tiny cardboard boxes, others expired, having been smashed by Hot Sausage's hand, the rats crushed by his shovel and lying underneath old carburetors and discarded fenders, amidst brooms and on dustpans, sprinkled with lime for later incineration in the giant coal furnaces that heated the Cause Houses. After supping on them, the ants turned upward, filing in a thick line up the broken toilet pipe to Flay Kingsley's apartment in 1B, where there was little food or garbage to be found, since Miss Flay's family of eight actually used apartment 1A across the hall, which had been empty since Mrs. Foy, the sole tenant, died four years previous and forgot to tell the welfare department about it, which created the perfect scenario for the welfare department and housing to blame each other about it—since one department didn't tell the other. The apartment was quiet. Welfare paid the rent. Who knew? From there the ants moved up to Mrs. Nelson's apartment, 2C, munching on the old watermelon rinds and coffee grounds she kept in a garbage can for her outdoor tomato garden, then up the waste pipe to 3C, Bum-Bum's place, which was slim pickings, then across the hallway via outdoor viaduct to Pastor Gee's place in 4C, which had no pickings at all, since Sister Gee kept a spotless house, then through Miss Izi's bathroom in 5C, where they sampled all manner of delicious soap from Puerto Rico, which Miss Izi every year forgot to store in glass containers in the fall knowing they were coming, and finally to the outer roof, where they attempted to perform a high-wire act by trooping across a stepladder that connected the roof of Building 17 to the roof of Building 9 next door—where they met their death care of a group of clever schoolboys: Beanie, Rags, Sugar, Stick, and Deems Clemens, the best pitcher the Cause Houses had ever seen, and the most ruthless drug dealer in the history of the Cause Houses.

As he lay in bed in apartment 5G of Building 9, his head wrapped in gauze, his mind fogged by painkillers, Deems found himself wondering about the ants. He had dreamed of them many times since he'd been hospitalized. He'd been home in bed three days, and the fog of painkillers and the constant ringing on the right side of his head had brought on odd memories and vivid nightmares. He had turned nineteen two months before, and for the first time in his life, he found himself unable to focus and remember things. He discovered with horror, for example,

that his childhood memories were fast disappearing. He couldn't remember his kindergarten teacher's name, nor the name of the baseball
coach from St. John's University who had called all the time. He couldn't
remember the name of the subway stop in the Bronx where his aunt
lived, or the name of the dealership in Sunset Park where the car sales-
man sold him his used Pontiac Firebird and then drove it home for him
because Deems himself couldn't drive. There was so much going on,
everything was a spinning whirlwind, and for a kid whose almost-perfect
memory once allowed him to collect illegal numbers for the local numbers runners needing neither paper nor pencil, the whole business of losing his past was troubling. It occurred to him, as he lay in bed that
afternoon, that the shrill buzz on the right side of his head where what
was left of his missing ear now lived might be the cause of the problem,
or that if there are a thousand things you should remember in life, and
you forget them all but the one or two useless things, maybe those things
aren't so useless. He couldn't believe how good it felt to remember the
dumb ants from Building 17. It had been ten years since he and his buddies had dreamed up wonderful ways to stop them from invading their
beloved Building 9. He smiled at the memory. They tried everything:
Drowning. Poison. Ice. Firecrackers, aspirin soaked in soda, raw egg
yolk sprayed with bleach, cod liver oil mixed with paint, and one year a
possum that his best friend, Sugar, produced. Sugar's family visited relatives in Alabama, and Sugar hid the creature in the trunk of his father's
Oldsmobile. The possum arrived in Brooklyn sick and prostrate. He was
tossed into a cardboard box taped shut with an entry hole and placed in
the ant path on the roof of Building 9. The ants arrived and obediently
climbed into the box and began to politely devour the possum, at which
point the possum came to life, writhing and hissing, which caused the
frightened boys to toss a glass of kerosene on the box and set it on fire.
The sudden whoosh of flames caused panic and they kicked the whole
business off the roof, where it landed in the plaza six stories below—a

bad idea, since that was sure to bring the wrath of adults of one kind
or the other. It was Deems who saved them. He grabbed a five-gallon
bucket left on the roof by a work crew and, scampering downstairs,
scooped the remnants of the whole business into the bucket and dashed
to the harbor, dumping everything at the water's edge. He became their
leader then, at ten, and had remained their leader since.

But leader of what? he thought bitterly as he lay in bed. He turned on
his side, groaning. "Everything," he muttered aloud, "is falling apart."

"Say what, bro?"

Deems opened his eyes and was surprised to see two of his crew,
Beanie and Lightbulb, sitting by his bed staring at him. He had thought
he was alone. He quickly turned to the wall, away from them.

"You all right, Deems?" Lightbulb said.

Deems ignored him, staring at the wall, trying to think. How had this
started? He couldn't remember. He was fourteen when his older cousin
Rooster dropped out of CUNY and started making big bucks selling
heroin, mostly to junkies from the Watch Houses. Rooster showed him
how to do it, and bang, five years passed. Was it that long ago? Now he
was nineteen, had $4,300 in the bank; his mother hated his guts; Rooster
was dead, killed in a drug robbery; and he was lying in his bed without
his right ear.

Fucking Sportcoat.

Lying there staring at the wall, the smell of the lead paint wafting into
his nostrils, Deems thought of the old man not with rage, but rather
with confusion. He could not understand it. If there was one person in
the Cause who had nothing to gain by shooting him, it was Sportcoat.
Sportcoat had nothing to prove. If there was one person in the Cause
who could get away with backtalking him, charming him, yelling at
him, calling him names, kidding him, jiving him, lying to him, it was old
Sportcoat. Sportcoat had been his baseball coach. Sportcoat had been
his Sunday school teacher. *Now he's a straight drunk*, Deems thought

bitterly, *though that's never affected anything before.* As far back as he could remember, he realized, Sportcoat had been a drunk more or less, but more important, he'd been the same—consistent. He never complained, or gave opinions. He didn't judge. He didn't *care.* Sport had his own thing, which is why Deems liked him. Because if there was one single thing in the screwed-up Cause Houses—in all of Brooklyn, for that matter—that Deems hated, it was people who complained about nothing. People with nothing complaining about nothing. Waiting on Jesus. Waiting on God. Sport wasn't that way. He liked baseball and booze. Real simple. Sportcoat did the Jesus thing, too, Deems noted, when his wife, Miss Hettie, used to make him. But even then he could see the old man and he were the same. They were stuck in Jesus houses.

Deems had long ago decided that Sport was different from the Jesus nuts of his life. Sport didn't need Jesus. Of course he acted like he did, just like a lot of grown-ups at Five Ends church. But Sportcoat had something that nobody at Five Ends, nobody in the projects, nobody Deems Clemens had known in his entire nineteen years of growing up in the Cause Houses, had.

Happiness.

Sport was happy.

Deems sighed heavily. Even Pop-Pop, his grandfather, the only man he'd ever known as a father, had not been happy. Pop-Pop had spoken in grunts and ruled his house with an iron fist, collapsing into his armchair at night after work with a beer in his hand, listening to the radio all night until he fell asleep. Pop-Pop was the only person who visited him when he went to juvy prison. His mother didn't bother. As if hours of talking about Jesus and the Bible would substitute for a kiss, a smile, a solitary meal together, a book read to him at night. She wore his ass out with her switch for the least offenses, rarely found anything good in what he did, never went to his baseball games, and dragged him to church on Sundays. Food. Shelter. Jesus. That was her motto. "I sling eggs and sugar and bacon twelve hours a day and you don't even thank Jesus that you got a place to live. Thank you, Jesus." *Jesus my ass.*

He wanted her to understand him. She could not. There was no one in his house who could. He wanted to be an equal. He saw how stupid the whole thing was, even as a child, all these people crowded into these shitbox apartments. Even a blind person like Pudgy Fingers could see it. He'd even talked to Pudgy about it, years ago, when they were in Sunday school. He was nine and Pudgy was eighteen. Even though he was a teenager, Pudgy was sent down to stay in Sunday School with the little kids during service because he was said to be "slow." Deems once asked if he minded. Pudgy simply said, "Nope. The snacks are better." They were in the basement and some Sunday school teacher was prattling on about God and Pudgy was sitting behind him and he saw Pudgy feeling the air with his hand until his hand landed on Deems's shoulder and Pudgy leaned over and said, "Deems, do they think we're retarded?" That surprised him. "Of course we ain't retarded," he snapped. Even Pudgy knew. Of course he knew. Pudgy wasn't slow. Pudgy was smart. Pudgy remembered things that nobody else remembered. He could remember how many singles Cleon Jones of the New York Mets hit against the Pittsburgh Pirates in spring training last year. He could tell you when Sister Bibb playing the organ in church was feeling sick just because of the way he heard her feet on the pedals. Of course Pudgy was smart, because he was Sportcoat's son. And Sport treated kids like equals, even his own. When Sportcoat taught Sunday school, the Lord's word was all candy and bubblegum, games of catch played in the church basement with balled-up church programs while the congregation sang and yelled upstairs. Sportcoat even took the class on a Sunday morning "outing" to the harbor once, where he'd hidden a fishing pole, tossing the fishing line into the water while Deems and the other kids played and muddied up their clothes. As for baseball, Sportcoat was a whiz. He organized the All-Cause team. He taught them how to catch and throw a ball properly, how to stand in the batter's box, how to block the ball with your body if need be. After practice on lazy summer afternoons, he'd gather the kids around and tell stories about baseball players long dead, players from the old Negro leagues with names that sounded like brands of candy: Cool Papa Bell, Golly Honey Gibson, Smooth Rube Foster, Bullet Rogan, guys who knocked the ball five hundred feet high into the hot August air at some ballpark far away down south someplace, the stories soaring high over their heads, over the harbor, over their dirty baseball field, past the rude, red-hot projects where they lived. The Negro leagues, Sport said, were a dream. Why, Negro league players had leg muscles like rocks. They ran the bases so fast they were a blur, but their wives ran faster! The women? Lord . . . the women played baseball better than the men! Rube Foster hit a ball so far in Texas it had to take the train back home from Alabama! Guess who brought it back? His wife! Bullet Rogan struck out nineteen batters straight until his wife took a turn and knocked his first pitch out of the yard. And where you think Golly Honey Gibson got his nickname? His wife! She's the one made him good. She'd hit line drives at him for practice, the ball traveling like a missile at the height of your face for four hundred feet, so hard he'd jump out the way, yelling "Golly, honey!" If Golly Honey Gibson was any better, he'd be a girl!

The stories were crazy, and Deems never believed them. But Sportcoat's love of the game washed over Deems and his friends like rain. He bought them baseball bats, balls, gloves, even helmets. He umpired the annual game against the Watch Houses and coached it at the same time, wearing his hilarious umpire costume—mask, chest protector, and black umpire's jacket—running around from base to base, calling runners safe when they were out and out when they were safe, and when either side argued, he'd shrug and switch his rulings, and when there was too much yelling, he'd holler, "Y'all driving me to drink!" which made everybody laugh more. Only Sportcoat could make the kids from those two housing projects, who hated each other for reasons long ago forgotten, get along on the ball field. Deems looked up to him. Part of him wanted to be like Sportcoat.

"The fucker shot me," Deems murmured, still facing the wall. "What'd I ever do to him?"

Behind him, he heard Lightbulb speaking. "Bro, we got to talk."

Deems shifted around and opened his eyes, facing them both. They had moved to the window ledge, Beanie smoking nervously, glancing out the window, Lightbulb staring at him. Deems felt his temple. There was a huge lump of bandage there, wrapped around his head. His body felt as if it had been squeezed in a vise. His back and his legs still burned, aching from his fall off the plaza bench. The ear, the one that was wounded, itched badly—what was left of it.

"Who's covering the plaza?" he asked.

"Stick."

Deems nodded. Stick was only sixteen, but he was original crew, so he was okay. Deems checked his watch. It was early, only eleven a.m. The usual customers didn't show up at the flagpole until noon, which gave time for Deems to establish his lookouts on the four buildings that directly faced the plaza to spy for the cops and hand-signal any trouble.

"Who's the lookout on Building Nine?" Deems said.

"Building Nine?"

"Yeah, Building Nine."

"Nobody's up there right now."

"Send somebody up there to look out."

"For what? You can't see the flagpole plaza from there."

"I want 'em up there looking out for the ants."

The boys stared at him, confused. "For the ants?" Lightbulb asked. "You mean the ants that come 'round that we used to play with—"

"What'd I say, man? Yes for the fucking ants—"

Deems snapped to silence as the door opened. His mother marched into the room with a glass of water and a handful of pills. She placed them on the nightstand next to his bed, glanced at him and at the two boys, and departed without a word. She hadn't said more than five words to him since he'd gotten out of the hospital three days before. Then again she never said more than five words to him anyway, other than: "I'm praying that you change."

He watched her as she moved out of the room. He knew the yelling, the screaming, and the cursing would come later. It didn't matter. He had his own money. He could take care of himself if she made him move out . . . maybe. It was coming soon anyway, he thought. He stretched his neck to ease the tension and the movement sent a flash of pain firing across his face and ear and down his back like an explosion. It felt like the inside of his head was being torched. He belched, blinked, and saw a hand extended at his face. It was Lightbulb, holding out the water and the pills.

"Take your medicine, bro."

Deems snatched the pills and water, gulped them down, then said, "Which apartments did they get into?"

Lightbulb looked puzzled. "Who?"

"The ants, bro. What apartments did they get into last year? They follow the same trail like always? They come up from Sausage's basement in Seventeen?"

"What you worrying about them for?" Lightbulb said. "We got a problem. Earl wants to see you."

"I ain't studying Earl," he said. "I asked about the ants."

"Earl's mad, bro."

"About the ants?"

"What's the matter with you?" Lightbulb said. "Forget the ants. Earl says Sportcoat got to be dealt with. He's saying we gonna lose the plaza to the Watch Houses if we don't do something."

"We'll deal with it."

"We ain't got to. Earl says he'll deal with Sportcoat hisself. Mr. Bunch told him to."

"We don't need Earl in our business."

"Like I said, Mr. Bunch ain't happy."

"Who you working for? Me? Or Earl and Mr. Bunch?"

Lightbulb sat in silence, cowed. Deems continued: "Y'all been out there?"

"Every day at noon," Lightbulb said.

"How's business?"

Lightbulb, always a goof, grinned and pulled out a round wad of bills and held it out to Deems, who glanced at the door where his mother had disappeared and said in a hushed voice, "Put that up, man." Lightbulb sheepishly pocketed the money.

"Light, anyone come through from the Watch Houses?" Deems asked.

"Not yet," Lightbulb said.

"What you mean not yet? You hearing they gonna come through?"

"I don't know, man," Lightbulb said forlornly. "I ain't never been through this before."

Deems nodded. Lightbulb was scared. He didn't have the heart for the game. They both knew it. *It was just friendship that kept them close*, Deems thought sadly. And friendship was trouble in business. He looked at Lightbulb again, his Afro covering his oddly shaped scalp that resembled from a side view a sixty-watt lightbulb, thus his nickname. The beginnings of a goatee were growing on his chin, giving Lightbulb a cool, almost hippie look. *It doesn't matter*, Deems thought. *He'll be shooting heroin in a year.* He had that smell on him. Deems's gaze shifted to the small, stout Beanie, who was quiet, more solid.

"What you think, Beanie? The Watches gonna try to move on our plaza?"

"I don't know. But I think that janitor's a cop."

"Hot Sausage? Sausage is a drunk."

"Naw. The young guy. Jet."

"I thought you said Jet got arrested."

"That don't mean nothin'. You check out his sneakers?"

Deems leaned back on the pillow, thinking. He *had* noticed the sneakers. Cheap PF Flyers. "They were some cheap joints," he agreed. Still, Deems thought, if Jet hadn't hollered, Sportcoat would've . . . He rubbed his head; the ringing in his ear had now descended into a tingling pain, working its way down to his neck and across his eyes despite the medicine. He considered Beanie's theory, then spoke. "Who was lookout on the roof of Building Seventeen and Thirty-Four that day?"

"Chink was on Seventeen. Vance was on Thirty-Four."

"They didn't see nothing?"

"We didn't ask."

"Ask," Deems said, then, after a moment, added, "I think Earl sold us a bunch of goods."

The two boys glanced at each other. "Earl didn't pop you, bro," Lightbulb said. "That was Sportcoat."

Deems didn't seem to hear. He ran through several quick mental checkoffs in his mind, then spoke. "Sportcoat's a drunk. He got no crew. Don't worry about him. Earl . . . for what we paying him, I think he double-crossed us. Set us up."

"Why you think that?" Lightbulb asked.

"How's it that Sportcoat could walk up on me without nobody calling it out? Maybe it ain't nothing. Probably old Sport just lost his head. But selling horse is so hot now . . . it's taking off. Easier to just rob somebody than stand out on the corners selling scag and smack in five- and ten-cent bags. I been telling Earl's boss we need more protection down here—guns, y'know. Been saying it all year. And we need more love on the money tip. We're only making four percent. We oughta be pulling five or six or even ten, as much shit as we move. I had all my collection money on me when I was shot. I woke up in the hospital and the money was gone.

Cops probably took it. Now I got to pay that back, plus the ten percent Bunch charges for being late. He don't give a shit about our troubles. For a lousy four percent? We could do better getting our own supplier."

"Deems," Beanie said. "We doing okay now."

"How come I got no muscle to protect me then? Who did we have out there? You two. Chink on Building Seventeen. Vance on Thirty-Four. And a bunch of kids. We need men around. With guns, bro. Ain't that what I'm paying Earl for? Who's watching our backs? We moving a lot of stuff. Earl shoulda sent somebody."

"Earl ain't the boss," Beanie said. "Mr. Bunch is the boss."

"There's a bigger boss than him," Deems said. "Mr. Joe. He's the one we should be talking to."

The two boys looked at each other. They all knew "Mr. Joe": Joe Peck, whose family owned the funeral home over on Silver Street.

"Deems, he's mob," Beanie said slowly.

"He likes money just like us," Deems said. "He lives three streets over, bro. Mr. Bunch is just a middleman, from way out in Bed-Stuy."

Beanie and Lightbulb were silent. Beanie spoke first. "I don't know, Deems. My daddy worked the docks with them Italians a long time. He said they ain't nothing to mess with."

"Your daddy know everything?" Deems asked.

"I'm just saying. Supposing Mr. Joe is like the Elephant," Beanie said.

"The Elephant don't do dope."

"How you know?" Beanie said.

Deems was silent. They didn't have to know everything.

Lightbulb spoke up. "What y'all talking about? We ain't got to mess with the Elephant or Mr. Joe or nobody else. Earl said he'd handle it. Let him handle it. It's old Sportcoat that's the problem. What you gonna do about that?"

Deems was silent a moment. Lightbulb had said "you" rather than "we." He filed that thought for later, and it made him feel sad all over

again. First he'd mentioned the ants and they'd hardly remembered. Protecting our building! That's what the aim was. The Cause. Protect our
territory! They didn't even care about that. Now Lightbulb was already
talking "you." He wished Sugar were here. Sugar was loyal. And had
heart. But Sugar's mother had sent him to Alabama. He'd written to
Sugar and asked to visit and Sugar wrote back saying "come on," but
when Deems wrote him a second letter, Sugar never wrote back. Beanie,
Chink, Vance, and Stick were all he could trust now. That wasn't much
of a crew if the Watch Houses came calling. Lightbulb, he thought bitterly, was out.

He turned to Beanie and the pain from his ear shot through his head.
He grimaced and asked, "Sportcoat been 'round these parts?"

"A little bit. Drinking like always."

"But he's around?"

"Not like always. But he's still around. So's Pudgy Fingers," Beanie
said, referring to Sportcoat's blind son. Pudgy was a beloved fixture in
the Cause Houses, wandering around freely, often brought to his door
by any neighbor he happened to run across. The boys had known him all
their lives. He was an easy target.

"Ain't no need to touch Pudgy Fingers," Deems said.

"I'm just saying."

"Don't fuck with Pudgy Fingers."

The three were silent as Deems blinked, deep in thought. Finally he
spoke. "Okay, I'll let Earl take care of my business—just this once."

The two boys immediately looked glum. Now Deems felt worse. They
had wanted to take care of Sportcoat, now he'd agreed, and now they
were sad. Goddamn!

"Stop being crybabies," he said. "You said we got to do it, and now
it's done. Otherwise, the Watch Houses is gonna come gunning for the
plaza. So let Earl deal with Sport."

The two boys stared at the floor. Neither looked at the other.

"That's how it is out here."

They remained silent.

"This is the last time we let Earl take care of our business," Deems said.

"Thing is . . ." Beanie said softly, then stopped.

"Thing is what?"

"Well . . ."

"What the fuck's the matter with you, man?" Deems said. "You so scared of Earl you want him to take care of our business. Okay, I said let him. It's done. Tell him go 'head. I'll tell him myself when I get on my feet."

"There's something else," Beanie said.

"Spit it out, man!"

"Thing is, when Earl come around yesterday, he was asking about Sausage, too."

Another hit. Sausage was a friend. He'd helped out Sportcoat with baseball in the old days. Sausage gave out the cheese to their families every month. Everybody knew about Hot Sausage and Sister Bibb, the church organist for Five Ends. She was also Beanie's aunt.

That's the problem, Deems thought. *Everybody's related to everybody in these goddamned pisshole projects.*

"Earl probably thinks Sausage is hiding Sportcoat," Beanie said. "Or that Sausage is diming us out to the cops."

"Sausage ain't diming nobody," Deems scoffed. "We working right in front of Sausage's face. He ain't no stoolie."

"Everybody in the Cause knows that. But Earl ain't from the Cause."

Deems glanced at Beanie, then at Lightbulb. One looked concerned, the other frightened. He nodded. "All right. Leave it to me. Earl ain't moving on Sausage. I'll talk to him. In the meantime, listen: In the next week or two, it's the March of the Ants. You two take turns setting on top of Building Nine like we used to. Let me know when the ants come. You the only ones that know how to do that."

"What for?" Lightbulb asked.

"Just do it. When you see signs they're coming, wherever I'm at, come fetch me. The first sign you see, come get me. Got it? You remember the signs, right? You know what to look for?"

They nodded.

"Say it."

Beanie spoke up: "Mice and rats running in that little hallway near the roof. Bunch of roaches running up there, too."

"That's right. Come get me if you see that. Understand?"

They nodded. Deems looked at his watch. It was almost noon. He felt sleepy; the medicine was taking effect. "Y'all get down there and help Stick make us some money. Post all the lookouts on the buildings and pay 'em afterward, not before. Beanie, check the roof of Nine before you go to the plaza."

He saw the look of worry on their faces.

"Just be cool," he said. "I got a plan. We'll get everything back to normal in no time."

With that, Deems lay sideways, his bandaged ear toward the ceiling, closed his eyes, and slept the sleep of a troubled boy who, over the course of an hour, had suddenly become what he'd always wanted to be: not a boy from one of New York City's worst housing projects, an unhappy boy who had no dream, no house, no direction, no safety, no aspiration, no house keys, no backyard, no Jesus, no marching-band practice, no mother who listened to him, no father who knew him, no cousin who showed him right or wrong. He was no longer a boy who could throw a baseball seventy-eight miles an hour at the of age thirteen because back then it was the one thing in his sorry life he could control. All that was past. He was a man with a plan now, and he had to make a big play, no matter what. That was the game.

8

THE DIG

THREE DAYS AFTER HOT SAUSAGE PREDICTED HIS DOOM, Sportcoat decided to stop in at the Watch Houses to see his buddy Rufus.

Despite Sausage's prediction that the world was going to end, Sportcoat hadn't seen a sign of it. He teetered through Building 9 as always, arguing with Hettie in the hall, then wandered over to the Social Security office in downtown Brooklyn, where they ignored him as usual, then on to his various jobs. The church ladies at Five Ends stepped in to walk Pudgy Fingers to the bus stop to take him to the social center and even kept Pudgy overnight, cycling Pudgy between them. "Five Ends takes care of their own," Sport bragged to his friends, though he had to admit to himself that his friends were fewer and fewer with Hettie gone and that Christmas money missing. The church ladies helping with Pudgy Fingers hadn't said a word about it, which made him feel even more guilty about not knowing where it was. He'd seen them place their precious envelopes bearing dollars and quarters into the Christmas Club collection tray every week. He'd already sought out Pastor Gee in his office after Bible study to clear the air.

"I didn't hide that money," he told Pastor Gee.

"I understand," Pastor Gee said. He was a humorous, good-natured man, handsome, with a cleft chin and a gold tooth that sparkled when he smiled, which was often. But he had no smiles that day. He looked troubled. "Some in the congregation are in a snit about it," he said carefully. "The deacons and deaconesses had a meeting about it yesterday. I stepped in there for a minute. There were a few hot words thrown around."

"What did you say?"

"Nothing I could say. Nobody knows how much was in the box, or who put in what. This one claims he's got a certain amount in there. That one says she got much more. The deaconesses are with you; they understand Hettie. The deacons ain't." He cleared his throat and lowered his voice. "You sure it ain't stuffed in a drawer someplace at home?"

Sportcoat shook his head. "It ain't no advantage to a man with a fever to change his bed, pastor. I'm about sick of the whole deal. If I ain't looked for that thing every day since Hettie died, you can throw a dipper of water in my face right now. I done looked in every nook and cranny. And I'll look again," Sportcoat said, feeling doubtful. He had looked everywhere in the apartment he could think of and came up with nothing. Where the *hell* did Hettie put it?

He decided to seek out Rufus, who was from his home country back in South Carolina. Rufus always had good ideas. Sportcoat took the bottle of Seagram's 7 Crown that he had clipped on his way out of Itkin's store last Thursday and headed over to the boiler room at the Watch Houses, where Rufus worked. He figured to trade the Seagram's for a bottle of Rufus's Kong and in the process hear Rufus's thoughts and advice.

He found Rufus—a slender, chocolate-skinned man—on the floor in his boiler room, wearing his usual blue grease-covered Housing Authority uniform, his hands and nearly his feet stuffed inside the guts of a large electric generator that was roaring in agony. The generator engine was accessed by an open panel door and Rufus's body was nearly completely inside it.

The generator was roaring so loud that Sportcoat had to stand behind Rufus and yell until Rufus glanced up from the floor at him and grinned, displaying a mouth full of gold teeth.

"Sport," he yelled. He adjusted the machine quickly and cranked it down a decibel, then pulled a long hand from the jumble of wires jutting from the machine to shake hands.

"Why you wanna wrong me, Rufus?" Sportcoat said, frowning, stepping away from the outstretched hand.

"What'd I do?"

"You know it's bad luck to greet a friend with your left hand."

"Oh. Sorry." Rufus hit a button and the machine whirred down to a slow grumble. Still seated with his legs splayed apart, Rufus wiped his right hand with a nearby rag and offered it. Sportcoat shook, satisfied. "What you got?" he said, nodding at the generator.

Rufus peered at it. "This thing acts up every week," he said. "Something's chewing on the wires."

"Rats?"

"They ain't that stupid. There some bad things going 'round Brooklyn, Sport."

"Tell me 'bout it," Sportcoat said. He reached into his pocket and produced the new bottle of Seagram's. He looked at the fresh liquor and sighed, deciding not to exchange it for some Kong after all. Rufus would give him the Kong anyway. Better to share, he thought. He cracked the label, then pulled a crate next to Rufus, sat down, sipped, then said, "Fella from our home country come into Mr. Itkin's to buy some wine. Said he woke up in the morning and found some leftover jelly in his wife's sifter."

"No kidding. She was baking?"

"Baked cookies the night before. He said she cleaned off everything afterward. She let the dishes dry overnight. Then this fella, her husband, he come into the kitchen in the morning and seen that jelly in her flour sifter."

Rufus produced a low whistle.

"Mojo?" Sportcoat asked.

"I reckon somebody mojoed him," Rufus said. He reached for the bottle and took a sip.

"I bet his wife done it," Sportcoat said.

Rufus took a satisfied swallow and nodded in agreement. "You still worried about Hettie?"

Instead of answering, Sportcoat held out his hand for the bottle, which Rufus surrendered. He took a deep drink and swallowed before he said, "I got to replace the church's Christmas Club money. Hettie kept track of it. She never told where she put it. Now the whole church is bellowing like a calf about it."

"How much is in it?"

"I don't know. Hettie never told. But it's a lot."

Rufus chuckled. "Tell them sanctifieds to pray for it. Get Hot Sausage to do it."

Sportcoat shook his head sadly. Rufus and Sausage didn't get along. It didn't help that Rufus had been a founding member of Five Ends Baptist Church and had quit fourteen years ago. He hadn't walked into a church since. Sausage, whom Rufus actually recruited to join Five Ends, was now a sanctified deacon, which had been Rufus's old job.

"How you gonna replace something you don't know what it is? It could be nothing in there but some thimbles and three teeth from the tooth fairy," Sportcoat said.

Rufus thought a moment. "There's an old somebody from Five Ends who might know where it's at," he said thoughtfully.

"Who?"

"Sister Pauletta Chicksaw."

"I remember Sister Paul," Sportcoat said brightly. "Edie Chicksaw's momma? She still living? She got to be well over a hundred if she is. Edie's long been dead."

"Long dead, but Sister Paul's yet living to my knowledge," Rufus said. "She and Hettie was friends. Hettie used to go out and visit her at the old folks' home out in Bensonhurst."

"Hettie never told me nothing about it," Sportcoat said, sounding hurt.

"A wife never tells her husband everything," Rufus said. "That's why I never got married."

"Sister Paul don't know nothing about church business. Hettie done all that."

"You don't know what Sister Paul knows or don't know. She's the se-niorest member of Five Ends. She was there when the church was built."

"So was I."

"No, old man, *Hettie* was there. You was still back home getting your toes sawed off. You come a year later, after the foundation was dug. Het-tie was there when the church was built. I mean the building itself. When the foundation was dug out."

"I was there for some of it."

"Not when they was digging the foundation and doing the brick-work, son."

"What's that prove?"

"It proves you don't remember nothing, for in them early days, Sister Paul collected the Christmas Club money. She done that *before* Hettie's time. And I do believe she might know something about where that money might be now."

"How you know? You quit Five Ends fourteen years ago."

"Just 'cause a man ain't sanctified no more don't mean he's missing his marbles. Sister Paul lived in this building, Sport. Right here in the Watch Houses. In fact, I seen that Christmas box."

"If you was a child, Rufus, I'd pull my switch out and send you hooting and hollering down the road for lying. You ain't seen no Christmas box."

"I walked Sister Paul to and from church many a day. When things got bad around here, she was afraid someone would knock her over the head for it, so she'd ask me to walk her to service from time to time."

"She ain't supposed to walk around with the Christmas box."

"She had to hide it someplace after she collected for it. Normally she hid it at church. But she didn't always have time to wait for church to empty out. Sometimes folks would linger eating fish dinners or the pastor would preach overtime or some such thing and she had to go home, so she brung it home with her."

"Why didn't she lock it in the pastor's office?"

"What fool would keep money 'round a pastor?" Rufus replied.

Sportcoat nodded knowingly.

"Sister Paul told me once she had a good hiding place for that box in the church," Rufus said. "I don't know where. But if she couldn't keep it there, she'd bring it home till the following Sunday. That's how I know she had it. 'Cause she'd come down and ask me to walk her over. And of course I was happy to do it. She'd say, 'Rufus Harley, you're a man and a half, that's what you are. Whyn't you come back to church again? You're a man and a half, Rufus Harley. Come back to church.' But I ain't a church man no more."

Sportcoat considered this. "That was years ago, Rufus. Sister Paul got nothing to help me now."

"You don't know what she got. She and her husband was the first coloreds to come to these projects, Sport. They come back in the forties, when the Irish and Italians 'round these parts was beating coloreds' brains out for moving into the Cause. Sister Paul and her husband started the church in their living room. In fact, I was there when Five Ends was digging out its foundation for the building. Weren't but four of us doing all that digging: me, her daughter Edie, your Hettie, and this crippled Eye-talian man from 'round these parts."

"What cripple?"

"I done forgot his name. He's long dead. He done a lot of the work on Five Ends. I can't recall his name, but it was an Italian name: Ely or some such thing. Ending with an 'i.' You know how them Italians' names go. Odd man. A cripple, that fella. Only had one good leg. Never said a mumbling word to me nor nobody else. Wouldn't give a Negro the time of day. But he was all for Five Ends Baptist. He had some money, too, I reckon, because he had a backhoe and hired a bunch of Eye-talians who didn't speak a lick of English, and they finished the job of digging out the foundations and painting the back wall with a picture of Jesus that's there. That picture of Jesus out back? That Jesus was painted by Eye-talians. Every speck of him."

"No wonder he was white," Sportcoat said. "Pastor Gee had me and Sausage help Sr. Bibb's son Zeke color him up."

"That was stupid. That was a good picture."

"He's still there. But he's colored now."

"Well, you shoulda left it like it was, on account of the man who brung his front loader and all them Eye-talians. I wish I could remember his name. Sister Paul would remember. Them two got along good. He liked her. She was quite the beauty in them days, y'know. She was well up in age, had to be north of seventy-five, I reckon, but Lord, she was . . . I wouldn't throw her outta bed for eating crackers, that's for sure. Not back then. She was well upholstered."

"You think there was . . ." Sportcoat moved his hand in a shaking motion.

Rufus grinned. "Y'know, there was always a lot of tipping going 'round in them days."

"Wasn't she married to the pastor?" Sportcoat asked.

"Since when did that monkey stop the show?" Rufus snickered. "He wasn't worth two cents. But to be honest, I don't know if she and that Eye-talian was doing the ding-a-ling, knock-a-boo thing or not. They got along good, is all. She was the only one he'd talk to. We wouldn't have built Five Ends without him. When he come along, we got all that digging done. And there was quite a lot of it. That's how that little church was built, Sport."

Rufus paused, remembering. "You know he gived the church its name? It was supposed to be *Four* Ends Baptist, see: north, south, east, and west, representing God's hand coming from all them directions. That was the pastor's idea. But when the Eye-talian added that back wall painting, somebody said let's make it Five Ends, since Jesus is an end to Himself. The pastor didn't like it. Said, 'I didn't want the picture up there in the first place.' But Sister Paul put her foot down and that was it. That's how it come to be *Five* Ends and not Four Ends. They still got that picture on the back wall, by the way?"

"Sure do. Weeds and all is up around it, but it's there."

"Do it still say over the top, 'May God Hold You in the Palm of His Hand'? Y'all ain't paint over that, did you?"

"Lord no. We ain't painted over them words, Rufus."

"Well, you ought not to. That's a credit to him, see, that Eye-talian. Long dead now. Doing God's work. A man ain't got to stand in church every Sunday to do God's work, y'know, Sport."

"That ain't telling me nothing."

"You asked me about Sister Paul, Sport. And I told it. You ought to take a ride out there and see her. She might know something about where that box is. Maybe she told Hettie where to hide it."

Sportcoat considered this. "That's a long subway ride."

"What you got to lose, Sport? She's the only one living from that time. I'd go with you. I'd like to see her. But them white folks out in Benson-hurst is a rough shuffle. They'll throw a pistol on a Negro in a minute."

At the mention of "pistol," Sportcoat blanched and reached for the

Seagram's again. "This world is damn complicated," he said, sipping deeply.

"Maybe Sausage'll go with you."

"He's too busy."

"Doing what?"

"Oh, he's in a frolic about something or other," Sportcoat said. "Running around accusing people of doing stuff they don't remember." To change the subject, he nodded at the generator. "Can I help? What's wrong with it?"

Rufus peered back into the guts of the old machine. "Ain't nothing wrong with it that I can't fix. G'wan out to Bensonhurst and take care of your business and look in on Sister Paul for me. Leave the bottle, though. A man needs a little shake and shimmy."

"Ain't you making some homemade King Kong?"

Rufus crouched down onto one knee and stuck his head back in the generator. "I'm always making King Kong," he said. "But it's a two-part thing. You got to make the 'King' first, then the 'Kong.' The 'King' part is easy. That's cooked and ready. I'm waiting for the 'Kong.' That takes time."

He hit a button on the side of the machine and the generator sputtered, coughed for a few seconds, howled in agony, then roared to life.

He glanced at Sportcoat, yelling over the din: "G'wan look in on Sister Paul! Let me know how she's doing. Wear your running shoes out in Bensonhurst!"

Sportcoat nodded, took a last sip of the Seagram's, and headed out. But instead of using the back emergency exit door, he took the door that led to a short hallway and stairs to the front door, which opened to the plaza. As he opened the outer door, a tall figure in a black leather jacket emerged from a broom closet underneath the stairwell that led upstairs and silently crept up behind him with a raised pipe. The man was two steps away when a baseball suddenly whipped down the stairwell from behind, struck the man in the back of the head, and sent him clattering back into the broom closet and out of sight. The next instant two boys, no older than nine, scampered down the stairs, whipping past a surprised Sportcoat. One of them scooped up the ball, which had come to a rest near the door, and blurted a hasty "Hey, Sportcoat!," then the boys vanished out the entrance, leaping down the front steps and out of sight, both of them laughing.

Sportcoat, irritated, quickly stepped out the door into the outside plaza to yell at their backs: "Slow your roll! Ain't y'all ever heard of a baseball field?" He marched down the steps in their direction, never noticing the man behind him.

Inside the broom closet, Earl, Bunch's hit man, lay sprawled on his rear end with his feet protruding out of the partially opened door, his back resting on the wall. He shook his head to clear his brain. He had to move, quick, before somebody else came downstairs. He smelled bleach. He suddenly realized his rear end was wet. His feet were atop a wheeled yellow bucket full of dirty water that had overturned. He inched his back off the wall, placed his hands on the floor to brace himself, and found his right hand landing on the wet end of a mop. The other hand was on some kind of contraption. He shifted and kicked the door open wide with his feet. In the light he saw, to his horror, that his left hand was sitting on a sprung rat trap—with a furry dead customer inside. He jumped to his feet with a yelp and burst out of the closet, down the hallway, out the front door of the building, speed walking through the plaza toward the nearby subway, wiping his hand frantically on his leather jacket, feeling the cold air blowing at his drenched pants and sneakers.

"Fucking old man," he muttered.

9

DIRT

THE TWO UNIFORMED COPS WALKED INTO THE FIVE ENDS
Baptist Church choir rehearsal five minutes after the fight between the
Cousins broke out. The fight had actually started twenty-three years
before. That's how long Nanette and her cousin Sweet Corn had been
arguing.

Sister Gee, a tall, handsome woman of forty-eight, sat in the choir
pew fiddling with her house keys and staring down in her lap as the
Cousins railed. "Lord," she murmured as the Cousins hissed at each
other, "please rein in them mules."

As if in answer, the back door of the church opened and two white
cops stepped through the tiny vestibule and into the sanctuary, the light
of the bare bulb glinting off their shiny badges and brass buttons. The
tinkling of their keys clanking against each other sounded like tiny bells
as they made their way up the sawdust-covered aisle to the front, their
leather gun holsters slapping against their hips. They stopped when they
reached the pulpit, facing the choir of five women and two men, who
stared back at them, with the exception of Pudgy Fingers, Sportcoat's

son, who sat at the end of the choir pew, his sightless eyes covered by shades.

"Who's in charge here?" one of the cops asked.

Sister Gee, sitting in the first row, took him in. He was young, nervous, and thin. Behind him stood an older cop, a thick man with wide shoulders and crow's-feet around blue eyes. She watched the older cop's eyes quickly scan the room. She had the impression she had seen him before. He removed his cap and spoke softly to the younger cop in a voice with a slight Irish lilt. "Mitch, take your cap off."

The younger cop obliged, then asked again, "Who's in charge?"

Sister Gee felt every eyeball in the choir swing toward her.

"In this church," she said, "we says hello to a person before we states our business."

The cop held up a blue folded sheet of paper in his hand. "I'm Officer Dunne. We got a warrant here for Thelonius Ellis."

"Who?"

"Thelonius Ellis."

"Ain't nobody here by that name," Sister Gee said.

The young cop looked at the choir behind Sister Gee and asked, "Anybody know him? We got a warrant here."

"They don't know nothing about no warrant," Sister Gee said.

"I'm not talking to you, miss. I'm talking to them."

"Seems to me you ain't made up your mind about who you come to talk to, Officer. First you come in and ask who's in charge, so I told it. Then instead of talking to me, you turns around and talks to them. Who you come to talk to? Me or them? Or is you just come by to make a bunch of announcements?"

Behind him, the older cop spoke. "Mitch, check the outside, would ya?"

"We already did that, Potts."

"Check it again."

The young cop turned, smartly snapped the blue warrant into Potts's waiting hand, and vanished out the vestibule door.

Potts waited until the church door closed, then turned to Sister Gee apologetically. "Young people," he said.

"I know it."

"I'm Sergeant Mullen from the Seven-Six. They call me Sergeant Potts."

"If you don't mind my asking, what kind of name is Potts, Officer?"

"It's better than pans."

Sister Gee chuckled. There was something about him that glistened, something warm that churned and billowed about, like a smoke cloud filled with sparklers. "I'm Sister Gee. You got a real first name, sir?"

"Not worth using. Potts is it."

"Was somebody bald-headed, or looking on the bright side, or wanting to steal or tell the world something when you was born, on account of your people giving you that kind of name?"

"I made a complete haymes of some potatoes once, back when I was a wee lad, so my grammy gave me that nickname."

"What's haymes?"

"A mess."

"Well, that's a mess of a name."

"That'd make your name fair play, wouldn't it? Gee, you said? I'll leg it out the door if you say your first name's Golly."

Sister Gee heard one of the choir chuckle behind her, and felt herself stifling a smile. She couldn't help it. Something about this man made her insides lift. "I seen you someplace before, Officer Potts," she said.

"Just Potts. You mighta seen me around. I grew up four blocks from here. A long time ago. I was a detective in the Cause."

"Well now . . . maybe that's where I seen you."

"But that was twenty years ago."

"I was here twenty years ago," she said thoughtfully. She rubbed her cheek, staring at Potts for what seemed a long time, then her eyes sparkled as her face unfolded into a sly smile. Her smile displayed a raw, natural beauty that caught Potts off guard. The woman, he thought, was all good handwriting.

"I know," she said. "On Ninth Street near the park. At that old bar there. The Irish place. Rattigan's. *That's* where I seen you."

Potts reddened. Several choir members smiled. Even the Cousins grinned.

"I've been known to have a business meeting there from time to time," he said wryly, recovering. "If you don't mind my asking, were you having one there too? At the same time? When you saw me?"

"*Ohlord!*" came a hushed laugh from someone in the choir. The two words mashed together like two coins: *ohlord!* This thing had gotten delicious. The choir laughed. Now it was Sister Gee's turn to blush.

"I don't go to no bars," Sister Gee said hurriedly. "I does day's work straight across the street from Rattigan's."

"Day's work?"

"Housework. I clean that big brownstone house there. Been cleaning for that family fourteen years. If I had a nickel for every bottle I pick up on the curb from Rattigan's on Mondays, I'd have me something."

"I keep my bottles inside the bar," Potts said in an offhand way.

"It ain't a bother to me where your bottles goes," Sister Gee said. "My job is to clean. It don't matter what I clean. Dirt's the same wherever it goes."

Potts nodded. "Some kind of dirt's harder to clean than others."

"Well, that do depend," she said.

The lightness in the room seemed to be leaving, and Potts felt some resistance coming. They both did. Potts glanced at the choir. "Can I have a private word?"

"Surely."

"Maybe in the basement?"

"It's too cold down there," Sister Gee said. "They can rehearse down there. There's a piano."

The choir, relieved, quickly got up and filed out toward the back door of the sanctuary. As Nanette passed, Sister Gee grabbed her wrist and said softly, "Take Pudgy Fingers."

The remark was casual, but Potts saw the glance between the two women. There was something about it.

When the door closed, she turned to him and said, "We was talking about something before, now?"

"Dirt," Potts said.

"Oh yes," she said, sitting down again. He saw now she was not just handsome, but rather had a quiet, cumulative beauty. She was a tall woman, middle-aged, whose face was not etched with the stern lines of church folks who've seen too much and done little about it other than pray. Her face was firm and decisive, with smooth milky brown skin; the thick hair with a bit of gray, neatly parted; her slender, proud frame clad in a modest flower-print dress. She sat erect in the pew; her poise was that of a straight-backed ballet dancer, yet with her slim elbows dangling on the rail in front of her, jingling her keys lazily in one hand, eyeing the white cop, she had an ease and confidence he found slightly unsettling. After a moment, she leaned back and placed a slender brown arm on the top edge of the pew, the small movement graceful and supple. She moved, Potts thought, like a gazelle. He suddenly found himself struggling to think clearly.

"You said some kind of dirt's harder to clean than others," she said. "Well, that's my job, Officer. I'm a house cleaner, see. I work in dirt. I chase dirt all day. Dirt don't like me. It don't set there and say, 'I'm hiding. Come get me.' I got to go out and find it to clean it out. But I don't hate dirt for being dirt. You can't hate a thing for being what it is. Dirt makes me who I am. Wherever I try to rid the world of it, I'm making things a little better for somebody. Same with you. The fellers you seek, crooks and all, they ain't saying 'Here I am. Come get me.' Most of 'em, you got to seek out, scoop up in some form or fashion. You brings justice to things, which makes the world a little nicer for somebody. Me and you has got the same job, in a way. We clean dirt. We clean up after people. We collects other people's mess, though I reckon it's not fair to call someone living a wrong life a problem, or a mess . . . or dirt."

Potts found himself smiling. "You oughta be a lawyer," he said.

Sister Gee crinkled her brow, looking suspicious. "You funning me?"

"No." He laughed.

"You can tell by the way I talk I'm not a book-learned person. I'm a country woman. I wanted to go to school for something," she said wistfully. "But that was long ago. Back when I was a child in North Carolina. Ever been to the South?"

"No, ma'am."

"Where you from?"

"I told you. Here. The Cause District. Silver Street."

She nodded. "Well how 'bout that."

"But my folks were from Ireland."

"Is that an island?"

"It's a place where folks can stop and think. The ones with brains, anyway."

She laughed, and as she did, Potts felt as if he were watching a dark, silent mountain suddenly blink to life, illuminated by a hundred lights from a small, quaint village that had lived on the mountainside for a hundred years, the village appearing out of nowhere, all the lights aglow at once. Every feature of her face glowed. He found himself wanting to tell her every sorrow he ever knew, including the knowledge that the Ireland of the vacation folders wasn't Ireland, that the memory of his ancient grandmother from the old country walking down Silver Street holding his hand when he was eight, clasping her last nickel in her palm, biting her lip as she hummed a sad song from her childhood of poverty and privation, wandering the Irish countryside looking for home and food, would kick through his arteries and bust into his heart until he was a grown man:

> *The grass waves green above them; soft sleep is theirs*
> *   for aye;*
> *The hunt is over, and the cold; the hunger passed away . . .*

Instead, he said simply, "It wasn't so nice."

She chuckled uneasily, surprised by his response, and watched him blush. Suddenly she felt her heart flutter. A charged silence descended on the room. They both felt it, felt themselves suddenly being propelled along a large chasm, feeling the irresistible urge to reach out, to reach across, to stretch their hands from opposite sides of a large, cavernous valley that was nearly impossible to cross. It was way too large, too far, just unreasonable, ridiculous. Yet . . .

"This fella," Potts said, breaking the silence, "this fella I'm looking for, he's uh . . . if his name's not Thelonius Ellis, what is it?"

She was silent now, the smile gone, looking away, the spell broken.

"It's all right," he said. "We know what happened with the shooting, more or less." He meant to say it lightly, as a comfort, but it sounded official and he didn't want that. The lack of sincerity in his own voice surprised him. There was an ease, a gentle filter in this long, chocolate woman that opened up a part of him that normally stayed closed. He had only four months to retirement. It was four months too long. He wished it were yesterday. He felt a sudden urge to take off his uniform, throw it to the floor, and walk downstairs with the choir and sing.

He found himself blurting: "I'm retiring soon. A hundred twenty days. Going fishing. Maybe I'll sing in a choir too."

"That ain't no way to spend the rest of your life."

"Singing in a choir?"

"No. Fishing."

"I can think of nothing better."

"Well, if that floats your boat, go ahead on. I reckon that's better than the funerals and going to large drinking gatherings."

"Like Rattigan's?"

She waved her hand. "That place don't bother me. They fight and squabble in every drinking hole from one to the next all over this world. It's the God-fearing places that's the worst. God is the last thing in some of these churches out here. Seems like they do more fighting than praying in the church today than they do on the street. Ain't nowhere safe. It didn't used to be that way."

Her words brought Potts around. With effort he returned to business. "Can I ask you about this fella, Thelonius Ellis?"

Sister Gee raised her hand. "Hand before God, ain't nobody 'round this church by that name that I know of."

"That's the name we got. Got it from an eyewitness."

"Must've been Ray Charles who told it. Or maybe it's somebody from another church."

Potts smiled. "You and I know he went to this church."

"Who?"

"The old man. The shooter. Drinks a lot. Knows everybody."

Sister Gee smiled grimly. "Why ask me? Your man knew him."

"What man?"

Sister Gee tilted her head at him. The tilt of that lovely face rendered him momentarily helpless. He felt as if a bird's wing had suddenly brushed his face and pushed a cool puff of misted air into it, the mist fluttering down onto his shoulders. His eyebrows lifted as he blinked at her, then his gaze shifted to the floor. He felt the emotional door he'd managed to close moments before swing open again. Staring at the floor, he found himself wondering how old she was.

"The cop who worked for Hot Sausage," she said.

"Hot who?"

"The cop," Sister Gee said patiently, "who worked for Hot Sausage. In the basement boiler room. Hot Sausage is the head janitor and boiler man. The janitor under him. The young guy. He was your guy."

"What's Hot Sausage's real name?"

She chuckled. "Why you trying to confuse me? We talking about your man. Hot Sausage is the janitor at Building Seventeen. The colored boy that was janitoring under him . . . *he* saved Deems's life, not nobody else. Folks 'round here don't know whether to thank him or throw a bucket of water on him."

Potts was silent. Sister Gee smiled.

"Everybody in the Cause knowed he was a cop. Don't you know your own people?"

Potts found himself resisting an urge to sprint out of the room, run back to the precinct, and beat the captain silly. He felt stupid. This was cleaning up garbage for the captain. Jet, Mr. First Black Everything. The kid didn't have the stuff to be a detective. Too young. No experience. No savvy. No allies, no mentors, except maybe him. The captain had insisted, "We need Negroes down in the Cause Houses." The guy had a soundproof head. How stupid can the captain be?

"That kid's transferred out to Queens," he said. "I'm glad. He's a good kid. I trained him."

"Is that why you're here?" Sister Gee asked.

"No. They asked me to step in because I know the area. They're . . . trying to make a move on these new drug dealers."

He saw her expression change slightly. "Can I ask you a personal question?" she asked.

"Surely."

"How does a detective go back to putting on a uniform?"

"That's a long story," he said. "I grew up here, as I said. I like the hours. I like the people. If the cops want to make a move on these drug lords, I'll be a Holy Joe about it."

Sister Gee could not completely keep a smirk from climbing across her face. "If this is the move they're making, it's sideways," she said. "Sportcoat's seventy-one. He ain't no drug dealer."

Potts continued, "We'd like to talk to him."

"You won't have no trouble finding him. He's a deacon in this here church. Some call him Deacon Cuffy. But most call him Sportcoat on account of him liking to wear them things. You can get his name easily enough from that. That's the most I can offer you. I got to live here."

"You know him well?"

"Twenty years. Since I was twenty-eight."

Potts quickly did the math in his head. *She was ten years younger than me,* he thought. He found himself straightening his jacket to cover his slight paunch. "What's his job?" he asked.

"Odd jobs mostly. Does a bit of everything. Works over at Itkin's Liquors some days. Cleans our basement other days. Takes out the trash. Gardens for a few white folks around these parts. He's got a real green thumb. Can do just about anything with plants. He's known for that. And for drinking. And baseball."

Potts thought a moment. "Is this the umpire from the baseball games between you and the Watch Houses? The one that yells and runs around all the bases?"

"One and the same."

Potts laughed. "Funny fella. I saw those games when I was on patrol sometimes. There was a hell of a ballplayer down there. Some kid . . . he was about fourteen or so. He could pitch like the dickens."

"That's Deems. The one he shot."

"You're kidding."

She sighed and was silent a moment. "Deems sat right where you is every Sunday till he was twelve or thirteen. Sportcoat—Deacon

Cuffy—he was Deems's Sunday school teacher. And his coach. And everything else to him. Till Hettie died. That's his wife."

This is why, Potts thought bitterly, *I got to get out of the business.* "What happened to her?"

"She fell in the harbor and drowned. Two years ago. Nobody ever did figure that out."

"You think your man had anything to do with that?"

"Sportcoat ain't my man. I been low in my life, but not that low. I'm married. To the minister here."

Potts felt his heart fall. "I see," he said.

"He ain't had nothing to do with Hettie dying—Sportcoat, I'm talking about. It's just how things work around here. Fact is, he was one of the few around here who really loved his wife."

She sat very still as she spoke, but her lovely olive eyes bore a softness and a hurt so deep that when he looked in them he saw the swirls of pools beneath; he felt as if he were looking at a piece of ice cream left on a picnic table in the hot sun too long. Regret poured out of her eyes like water. She seemed to be breaking apart in front of him.

He felt himself reddening and looked away. He was about to blurt an apology when he heard her say, "You looks a lot better in street clothes than you do wearing that fancy uniform. I guess that's why I remember you."

Later, much later, it occurred to him that maybe she remembered him because she had been watching him, sitting outside the bar with his friends listening to the bitter soldiers of the IRA swear at the British and complain about the neighborhood going down because the Negro and the Spanish had arrived with their civil rights nonsense, taking the subway jobs, the janitor jobs, the doorman jobs, fighting for the scraps and chicken bones the Rockefellers and all the rest tossed to them all. He found himself stammering, "So I needn't look into her death?"

"Look all you want. Hettie was a hard woman. She was a hard woman because she lived a hard life out here. But she was good through and through. She wore the pants in that house. Sportcoat did everything she told him. Except," she chuckled, "when it came to that cheese."

"Cheese?"

"They give out free cheese in one of the buildings every first Saturday of the month. Hettie hated that. The two of them fought about it all the time. But other than that, they were good together."

"What do you think happened to her?"

"She walked into the harbor and drowned herself. Things ain't been right around this church since."

"Why'd she do it?"

"She was tired, I reckon."

Potts sighed. "Should I write that in my report?"

"Write whatever you want. The truth is, I hope Sportcoat's run off. Deems ain't worth going to jail for. Not no more."

"I understand. But your guy's armed. Maybe unstable. That creates instability in a community."

Sister Gee snorted. "Things got unstable 'round here four years ago when that new drug come in. This new stuff—I don't know what they call it—you smoke it, you put it in your veins with needles . . . however you do it, once you do it a few times you is stuck with it. Never seen nothing like it around here before, and I seen a lot. This projects was safe till this new drug come in. Now the old folks is getting clubbed coming home from work every night, getting robbed outta their little payday money so these junkies can buy more of Deems's poison. He ought to be ashamed of hisself. His grandfather would kill him if he was living."

"I understand. But your man can't take the law into his own hands. That's what this is for," he said, holding up the warrant.

Now her face hardened, and a space opened up between them again. "Warrant on. And while y'all is throwing them warrants around, maybe y'all can throw a warrant at the person who stole our Christmas Club money. There's a couple thousand in there, I expect."

"What's that about?"

"Christmas Club. We gathered that money every year for us to buy our kids toys at Christmas. Hettie was the one who collected the money and kept it in a little box. She was good about it. Never told a soul where she put it, and every Christmas she handed you your money. Problem is, she's gone now and Sportcoat don't know where it is."

"Why not ask him?"

Sister Gee laughed. "If he knew, he'da gived it back. Sportcoat wouldn't steal from the church. Not for drink even."

"For drink, I seen people do worse."

Sister Gee frowned at him, frustration etched across her clear, pretty face. "You's a kind person, I can tell. But we is poor folks here in this church. We saves our little dimes for Christmas presents for our children. We pray for each other and to a God that redeems, and that does us well. Our Christmas money's missing and likely gone for good, and that's God's will, I reckon. To y'all police, that don't mean nothing other than maybe old Sportcoat mighta took it. But you're wrong there. Sportcoat would throw hisself in the harbor before he'd take a penny from any soul in this world. What happened was, he got drunk out of his mind and tried to clean this place up in one big swoop. And because of it, you ain't never seen so many cops turning up rocks trying to get hold of him. What's that say to us?"

"We want to protect him. Clemens works for a pretty rough bunch. That's who we're really going after."

"Then arrest Deems. And the rest of 'em who's selling whatever the devil wants."

Potts sighed. "Twenty years ago I could've done it. Not now."

He felt the space between them close up, and he wasn't imagining it.

Sister Gee felt it as well. She felt his kindness, his honesty and sense of duty. And she felt something else. Something big. It was as if there were a magnet somewhere inside him pulling her spiritually toward him. It was odd, exciting, thrilling even. She watched as he rose and moved toward the door. She quickly stood and walked down the aisle with him, Potts humming nervously, picking his way past the woodstove and down the sawdust-covered aisle to the door as she watched him out the corner of her eye. She hadn't felt that way about a man since her father showed up at school one afternoon to walk her home after a boy in her class got beat up by some white kids, the feeling of comfort and safety that radiated from someone who cared about her so deeply. And a white man, no less. It was an odd, wonderful gush to feel that coming from a man, any man, especially a stranger. She felt like she was dreaming.

They stopped at the vestibule door. "If the deacon turns up, tell him he's safer with us," Potts said.

Sister Gee was about to respond when she heard a voice from the vestibule say, "Where's my daddy?"

It was Pudgy Fingers. He'd wandered upstairs and was seated in a folding chair in the dark next to the church front door, his eyes covered with their customary shades, rocking back and forth as he always did. In the basement, the choir sang, obviously no one bothering to fetch him, since Pudgy Fingers knew his way around the church as good as anyone and often liked to wander about the tiny building on his own.

Sister Gee placed a hand on his elbow to stand him up. "Pudgy, g'wan back to rehearsal," she said. "I'll be right there."

Pudgy Fingers reluctantly stood. She carefully spun him around and placed his hand on the stair railing. They watched him work his way downstairs and disappear into the basement.

When he was out of sight Potts said, "I expect that's his son."

Sister Gee was silent.

"You never told me what building your man lives in," he said.

"You never asked it," she said. She turned to the window, her back to him, and rubbed her hands nervously as she gazed out the window.

"Should I go down and ask his son?"

"Why would you do that? You see the boy's not all the way there."

"He knows where he lives, I'm sure."

She sighed and continued to stare out the window. "Lemme ask you, what good does it do to squeeze the one person around here who done the little bit of good that's been done?"

"That's not my call."

"I already told you. Sportcoat is easy to find. He's around these parts."

"Should I write that down as a lie? We haven't seen him."

Her expression darkened. "Write it down however you like. However the cut comes or goes, once y'all take Sportcoat to jail, social services will have Pudgy Fingers. They'll ship him up to the Bronx or Queens someplace and we won't see him no more. That's Hettie's boy there. Hettie was in her forties when she had him. For a woman, that's old to have a child. And for someone who lived a hard life like she did, that's very old indeed."

"I'm sorry. But that's not my department either."

"Course not. But I'm the type of person that goes to sleep if something comes along that don't interest me," Sister Gee said.

Potts laughed bitterly. "Remind me to eat some knockout pills next time I go to work," he said.

Now it was her turn to laugh. "I didn't mean it that way," she said. "Hettie done a lot for this church. She was here at the very beginning of it. She never took a penny of the Christmas money for herself, even when she lost her job. Do what you will or may, but once you arrest Sportcoat, they'll roll Pudgy Fingers up in, too, and that's a different pack of crackers altogether. I reckon we'd make a fight of it 'round him."

Potts, exasperated, held out his hands. "You want I should pass out free jawbreakers to every kid in the projects with a gun? The law's the law. Your guy is a triggerman. He shot somebody. In front of witnesses! The guy he shot ain't a choirboy—"

"He *was* a choirboy."

"You know how it works."

Sister Gee didn't move from the vestibule window. Potts watched her, straight-backed, tall, staring outside, breathing slowly, her breasts moving like two nodding headlights. Her face turned in profile as her olive eyes searched the streets, the fragility and gentleness gone, the cheekbones, the strong jaw, the wide nose that flared at the tip, angry again. He thought of his own wife, back home in Staten Island in her bathrobe, cutting coupons from the *Staten Island Advance,* the local paper, her eyes moist from boredom, complaining about getting her nails done on Thursday, her hair done Friday, missing bingo night on Saturday, her waist growing wider, her patience growing thinner. He saw Sister Gee rub her neck and found himself pondering the notion of placing his fingers there, then down her long arched back. He thought he saw her mouth move, but he was distracted and couldn't hear. She was saying something and he caught just the end of it, and only then did he realize it was he who was talking, not her, him saying something about how he had always loved the neighborhood and came back to the Cause District because he'd had some trouble at another precinct trying to be an honest cop, and the Cause was the only place he felt free because he'd grown up just a few blocks away and the neighborhood still felt like home. That's why he was back, to finish his career here, to be home at the end. And this case, he said, was "just a doozy, in every way. If this was any other part of Brooklyn, it might disappear. But your choirboy Deems is part of a big outfit. They got interests all over the city, with the mob, politicians, even the cops—and you didn't hear that last part from me. They'll hurt anyone who bothers their interests. That's got to be dealt with. That's just how it is."

She listened in silence as he spoke, staring out the window at the darkened projects, at the Elephant's old boxcar on the next block, the worn, battered streets with newspapers blowing about, the hulks of old cars that sat at the curbs like dead beetles. She could see Potts's reflection in the window as he talked behind her, the white man in a cop's uniform. But there was something inside the blue eyes, in the drift of his broad shoulders, in the way he stood and moved, that made him different. She watched his reflection in the window as he talked, his face downcast, fiddling with his hands. There was something large inside him, she concluded—a pond, a pool, a lake maybe. The lovely Irish brogue in his voice gave him an air of elegance, despite his wide shoulders and thick hands. A man of reason and kindness. He was, she realized, as trapped as she was.

"Let it roll as it will then," she said softly to her reflection.

"You can't leave it there."

She looked at him sideways, tenderly. Her dark eyes glistened in the vestibule.

"Come 'round and see me again," she said. With that, she opened the church door for him.

Potts, without a word, placed his NYPD cap on his head and stepped out into the dark evening, the smell of the dirty wharf drifting into his nose and consciousness with the ease of lilacs and moonbeams, fluttering around his awakened heart like butterflies.

10

SOUP

THE MORNING AFTER HE VISITED RUFUS, SPORTCOAT LAY
in bed trying to decide, with Hettie's help, whether to wear his plaid
sport coat or go with the straight yellow.

She was in a good mood and they were getting on quite well when the
twang of an errant guitar interrupted them. Hettie vanished as Sportcoat, irritated, lumbered over to the window and looked down, frowning
as a crowd gathered in the plaza at the front steps of Building 17, which
faced his Building 9. On the front steps four musicians—one guitarist,
one accordion player, and two playing bongos and congas—had already
gathered. From his fourth-floor view, Sportcoat saw several other bongo
and conga players approaching the plaza, toting their instruments.

"Geez," he grumbled. He looked back into the room. Hettie had
gone. And they were getting on so good too.

"It ain't nothing, Hettie," he said aloud to the empty room. "Just Joaquin and his bongos. C'mon back." But she was gone.

Irritated by her disappearance, he crawled out of bed, having slept in
his pants, and put on a shirt and a sport jacket—the yellow one that

Hettie had favored—and sipped a quick bracer from a leftover bottle of Kong, which Hettie did not favor, but that was what she got for leaving. He stuck the bottle in his pocket and stumbled out into the plaza, where a crowd had gathered around the front stoop of Building 17 to hear Joaquin and his band Los Soñadores (the Dreamers).

Joaquin Cordero was the only honest numbers runner in Cause Houses history, as far as anyone could remember. He was a short, squat, brown-skinned man whose good looks were squeezed into a head that resembled a ski jump in that the back of his head was flat as a pancake and the top of his head sloped downward like a ski slope, thus his childhood nickname "Salto," or "jump" in Spanish. He didn't mind. Joaquin was what he called a "people person," and like any good people person who wasn't in politics, he had many jobs. He collected numbers from a custom-made countertop window at his first-story apartment in Building 17—the window accessible to pedestrians, with a special cabinet beneath the inside window ledge he'd constructed himself, from which he sold loose cigarettes, whiskey shots, and wine in paper cups to customers who needed a boost of happy sauce in the mornings. He also ran a part-time taxi service, charged a reasonable price for doing laundry for busy workers, repaired chair seat bottoms for anyone who asked, chased the occasional bored housewife, and played guitar and sang. Joaquin was, as they say, multitalented. He was the maestro of the Cause and his merry band was the hometown favorite.

It was hard for anyone in the Cause to say whether Joaquin and Los Soñadores were actually any good. But there wasn't a wedding, an event, or even a funeral where Los Soñadores were not participants, if not in person, then at least in spirit, for while they sounded like a diesel engine trying to crank on a cold October morning, it was the effort that counted, not the result. It didn't matter that Joaquin's ex-wife, Miss Izi, declared the only reason Los Soñadores played at all the Cause events was because Joaquin was piping Miss Krzypcinksi, the young white social worker with big boobs who couldn't clap on beat and wouldn't have known a salsa rhythm if it were dressed like an elephant in a bathtub, but whose wide hips moved with the kind of rhythm every man in the Cause could hear a thousand miles away. Miss Krzypcinksi ran the Cause Houses Senior Center, which doled out money and tidbits for special events all over the projects. And it did seem odd that the senior center, which constantly cried broke, always seemed to find the funds to pay Los Soñadores to play lumpty-dumpty music for every occasion in the Cause Houses when Hector Vasquez in Building 34 played trombone for Willie Bobo and Irv Thigpen in Building 17 played drums for Sonny Rollins. Couldn't she get those guys to play around here sometime?

It didn't matter. Whenever Los Soñadores played, clunking along like four jalopies in tandem, they drew a crowd. The Dominicans nodded politely and chuckled among themselves. The Puerto Ricans shrugged and said only God was greater than Celia Cruz and that crazy Eddie Palmieri, who stirs up salsa jazz so hot you *charanga* away all your money in the nightclub, so what difference does it make? The blacks, mostly Southern-born Christians who grew up in churches where preachers packed pistols, slung cotton, and could, without warning or warmup, toss their voices across half a state from their pulpits while holding a bale of cotton with one hand and fingering a female choir member with the other, liked any kind of music, so what's the bother? They all danced along and got along, and why not? Joaquin's music was free, and music came from God. Anything from God was always a good thing.

Sportcoat wandered to the back edge of a crowd surrounding the front steps of Building 17, where Los Soñadores, their amps and drums set up on the top plateau of the building entrance steps, plunked on. An electric extension cord strung raggedly across the makeshift stage supplied power to the amps. The cord led to the first-floor window of Joaquin's place, the window located right next to the main entrance of the building. On the building awning over the band members, a banner stretched across the doorway, which Sportcoat, standing at a distance, could not read.

He stopped and watched from the back of the crowd as Joaquin, croaking away in Spanish, came to a particularly moving passage and lifted his voice to a higher pitch, causing his merry musicians to saw away at the accordion and bang their bongos with even more gusto.

"G'wan, Joaquin!" Sportcoat said. He gulped a sip of King Kong and grinned at a woman standing next to him, displaying several yellowed teeth that stuck out of his front gums like sticks of butter. "Whatever they doing," he said, "it ain't no put-down."

The woman, a young Dominican mother with two little children, ignored him.

"G'wan, Joaquin! The more I drink, the better you sound," he yelled to the stage. Several people nearby, awed by the display of musicianship, smiled at the remark, but their gazes were trained on the band. Joaquin was on a roll. The band chunked forward. They did not notice Sportcoat.

"Cha cha cha!" Sportcoat blurted cheerfully. "Play it, fellas!" He took another sip of the Kong, shook his hips, then hooted, "Best bongo music in the world!"

That last crack brought a smile to the face of the mother next to him and she glanced at him. When she saw who it was, her smile disappeared and she backed away, pulling her children protectively to her. A man nearby saw her step away, spotted Sportcoat, and he too backed off, followed by a second.

Sportcoat didn't notice. As the crowd peeled away from him, he spotted at the front of the crowd near the band the familiar porkpie hat of Hot Sausage, nodding to the *bachata* music, holding a cigar in his teeth. Sportcoat worked his way forward through the crowd and tapped Hot Sausage on the shoulder. "What's the party for?" he asked. "And where'd you get that cigar?"

Sausage turned to him and froze, his eyes wide. He glanced around nervously, yanked the cigar from his mouth, and hissed, "What you doing here, Sport? Deems is out."

"Out where?"

"Out the hospital. Out the house. Around."

"Good. He can get back to baseball," Sportcoat said. "You got another cigar? I ain't had a cigar in twenty years."

"Ain't you heard me, Sport?"

"Stop fussing at me and gimme a cigar." He nodded his head toward his hip jacket pocket, where the Kong bottle was stashed. "I got the gorilla here. Want some?"

"Not out here," Sausage hissed, but then took a quick glance in the direction of the flagpole, saw the coast was clear, snatched the bottle out of Sportcoat's pocket, and nipped quickly, slipping the bottle back in Sportcoat's pocket when he was done.

"What's the cigar for?" Sportcoat asked. "You get Sister Bibb pregnant?"

The reference to Hot Sausage's part-time lover and the church organist, Sister Bibb, did not please Hot Sausage. "That ain't funny," he grunted. He took the cigar out of his mouth, looking uncomfortable. "I won a bet," he murmured.

"Who's the sucker?" Sportcoat asked.

Hot Sausage glanced at Joaquin, who from the front steps was staring at somebody and suddenly went pale. Indeed, Sportcoat noticed the entire Los Soñadores band staring at somebody now: him. The music, which had loped along poorly before, dropped to an even slower clip-clop.

Sportcoat pulled the bottle of Kong out his pocket and finished the last corner, then nodded at Los Soñadores. "Let's face it, Sausage. They ain't Gladys Knight and the Pips. Why'd Joaquin bring 'em out of mothballs?"

"Can't you see the sign?"

"What sign?"

Sausage pointed to the sign above the band scrawled on a piece of cardboard, which read *Welcome Home, Soup.*

"Soup Lopez is out of jail?" Sportcoat said, surprised.

"Yes, sir."

"Glory! I thought Soup got seven years."

"He did. He came out in two."

"What was he in for again?" Sportcoat asked.

"I don't know. I reckon they went broke feeding him and cut him loose. I hope he ain't hungry today."

Sportcoat nodded. Like most in the Cause, he had known Soup all his life. He was a mild, scrawny, quiet runt who got his exercise mostly by running from the local bullies. He was also the worst player on Sportcoat's baseball team. Little Soup preferred to spend his afternoons at home watching *Captain Kangaroo*, a children's show about a gentle white man whose gags with puppets and characters like Mr. Moose and Mr. Green Jeans delighted him. At nine, Soup hit a growth spurt the likes of which no one in the Cause had ever seen. He grew from four foot nine to five foot three. At ten he mushroomed to nearly six feet. At eleven he topped off at six feet two inches and had to sit on the floor of his mother's living room and strain his neck to peer down at the small black-and-white screen to watch *Captain Kangaroo*, whose puppet tricks and gags he found, at that age, increasingly boring. At fourteen he abandoned *Captain Kangaroo* altogether and later favored a new TV show, *Mister Rogers' Neighborhood*, about a gentle white man with better puppets. He also added three inches to his frame. By sixteen he topped six foot ten, two hundred seventy-five pounds, all of it muscle, with a face scary enough to make the train leave the track, with the kind disposition of a nun. But, alas, Soup played baseball like one too. Despite his size he remained the worst player on Sportcoat's team, in part on account of he was so tall he had a strike zone the size of Alaska. Plus the idea of striking a ball, or anything else, was foreign to Soup.

Like most of Sportcoat's team, Soup disappeared from adult radar at the Cause when he entered the labyrinth of his teenage years. One minute he was striking out to the guffaws of the opposing team, the Watch Houses, the next minute word got out that Soup was in jail—adult jail— at seventeen. What put him there, no one seemed to know. It didn't matter. Everybody went to jail in the Cause eventually. You could be the tiniest ant able to slip into a crack in the sidewalk, or a rocket ship that flew fast enough to break the speed of sound, it didn't matter. When society dropped its hammer on your head, well, there it is. Soup got seven years. It didn't matter what it was for. What mattered was that he was back. And this was his party.

"I think it's dandy that he's out," Sportcoat said. "He was a . . . well, he wasn't a solid ballplayer. But he always showed! Where's he at?"

"He's running late," Sausage said.

"We could use him as a coach for the team," Sportcoat said gaily. "He can help us get the game rolling again."

"What game?"

"The game against the Watch Houses. That's what I come to talk to you about."

"Forget the game," Sausage snapped. "You can't show your face out here, Sport."

"What you chunking at me for? I ain't the one out here making cha-cha at nine o'clock in the morning. Joaquin is the one you oughta be humping at. He should be taking numbers in his window right now. People got to get to work."

As if the band heard him, the music ground to a halt. Sportcoat looked up to see Joaquin heading inside.

"Soup ain't here yet!" someone said loudly.

"I gotta open for business," Joaquin said over his shoulder. He disappeared through the front door, followed by his band.

"He ain't worried about no business," Sausage grumbled. "He wants to be inside when the shooting starts."

"What shooting?"

Several people shoved past Sportcoat and Hot Sausage, forming a sloppy line beneath Joaquin's window. Slowly, reluctantly, Joaquin opened the window and stuck his head out. After peering both ways to make sure the coast was clear, he began taking number bets.

Sportcoat nodded at the window and said to Hot Sausage, "You gonna play today?"

"Sport, get the hell outta here and back ins—"

"Sausage!" a shrill voice hollered. "Are you gonna raise the flag or not?" Sausage had been interrupted by the high-pitched yammer of Miss Izi, who strode up with her hands folded across her chest, followed by Bum-Bum and Sister Gee. "We been waiting at the bench for a half hour. Where's the doughnuts? Did you know Soup Lopez is back?"

Sausage pointed to the sign over the building entrance. "Where you been? Alaska?"

Miss Izi looked at the sign, then back at Sausage, until her gaze slipped over to Sportcoat and she blinked in surprise.

"Oh, *papi*. What you doing here?"

"Nothing."

"*¿Papi, olvidaste lo que le hiciste a ese demonio Deems? Su banda de lagartos te va a rebanar como un plátano.* You got to leave, *papi*."

Sister Gee stepped forward and said evenly to Sportcoat, "Deacon, the police came by the church asking for you."

"I'mma find that Christmas money, Sister. I told the pastor I'm gonna and I'm gonna."

"They wasn't fretting about that. They was asking about somebody named Thelonius Ellis. You know him?"

Sausage had taken a seat on the top step of the building entrance when the women arrived. From his seat on the step, Sausage looked up, stunned, and then blurted, "What they want me for? I didn't shoot Deems!"

At the mention of "Deems," there was a pregnant silence. Several people standing in line to play numbers slipped away before placing their bets. The rest of the people stood in anxious silence, staring straight ahead, number papers in hand, edging forward, one eye in the direction of the flagpole where Deems worked, pretending not to have heard anything. This was juicy indeed, juicy enough to risk your life over but not juicy enough to get involved.

"I didn't know Thelonius Ellis was your name," Sister Gee said to Hot Sausage. "I thought you was Ralph, or Ray . . . something or other."

"What difference do it make?"

"Makes a big difference," she said, exasperated. "It makes me out to be a liar to the police."

"You can't be a liar 'bout what you don't know," Hot Sausage said. "The Bible says Jesus had many names."

"Well golly, Sausage, where's it say in the Bible that you're Jesus?"

"I ain't said I was Jesus. I said I ain't stuck with just one name."

"Well, how many names you got?" Sister Gee demanded.

"How many do a colored man need in this world?"

Sister Gee rolled her eyes. "Sausage, you never said nothing about having no other name. I thought your real name was Ray Olen."

"You mean Ralph Odum, not Ray Olen. *Ralph* Odum. Same thing. It don't matter. That's not my real name nohow. Ralph Odum's the name I gived to Housing when I come on staff twenty-four years ago. Ellis is my real name. Thelonius Ellis." He shook his head, pursing his lips. "Now the police want me. What I done?"

"They don't want you, Sausage. They *want* the Deacon here. I reckon they called your name thinking you was him."

"Well there it is," Hot Sausage fumed at Sportcoat, sucking his teeth. "You done pulled me into the swill again, Sport."

"What are you talking about?" Sister Gee asked.

But Hot Sausage ignored her. Boiling, he glared at Sportcoat. "Now the cops is hunting me. And Deems is hunting you! You happy?"

"This projects is going down!" Miss Izi exclaimed. "Everybody's hunting everybody!" She tried to sound disconsolate but instead sounded almost happy. This was high-grade gossip. Delicious. Exciting. The numbers players still in line who were listening shifted lustily, edging closer to the conversation, almost gleeful, their ears wide open, waiting for the next tidbit.

"How did this happen?" Sister Gee asked Sausage.

"Oh, I bought an old Packard back in fifty-two. I wasn't following the Ten Commandments back in them days, Sister. I had no license or papers or nothing when I come to New York, on account of I hoisted a shot, a sip, and a nip of spirits from time to time in them days. I bought that car and let Sport here register the dang thing for me. Sport's good at talking to white folks. He went down to motor vehicles with my birth certificate and got the license and all the papers and everything. One colored looks just like another down there. So . . ."

He removed his hat and wiped his head, glancing up at Sportcoat. "We keeps the license and switches off. One week he holds it. The next week I holds it. Now the cops is holding me to judgment on account of Sportcoat." Sausage barked at Sportcoat, "Somebody who seen you drop Deems in the plaza must've seen you beating it to my boiler room and told the cops." Then he said to Sister Gee, "They looking for him—with my name. Why I got to be burdened with his note? Only wrong I done to him is to place a bet."

"What bet?" Sister Gee asked.

Sausage glanced at Joaquin in the betting window, who, along with the line of bettors, was openly staring at them. Joaquin looked chagrined but remained silent.

"What difference do it make?" Hot Sausage said glumly. "I got bigger problems now."

"I'll explain it to the police," Sister Gee said. "I'll tell them your real name."

"Don't do that," Sausage said quickly. "I got a warrant out for me. Back in Alabama."

Sister Gee, Miss Izi, and Sister Billings stared at each other in surprise. Joaquin, and several people in line, watched with interest as well. This confession was unexpected but juicy.

"A warrant! Oh, that's bad luck, *papi*!" Joaquin piped up from his window. "You good people, too, bro." He said it so loudly that several people in line who had tuned out now tuned back in, staring at Hot Sausage.

Sausage glanced at them and said, "Whyn't you just put it on the radio, Joaquin?"

"That does change the bet, though, *papi*," Joaquin said.

"Don't try to twist out of it." Hot Sausage sucked his teeth. "I won the bet fair and square."

"What bet?" Sister Gee said.

"Well . . ." Sausage began, then trailed off. To Joaquin he said hotly, "I'd sleep in a hollow log before I give you a plugged nickel."

"Things happen, bro," Joaquin said sympathetically again. "I understand. But I still want my cigar."

"I'd fertilize my toilet with ten cigars before I give you one!"

"Could a grown-up speak here?" Sister Gee said impatiently. She turned to Sausage. "What was the bet?"

Sausage didn't address her, but rather turned to Sportcoat, looking sheepish. "Oh, it was about you, buddy—getting pulled in, arrested, y'see. I ain't mean nothing by it. I'da bailed you out—if I could. Best thing for you is to get arrested, Sport. But now I got to worry about my own skin." Hot Sausage looked away glumly, rubbing his jaw.

"A warrant ain't nothing, Sausage," Sportcoat said. "The police gives 'em out all over. Rufus over at the Watch Houses got a warrant on him too. Back in South Carolina."

"He does?" Sausage brightened immediately. "For what?"

"He stole a cat from the circus, except it wasn't no cat. It got big, whatever it was, so he shot it."

"Maybe it wasn't no cat he killed," Sausage snorted. "Rufus ain't got no moderation. Who knows what he done? That's the thing with a warrant. You don't know what it's for. When a person got a warrant on them, they coulda killed somebody!"

There was a pregnant silence as Miss Izi, Bum-Bum, Sister Gee, Joaquin, Sportcoat, and several people in line stared at Hot Sausage, who sat on the top step, fanning himself with his porkpie hat. Eventually he noticed them staring and said, "Well. What y'all looking at me for?"

"Did you . . . ?" Miss Izi asked.

"Izi, keep quiet!" Joaquin barked.

"Shut your talking hole, you evil gangster!" she snapped.

"Go take drowning lessons, woman!"

"Monkey!"

"Ape!"

"*Me gustaría romperte a la mitad, pero quién necesita dos de ustedes!*"

"Will y'all quit!" Sausage shouted. "I ain't ashamed to tell it. I was on a work crew in Alabama and runned off." He looked at Sportcoat. "So there."

"That's the difference between Alabama and South Carolina," Sportcoat said proudly. "In my home country, a man on a work crew *stays* on the work crew till the job is done. We ain't quitters in South Carolina."

"Can we rope this in and get to the problem!" Sister Gee said, her voice sharp. She turned to Sportcoat. "Deacon, you're gonna have to go to the police. Deems was a wonderful boy. But the devil's having his way with him right now. You can explain that to the police."

"I ain't explaining nothing. I done him no wrong that I recall," Sportcoat said.

"You don't remember humping Deems like a dog when you shot him?" Miss Izi said.

"I heard that too," a woman in line at Joaquin's window said to the man behind her.

"I was right there," Miss Izi said proudly. "He showed Deems who's boss."

The woman laughed and turned to Sportcoat. "Ooooh-wee! You a bad man, Mr. Sportcoat! Oh, well. Better to be a fat man in a graveyard than a thin man in a stew."

"What's that mean?" Sportcoat asked.

"Means Deems is gonna come meddlin'. And you best not be around," Hot Sausage said.

"Deems ain't gonna do nothing," Sportcoat said. "I known him all his life."

"It's not just him," Sister Gee said. "It's the folks he works for. I hear tell they're worse than a bunch of root doctors."

Sportcoat waved his hand dismissively. "I ain't come here to sit around talking all this who-shot-John nonsense. I come here," he said, glaring at Hot Sausage, "to talk to a certain boiler man about my umpire suit, which I put up in his boiler room."

"Well, since we is on the subject of taking back things, where's my driver's license with *your* picture on it using *my* name?" Hot Sausage asked.

"What you need that for?" Sportcoat said. "You's in trouble enough. Plus it's my week to hold it."

"It ain't my fault that your past is bad." Sausage held out his hand. "I'll take it now, please. You won't be needing it nohow."

Sportcoat shrugged and pulled out a weathered wallet, thick with papers, and from it produced the license, frayed around the edges, and handed it over. "Now gimme my umpire stuff so I can start up the game again. I'mma get these kids 'round here on the right track again."

"Is your cheese done slid off your cracker, Sport? These kids don't want no baseball. Them days ended the minute Deems walked off the team."

"He didn't walk off," Sportcoat said. "I threw him off for smoking them funny reefer cigarettes."

"Sport, you is more outta date than a Philadelphia nightclub. I know bartenders from Hong Kong smarter'n you. These children want tennis shoes now. And dungaree jackets. And dope. They whupping ass and robbing old folks to get it. Half of your baseball team works for Deems now."

"Soup don't work for him," Sportcoat said proudly.

"That's 'cause Soup was a guest of the state," Joaquin said from his window. "Give him time. You need to go, bro, just till things cool off. You can go stay with my cousin Elena in the Bronx if you want. She's never home. She got a good job working for the railroad."

Miss Izi snorted. "She's been boarded more times than the railroad too. Don't stay there, Sport. You'll get fleas. Or worse."

Joaquin's face reddened. "*Tienes una mente de una pista. Una sucia sucia!*"

"So does your mother!" Miss Izi said.

"All right already!" Sister Gee said, glancing around. The line of people waiting to play their numbers had quit, and most had taken seats on the stoop near Sausage to watch this theater, which was better than any numbers game. Sister Gee said, "Let's think this through," and as she spoke, the sound of the front door opening behind them was heard and she looked up over their shoulders, gaping in surprise. The rest followed her shocked gaze, glancing over their shoulders to a sight that brought them to their feet.

Standing behind them, Soup Lopez, a resplendent, smiling giant, in a crisp gray suit, white shirt, and splendid black bow tie—all six foot ten of him—stood on the top step, filling the open doorway of Building 17.

"Soup!"

"Soup Lopez! Back from the dead!"

"*¡Sopa! ¡Comprame una bebida! ¿De dónde sacaste ese traje?*"

"Home at last!" Soup roared.

Cries of greeting and handshakes all around as the crowd surrounded the big man, who towered over them. Joaquin, from his window, poured several quick whiskey shots into plastic cups, then abandoned the window altogether, emerging from the building with his guitar, followed by the bongo player of Los Soñadores, who hurriedly rushed out the building entranceway shouting in Spanish, "Nephew!" and hugged Soup, who lifted the small man like he was a pillow. Los Soñadores quickly plugged in and the horrible music began again, with even more gusto than before.

For the next hour and a half, Sportcoat's crisis was forgotten. It was still early, and Soup greeted all his old friends by amusing everyone with magic tricks. He picked up two women in one hand. He showed everybody one-handed push-ups he'd learned in prison. He showed off his shoes, size 18S, special made by the state of New York, and impressed his old coach, Sportcoat, by taking off one shoe and using it to swat a handball three hundred yards. "You always said I had good basics," he said proudly.

The joy encouraged a frolic, and several who were embarrassed to approach Sportcoat now came forward to shake his hand, pat him on the back, thank him for shooting Deems, and offer him drinks. One old grandmother gave him the two dollars she normally used to play the numbers, stuffing the money in his coat pocket. A young mother stepped forward and said, "You showed me how to can peaches," and kissed him. A thick-bodied Transit Authority worker named Calvin who manned the tollbooth at the local G train subway stop ambled up, shook Sportcoat's hand, and slipped five dollars into Sportcoat's pocket, saying, "My man."

The floodgates were open, and the crowd of onlookers who had fled when they first spotted him wandered back to marvel that he was still alive, gawk at him, and shake his hand.

"G'wan old-timer!"

"Sportcoat, you showed 'em!"

"Sport . . . *eres audaz. Estás caliente, bebé. Patearles el culo!*"

"Sportcoat, come bless my son!" a young pregnant mother shouted, her hands on her rounded stomach.

Sportcoat endured it all with a blend of awe, bashfulness, and pride, shaking hands and enjoying free drinks that were poured for him from Joaquin's window, paid for by his neighbors, the window now manned by Miss Izi, who apparently knew enough about her ex-husband to know he didn't give a hoot who poured the hooch so long as the fifty cents per shot was collected. Unbeknownst to him, she kept a quarter from each pour for herself. Handling charges.

The rush at Sportcoat was merry until Dominic Lefleur, the Haitian Sensation and Sportcoat's neighbor in Building 9, appeared with his friend Mingo, a horrid-looking old man with a pitted, pimply face. In his hand was a horrible-looking homemade doll, which consisted of three tiny couch pillows stuck together with a head that looked and felt suspiciously like four size-D batteries taped together covered by cloth. Dominic slapped Sportcoat on the back, held the doll out to him, and said, "You are now protected."

Bum-Bum, who had faithfully stood in line twenty minutes to play her number and who had lost her place twice since the party started and the line had been reduced to a line for whiskey shots, took umbrage.

"Why you spreading haints and spirits, Dominic?"

"It's good luck," Dominic said.

"He don't need luck. He got Jesus!"

"He can have this too."

"Jesus Christ don't need no witchery. Jesus don't need no ugly dolls. Jesus ain't got no limits. Look at Soup. Jesus brought him home 'cause we was praying for him. Ain't that right, Soup?"

Soup, in his suit and bow tie, towering over the party of folks drinking shots and a few now dancing to the horrific *bachata* of Los Soñadores, looked uncomfortable. "Truth is, Sister, I don't go to church no more. I'm a member of the Nation."

"What Nation?"

"The Nation of Islam."

"Is that like the United Nations?" Bum-Bum asked.

"Not really," he said.

"They got their own flag, like the Stars and Stripes?" Sausage asked.

"Them Stars and Stripes ain't mine, Brother Sausage," Soup said. "I got no country. I'm a citizen of the world. A Muslim."

"Oh . . ." Hot Sausage said, uncertain what else to say.

"See, Muhammad was the true Prophet of God. Not Jesus. And Muhammad didn't use no little dolls like Dominic here." Seeing the horror on Bum-Bum's face, Soup added, "But I agrees with you to a point, Miss Bum-Bum. Everybody needs something."

He was trying to be amenable, as Soup always was, but his words had a terrible effect. Bum-Bum stood with her hands on her hips, thunderstruck into silence. Dominic looked away in embarrassment. Sister Gee, Hot Sausage, and Sportcoat couldn't believe what they'd heard. Joaquin, noting a lull in the activity among them, unslung his guitar, slipped into the front door of the building as Los Soñadores chugged on, and emerged a minute later with a bottle of brandy.

"Welcome back, Soup. I saved this for you," Joaquin said.

Soup took the bottle in his giant hand. "I can't drink this," he said. "This is the white man's way of keeping the black man down."

"With Dominican brandy?" Joaquin said. "That's the best."

"It's piss compared to Puerto Rican brandy," Miss Izi said from Joaquin's window.

"Get out my window," Joaquin hissed angrily.

"I'm making money for you! Like before! Rabbithead!"

"Get out my window and take the midnight broom out of town, hussy!"

There was a fat glass ashtray at Miss Izi's elbow. She grabbed it and tossed it at her ex-husband. It was a mild, casual toss, flung like a Frisbee. She didn't even mean to strike him, and she didn't. Instead, the ashtray struck a pregnant woman in the shoulder. She was dancing near the front of the crowd with her boyfriend, and she quickly spun around and slapped Dominic, who was standing behind her, holding the doll. Being a gentleman, Dominic raised his hand to stop her from striking him a second time and inadvertently clunked the young mother's boyfriend on the head with the doll's hard battery head. In turn, the boyfriend reached his fist to whack Dominic, but instead his elbow struck Bum-Bum in the jaw, who had stepped over to help the young mother. Bum-Bum, furious at being hit, flung a punch at her assailant and struck Sister Gee, who fell into Eleanora Soto, treasurer of the Cause Houses Puerto Rican Statehood Society, who was sipping a cup of whiskey, which she spilled down the shirt of Calvin, the Transit Authority worker who had just given Sportcoat his five-dollar lunch money.

And just like that it was on. A fight, with biting, scratching, and kicking. It wasn't a free-for-all, but rather a series of skirmishes that exploded and quelled, breaking off here, starting again there, with referees and peacemakers scattered about, some taking knuckles in the face themselves, all on a hot morning when they should have been celebrating. Several fought till they got tired, sat down on the front steps in tears and exhaustion, and then, once they'd caught their breath, started up again, just as enraged. Others cursed out one another until one or the other got struck by an errant fist, and then they too joined the fray. Still others fought silently, resolutely, in pairs, working out old grudges they'd held for years. They were all so busy that no one seemed to notice a tall figure in a black leather jacket, Bunch Moon's enforcer Earl, a switchblade knife in his fist, slowly working his way from the back of the crowd to the front, slipping left and right, easing toward Sportcoat, who was still seated on the front steps in front of Los Soñadores next to Soup, both of them watching the fight in wonder as the terrible band played on.

"This is my fault," Soup admitted. "I shoulda stayed upstairs and watched television."

"Oh, the cotton and weeds comes together from time to time but it ain't nothing," Sportcoat said. "These things is good. They clears the air." As he watched the scrambling, cursing mob, it occurred to Sportcoat that Joaquin's unopened bottle of delicious Dominican brandy, standing on the bottom step just a few feet away, looked lonesome, with nobody to keep it company. He also realized he'd have to get moving soon. He had to do some yard work for the old white lady over on Silver Street who needed him in her garden planting. He usually went on Wednesday, but he'd missed last Wednesday because . . . well, because. He'd promised to come today, Monday, and the old lady didn't fool around, which made him determined. He'd even decided to skip playing Joaquin's numbers that morning and head straight out to the old lady's house, but Joaquin's lousy band woke him up and derailed him. Now he had to get moving.

Still, seeing the lonely brandy by itself on the bottom step, he decided it wouldn't hurt to take a quick nip. Nothing wrong with getting a little daily relief before the job.

He stood up and stepped down the stairs to grab the brandy on the bottom step. As he reached, someone kicked the bottle onto its back and it skidded onto the plaza and into the melee, unbroken but spinning on its side, stopping a few feet away. He followed it, wading into the crowd. Just as he reached it, the bottle was kicked again and slid between the legs of Sister Billings and the young pregnant mother, the two still tangling as Dominic and the woman's boyfriend sought to separate them. He followed it, only to watch it get kicked again. This time it took a bouncing, flipping ride before sliding past the feet of Sausage and Calvin the transit worker, slowing to a miraculous, agonizing, twirling stop between the legs of two women who were grappling with one another, each cursing and threatening to rip the other's wig off.

The bottle spun 'round and 'round beneath their legs, slowly coming to a stop.

Sportcoat crouched low, swiped it up, and was about to unscrew the lid when the bottle was suddenly swiped from his hand.

"This is the white man's poison, Mr. Sportcoat," Soup said calmly, holding the bottle. "We don't need this stuff 'round here no more."

He tossed the bottle casually over his shoulder, away from the crowd.

Soup, as a kid baseball player, never had much of an arm. But as a giant he had velocity. Several sets of eyes followed the bottle as it made a long, slow arc into the air, high up, twirling end over end, arching a bit as it reached its apex, then falling back to earth in a long, lazy, crazy spiraling curve—boinking Earl, Bunch's hit man, right on the noggin.

Amazingly the bottle remained intact after pinging off Earl's head, then struck the pavement before finally smashing into pieces. Earl fell next to it, crumpling to the ground like a paper doll.

The crash of the shattering glass and the sight of the fallen man stopped everyone. The crabbing and scratching ceased and everyone hustled over, gathering around the prostrate Earl, who was out cold.

In the distance, a police siren was heard.

"Now y'all did it," Joaquin said gloomily.

Everyone realized the crisis instantly. Joaquin's apartment would be searched. He'd be closed for days, weeks, even months. That meant no numbers. Even worse, Soup was on probation. Any kind of trouble would put him back in the clink. What a mean world!

"Everybody git," Sister Gee said calmly. "I'll take care of this."

"I'll stay too," Dominic said. "It's my fault. I got Bum-Bum stirred up."

"Can't no man stir me up, Dominic Lefleur," Sister Billings snapped defensively. "I don't need no *man* to stir my drink!"

"That depends on the straw and the man," Dominic said, smiling. "I'm the Haitian Sensation—emphasis on 'sensation.'"

"Don't try that scalawag sweet talk on me, mister! I know you don't mean it!"

Dominic shrugged as if to say "What do I do now?"

"We're wasting time," Sister Gee said. She turned to the crowd. "Get moving, y'all," she snapped. She turned to Calvin, the subway toll collector. "Calvin, you and Soup stay. You too, Izi." To the rest she said, "Hurry up, y'all. Git."

The crowd vanished. Most ran inside their buildings or hurried to work. But not everybody. Sportcoat and Hot Sausage returned to the stoop, where Joaquin and Los Soñadores were hastily packing up. Sausage nodded at the band. "If they was the O'Jays, this wouldn't have happened," he said.

"Bongo music," Sportcoat agreed, shaking his head. "I never did favor it."

"Is you gonna wait here to be arrested?" Sausage asked.

"I gotta get to work."

"Let's get a snort before we set out," Hot Sausage said. "I got some

Kong in the workshop. We can take the back door and cut through the coal tunnel under Building Thirty-Four. That'll puts us back at Nine."

"I thought that coal tunnel was closed up."

"Not if you the boiler man."

Sportcoat grinned. "Doggone it, you's a good rooster, Sausage. C'mon then."

The two disappeared inside. Behind them, Sausage noticed Soup hoisting Earl over one shoulder and trotting out of the plaza. By the time the cops rolled up minutes later, the plaza was deserted.

Twenty minutes later Earl came to and found himself on a bench on the platform of the Silver Street subway station. Seated on one side was the biggest Puerto Rican he'd ever seen, and on the other a handsome black woman in a church hat. He felt his head. He'd been struck on the same spot where the errant baseball had hit him days before. He had a lump there the size of Milwaukee.

"What happened?" he asked, his voice hoarse.

"You was hit in the head with a bottle," the lady said.

"Why's my clothes wet?"

"We doused you with water to get you up."

He felt in his pocket for his switchblade. It was gone. Then he noticed the handle of the folded knife poking out from the closed fist of the giant Puerto Rican, who had a face ugly enough to belong to a cadaver. His blade, Earl realized, wouldn't do shit on that Spanish elephant motherfucker but tickle him. Earl glanced nervously around the subway platform again. It was completely empty.

"Where's everybody?" he asked.

"We seen from papers in your pocket you is from Gates Avenue out in Bed-Stuy," the woman said. "So we is putting you on the train that way."

Earl started to curse, then glanced at the giant, who stared back at him, his eye steady.

"Seems to me," the woman began, "you favors a preacher I once knew over in Bed-Stuy. Reverend Harris at Ebenezer Baptist. A nice man, the reverend was. He died some years back. You any kin to him?"

Earl was silent.

"A good man, Reverend Harris was," she repeated. "Worked all his life. Janitored over at Long Island University, I do believe. I recollects when my church visited Ebenezer that Reverend Harris had a child or two that favored you. Of course this is going back a ways. I'm forty-eight. I can't remember nothing no more."

Earl stayed silent.

"Well, I do apologize for whatever misunderstandings you has had in the Cause," she said. "We seen from your wallet papers where you was from, and being God-fearing people, we brung you here so you could get home without no trouble from the police. We takes care of our visitors in the Cause." She paused a moment, then added, "We takes care of our own too."

She let that one sit a moment, then got up. She nodded at the giant. Earl watched in awe as the stoic man in a neat suit, bow tie, and crisp white shirt, clearly a member, he realized now, of the feared and re-spected Nation of Islam, stood up. Up and up he went, unfolding like a human accordion, his giant fist still clasping the switchblade. When he stood up to his full height, his head nearly scraped the lights of the sub-way platform. The giant opened his big palm and, with two massive fingers, gently placed the blade on the bench next to Earl.

"Well then, we bid you good day, son," the lady said. "God bless you."

She moved toward the stairs, followed by the lumbering giant.

Earl, still seated on the bench, heard the rumble of an incoming train and he looked down the tracks to see the graffiti-covered G train curv-ing out of the tunnel toward him. When it stopped, he rose as quickly as he could manage, slipped gratefully aboard, and watched through the window as the woman and her giant, the only two souls on the platform, stood at the top of the stairs watching the train roll out.

He was the only passenger to board. He noticed there were no other passengers on the entire platform. The whole situation seemed odd. Only when the train moved did the two turn away.

Sister Gee and Soup descended the stairs of the subway platform, then headed down an escalator that reached street level and the tollbooth. When they arrived, Sister Gee noticed a crowd of about fifteen impatient subway riders standing at all three entranceway turnstiles. All three were closed, each with an emergency cone blocking it. She glanced at the tollbooth, and Calvin, the tollbooth worker, quickly emerged and removed the cones without a word, then stepped back inside his booth. The subway riders rushed through the turnstiles and up the escalators.

Sister Gee watched them mount the escalators in a hurry toward the train platform. When they were out of sight, she didn't turn away but rather said softly to Soup, standing behind her, "Meet me outside, okay?" The big man lumbered toward the street exit as Sister Gee quickly crossed to the tollbooth, where Calvin stood at the counter, his face stoic. "I owe you one, Calvin," she said softly.

"Forget it. What happened after everybody left?"

"Nothing. We hightailed over here by the backstreets. Bum-Bum hid Joaquin's numbers in her bra. Miss Izi told the police she and Joaquin had one of their fights. It's all good. Joaquin's back in business. The cops are gone. I can't thank you enough."

"If you put two dollars on my number today, that'll square us," Calvin said.

"What number?"

"One forty-three."

"That's a good-sounding number. What's it mean?"

"Ask Soup," he said. "That's Soup's number."

She emerged from the Silver Street station and fell in beside Soup for the short walk back to the Cause Houses. "I reckon if your momma was alive, she wouldn't be pleased I put her son in a spot like this, cleaning up somebody else's mess. I don't know that I done right or not. But I couldn't carry that fella to the train myself."

Soup shrugged.

"Course he was up to no good," she said. "I reckon he come here to do wrong to old Sportcoat. What's this world coming to if common church folk can't stand up for one of their own?" She thought for a moment. "I reckon I did right. On the other hand, Sportcoat's in a little too thick for my taste. You can get in deep water quick fooling around with them drug dealers. Don't you do it, Soup."

Soup smiled sheepishly. He was so tall, she had to squint to see his face in the afternoon sun. "That ain't me, Sister Gee," he said.

"Why is Calvin playing your number? Is he in your new religion too?"

"Nation of Islam? Not at all," Soup said. "He and my ma was friends. We lived in the same building. He used to come by sometimes and watch my show with me. The number's from that."

"What show is that?"

"*Mister Rogers.*"

"You mean the nice little white man who sings? With the puppets?"

"That's Mister Rogers's address. One forty-three. You know what one forty-three means?"

"No, Soup."

His stoic face folded into a smile. "I would tell you, but I don't wanna spoil it."

11

POKEWEED

FOUR BLOCKS FROM THE SILVER STREET STATION, THE EL-
ephant sat at his mother's kitchen table griping about a plant. "Pokeweed," he said to his mother. "Didn't you say it was poisonous?"

His mother, a diminutive, olive-complexioned woman, was standing
at the countertop, her gray hair in wild tousles about her head, slicing at
several plants he had pulled out of her garden that morning: fiddleheads,
rootberry blossom, and skunk cabbage.

"It's not poison," she said. "Just the root. The shoots are good. They're
good for the blood."

"Get some blood thinners," he said.

"Doctor's medicine is wasted money," she scoffed. "Pokeweed cleans
you out—and it's free. It grows near the harbor."

"Don't plan on me digging around in the mud near the harbor today,"
Elefante grumbled. "I gotta go to the Bronx." He was going to see the
Governor.

"Go ahead," his mother said defiantly. "I got the colored man from
the church coming by."

"What colored man?"

"The Deacon."

"That old scooch? The way he drinks, solid food makes a splash in his stomach when he eats it. You keep him out of the house."

"Leave it alone," she snapped. "He knows more about plants than anybody around here," she added. "More'n you, that's for sure."

"Just keep him outside."

"Stop worrying. He's a deacon at the colored church there, the Four Ends or Deep Ends or whatever it's called."

"Five Ends."

"Well, he's there. A deacon." She chopped away.

Elefante shrugged. He had no idea what deacons did. He remembered the old guy faintly as one of the coloreds who came and went from the church a block from his boxcar. A drinker. Harmless. The church was on the far side of the street, while the boxcar was on the harbor side. Close as they were, separated by a weeded lot that ran the block's length, they were strangers to one another. But Elefante considered coloreds perfect neighbors. They minded their own business. Never asked questions. That's the reason his guys pulled that poor lady from the harbor when she came floating into the dock a few years ago. He'd watched her come and go from the church for years, waving hello to him, and he waved back. That was the extent of their conversation, which in the Cause, where the Italians and blacks lived side by side but rarely connected, was a lot. He never knew or heard the story of how she landed in the harbor—that wasn't his business—but he had a faint recollection she might be related to one or the other of the coloreds. He left his headman to keep up with details of folks like her, not him. He didn't have time. He only knew that every Christmas since his guys pulled that lady out of the water, the church coloreds had dropped off two sweet potato pies and a cooked chicken outside his railroad boxcar. Why couldn't more people get along that way?

He regarded his mother as she chopped. She had on his father's old construction boots, which meant she planned to go plant digging today too. With the boots, the housedress, the apron, and her wild hair, she looked, he knew, like something from the outer limits. But at eighty-nine, she could do what she wanted. Still, he fretted about her health. He noticed the difficulty she had chopping, her arthritic hands curled and gnarled. Rheumatoid arthritis, diabetes, and a leaking heart were taking their toll. She had fallen several times in the past few weeks, and the doctor's murmurings about heart trouble were no longer murmurings, they were explicit warnings, outlined in red pen on her prescriptions, which she ignored, of course, in favor of the plants she swore fostered good health or simply needed to be had for the sake of having them, the names of which he'd memorized from childhood: black cherry, Hercules' club, spicebush, and now, pokeweed.

He watched as she struggled with the knife. He suspected the old colored gardener did all the chopping once he left. He could tell by the neat cut of the plants, their stems tied tightly with rubber bands, others with stems and roots cut just so. He was secretly glad she ignored his disapproval of allowing someone inside the house. Someone was better than no one. She was near the end, they both knew it. Three months ago, she'd paid Joe Peck, whose family ran the last Italian funeral home in the Cause District, to send a man to disinter his dad's body over at Woodlawn Cemetery and bury it deeper. The overcrowded cemetery had no more space for new graves, so her plan was to be buried atop his father in the same plot. That required his father's casket be reburied eight feet down instead of the usual six. Peck had assured her he had done the job himself. But the Elephant was suspicious. Anything Joe Peck said could be a lie.

"Did you get someone to sound that plot Joe Peck said he dug out?" he asked.

"I told you already. I can take care of my business," she said.

"You know Joe says one thing and does another."

"I'll get my colored man to check it."

"He can't poke around the cemetery. He'll get arrested."

"He knows what to do."

Elefante gave up. At least there would be a set of eyes in the house while he ran up to the Bronx to check out the Governor's tip.

He sighed, rose from the kitchen table, reached for his tie on a nearby doorknob, placed it around his neck, and then stepped to the parlor mirror to tie it, feeling a blend of relief and, despite himself, a small bit of excitement. He'd already decided that the Governor's story about this so-called hidden loot, this great treasure that his father had somehow hidden someplace in his boxcar or in his storage warehouse, was a fable. Yet a few discreet phone calls and a query to his mother proved that the Governor's story was, at least, partly true. Elefante had confirmed that the Governor had been his dad's sole friend and cellmate for two years in Sing Sing. His dad had also mentioned the Governor to his mother several times as he drifted toward death, but she swore she'd paid little attention. "He said he was holding something for a friend and it was in God's hands," she told him. "I paid it no mind."

"Did he say in God's hand, or the palm of His hand?" Elefante asked, remembering the poem the Governor cited.

"You were there!" she snapped. "Don't you remember?"

But Elefante did not. He had been nineteen, about to inherit a business that was beholden to the Gorvino family. His father was dying. He had to take over. There was a lot to think about. He was drowning in his own confused, bottled-up emotions at the time. God was the last thing on his mind.

"No I don't," he said.

"He was talking out of his head at the end there," his mother said. "Poppa hadn't been in church since he was out of prison, so I paid it no mind."

Elefante had checked all his storage places—the ones he had access to, which was more than he cared to let his customers know about—and come up empty. He raked through his own memories as well, but they played tricks on him. As a boy, he remembered his father saying to him several times . . . *Look out for the Governor. He's got that crazy poem! Pay attention.* But what teenager paid attention to his dad? His father didn't speak in detail anyway. He spoke in nods and grunts. Giving words to ideas was too dangerous in their world. When Poppa did give words to something, though, it was for a reason. It had weight. So Poppa must have been giving him a message. But what? The more Elefante considered the matter, the more confused he became. Driscoll Sturgess, he decided, the Governor himself, might have the answer—if there was one at all. So he'd called and made arrangements to see him, to maybe get some peace on the question.

Elefante grabbed his jacket and car keys, feeling anxious and a little excited. The trip to the Bronx was more of a break for him than anything else. He paused one last time at the mirror in the front hall to straighten his tie and unrumple his suit, checking himself out sideways. He still looked good. A little heavy maybe, but his face was still tight, no wrinkles, no crow's-feet around the eyes, no kids, no cousins he trusted, no wife who cared for him, no one to take care of his mother either, he thought bitterly. At forty, Elefante was lonely. Wouldn't it be nice, he thought, as he straightened his tie one last time, if there was a real big score in it. Just once, something that would get him off that pier, out of that hot boxcar, out of the squeeze between Joe Peck and the Gorvinos, who controlled every dock in Brooklyn, and get him to an island in the Bahamas where he could spend the rest of his life sipping grape and watching the ocean. The stress of the job was beginning to wear at him. The Gorvinos were losing faith in him. He knew it. He could tell they were increasingly irritated by his resistance to drugs, a prejudice he'd inherited from his father. But that had been a different time, and they were different men. The old man had kept the Gorvinos satisfied by renting them cheap storage space, doing quick under-the-table construction jobs for them, and moving anything they wanted outside of dope. But that was before, in the age of graft, numbers, smuggling, and booze. Dope was the thing now. Big money, and Joe Peck, the only other made member of the Gorvino family in the Cause District, had jumped into the dope game with both feet, becoming a major distributor, pulling Elefante in by the nose. There were plenty of docking points in Brooklyn, but Elefante was under constant pressure to keep his dock active because Peck was in his area, and Joe moved dope from water to shore in whatever stupid form he could dream up: in cement bags, in gasoline tanks, in the back of refrigerators, stuffed into TV sets, even in car parts. It was risky. He hated the whole tuna. Drugs were a damn stinking fish, the smell of it taking over everything. Gambling, construction, cigarettes, booze were all second-rate now. Ironically, the Gorvinos weren't wild about dope or Joe Peck either—they knew how stupid and impulsive Peck was—but they lived in Bensonhurst and not in the Cause. That might as well have been the moon as far as Elefante was concerned. They never got to see Joe's stupidity up close, which always complicated matters. Peck had his head so far up his ass he couldn't see the order of things. He made deals with the colored, the Spanish, and every two-bit crooked cop who could put two nickels together—without one bit of trust between them. That was a recipe for disaster and a ten-year stretch in the workhouse. To make it worse, Victor Gorvino, head of the Gorvino family, was old as the hills and half-demented, fucked up in his head. Gorvino was under a lot of heat from the cops now. Getting in to see him to explain Joe Peck's stupidity was difficult. To top it off, Gorvino and Peck were Sicilian. The Elefantes were from Genoa, northern Italy, which fell right into his father's admonition. "Remember," he'd remind his son, "we're just a bunch of Genoans." They were always on the outside.

When his father was alive, that difference between the northern and southern Italians didn't matter as much. His father and Gorvino were old-school. They went back to the days of Murder, Inc., Brooklyn's enforcement arm of the Mafia, where silence was the golden rule and cooperation was the key to a long life. But as far as Gorvino was concerned, the son was not the father, and now that Gorvino was half-cocked and not able to pull up his pants without help from his lieutenant Vinny Tognerelli—a Gorvino underling Elefante didn't know well—the tight space that Elefante lived in had gotten even tighter.

At the front door, he turned to his mother, who was still busy whacking away at the plants on her countertop, and said in Italian, "What time is the colored coming?"

"He'll be here. He's always late."

"What's his name again?"

"Deacon something or other. They call him something else too. Suit Jacket, or something."

Elefante nodded. "What does a deacon do?" he asked.

"How should I know?" she said. "They're probably like priests, but make less money."

Elefante exited the wrought-iron fence surrounding his yard, stepped to his Lincoln at the curb, and had placed his key in the door when he heard the sound of Joe Peck's GTO turn the corner and roar up the street toward him. Elefante frowned as the GTO slowed and stopped as the passenger window rolled down.

"Take me with you, Tommy," Peck said.

Peck, seated in the driver's seat, was clad in his usual dark open-collared shirt and cleanly pressed pants, his handsome blond features curled into his usual queer smile. The crazy pretty boy. Elefante ducked his head inside the car so the two couldn't be heard from the street.

"I'm going to mix business with business, Joe. No pleasure in it. You don't wanna come."

"Wherever you go, there's money in it."

"See ya, Joe." Elefante turned away and Peck called out, "Gimme a minute, will ya, Tommy? It's important."

Elefante frowned and stuck his head inside the cab again, the two men's faces close together as the GTO rumbled. "What?" he said.

"Change of plans," Peck said.

"What plans? We going to the prom? We got no plans."

"About that shipment from Lebanon," Peck said.

Elefante felt the blood rush to his face. "I already told you. I ain't doing that."

"C'mon, Tommy!" Peck pleaded. "I need you on this one. Just this one."

"Get Herbie over in the Watch Houses. Or Ray out in Coney Island. Ray's got a whole crew now. He's got new trucks and everything. He'll take care of it for you."

"I can't use them. I don't like those guys."

"Why not? That's two guys. If you put 'em together, they'd make one man."

Peck's temple's bulged and he grimaced, a look that Elefante knew spelled anger. That was Joe's problem. His temper. He'd known Joe Peck since high school. Three thousand kids at Bay Ridge High and the only one stupid enough to pull out an X-Acto knife in auto shop and use it over a lost wrench was Joe Peck, the small, scrappy kid from the Cause District with a girly face and a brain the size of a full-grown pea. Elefante had been forced to beat Joe down himself four or five times at Bay Ridge High, but Peck had an amazingly short memory for losses. When he blew his top he didn't care what happened, who was involved, or why. It made him a bold gangster but a prime candidate to land in an urn in his own family's funeral parlor one day, Elefante was certain. Amazingly, the years had not mellowed him.

"The niggers at the Cause Houses are crapping on my business," Peck said. "They shot a kid. Great kid. Negro. He turned over a lot of stuff for one of my customers. They say he's a real whiz kid, just a great kid. Doing great, till he got shot."

"If he's so great, why not give him one of those Negro scholarships, Joe?"

Peck's face flushed and Elefante watched, half-amused, as Peck beat back the rage, ignoring the insult. "Thing is . . ." Peck glanced through the front windshield, then through the rear one, to make sure no one was nearby listening. "The kid was shot by some old geezer. So my customer in Bed-Stuy sends one of his guys to even things out. He's tracking the old gunner to squeeze him. But the old bum don't wanna get caught."

"Maybe he's a humble man who don't like attention."

"Can't you fucking listen for a minute?"

Elefante felt his pulse racing. He resisted the urge to reach across the seat, yank Peck out by his shirt collar, and part his pretty, girly face with his fist. "Get your blockers outta the backfield and get moving downfield, would ya, Joe?"

"What?"

"Just tell me what you want. I got stuff to do."

"The guy they sent out to even things, he screwed up. The cops got hold of him. Now he's singing to the Seven-Six. A bird I know over there tells me the guy is singing like a robin—telling the cops everything. So before they cut him loose this snitch tells the cops that my main colored customer up in Bed-Stuy wants to cut me out. The coloreds don't want me supplying them no more. How do you like that? Ungrateful niggers! I set them up and now they wanna double-cross me. They're gonna start a race war."

Elefante listened in silence. *This is what happens when you deal with people you don't trust,* he thought bitterly. *It doesn't matter if it's drugs or cereal. Same problem.*

"I ain't involved," he said.

"Gorvino won't like it."

"Did you talk to him?"

"Yeah . . . well, not yet. I talked to his guy, Vincent. He says Gorvino will get back to me, but Bed-Stuy is our area, that's what Vincent says. He says we got to deal with it."

"It's *your* area, Joe. Not mine."

"It's our dock."

"But it's *your* dope."

He saw Peck's face darken; he was fighting back his boiling temper, just a string away from busting loose. With great effort, Peck checked himself again.

"Would you roll with me just this one time, Tommy?" he said. "Just this once? Please? Move this Lebanon shipment for me and I won't ask you ever again. Just this one fucking time. With this one shipment, I'll make enough to muscle them niggers off and tell them to fuck off forever. And I can clean up things with Gorvino too."

"Clean up things?"

"I'm into him for a few thousand," Joe said, adding hastily, "but I get this shipment and I can clean that up easy and I'm outta dope forever. You're right, by the way. You've always been right about the dope. It's too risky. This is my last job. I'll clean things up and I'm out of it."

Elefante stared at Peck in silence for a long moment.

"C'mon, Tommy," Peck pleaded. "For old times' sake. You haven't taken one goddamn shipment in six months. Not one. I'll give ya eight grand. It'll take an hour. One fucking hour. Straight off a freighter, to the dock, and out. No unloading tires or nothing fancy. Just grab the stuff and get it to me. One hour. That's how long it'll take to get it outta your hair. One hour. You can't make that much slinging cigarettes in a month."

Elefante nervously tapped one hand on the car roof. The GTO rumbled, shaking, and Elefante felt his resolve shaking with it. *Just an hour,* he thought, *to risk everything.* It sounded easy. But then his mind ran through the scenario quickly. If the crap came in from Lebanon, it'd be on a freighter, probably out of Brazil or Turkey. That meant getting a fast boat to retrieve it, because a freighter would not dock in the Cause. The waters were deep enough, but only barges came to Brooklyn, which meant probably taking the speedboat to the middle of the harbor from the Jersey side to be safe. That meant slipping past harbor patrol on that side, grabbing the loot in the middle of the harbor, racing back to shore, getting the stuff to an untraceable car that would likely have to be stolen, and then moving it to wherever Joe Peck wanted it. Knowing how the feds were everywhere now, it might be that Peck had the feds watching his front door and the Gorvino family watching the back door, since he owed the Gorvinos money. He didn't like it.

"Get Ray out at Coney Island."

Peck's temper broke through. He banged the steering wheel furiously with his fist. "What kind of fucking friend are you?!"

Elefante's top teeth met the bottom of his folded lip as he felt the dreadful silence descend on him. The day, once hopeful and full of promise, with a pleasurable trip to the Bronx ahead to sound out a possible treasure, was ruined. Even if that so-called treasure was the pipe dream of an old Irish con artist who was likely full of shit, the idea of tracking it down to zero was still a reprieve from the day-to-day of his own trapped, screwed-up life. Now the lightness of the day was gone. Instead, a familiar seething spread inside him, like a black oil slick sliding into place, and the silence took over. It wasn't rage, uncontrolled and raw, but rather a cool anger that launched a terrible, unstoppable determination within him to squelch problems with a speed and dispatch that even the most hardened mobsters of the Gorvino family found unsettling. His ma said it was the Genoan in him, because Genoans learned to live unhappily and trudged forward no matter what, just finishing things up, dealing with it, bearing up doggedly till the job was finished. The Genoans had been doing that, she said, ever since the ancient days of Caesar. He'd been to Genoa with his parents, and he'd seen it himself, a city of dull, exhausting hills, the dreary, ancient, gray buildings, the solid stone walls, the bleak cold weather and miserable rain-soaked cobblestone and brick streets, the unhappy souls wandering about in tight circles, from home to work and back home again, grimly walking past one another, tight-lipped, pale, never smiling, marching stolidly down the small, drenched streets as the cold sea splashed over the sidewalks and even over them and them not noticing it, the smell of stinking sea and nearby fisheries climbing onto their clothing, into their miserable tiny houses, their drapes, and even into their food, the people ignoring it, plodding forward with grim determination like robots, having accepted their fate as unhappy sons of bitches living in the shadow of happy Nice, France, to the west and under the sunshine disdain of their poor dark cousins to the south, Florence and Sicily, who laughed like dancing Negroes, happy and content to be the black Ethiopians of Europe, while their smiling cousins on the Mediterranean Sea, the French, sunned themselves topless on the lovely beaches of the Riviera. All the while the hardworking, joyless Genoans marched on grimly, eating their fucking focaccia. No one appreciated Genoan focaccia except the Genoans. "Best bread in the world," his father used to say. "It's the cheese." Elefante tried it once and understood then why Genoans were a miserable lot, because life was nothing compared to the delicious taste of Genoan food; once they got to the food, the business of life, whatever that business was—loving, sleeping, standing at the bus stop, shoving each other at the grocery store, killing each other—had to be done with speed so as to get to the food, and they did it with such silent grit, such determination and speed, that to get in the way of it was like stepping into a hurricane. Christopher Columbus, his mother pointed out, was a Genoan who wasn't looking for America. He was looking for spices. For food.

A real Genoan, she said, would hang themselves before they'd let anyone destroy the one or two things in life that gave them a little relief from the difficulties of the devil's world.

Elefante found the whole business of his own anger frightening, because that's what his great furious silences were. Relief. A pressure cooker blown open. To his utter disgust, he'd found himself liking when the great silences came upon him. He hated himself later for those moments. He'd done some terrible things during those times. Many times afterward, in his darkest hours, in the late nights when Brooklyn slept and the harbor was dark, lying in bed in his lonely, empty brownstone with no wife and no children snoring in another room, with his widowed mother clomping around the house in her late husband's construction boots, the things he did during the spells when the silence came upon him tortured him with a searing brutality that caused him to sit up in the dark and check his pajamas for blood, feeling like his soul had been sliced into quarters, sweat bursting out of his pores and tears running down his face. But there was nothing to do then. The moment was over. The rage had already poured out of him like lava, unrelenting and merciless, steaming over whoever or whatever was in the way, and the sorry soul on the receiving end saw nothing more than a blank stare of cold clarity. Were they seeing the eyes of Tommy Elefante, the lonely man with the kind heart who ordered his obedient crew to pull poor old colored women out of the harbor who had landed there for one reason or other, and why shouldn't they, since New York was shit? Or were they seeing the eyes of Tommy Elefante, the shy Brooklyn bachelor who dreamed of escaping Brooklyn to move to a farm in New Hampshire and marry a fat country girl and even had the looks and charm to find one, but was too kind to drag any woman into his life of brutality and stealth, which had made his mother a prison widow and half-mad eccentric, a life that had diced his father's kindness into bits? Perhaps they saw neither; perhaps they saw only the outer shell: the silent, cold, brutal

Elephant, whose calculating calm and mum stare said, "You are finished," and who dispatched them with the matter-of-fact speed and brutality of a Category 5 hurricane, ripping everything apart as he went.
The Elephant's stare reduced the hardest men to terror. He'd seen the
fright explode across their faces when his silent business face emerged,
and try as he could, he could not wipe those expressions of fright from
his own memory, the most recent being the colored kid Mark Bumpus
and his two hooligans at the abandoned factory on Vitali Pier three years
ago, when he'd caught them red-handed trying to steal fourteen grand
from him. *I'll help you*, Bumpus had pleaded. *I'll help you fix things*, he
wailed. But it was too late.

Peck found himself staring at Elefante's silence at that moment, a silence so palpable that to Joe, it was almost like hearing it and seeing it at
the same time, for Peck had experienced it several times when they were
teenagers, and his own inner alarm sounded off as loud as the blaring of
a ship's bullhorn. Peck realized he'd gone too far. His angry facial features twisted into blinking alarm as Elefante's blank stare combed his
face, the interior of the car, and Joe's hands, which, they both noted,
remained on the steering wheel—where they should be, Joe noted
ruefully—and had better stay.

"Don't come at me like that again, Joe. Find somebody else."

Elefante withdrew from the GTO and stood with his hands at his
sides as Joe threw the GTO in gear and roared off. Then he placed his
hands in his pockets and stood in the middle of the street alone, giving
the silent roaring rage inside him time to ease down and out, and after
several long minutes he once again became who he was, a solitary
middle-aged man in the August of life looking for a few more Aprils, an
aging bachelor in a floppy suit standing on a tired, worn Brooklyn street
in the shadow of a giant housing project built by a Jewish reformer
named Robert Moses who forgot he was a reformer, building projects
like this all over, which destroyed neighborhoods, chasing out the work-

ing Italians, Irish, and Jews, gutting all the pretty things from them, displacing them with Negroes and Spanish and other desperate souls clambering to climb into the attic of New York life, hoping that the bedroom and kitchen below would open up so they could drop in, and at minimum join the club that to them included this man, an overweight bachelor in an ill-fitting suit, watching a shiny car roaring away, the car driven by a handsome young man who was pretty and drove away as if he were barreling into a bright future, while the dowdy heavyset man watched him jealously, believing the man so pretty and handsome had places to go and women to meet and things to do, and the older heavyset man standing behind eating his fumes on a sorry, dreary, crowded old Brooklyn street of storefronts and tired brownstones had nothing left but the fumes of the pretty sports car in his face. A dreamless, friendless, futureless, sorry-ass New York guy.

Elefante watched the GTO turn the corner. He sighed and headed back to his Lincoln. He slowly slid his key into the lock, entered the car, and sat behind the steering wheel in silence, staring. He sat in the soft leather of the car for several long moments. Finally, he spoke aloud.

"I wish," he said softly, "somebody would love me."

12

MOJO

SPORTCOAT SAT ON A CRATE INSIDE SAUSAGE'S BOILER ROOM clasping a bottle of King Kong. He was in no hurry now. The disappointment of chasing the bottle of brandy around the plaza before it was destroyed by Soup that morning was softened by this pit stop at Sausage's headquarters. Sausage was nowhere to be found and that was fine. Sportcoat had spent the rest of morning there, cooling his heels with some Kong. He felt better now. Evened out. *Noooooo hurry*, he thought happily, clasping the bottle. He thought he might get up to look at the clock to check the time, but by the tilt of sunlight in the tiny basement window he got the general idea. Afternoon. He stretched and yawned. He was supposed to be at work at the old lady's garden on Silver Street at least two hours ago. He tried for a moment to remember her name, but couldn't. It didn't matter. It was Italian and ended with an "i" and she paid cash, that's what was important. She didn't mind too much if he was late—he always stayed late if he arrived late—but she had seemed a bit unsteady on her feet in the past few weeks. *Getting old*, he thought wryly. *You got to be strong to get old*. He was about to put the Kong away and head out when Hettie suddenly appeared.

"If you gonna come at me hanking about what happened at Soup's party today, don't bother," he said.

She chortled bitterly. "I don't care what you done," she said. "Fact is, when you walk about being spit on, it don't much matter what else you think you done."

"Who spit on me? Nobody spit on me."

"You spit on yourself."

"Get gone with that foolishness. I'm going to work."

"Well git on then."

"If it pleases me to stop for a bracer while I ruminates on getting my baseball game going again, that's my business."

"That game don't mean nothing to these children around here," she said soberly.

"How would you know? You didn't see a game I umped in ten years."

"You didn't invite me in ten years," she said.

That stumped him. Like most things he did most of his adult life, he couldn't remember exactly what happened, largely because he was drunk at the time, so he said, "I was the best umpire the Cause Houses ever seen. I gived joy to everyone."

"Except your own wife."

"Oh hush."

"I was lonely in my marriage," she said.

"Stop complaining, woman! Food on the table. Roof over our heads. What else you want? Where's the damn church money, by the way? I'm in a heap of trouble on account of it!"

He lifted the Kong to his lips and gulped down a long swallow. She watched him silently, then after a moment said, "Some of it's not your fault."

"Sure ain't. You the one hid that money."

"I ain't talking about that," she said, almost pensively. "I'm talking about the old days when you was a child. Everything ever said to you or done to you back then was at the expense of your own dignity. You never complained. I loved that about you."

"Oh, woman, leave my people out of it. They long dead."

She watched him thoughtfully. "And now here you are," she said sadly, "an old man funning around a ball field, making folks laugh. Even the boys don't follow you no more."

"They'll follow me plenty when I get 'em back on the field. But I got to get off the hook 'bout them Christmas Club chips first. You kept the money in a little green box, I remember that. Where's the box?"

"The church got plenty money."

"You mean the box in the church?"

"No, honey. It's in God's hands. In the palm of His hand, actually."

"Where's it at, woman?!"

"You ought to trade your ears in for some bananas," she said, irritated now.

"Stop talking in circles, dammit! Pastor declares the church got three thousand dollars in claims for that money. We got liars falling out of the trees now. There's more folks at Five Ends on Sunday mornings hankering about that money than you'd see in a month of Easter Sundays. Every one of 'em's got eyes for that box. Digs Weatherspoon says he got four hundred dollars in there, and that fool ain't had two nickels to rub together since Methuselah got married. What I'mma do about that?"

She sighed. "When you love somebody, their words oughta be important enough for you to listen."

"Stop lumping on about nothing!"

"I'm telling you what you wanna hear, fool."

Then she was gone.

He sat in a huff for several minutes. There was no money in the church. He and Hot Sausage had searched the small building a dozen times. He felt thirsty and turned the bottle of Kong, only to discover it was dry. But there were other joy juice hiding places in that basement. He rose, dropped to one knee, and ran his hand under a nearby cupboard, finding it bare, then heard, over his shoulder, the sound of the door opening and saw the back of Hot Sausage's head as Sausage walked in and strode out of sight behind a large generator on the other side of the room. He said, "Sausage?"

There was no answer. He could hear Sausage grunt and the clattering of tools being moved around. So he said, "You ain't got to hide from me. There was three bottles of Kong down here to my recollection."

As if in answer, there was a sparking sound and the huge generator fired up with a roar, the sound filling the room. Sportcoat rose and shuffled around to the side of the generator to find Hot Sausage nearly prone on the floor, stretched out with his head inside the motor of the same model of ancient roaring electric generator that befuddled Rufus in the Watch Houses boiler room. Sausage stretched out on his hip sideways, offered a quick sullen glance, then turned his attention back to the generator, which sputtered unhappily.

Sportcoat grabbed a crate and slid next to him. Sausage had removed his porkpie hat. His blue Housing Authority uniform was ragged and grease stained. He glanced at Sportcoat again, then back to the roaring engine. He didn't say a word.

Sportcoat yelled over the din. "I'm sorry, Sausage. I'll go to the police myself to straighten it out. I'll explain it all and ask 'em to tell me how long I have to leave town."

Sausage, peering into the roaring engine, chuckled. "You a doggone fool."

"I didn't mean in no way, shape, or form to get you mixed up in no nonsense, Sausage."

Sausage lightened and pulled a long hand out of the machine to shake.

Instead of shaking it, Sportcoat stared at the hand, frowning. "I done apologized. So why the left hand? You know that's bad luck."

"Oh. Sorry." Hot Sausage hurriedly pulled his right hand out of the generator and extended it. Satisfied, Sportcoat shook it and sat on a nearby crate. "Where's the Kong?" he shouted over the din.

Sausage reached under a nearby tool bench and produced a quart-sized glass jug full of clear fluid, carefully sliding it over to Sportcoat, then he turned his attention back to the generator, peering inside. "This thing quits every week," he said.

"Rufus got the same problem over at the Watch Houses," Sportcoat yelled. "These projects was built the same year. Same apartments, toilets, generators, everything. Bad junk, these generators."

"But I takes care of my generators."

"Rufus says it ain't the generators. It's bad spirits."

Sausage sucked his teeth, made a few adjustments, and the machine's decibel level lowered to a bearable volume. "It ain't no damn spirits."

"Rats? Ants maybe?"

"Not this time of year. Even ants ain't stupid enough to climb inside this thing. It's cockeyed wiring is what it is. Old as Methuselah. Been fiddled with a lot too. Whoever done it was pulling his privates with one hand and fiddling at the wires with the other."

Sportcoat sipped from the whiskey jug again and held it out to Sausage, who took a generous gulp, handed it back to Sportcoat, then peered back into the guts of the old machine. "Dumbest thing in the world," he said. "There's thirty-two units in this building. This thing runs electric to only four of 'em. It's wired to the other one over there." He nodded toward a second large generator on the wall on the far side of the room, separated from the first by a sea of junk that cluttered the basement: old sinks, bricks, brooms, refuse, pieces of bicycles, mops, toilet parts, and Sausage's old wooden pendulum clock. "Whoever built this place was drunk, I reckon, to set 'em apart that way, instead of making 'em just one."

Sausage sipped again, placed the bottle on the floor next to the generator, stuck his long hands into the machine, and tied two wires together. The generator sputtered, coughed a moment, then chugged onward.

"I got to replace the church's Christmas Club money somehow, Sausage."

"That's the least of your problems."

"Oh, cut that nonsense. This is real money here we talking. Hettie never told me how much was in that Christmas box. Or where she hid it. Or who put what in. Now Pastor Gee says there's three thousand dollars in claims on it. Everybody and their brother's swearing they got money in it."

"That don't include the fourteen hundred dollars I throwed in," Sausage said.

"Very funny."

"No wonder you seeing Hettie's ghost, Sport. I'd be chickenhearted too with that kind of money floating north of me. You got trouble all 'round. You did lock that door behind you coming in, didn't you? Deems ain't got nothing against me, but outside of a child in pain, the worst sound in the world is an old man begging for his life while he's at work. What's to stop him from coming in here blasting?"

"Stop fussing about nothing," Sportcoat said. "Ain't nobody following me. And I ain't talking to Hettie's ghost. It's a nag that's bothering me, Sausage. What I'm talking to is a nag. A nag ain't a ghost. It's a mojo. A witch. Playing tricks. It looks like a person, but it ain't. It's just a witch. The old folks talked about that back home all the time. A witch can take any form she wants. That's why I know it ain't my dear Hettie talking. She never talked that way, calling me an idiot and carrying on. That's a witch."

Sausage chuckled. "That's why I never got married. My uncle Gus married a girl like that. He met a girl down in Tuscaloosa and got into a hank with her daddy. One of his cows ate some of her daddy's corn. Her daddy wanted forty cents for that corn. Uncle Gus didn't pay it. His wife hollered at him but he wouldn't, and then she died and put a wangature on him. Baddest mojo I ever seen. His chest bone growed out like a chicken's breast. The hair on the sides of his head smoothed out. The top of his hair stayed kinky. That was a weird-looking nigger. He looked like a rooster till he died."

"Whyn't he just pay her daddy back?" Sportcoat said.

"Too late then," Hot Sausage said. "Forty cents ain't gonna stop no mojo. Four hundred cents would stop it, once it gets going. His wife put a nag on him, see, like Hettie done to you."

"How you know Hettie done it?"

"It don't matter who done it. You got to break it. Uncle Gus broke his by taking a churchyard snail and soaking it in vinegar for seven days. You could try that."

"That's the Alabama way of breaking mojos," Sportcoat said. "That's old. In South Carolina, you put a fork under your pillow and some buckets of water around your kitchen. That'll drive any witch off."

"Naw," Sausage said. "Roll a hound's tooth in cornmeal and wear it about your neck."

"Naw. Walk up a hill with your hands behind your head."

"Stick your hand in a jar of maple syrup."

"Sprinkle seed corn and butter bean hulls outside the door."

"Step backward over a pole ten times."

"Swallow three pebbles . . ."

They were off like that for several minutes, each topping the other with his list of ways to keep witches out, talking mojo as the modern life of the world's greatest metropolis bustled about them. Brooklyn traffic roared aboveground. In Borough Hall, twenty blocks away, the Brooklyn borough president was welcoming Neil Armstrong, the first man to walk on the moon. In Flushing, Queens, the New York Mets, the former dogs of baseball and now the toast of the town, were warming up for a game at Shea Stadium under TV lights with fifty-six thousand people in the stands. On Manhattan's Upper West Side, Bella Abzug, the flamboyant Jewish congresswoman, was meeting with fund-raisers to consider a run for president. Meanwhile, the two old men sitting in the basement sipping moonshine were having a mojo contest:

"Never turn your head to the side while a horse is passing . . ."
"Drop a dead mouse on a red rag."
"Give your sweetheart an umbrella on a Thursday."
"Blow on a mirror and walk it around a tree ten times . . ."

They had reached the remedy of putting a gas lamp in every window of every second house on the fourth Thursday of every month when the generator, as if on its own, roared up wildly, sputtered miserably, coughed, and died.

The basement went nearly dark, the lights dimming low, and they would have gone almost completely black but for the second generator, which sputtered onward, powering a single bulb in a far corner of the basement. It shone brightly, as did the exit light over the hallway door through which Sportcoat had entered and which he had tightly closed upon entering.

"Now you done it," Sausage grumbled in the near dark. "Coming down here carrying on about witches and all, you put a spell on the damn thing."

He knelt, groped inside the generator, and made a few adjustments. The generator coughed miserably, sputtered, and grumbled back up. The lights in the room came up full again.

Sportcoat glared at the generator, puzzled. It seemed louder than ever, roaring at a speed that was unusual, powering along with a shake-rattle so loud that Hot Sausage had to shout over it at the top of his lungs.

"I think it's got a short," he shouted over the roar.

Sportcoat nodded. "But if it's connected to four apartments upstairs," he yelled, "why's the lights going out down here?"

"What?"

"Forget it," he yelled. "I got to get to work. Where's my umpire uniform?"

"What?"

Sportcoat pointed to the roaring generator. Sausage knelt and adjusted the machine, and the roar kicked back a decibel. From his crouch he repeated, "What?"

"I'm getting the baseball game going again," Sportcoat said. "I need my umpire uniform, remember? I know it's down here someplace."

"What you need that for? We ain't got no pitching. Our star pitcher ain't got no ear. And he's gunning for you."

Sportcoat, irritated again, took another sip of King Kong. "Just git it."

"It's right where you put it last," Sausage said, taking the bottle and nodding at a closet in a far corner. Sportcoat gazed at the pile of refuse that stood between them and the closet. He looked down at his plaid sport coat. "I'mma mess up my jacket digging through that."

Sausage sucked his teeth, handed the bottle to Sportcoat, and disappeared into the cacophony of junk. After several clangs, grunts, kicks, and shoves, he reappeared moments later with a black plastic bag, which he tossed on the floor.

At that moment, the generator emitted a horrible burst, coughed, sputtered, sparked, and died again. A moment later, the second generator quit as well.

The room went completely dark this time, save the exit sign over the door. The door, which neither noticed, now stood slightly ajar.

"Goddamn," Sausage said in the silence. "This one here musta shorted out the other one. Gimme a flashlight, Sport."

"That ain't something I normally carries about, Sausage."

"Stay here. I'mma check the generator on the other side."

There was more clattering as Sausage scrambled to the other side of the room. Sportcoat sipped his Kong nonchalantly, felt for the crate with his feet, found it, and sat down.

Neither of them noticed the tall figure in the leather jacket who had slipped into the room through the door underneath the exit sign.

"Do this happen all the time?" Sportcoat said in the silence.

"Never like this," Sausage said from across the room. "Course when you calling on witches and so forth . . ." Sportcoat heard him curse and grunt, then heard a noise near the door and glanced at it. In the light of the exit sign he saw—or thought he saw—a shadow move past it.

"Sausage, I think there's somebo—"

"I got it!" Sausage called. "Okay. There's a switch box behind that generator where you're at. Go back behind it and throw it when I tell you. That'll bring the lights up."

"Throw what?"

"The switch. Behind the generator where you're standing. Feel 'round that generator and throw that switch there," Hot Sausage said. "That'll fire 'em both."

"I don't know nothing about no switches."

"Hurry up, Sport. There's thirty-two apartments upstairs. Them Negroes is cooking collards and scrambled eggs and gotta get to work. Ain't nothing to it, Sport. Just go 'round back of the generator. Stick your hand behind it and feel a thick wire coming out. Follow that wire to the wall with your hand. You'll feel a box there. Open that box and throw the switch in there backward and forward one time."

"If it's all the same to you, I'd rather cook what little brains I got left with whiskey," Sportcoat called out. "I can't see nothing. Plus there's somebo—"

"Git up and do it before them fools upstairs come down here raising hell!"

"I don't know nothing about no boxes."

"You can't get electrocuted back there," Sausage snapped, trying not to sound impatient. "It's all grounded. That generator there's two hundred forty volts. This one here's two hundred twenty." He paused, then said, "Or is it the other way around?"

"Make up your mind now."

"Just go throw that danged switch in the box, please. You got nothing to worry about, Sport. This is the circuit breaker here. The juice is here. It ain't over there where you at."

"If it's over there, whyn't you throw the switch over there?"

"Stop being light-headed, nigger! Hurry up before them Negroes upstairs git here hollering—or even worse, call up Housing."

"All right," Sportcoat said, irritated. He groped his way through the dark, found the generator, ran his hand along the wall behind it until his fingers found a thick wire. He groped the wire, following it to the wall, turned to address Sausage, and saw again the shadow of a man cross the exit light and move toward the middle of the room. This time he was sure of it.

"Sausage?"

"Throw the switch."

"There's somebo—"

"Will you throw it already?"

"All right. What about this wire?"

"Forget the wire now. You don't need it. Throw the switch."

"I don't need this wire? This loose one?"

There was a long silence from Sausage. "Did I forget to tie that thing off?" he muttered.

"Tie off what?"

"The wire."

"There's two."

"Wires or boxes?"

"Both."

"Well don't worry about that," Sausage called, more impatient now. "Just find a box. Any box. Throw the switch in any box you touch and make sure the wire don't touch the generator. I'm holding the panel to this generator box open. I can't hold it much longer, Sport. It's heavy. There's a spring on it."

"But the wire—"

"Forget the wire. It's all grounded, I tell you."

"What's grounded mean?"

"Nigger, you want math and a marching band too? Just throw the goddamn switch! I'll fix everything when we get the lights going. Hurry up before the whole building riots on us down here!"

Sportcoat chose the box nearer to him. He opened it and felt inside. There were two switches in it. Not knowing what to do, he placed the bare wire on the generator and threw both switches. There was a flickering spark, a grunt, and the squealing howl of a human. As the roar of the generator fired and the lights came back up, he caught sight of two boots flying upward in the air.

From the other side of the room, Sausage angrily approached, clattering over the piles of benches, cinder blocks, sinks, and bicycle parts, jawing as he came. "What's the matter with you, Sport? How hard can it be to throw a switch?"

Then he stopped, silent, and stared wide-eyed at something in the middle of the floor. From his side of the room, Sportcoat clambered over the junk and the two of them stood over Earl, Bunch's triggerman. He lay on his back, out cold, his black leather jacket scorched from where the electricity had coursed through him. A shiny watch protruded from his wrist, its crystal broken, and a revolver was squeezed tight in his hand.

"Good God," Sausage said. "That's the feller from Soup's party. How'd he get back so fast? I thought they carried his ass off."

Sportcoat stared at him. "Is he dead?"

Hot Sausage knelt, feeling Earl's neck for a pulse. "He's yet living," he said.

"He'da been ramped up good if they let him drink that brandy rather than letting Soup waste it by busting it on his head. You wanna call the police?"

"Hell no, Sport. Housing'll blame me."

"You ain't done nothing wrong."

"Don't matter. However the cut comes or goes, if the police show up at Housing it means they got to write a report. That means they got to do something down there other than take naps and sip coffee. Anyone who disturbs them from doing that gets walking papers. I'll be outta my job."

He looked down at Earl. "He got to go, Sport. Let's put him out."

"I ain't touching him."

"What you think he come here for? To teach you letters? He crawling 'round here with a pistol. He's somebody Deems put on you."

"Deems is a boy, Hot Sausage. This here's a man. Plus little Deems ain't got no money to hire nobody to do nothing."

"Little Deems got a Firebird car."

"He do? Glory. That boy's running a big mill, ain't he!"

"Goddammit, Sport, I'll take my baseball bat and send you hooting and hollering out that damn door! You brung trouble to my job! Now he got to go! And you got to help!"

"All right. You ain't got to get all tied up in a knot about it."

But Sausage was already moving. He yanked a four-wheel dolly from the junk pile in the middle of the floor, wheeled it over to Earl, then, kneeling over him, checked his pulse again. "I been shocked by that generator before," he said. "It's gonna take him awhile to come to hisself, but he'll be all right. In the meantime, let the devil have him."

They set to work.

Twenty minutes later, Earl woke up in the alley behind Building 17. He was lying on his back. His burned leather jacket smelled like scorched hair. His arms ached so bad he was afraid he'd broken both. His head, knotted with a lump from where the bottle had knocked him cold, felt as if a jackhammer were banging away at it. He raised his right arm, a movement that sent pain roaring down his shoulder, and checked his watch. The crystal was broken. The watch was dead. His moved his left arm, found it alive, and pulled his gun out of his left pocket. He noted the bullets had been emptied from it. He shoved it back into his pocket and sat up. His feet were wet. So were his legs. He'd wet himself. He looked up at the sky and the windows above him. He saw no faces peering at him but could tell by the sun's position in the sky that it was afternoon. He was late. He was supposed to collect yesterday's take from Bunch's Bed-Stuy street dealers by noon.

He got to his feet slowly, every muscle in his body protesting, and staggered toward the nearby Silver Street subway, leaning on the wall as he went. He felt like he was falling to pieces, but moved faster as he got his wind, keeping one eye out for the giant who had escorted him there that morning. He had to make it to Bed-Stuy to pick up Bunch's cash before heading back to the boss's house. The least he could do was to show up with Bunch's rocks. It might keep the boss from killing him.

13

THE COUNTRY GIRL

ELEFANTE AND THE GOVERNOR SAT IN THE LIVING ROOM of the Governor's modest two-family brick house in the Morris Heights section of the Bronx, a calm enclave of apartment buildings dotted with a few leafy trees amid coming urban decay, when the door burst open and a mop swept into the room, followed by an attractive woman pulling a wheeled bucket full of soapy water. Her head was down and she mopped at the floor with such speed and intensity that at first she didn't notice the two men sitting in the room. Elefante was in the rocking chair with his back to the door. The old man was on the couch. The woman swept from left to right and then hit the leg of the rocking chair and saw a foot. She looked up in surprise at Elefante, her face flushed a deep red, and at that moment Elefante saw his future.

She was a heavyset woman, getting on in years but with a sweet face that could not bridle the shyness that emanated from it, with wide brown eyes that, at the moment, blinked in surprise. Her brown hair was pulled back to a bun, and a long, cute, dimpled chin lived beneath a pleasant mouth. Though heavy, she had the frame of a tall, thin woman, her neck was long, and she hung her head a bit, as if to deemphasize her height. She wore a green dress and her feet were bare.

"Whoops. I was just coming in to clean." She backed out of the room quickly and slammed the door. Elefante heard her footsteps retreating to the back of the apartment.

"Sorry," the Governor said. "That's my lass, Melissa. She lives downstairs."

Elefante nodded. He had not seen Melissa long but he had seen her long enough. It was the barefoot part, Elefante thought later, that did it. The no shoes. What a beauty. A country beauty. The type he'd always dreamed about. He liked heavy women. And she was deeply shy. He saw that immediately. It was the way she moved, with slight clumsiness, her head down, that long neck swinging that pretty face away from what was happening. In that moment, he felt an inside part of his tightly wound heart loosen, and understood, with certainty, the Governor's problem. He doubted that shy beauty had the guile to run a bagel shop, much less take care of whatever business the Governor had with this piece that he wanted to dump for dollars, whatever it was. *That type ought to be running a country store someplace*, he thought dreamily. *Running it with me.*

He shook the thought as he saw the Governor watching him, a slight smile on his lined face. They had spent the afternoon together. The old man had been cordial. He'd greeted Elefante like they were old friends. The bagel shop was just two blocks away, and despite the Governor's wheezing and poor health, he insisted they walk over. He proudly showed Elefante the entire operation, the large eating area, the display cases, the store crowded with customers. He showed him the back garage area where he kept his two delivery trucks, and finally the kitchen, which he saved for last, where the two Puerto Rican cooks were finishing up. "We start at two a.m.," the Governor explained. "By four thirty the bagels are hot and rolling out the door. By nine we've moved eight hundred bagels. Sometimes we move a couple thousand a day," he said proudly. "Not just for us. We sell to shops all over the Bronx."

Elefante was impressed. It wasn't so much a bagel shop as it was a factory. But now the two men were back in the Governor's two-family house, in the upper apartment where he stayed, and with the pretty daughter apparently safely down in her apartment below he was eager for the real talk. One look at the daughter told Elefante all he needed to know: if the Governor was telling the truth, he had no real plan.

"It's not my business," Elefante said, "but does your daughter know anything about . . . what I'm here to discuss?"

"Christ, no."

"Don't you have a son-in-law?"

The Governor shrugged. "I can't tell you the ways of the young. In the old days, Irish legend had it that the seals on the beach in Ireland were really dashing young princes who slipped out of their skin to become seals and marry the merry mermaids. I think she's looking for a seal."

Elefante said nothing.

The Governor suddenly appeared tired, and he leaned back into the couch, his head tilted up toward the ceiling. "I've no son. She's my heir, that one. She'd give it the full shilling if I told her about this business, but she'd make bags of it. I want her out of it."

He seemed by nature a lighthearted man, but the tone of that statement let Elefante know that the door was open to his taking full charge of the affair and negotiating a better price for himself, if there was indeed anything to the old man's story at all. The man was exhausted. That small bit of walking to his shop and the tour of it had worn him out completely. "I'm a bit jaded and might have to rest my head on me couch in a while," he said. "But I can still talk. We can get started now."

"Good, 'cause I'm not sure what you're selling."

"You'll know now."

"Talk then. It's your party. I already asked around. My poppa had some friends who remember you. My mother says my poppa trusted you and that you two did talk. So I know you're okay. But you have a good operation here. This isn't a bagel shop. It's a factory. It's clean. It makes money. Why get flashy and monkey with trouble when you're making good guineas now? How much dough do you need?"

The Governor smiled, then coughed again and grabbed a handkerchief and spat in it. The glob he spat into that handkerchief, Elefante saw, was big enough that the Governor had to fold the handkerchief in half to use it again. *This Irish* paisan, he thought, *is sicker than he's letting on.*

Instead of answering the question, the old man tilted his head back again and said, "I got this place and the bagel shop in forty-seven. Well, my wife got the shop, actually. I was in jail that year with your father.

"Here's how we got it. I had some money put up. How I got that money doesn't matter, but it was a good amount of chips. I made the mistake of telling my wife where it was while I was in prison. She came to visit one day and said, 'Guess what? Remember the old Jewish couple on the Grand Concourse with the bagel shop? They sold it to me cheap. They wanted out fast.' She said she couldn't reach me to make a decision. She just went for it. Bought the whole fecking building. With my stash."

He smiled at the memory. "She told me about it in the visitors' room. I ate her head off. I blew my top so bad the prison guards had to collar me to keep me from wringing her neck. It was weeks before she even wrote to me. What could I do? I was in the slammer. She burned up every penny we had—on bagels. I was shook. Mad as a box of frogs."

He stared at the ceiling, his face wistful.

"Your father thought that was funny. He said, 'Is it losing money?' I said, 'How the hell would I know? There's niggers and spics all over.'

"He said, 'They eat bagels too. Write to your wife and tell her you're sorry.'

"I did, blessed God, and she forgave me. And now I thank her every day for buying that place. Or would. If she was here."

"When did she pass away?"

"Oh, it's been . . . I don't keep track." He sighed, then sang softly,

> Twenty years a-growing,
> Twenty years in blossom,
> Twenty years a-stooping,
> Twenty years declining.

Elefante found himself softening, the inside part of him, the part that he never let the world see, the part that had loosened when the man's daughter swept her mop into the room. "Does that mean you have a clear conscience on the whole bit? Or just a bad memory?"

The Governor stared at the ceiling a bit longer. His eyes seemed fixed on something far distant. "She lived long enough to see me come out of prison. She and my Melissa, they built the business while I was in jail. Three years after I came out, my wife took ill, and now I'm a little under the weather myself."

A little under the weather? Elefante thought. He looked ready to keel over.

"Luckily Melissa's ready to take it over," the Governor said. "She's a good lass. She can fly the business. I am lucky she's so good."

"All the more reason to keep her out of trouble."

"That's where you come in, Cecil."

The Elephant nodded, uncomfortable. The reference took him by surprise. He hadn't been called that in years. "Cecil" was a childhood nickname his father had given him. His real name was Tomaso, or Thomas. He bore his father's name as a middle name. Cecil was his father's creation. Where it came from, and why his father chose it, he never knew. It was more than a name of adoration; it was a sign between

father and son that they needed to talk privately. His poppa was bedridden in his last year, still running the business, and there were often
other people about his bedroom, men who worked in the boxcar, in construction, and in the storage house. When Poppa said "Cecil," there was
important business, private business about, and they needed to discuss it
when the room cleared. The Governor's knowledge of the name was a
further sign of credibility—and also, Elefante thought glumly, responsibility. He didn't want to be responsible for this guy. He had enough
responsibility.

The Governor eyed him a long moment, then gave in to his fatigue.
He shifted and pulled his legs on the couch and lay down, stretching out,
an arm on his forehead. He raised his other arm and pointed a finger
to a desk behind Elefante. "Hand me a pen and paper from that desk,
would ya? They're right on top."

Elefante did as he was told. The Governor scratched something on the
paper, folded it tightly, and handed the paper to Elefante. "Don't open it
yet," he said.

"You want I should stuff ballot boxes for you too?"

The old man smiled. "That's not a bad thing to know, considering
what happens to old codgers like me in our game. You get tired, y'know.
Your father understood that."

"Tell me about my poppa," Elefante said. "What'd he like to talk
about?"

"You're trying to trick me," the Irishman said with a low chuckle.
"Your father played checkers and said six words a day. But if he said six
words, five of them were about you."

"He didn't show me that side much," Elefante said. "After he came
back from prison, he'd already had the stroke. So talking was hard.
He was in bed a lot. He was about survival in those days. Keeping the
boxcar busy, working for the fami—" He paused. "Working for our customers."

The Governor nodded. "I've never worked for the Five Families," he said.

"Why not?"

"A true Irishman knows the world will one day break your heart."

"What's that mean?"

"I like breathing, son. Most people I knew who worked for the families ended up getting dragged across the quit line in pieces. Your father was one of the few who died in bed."

"He never trusted them completely," Elefante said.

"Why?"

"Lots of reasons. We're northern Italian. They're southern Italian. I was young and stupid. He didn't think I'd live long when I got made. He kept me busy running that dock. He gave orders. I followed them. That's how it was. Before he went to jail and after. He was the puppet master, I was the puppet. Work the boxcar, move the stuff, ship it here, there, store this, pay this guy, pay that guy. Pay your men well. Say nothing. That was the gig. But he always kept a foot in other things: construction, a little loan business, even a gardening business for a while. We always had other interests."

"You had other interests because your father did not trust."

"He *did* trust. He was just careful about the people he trusted."

"Because . . . ?"

"Because a man who doesn't trust cannot be trusted."

The Governor smiled. "That's why you're the right lad for the job."

He looked so satisfied Elefante blurted, "If you feel a song coming on, don't bother. I had Cousin Brucie on the radio in the car all the way over. He played Frankie Valli. Nobody sings better than him."

The old man chuckled, then raised a frail hand and pointed at the piece of paper in Elefante's closed fist. "Read it."

Elefante unfolded the paper and read: *"A man who does not trust cannot be trusted."*

"I knew your father well," the Governor said gravely. "As good as I knew any man in this world."

Elefante didn't know what to say.

"Now I *am* gonna sing," the Governor said brightly. "And it's gonna be better than Frankie Valli."

And he proceeded to talk.

As Elefante drove his Lincoln down the Major Deegan heading home that evening, the note still folded in his shirt pocket, his mind was spinning. He thought not of the story the governor told him, but of the country-looking farm girl who'd come into the room and backed out the door apologizing, excusing herself. A shy, pretty Irish girl. Fresh as spring. She was a little younger than him, thirty-five or so he guessed, which was old not to be married. She seemed so shy, he wondered how someone so meek could run a business. *Then again*, he thought, *I've never seen her in action. Maybe she's like me*, he thought. *All show business at work, gruff and bitter, but at home, at night, crowing to the stars for love and company.*

Or maybe I'm a moron, he thought bitterly. *Just an aching heart—in a city full of them. Geez.*

He gunned onto a ramp that exited to the FDR Drive, then zipped down the east side of Manhattan toward the Brooklyn Bridge. He was glad to be driving. It allowed his mind to roam and the confusion to quell. It was just past four thirty p.m. and traffic was still moving smoothly. He turned on the radio and the music jarred him back to reality. He scanned the East River, checking the line of barges moving along. Some of them he knew. A few were run by honest captains who refused hot items. They wouldn't move a stolen tire if you paid them a thousand bucks. Others were captained by blithering idiots who would kick their scruples out the window for the price of a cup of coffee. The first type were honest to a fault. They just couldn't help it. The second type were born crooks.

Which one am I? he wondered.

Am I good or bad? he thought as he maneuvered the Lincoln through traffic. He thought about getting out of the game altogether. It was an old dream. He had plenty saved up. He'd made enough to live. That's what Poppa wanted, right? He could sell his two rental houses in Bensonhurst, sell the boxcar to Ray out in Coney Island, and step out once and for all. *To do what? Work in a bagel shop?* He couldn't believe the thought entered his mind. The Governor's daughter didn't even know who he was and he was already putting himself in her kitchen. He pictured himself ten years from now, a fat husband in a cook's outfit, slinging dough and slamming it into an oven at three a.m.

On the other hand, what was life all about? Family. Love. That woman was concerned about her father. She was loyal to family. He understood that feeling. It said a lot about her.

He'd talked to her briefly before he left. The Governor had fallen asleep on his couch after their conversation, and Elefante went to the door to let himself out. She was coming up the stairs to check on her father and caught him. He'd guessed she heard him leaving and wanted to make sure her father was okay. That's what he would have done. Check that her father was breathing, maybe make sure the stranger wasn't some goombah from years past who showed up wanting to even things. That said a lot about her too. She was shy, but clearly not that shy, and not stupid. And not afraid.

They'd met in the hallway by the front door. They'd talked maybe twenty minutes. She was immediately open and candid. He was someone her father trusted. So she trusted him.

"I can handle things," she said when he asked her about running the bagel shop on her own. He had joked about her tearing into the room, mop first, holding the bucket and using the mop as a spear. She laughed and said, "Oh, that. My poppa cleans like a kindergartner."

"Well, he's worked hard enough."

"Yes, but he leaves his place a mess, and he falls asleep so easily."

"My feet fall asleep when I'm running for the bus."

She laughed again, and opened up more, and in the ensuing chat showed that behind the gentle veneer lay qualities more like those of her father, lighthearted, funny, but with a firmness and cleverness he found alluring. They chatted easily together. She knew he was there for important business. She knew their fathers had been close friends. Yet he still sensed a tentativeness. He probed her gently. That was his job, he thought bitterly, as a goddamned smuggler working with lowlife drug dealers like Joe Peck and murderers like Vic Gorvino: to sense weakness in others. Standing there, he felt her probing him as well. He felt her size him up and squeeze him—gently—for information. Try as he might, he couldn't block it, couldn't prevent her from seeing the part that most never saw, that while he was firm and tight on the surface, all business, maybe a little too Italian in his manner and speech, beneath it he bore the heavy sense of responsibility for his mother and those he cared about with kindness that was safer to hide. He was the man her father trusted. But why him? Why not a cousin or an uncle? Or at least a fellow Irishman? Why an Italian? In those twenty minutes the war between the races, the Italians versus the Irish, was waged, the two representatives of the black souls of Europe, left in the dust by the English, the French, the Germans, and later in America by the big boys in Manhattan, the Jews who forgot they were Jews, the Irish who forgot they were Irish, the Anglos who forgot they were human, who got together to make money in their big power meetings about the future, paving over the nobodies in the Bronx and Brooklyn by building highways that gutted their neighborhoods, leaving them to suffer at the hands of whoever came along, the big boys who forgot the war and the pogroms and the lives of the people who survived World War I and World War II sacrificing blood and guts for their America, so they could work with the banks and the city and state to slap expressways in the middle of thriving neighborhoods and send the powerless suckers who believed in the American dream scrambling to the suburbs because they, the big boys, wanted a bigger percentage. He felt it, or thought he felt it, as they stood by the front door. There was a connection: a man whose father was dead and a woman whose father was about to die, a sense of wanting to belong, standing in the warm vestibule, she in her farm-girl dress, with a job that paid taxes and drew no cops, no Joe Pecks, no complicated phone calls from complicated people trying to pick your pocket with one hand while saluting the flag with the other, and he feeling a sense of belonging he hadn't felt in years.

She laughed easily, asking questions, the shyness gone now, while he nodded silently. She talked the entire twenty minutes, which seemed to pass in seconds, and all the while he felt like shouting, "I'm the seal on the beach. If you only knew me." But instead he was light and firm, halfheartedly trying to block her questions by pretending to be aloof and distrustful. She saw through it all, he could tell. She saw him clearly. He felt naked. She wanted to know why he was there. She wanted to know everything.

But she could never know.

That was part of the arrangement. He had agreed to the Governor's harebrained scheme, of course. In part because he loved his father. The parts of his father that he knew ran deepest were all about trust. Any man his father trusted had to be a loving, good man. There was no doubt. Guido Elefante had never backed out on his word with a man he trusted. Neither did his father care what others thought of him. Poppa loved his mother, no doubt because Momma was anything but the typical Brooklyn Italian housewife like so many on his block, the women who chatted about nothing, tossing cannolis around, filing obediently into mass at St. Andrew's every morning praying for their husband's redemption and, by extension, their own, complaining about the niggers and the spics taking over the neighborhood while their husbands ran liquor and shot anyone who opened their mouth wrong about their gambling operations and horse-racing fixes and their running roughshod over the coloreds. His mother didn't care about the coloreds. She saw them just as people. She cared about plants, and digging for them in the empty lots around their neighborhood—plants, she insisted, that had kept her husband alive long after most expected him to be gone. And as for their son, she never asked questions of Thomas; she respected Elefante when he was but a boy because she understood, instinctively, that her son would be different from most of the Italians in the neighborhood, had to be different just like she and her husband had to be different to survive. She never made apologies for her family. The Elefantes were what they were. That was all there was to it. Poppa had welcomed the Governor into his world. And so Elefante did as well. They were partners now. That was decided.

Also, there was the intrigue of the whole business.

And of course, the money.

Was it about the money? he asked himself.

He glanced at the folded paper on the car seat next to him. It was the paper that the Governor had placed in his fist when they spoke of Poppa.

"A man who does not trust cannot be trusted."

Elefante swung the big Lincoln to the off ramp of the FDR just past Houston Street. The silhouette of the Brooklyn Bridge loomed ahead. He thought of their conversation again, and the Governor's story.

"I'm losing my mind," he murmured.

It had been late afternoon and the Governor was nearly asleep when he told Elefante the story of the "soap" he'd given to the younger man's father. Lying on the couch, he spoke to the ceiling while a fan overhead creaked ceaselessly:

"For almost a thousand years, the Church of the Visitation in Vienna, Austria, had these precious treasures," he said. "Manuscripts, candleholders, altar cups. Most of it would be biscuits to a bear to you and me. Stuff used during mass, altar cup to drink our savior's blood, candleholders, that sort of thing. Some gold coins. All of it was made to last. It's hundreds of years old, this stuff. Passed down through generations. When World War II came, the church hid it from the Allies.

"That's where my younger brother Macy was stationed. He was sent there in forty-five during the war. America kept troops there after the war and Macy stayed on. Macy was eight years younger than me, a lieutenant in the army, an odd fellow. He was, um . . ." The Governor thought a moment. "A ponce," he said.

"A ponce?" Elefante repeated.

"Light as a feather. They'd call him a sissy today, I guess. He had a taste for the finer things in life. Always liked art. Even when he was little. He knew all about it. He read books on art. Just had a taste for it. Well, the city was all torn up after the war, patrolled by different armies here and there, and somehow Macy found this stash of stuff. It had been hidden by the Nazis. In a cave near a place called Altenburg."

The Governor paused, thoughtful.

"How Macy found that cave, I never knew. But there was valuable stuff in there. A lot of it. And he helped himself to it: manuscripts, tiny little boxes decorated with diamonds, with little panels of ivory. And some reliquaries."

"What's that?"

"I had to look it up five times before I understood it," the Governor said. "They're tiny boxes like coffins, made of gold and silver. Some are trimmed with diamonds. The priests kept jewelry, art, relics, even old bones of saints in them. This stuff was heavy loot. The spoils of war, m'lad. Macy got hold of a good gob of it."

"How do you know?"

"I saw it. He had them in his house."

"How'd he get all of it home?"

The Governor smiled. "He used his noodle and shipped it to himself by the US Military Postal Service. Little by little. I guess that's why he stayed in the service so long. The stuff was small. Then after the war, he got a job at the post office so he could move it when he wanted without nobody making a stink. Simple as that."

He chuckled, and had to raise himself as he coughed a large amount of phlegm into his handkerchief. When he was done, he folded the handkerchief, put it back into his pocket, and continued.

"It always seemed odd to me that Macy lived too well to work at the post office," the Governor admitted. "He had an apartment in the Village the size of a rugby field. Full of fancy things. I never asked. He had no kids, so I figured it wasn't anything. My poppa couldn't stand Macy. He used to say, 'Macy likes boys.' I told Poppa, 'There was a priest at Saint Andrew's who's said to like boys.' But he didn't want to hear it. I was a young man back then, fast on my feet and a bit of a wanker, but even then I knew the difference between a sick man who likes children and a man sweet on men. I knew because Macy talked me out of killing that half-langered Rale Bulgarian priest at Saint Andrew's who acted the maggot with a lot of kids in the parish. I found out about him when Macy grew up and we started adding up crib notes on him. But Macy said, 'He's a sick man. Don't go to jail for him.' He was my kid brother and he was smarter than me in a lot of ways. So I listened, and went to jail on my own! Even in prison, Macy's smarts helped me. If you walk into the slammer not looking for a hop on, knowing that what a man does in his private time is his own damn business so long as he doesn't make things worse for you, well, you're all right. So I loved Macy for what he showed me. And he trusted me."

The Governor sighed and rubbed his head as he plowed through the memory. "He didn't live long after the war. First our mother died. Then a couple of years later, cancer got him. That and a broken heart, poor lad, because his father didn't want him. Toward the end of his life, he came to me and confessed everything. He took me to a closet in his house and showed me what he had. He kept all those things from the cave in a closet, imagine that. Wonderful things: Bibles with solid-gold covers. Relics. Manuscripts rolled into tubes made of gold. Gold coins. Diamond reliquaries with the bones of old saints inside. He said, 'This stuff is a thousand years old.' I said, 'You're a millionaire.'

"He said, 'I hardly sold any of it. I made a good living at the Postal Service.'

"I laughed at him. I said, 'You're a stock.'"

"A stock?" Elefante repeated.

"A fool."

"Oh."

"He said, 'I didn't want to sell them. I just liked looking at them.'

"I said, 'Macy, it's not good. These are things from the church.'

"'The church doesn't care for people like me,' he said.

"Oh, it broke my heart when he said that. I said, 'Macy, my boy. Our dear mother in heaven would fall to fever at God's throne knowing you sit here with stolen things from her Lord and Savior. It would break her heart.'

"That brought a tear to his eye. He said, 'I have to live. Maybe I'll find a way to return a few things.'"

The Governor looked at Elefante. "And return them he did. Oh, he sold one or two more things in droves to keep his lifestyle before he died. But most of the things he returned. He got them back to Vienna the same way he got them here. He mailed them back little by little. He returned them in a way so he could never get caught. But there was one item he didn't return.

"And what was that?"

"Well, it was something I wanted. A little statue."

"Statue of what?"

"A fat girl. The Venus of Willendorf."

Elefante wondered if he was dreaming. A statue of a fat girl? The Governor's daughter was like that. A beautiful one. Could this be a trick? A coincidence?

"Is that the name of a soap?" he asked.

The Governor smirked at him, irritated.

"I'm just asking," Elefante said.

"Macy said it was the most valuable piece in his collection."

"Why was that?"

"I can't say. Macy knew why but I don't know those things. It's reddish gold. It's very small. Made of stone. No bigger than a bar of soap."

"If it's not gold, why is it worth so much?"

The Governor sighed. "I'm thicker than a bag of spuds when it comes to art, son. I don't know. Like I said, I had to look up the word 'reliquary' five times before I understood it. This statue was in one of those reliquary things. A tiny container, like a coffin, the size of a bar of soap. It's from thousands of years ago. Macy said the box alone was worth a fortune. He said the little fat girl, the Venus of Willendorf, was worth more than anything he had."

"Then it likely lives in one of those big castles in Europe where the welcome mat's printed in old English, and he was holding a fake. Or the real one's living in a museum. How come it's not in a museum? A museum would know if it's a fake, by the way."

"So what. Son, your pop and I were in prison with several sweet-tongued buncos who could sell ice to an Eskimo. These blokes could even out your bank account to a flat zero faster than a fly can mount shit. They knew more insurance swindles, bank diddles, and hand tricks than a Philadelphia bartender. Smooth as taffy, these fellas. And each one will tell you that most times the trout who gets hooked or bamboozled hushes up tight about it. They want that kind of news kept quiet.

The fancy hoofers running your museums are no different. If they're holding a fake, why would they blast it to the world? So long as a cad is paying a shilling to eyeball it, who's to know the difference?"

Elefante was silent, taking this in.

"You think I'm having you on?" the Governor asked.

"Maybe. Did you ever ask your brother why it was worth so much?"

"No, I didn't ask him. I took it before he changed his mind. Then he died."

"The Venus of Willendorf. That sounds like the name of a soup."

"It's not a soup. It's a fat girl," the Governor insisted.

"I knew a fat girl in high school who was a real treasure. But nobody made a statue of her."

"Well this one will fit in the palm of your hand. I stashed it before I went to prison. Your father got out two years before me. I was afraid someone would find it, so I told him to fetch it and hold it for me. He told me he did. So you have it someplace."

Elefante held his hands out. "I swear on the Blessed Virgin, my poppa didn't tell me where he put it."

"Nothing?"

"He just told me about that stupid song you sing, about the palm of God's hand."

The Governor nodded in satisfaction. "Well, that's something."

"That's nothing. How can I look for a thing if I don't know where it is or what it looks like?"

"She's a fat girl."

"There must be a million statues of fat girls. Does she have a bump on her nose, or is she fat like a blob? Does she look like a horse if you turn her sideways? Are the head and stomach the only parts you want to go pokey at? Or is it like one of those crappy things where a guy throws paint on a canvas and art slobs cream all over it? Does she have one eye? What?"

"I don't know what. *It's a fat girl*. From thousands of years ago. And there's a guy in Europe who will pay three million dollars cash for it."

"You said that before. How do I know he's the real deal?"

"He's real, all right. Macy sold him one or two pieces before he died. He told me how to reach the guy, but Macy died while I was in prison. I couldn't call nobody from Sing Sing. So I left it alone. You can end up in an urn in somebody's cemetery playing tricks with a fella you never seen before and done no business with. I never called him before I went to prison. After I got out, my wife got sick, I had to take care of her, and I didn't want to go back to the joint. Then a couple months ago, when the doctor told me I had this . . . sickness, you see, I called the guy in Europe and he was still alive. I told him I was Macy's brother and told him what I have. He didn't believe me, so I sent him the one picture I had. I'm an old crook. I'm too stupid to keep copies. Saints be praised, he got the picture and got serious. He calls me almost every week now. He says he can move it. At first he offered four million dollars, and I said, 'How can you get that much money?' He said, 'That's my business. I'll give you four, because I can sell it for twelve million. Or even fifteen. But you need to get it here.' He said he's in Vienna.

"I smelled a rat then. I almost backed out. I didn't trust him. So I said, 'If you're the guy my brother said you are, wire me ten grand and tell me the name of one thing my brother sold you.' He did. I ain't daft. I didn't tell the guy where I lived. He thinks I live in Staten Island. That's the return address I put on the envelope with the picture I sent him. He wired the dough to the bank in Staten Island I told him to. I sent him the ten grand back and said okay.

"But I got no muscle to move this thing. I can't get it to Europe now. Even if I could, I wouldn't go all the way over there and have the guy lay boots on me or worse, then bag the thing and run off. So I says to him, 'You come here and get it and I'll let it go for three million dollars. You can keep the extra million for your troubles.'

"I was just talking," the Governor said. "I thought he'd say 'Get lost.' I didn't think he had the balls to do it. He said, 'Let me think about it.' After a week, he called back and said, 'Okay. I'll come get it.' That's when I come to you."

"You're throwing a pretty long pass here, mister. What makes you think I'd give it to you—or to him—if I found it?" Elefante said.

"Because you're your father's son. I ain't just flying it, son. I asked around about you. See, your poppa and me, we knew who we were. We were always little guys. Moving guys. We never wanted muscle or trouble. We moved stuff. This guy from Europe I'm talking to, he's a head guy. He talks smart. With an accent. Smooth. Head guys like that are always one step ahead of you. No matter how smart you think you are, they got a leg up on you. That's why they're head guys. You fool with a head guy, you better be the full shilling. Your poppa always said you were the full shilling."

Elefante thought that one over and said softly, almost to himself, "I'm not really a head guy."

"For three million chips you are."

The Governor was silent a moment, then continued. "I took it as far as I could. I called the guy and said, 'Let's arrange a meet.' He said, 'Put it in a locker and let me come get it and I'll leave your dough.' That was the idea. We meet at Kennedy. Make the switch in a locker there, and go on. We didn't talk about the exact switch, how we'd do it, but I agreed on the locker bit."

"Then work out the last bit and go make your money, for Chrissakes."

"How can I do that if I don't know where the statue is?"

"You did know," Elefante said. "You had it before my poppa did."

"He stashed it!" The Governor paused. "Look, I had it before I went to prison. I couldn't tell my wife about it. She'd already spent my dough on fuckin' bagels. The statue wasn't in a safe place. I told your poppa where it was when we were in Sing Sing. He got out two years ahead of me. He agreed to get it and hold it. I told him, 'After I get out, when things cool off, I'll come for it. And I'll give you a piece of it.' He said, 'Okay.' But he had that stroke in prison just before he got out, and I didn't see him no more. I tried passing word to him when he was in the prison hospital, but he was gone before I could reach him. They released him after his stroke. He passed word to me after he got out. He sent a letter. It said, 'Don't worry. I got that little box of yours. It's clean and safe and in the palm of God's hand like that little song you used to sing.' So I know he got it somehow. And I know he kept it someplace."

"In God's hand? What's that mean?"

"I don't know. He just said the palm of God's hand."

"You got the wrong guy then. My pop didn't write that letter. He never went to church."

"Weren't you Catholic?"

"My mother dragged me to Saint Augustine till I was big enough to quit. But my father never went. Until he was dead, he never went into a church. We had his funeral. That's when he went to church."

"Maybe he left it in a church. Or in his coffin."

Elefante thought for a moment. His mother did say she wanted his father's coffin exhumed so she could get in the same grave. And Joe Peck had promised to do the job himself. The thought of that pea-brained idiot Joe Peck digging through his father's remains, flipping his poppa's corpse around, working through the pockets of his dad's best suit, drilling through his poppa's brains with a screwdriver, trying to find whatever the hell the fat girl's name was that was worth three million dollars threw him, and for a moment Elefante felt out of breath. After a moment, he regained his composure and said: "He wouldn't leave it in a church. He had no contact with churches. There's no one in any church he'd trust. He wouldn't be dumb enough to bury it with himself either. He wouldn't do that to my mother."

"I agree," the Governor said. "But you have a storage place. You move stuff."

"I looked through every single storage rental we have. The ones I have access to."

"What about the ones you don't have access to?"

"I guess I could get in them," Elefante admitted. "But that'll take time."

"Time I ain't got," the Governor said. "The guy who wants to buy, he won't deal with nobody else. You don't call this type of guy. He calls you. I'm stalling him. I told him I had to think about the deal. He's skittish. He won't like it if there's a second person involved. As it is, I'm thinking he might make a move on me regardless. Which is the other reason I'm hoping you'll dig it up."

And there it was, Elefante thought bitterly. *He's got nobody. If a big shot in Europe wants a fucking artifact worth an arm and a leg and the only stumbling block between him and that dough is a bagel maker and his daughter . . . well there it is.*

"I thought you told him you're in Staten Island," Elefante said.

"People like that can find you," the Governor said. "On the other hand, he's like my brother Macy. These guys are fanatics. We got a little maneuvering room. I let him know that the minute I smell a rat, the statue is gone forever. Flushed down the toilet. Peeled to pieces. Tossed in the river. But I still think of Melissa here. So when I came to you . . . well, with you, knowing how your father was, I know I have at least one guy on my team who won't cut and run."

Elefante was silent. *"My team,"* he thought. *How the hell did I get on his team?*

The Governor sat up on the couch a moment, arched his back awkwardly, then reached under the couch and pulled out an envelope. "One more thing," he said.

He handed the envelope to Elefante, who instantly recognized the painful scrawls of his father's handwriting, which toward the end of his life was shaky and big. The envelope was addressed to the Governor.

"Where'd you get this?"

"Your poppa sent this to me when I was in prison."

Elefante opened the envelope. Inside was a simple greeting card, with a picture of the old Cause docks, taken perhaps in the 1940s, the familiar Statue of Liberty in the distance. On the back was taped the traditional Irish blessing, obviously clipped from a book or a newspaper:

> May the road rise up to meet you.
> May the wind be always at your back.
> May the sun shine warm upon your face,
> The rains fall soft upon your fields.
> And until we meet again,
> May God hold you in the palm of His hand.

Next to that was a sketch, in his father's hand, of a tiny box. Inside the box was a wooden stove, with small bits of firewood, crudely drawn, and a cross above it. The box had five sides; on one of the sides was a circle with a stick figure drawn in the middle, its arms outstretched.

"If this weren't his handwriting, I wouldn't believe he'd drawn it," Elefante said.

"Do you recognize anything?"

"No."

"It's an Irish blessing," the Governor said.

"I figured that much," Elefante said. "But what's with the firebox and the firewood?"

"Do you have a storage locker with something like that in it?" the Governor asked.

"No. That box could be anything. A garage. A house. A milk crate. A cabin in the woods. It could be anywhere."

"Yes, it could," the Governor said. "But where would Guido Elefante go?"

Elefante thought a long moment before he answered.

"My father," he said dryly, "never went anywhere. He never went three blocks outside the Cause District. Hardly ever. He couldn't walk very well. Even if he could, he wouldn't go far. Maybe to the store in Bay Ridge once in a while that sold food from Genoa. There was a place on Third Avenue that sold Genoese stuff, focaccia, cheese mostly from the old country, but he hardly went there."

"How do you know?"

"He never went anywhere, I tell you. He went to the boxcar every once in a while. He went to the storage place hardly ever. Maybe three times my whole life I saw him walk in there. I took care of the storage place, not him."

"What else is around you?"

"Nothing. Just the housing projects. The subway. Some abandoned buildings. That's it."

The Governor looked at him oddly. "You sure?"

"I'm sure."

"That box is somewhere. Sure as I'm living, it's sticking out like a blind cobbler's thumb someplace. Somewhere your poppa put it."

"How would I know where?"

The Governor yawned. "He's your father," he said sleepily. "A son knows his father."

Elefante stared at the paper in his hands a long time. He wanted to say, "But you weren't my father's son. You don't know how difficult he was. He was impossible to talk to." But instead he said, "That's not gonna be easy."

He looked over at the Governor. He was talking to himself. The old man had fallen asleep. As quietly as he could, he rose from the rocker, stepped out the door, and slipped silently out into the hallway just as Melissa was coming up the stairs.

14

RAT

BUNCH SAT AT THE TABLE OF HIS DINING ROOM IN HIS Bed-Stuy brownstone and chewed a chicken wing. A huge spread of wings and a platter of barbecue sauce were on the table. He motioned to the young man seated at the table across from him. "Help yourself, young brother."

Lightbulb, Deems Clemens's right-hand man, reached deep into the chicken wings, his fingers scooping out two, and then dipped them in the sauce. He sucked down the tender meat and reached for the plate again.

"Slow your roll, bro," Bunch said. "The chicken ain't going nowhere."

Lightbulb still ate fast—too fast, Bunch thought. Either the kid was starving or he might be a dope user already. He guessed the latter. The kid was awful thin and wore long sleeves to cover what might be tracks in his arms.

Lightbulb glanced at the end of the table where Earl, fresh from his painful electrocution in Sausage's basement boiler room, silently scratched at a crossword puzzle, his right arm in a sling and his head bandaged from where the bottle had smashed him at Soup's coming-home party. Earl kept his head down.

"So tell me about Deems," Bunch said.

"What you wanna know?" Lightbulb asked.

"How'd he win the flagpole?" he asked. "That's the busiest section of the Cause. Who was doing business there before Deems took over?"

"I want the flagpole plaza, by the way," Lightbulb said. "If this works out."

"How about a flagpole up your ass. I asked you about how Deems won it. I didn't ask you what you want."

"I'm just saying I can do a better job than him. I'd need the flagpole to do it."

"Who you think you talking to, kid, Santa Claus? I don't care about your needs. You ain't done nothing so far other than say what you need and lick your nasty fingers while eating my chicken."

Lightbulb blinked and started in. "Back when we was all playing baseball, Deems had an older cousin named Rooster. Rooster started selling first. He was making so much bank we quit ball to work under him. We ran customers to him. Junkies on the street. White boys from New Jersey cruising through, like that. Rooster got killed by somebody who tried to rob him. So Deems took over."

"Just like that? Y'all just let Deems be top dog?"

"Well . . . he done some things, Deems did."

"Like?"

"Well . . . a boy named Mark Bumpus was the first guy. He dead now."

"How'd he get that way? Was he a heavy sleeper? Did he fall down a flight of stairs?"

"Deems set him up."

"How so?"

"Well, Rooster died while we was all in jail. When we come out, Bumps—Mark Bumpus—ran things."

"And Deems didn't mind? Even though Rooster was his cousin?"

"We got, like, forty dollars a day. That's a lot of money."

"And Deems didn't say nothing?"

"I got to back up a minute to tell it right," Lightbulb said. "See, we was all in Spofford together," Lightbulb said, referring to the juvenile center. "Me, Beanie, Sugar, Deems, and Bumps. Deems and Bumps got into it in Spofford, in the rec room. It wasn't over Rooster. He was already dead."

"Over what then?"

"The TV. Deems wanted to watch baseball. Bumps didn't. They got into it. Deems whipped up on Bumps pretty bad. Then Deems's grandfather visited and gave Deems fifty dollars. The food was bad in Spofford, so Deems went to the commissary and bought some rice and beans. He shared it with his boys: me, Beanie, Sugar. Bumps wasn't his boys. When Bumps asked Deems for some rice and beans, Deems said no, I just share with my boys. So that night Bumps and a couple of his friends caught Deems alone in the shower and cut him up bad. They took his rice and beans and the rest of that fifty dollars.

"Deems never forgot that," Lightbulb said. "Bumps got out of Spofford before Deems did. When he come out Spofford a few months later, Bumps had taken over the plaza. Bumps was hot, man, selling dope, weed, acid, everything. By that time most of us was out of Spofford. We all needed money, so we went to work for Bumps. He paid forty dollars a day. He even hired Deems. He told Deems, 'Forget all that stuff from Spofford. You're with me now. We boys now.'

"Deems ran customers to Bumps better than any of us. Deems knew how to find dopeheads. Deems would go all the way downtown to get customers and run them over to Bumps. It got so that Bumps would let Deems carry dope to his far-off customers, because Bumps was rolling. He was selling to everybody. That's when Deems got him.

"He sent Deems out with thirty grams of coke to this Jamaican guy out in Hollis, Queens. Deems switched out the dope for some white soap flakes and flour and gived the bag to the guy. The guy used it and damn near died. He called on the phone and Deems had Beanie answer the telephone and Beanie told the guy 'Fuck off.' So the guy got his revenge. Deems took a bunch of us to the top of Building Nine where we could wait to watch the ants come—"

"What ants?"

"It don't matter. Just a bunch of ants that crawl up there every year. But you can see the plaza from there. You could see Bumps out there working. Deems said, 'Remember my rice and beans when we was in juvy? I'mma square that with punk-ass Bumps. Just watch.'

"Sure enough, a couple of nights later this pretty Jamaican girl come around to the flagpole saying to Bumps she wanted some dope but didn't have no money. She offered to, you know, service his rod if he let her shoot up afterward. Bumps said okay. He followed her to the alley behind the plaza and them Jamaicans was waiting for him. They damn near killed him. Cut his face, down his forehead, all down his eye, oh man, messed him up. They left him like that.

"Soon as they started whipping on him, Deems ran off the roof. He run off soon as they started cutting Bumps up. The minute them Jamaicans left Bumps laying in the alley, Deems came out the back door of Building Nine and ran over to Bumps holding a steaming pot of rice and beans. He must've had it cooking in his house. He said, 'Here's your rice and beans, Bumps.' He poured that whole pot on him.

"Bumps got crippled from that. He was never the same. He got out the dope game altogether. He tried fooling around on the dock, smuggling, trying to make money that way. He didn't last long. He was walking in the Elephant's territory then. You ever heard of the Elephant?"

"I heard of him."

"Yeah, well, that's the last anybody seen of Bumps."

Lightbulb paused, then reached for another piece of chicken and dipped it in the sauce. "That's how Deems won the flagpole," he said.

"Why didn't somebody from Bumps's crew take the flagpole plaza back?" Bunch asked.

"First of all, that ain't the only thing Deems done, bro. Second, ain't nobody smarter in the Cause than Deems."

"So people are afraid of him?"

"Well, yes and no. The old folks in the Cause like Deems. He was a church boy. The church folks sit around the flagpole in the mornings and talk and bullshit. Deems stays out of their way. He don't run his dope till the afternoons, when the church folks leave the plaza. He don't allow it before then. He's funny about them church people. He don't wanna make the church people mad. Some of 'em's old, but they can cause trouble. Some of 'em will shoot, y'know."

"I do know." Here Bunch glanced disgustedly at Earl, whose face was shoved so deep into his crossword puzzle he appeared to be cleaning the puzzle with his nose.

"Plus Deems was the star on the Cause Houses baseball team," Lightbulb said. "That's Sportcoat's old team. Deems's father wasn't around. His mother drank a lot. Deems's grandfather raised him. And his grandfather and Sportcoat was buddies. That's why Sportcoat ain't dead yet, I guess. Because Deems was on his baseball team and his grandfather was all for him doing that. He could play the shit outta some baseball. When his grandfather died, he left all that and went to selling the flour and rock. Good as he was in baseball, that's how good he is at moving that dip. Deems thinks stuff out. All day long, he thinks how to move that powder. He's to hisself too. He don't chase girls too much. He don't watch TV. And he don't forget. If you cross Deems, he'll let a year pass. Two years even. I seen him walk up to guys and choke them till they fall asleep for stuff they did to him two years before that they forgot all about. I seen him put a hot iron to a guy's neck to get the name of somebody who stole from him so long ago ain't nobody remembered it but Deems. He's smart, bro, like I said. He ain't been in jail since Spofford.

He don't carry a knife. Don't carry a gun. He's organized. He pays little-kid watchers to set on the buildings and watch out. He got watchers in the plaza. *They* got the weapons. Not him."

"So what's the matter with him now?"

"He's too strict, Mr. Bunch. He wants to be a cop now. Before he became a punk and let Sportcoat shoot him, he would sell to everybody. Now he won't sell to grandmothers. He won't sell to little kids. He won't sell to nobody from the church. He don't want nobody smoking near the church, or robbing the church, or falling asleep in the door of the church, like that. And like if somebody beats up their girlfriend over something, he won't sell to 'em. He wants to be telling folks what they should be doing. That's why Sportcoat shot him, I think, because he got pussified, talking about going back to baseball and all this, ordering folks around, telling folks what to do instead of making that money. It ain't gonna be long before the Watch Houses come take our territory. It's only a matter of time."

"What's that I'm hearing about you saying Deems wants Joe Peck to supply him?"

Lightbulb glanced at Earl.

"Did I say that?" Lightbulb said.

"I'm asking if *he* said it. Did he say that or not?" Bunch asked.

Lightbulb paused. He had told that to Earl in confidence, a kind of extra carrot he'd dangled to Earl to get himself an audience with the boss. But he realized now, looking at Bunch's operation for the first time, the brownstone, dilapidated on the outside and polished to a sheen on the inside, the busy factory a block away that Earl had shown him full of employees processing heroin, the large cars, and the fabulous modern furniture of Mr. Bunch's dining room, that this man was a major roller. Bunch, Lightbulb realized, was a real-life gangster. He realized, too late, that he was in over his head.

A cone of silence enveloped the room as Bunch stared at him, unblinking. Realizing his response could be a death sentence for Deems, Lightbulb said, "I might've said it. But I don't know if Deems really meant it."

Bunch sat for a moment, looking thoughtful, then the tension seemed to ease out of him. He spoke softly. "I appreciate you coming by, young blood. I appreciate you letting me and my man here know you got our best interests at heart."

"So I get the flagpole?"

"I'mma give you a break on that," Bunch said, reaching in his pocket and pulling out a roll of crisp bills.

Lightbulb smiled, relieved, grateful, and felt a sudden burst of guilt. "I just wanna say: I like Deems, Mr. Bunch. We go back a long way. But like I said, he wanna be a cop now. That's why I'm here."

"I understand," Bunch said calmly. He slowly, deliberately counted out four fifty-dollar bills and slid them across the table to Lightbulb.

"Take that and git gone."

"Do I get the flagpole?"

"Can a donkey fly?"

Lightbulb seemed confused but didn't speak at first, then asked, "Does that mean yes?"

Bunch ignored that. "You want a chicken wing on your way out?"

Lightbulb, flummoxed, found it suddenly hard to breathe. "So I don't get the flagpole?"

"I'll think on it."

"I done told you everything like I said I would. What do I get now?"

Bunch shrugged. "You get two hundred dollars. You can get a lot with that. Some soup. A bottle of beer. Some poontang. Even get a job with it in some places. I don't care what you get, so long as you stay out my business. And if I ever see your face here again, I'll part it with a hammer."

Lightbulb's eyes widened. "What'd I do wrong?"

Bunch turned to Earl. "He rats his own boy out. Rats out the guy who gave him his own rice and beans in the joint. The guy who gave him food from his own mouth practically. And he comes to me saying he wants to work for me?"

"Dig thaaaat," Earl said. He stood, menacingly.

Lightbulb, watching Earl out of the corner of his eye, slid his hand over to the money on the table. Bunch's hand suddenly slammed down on his.

"Need I remind you, young brother, to forget us?"

"No."

"Good. Because we will not forget you. Now git."

Lightbulb snatched the two hundred dollars off the table and fled.

After the front door closed, Bunch shrugged and reached for the newspaper. "We'll get back every penny of that dough. He's skin popping now."

"Dig thaaaat."

Bunch shot an irritated look at Earl. "You mucked it up, man."

"I can fix it," Earl said.

"You had three shots at it already. You get your head banged in twice, then get shocked like a clown. You're like the Three Stooges, bro, with a bag full of excuses. You made it worse."

"You said don't kill him. Killing and hurting's different. You hurt a guy, you gotta make so he can't see you, so he can't rat. Taking him out is—"

"Something I ain't asked you to do, bro."

Bunch reached for a chicken wing, dipping it in the sauce and chewing slowly as he scoured the newspaper. "The game's changed, Earl. I should've watched Deems closer."

"Lemme even it out, Bunch. It's my load. Let me carry it."

Bunch wasn't listening. He had placed the newspaper down and was staring out the window. There was so much to think about.

"Peck says this big shipment from Lebanon is coming soon. He says he's got a dock for it. But that idiot's so dumb he lights up a room by leaving it. And now this crap with this old motherfucker who shot Deems. If we can't shake up an old drunk, how the fuck we gonna run Peck's operation?" He shook his head, biting his bottom lip angrily. "All my luck is junior grade."

Earl felt the same way. He sat in silence, studying his fingers atop the crossword puzzle. His nerves felt as if they were sitting on a razor blade. He'd already been collared twice by that white cop, Potts, who'd promised him he'd look the other way when the cops dropped the hammer on Bunch—if he flipped on Bunch, which Earl had agreed to do with trepidation. But now, sitting before Bunch, he realized he'd underestimated Bunch's cleverness and forgotten the power of his rage, which seemed to ooze off him. If Bunch found him out, he was cooked. That suddenly seemed a possibility. Worse, the old woman from the Cause had recognized him as Reverend Harris's son. His father, he felt, was torturing him from the grave.

"I can straighten out the old man," Earl said.

"Don't need to," Bunch said matter-of-factly. "There's a nine-thirty train coming in tonight from Richmond. Take my car down to Penn Station in the city and pick up Harold Dean. You can do that without mucking it up, can't ya?"

"We don't need Harold Dean!"

"You think I'm running a summer camp? If Deems convinces Peck to sell to him instead of us, we'll be buying our groceries with Green Stamps, brother. We're done. Nobody will sell to us. Not Roy and them Italians out in Brighton Beach. Nobody from the West Side. Nobody in Harlem. It's the Elephant's dock or nothing. Peck's the only one who's still got a line to the Elephant. If Deems convinces Peck to go with him, then he's got the Elephant's dock, too, and we're outta business. Deems has got to go. And Peck. We got to flatten things out, get everything back to zero, before that Lebanon thing comes in. I'll talk to the Elephant myself. But first let's get rid of the old man. What's his name?"

"Something . . . Sport Jacket, they call him."

"Whatever the fuck he is, he got to be put to sleep. Now. Get off your spine and get Harold Dean. Make sure Harold Dean does the old man first. Nobody in the Cause has seen HD; that one will be quick and easy."

15

YOU HAVE NO IDEA
WHAT'S COMING

DOMINIC LEFLEUR OF BUILDING 9 SPENT DAYS APOLOGIZ-
ing to Bum-Bum for starting the fight at Soup Lopez's coming-home
party. He "accidentally" ran into her on three separate occasions as she
went about her business. The first time she was coming out of Five Ends.
She had gone inside to place a few cans of beans in the pantry, and when
she emerged he happened to be outside, which gave him the opportunity
to explain that the doll he tried to give Sportcoat was not bad luck.

"It's a custom back home in Haiti," he said. When she seemed doubtful, he explained defensively that black Americans had their own rituals:
black-eyed peas on New Year's Day, carrying a raw potato in the left
pocket for rheumatism, or "holding a copper coin under your tongue
during coitus."

"Coitus?" she asked.

"Doing the nature thing," Dominic said. "You hold the copper coin
under your tongue during . . . coitus . . . to keep from getting pregnant.
My first wife was from Tennessee."

Bum-Bum received this information with a snort. "What did they feed her down there, smog? I never ever heard such nastiness. Anyway, that ain't the same as witchery." Still, she let him walk her home.

The next time he "happened" to be across the street from the wall of Jesus painted on the back side of Five Ends Baptist, where she stopped every morning on the way to work to silently pray for the destruction of her ex-husband who ran off to Alaska, that his testicles might be pressed in a juice maker or lopped off with a saw. Dominic happened to be marveling at the wonderful artistry of the garbage piled high on the back wall of the church under the painting of Jesus—garbage that the church sexton, Sportcoat, had somehow forgotten to haul to the curb, being that he'd unexpectedly received a bottle of Haitian Creation from his wonderful neighbor Dominic that very afternoon, who had supplied it with the hope it would spark a binge and Sportcoat would forget the garbage altogether. Which is exactly what happened. That left Dominic with the task of informing Bum-Bum that since they happened to be at Five Ends together on a Tuesday morning when sanitation picked up, it was their civic duty as residents of the Cause and respecters of all religions to clean up the house of the Lord, as it wouldn't be right to leave garbage setting right under Jesus's nose for a full week before sanitation came again. Bum-Bum muttered that Five Ends' rival church, Mount Tabernacle, put its trash out faithfully, and Five Ends' garbage was Sportcoat's business, not hers, plus she was dressed for work in all white, being a home care attendant. But she agreed that no Christian person in their right mind could walk away while Jesus's painting stood above a pile of garbage. Which gave them a full twenty minutes of setting out the garbage that normally took thirty seconds, since Dominic refused to let her dirty her uniform and did all the lifting while he talked. That gave him twenty minutes to explain to Bum-Bum what a mojo could do.

"Mojos," he said patiently, as he swung a half-filled garbage bag toward the curb, "can work on a person for miles and miles."

"How many miles?" she asked.

"A hundred miles. Five hundred miles. A thousand miles even," he said, marching toward the curb as she followed. "As far away as, say, Alaska."

Bum-Bum, standing at the edge of the street in front of the garbage, worked hard to keep the lightbulb that went off in her brain from showing in her face. She frowned. So even the Haitian Sensation knew about her husband's running off to Alaska. She wondered if he'd heard the part about her ex taking up with a man. Probably, she thought. She shrugged. "It's better to pray for the saving of an enemy's soul than their ruination," she said, "but tell me about it anyhow," and allowed him to walk her to the subway as he explained the magic of rituals.

The third time he "happened" to be passing through her building, Building 17—a good fifteen-minute walk to her third-floor unit from his own apartment on the fifth floor of Building 9—it was a warm night, and Sam Cooke's "You Send Me" played out the window of an upper apartment. He arrived holding a plate of Haitian *mayi moulen ak sòs pwa, poul an sòs*—cornmeal with beans and stewed chicken. He knocked on her door, holding the plate and the doll, which he had ripped in half. "I'm going to make a pillow out of it," he explained, then handed her the plate and asked her out to the movies. Bum-Bum refused. "I'm a Christian woman and I don't do worldly things," she said firmly. "But I'm going to Five Ends tomorrow morning. We need folding chairs. And Mount Tabernacle is offering us some."

"I thought Tabernacle and Five Ends don't get along," Dominic said.

"We are Christian people, Mr. Lefleur. Their music is too loud and they fall out and speak in tongues and so forth when they gets filled with the Holy Spirit, and we don't do that here. But the book of Hebrews twelve fourteen says 'Strive for peace with everyone,' which means Mount Tabernacle too. Plus my best friend, Octavia, is a deaconess there and everybody knows the police is trying to shut our church down for protecting old Sportcoat, who helped me put in my washing machine

even though Housing says I'm not supposed to have one. Mount Tabernacle is with us for sure. We've always gotten along."

Thus it was the sight of Dominic Lefleur, Bum-Bum, Sister Gee, and
Miss Izi struggling toward the side door of Five Ends Baptist with seventeen folding chairs stuffed inside an old post office dolly, the chairs
stacked six feet high, that greeted Sergeant Potts Mullen as he swung his
Plymouth squad car to the front of Five Ends Baptist Church a week
after Soup's big party. Sister Gee didn't notice him when he pulled up.
Her back was to him. He watched as she peeled off from the others and
moved to the rear of the church, grabbing an old-fashioned weed chop-
per from the back wall and stepping into a field of high weeds. The weed
cutter was shaped like a golf club and she swung it high over her head,
slaying weeds as she went. Had he driven by the church three weeks ago
and seen that sight, he would've said to himself the woman looked like
a cotton picker on a plantation someplace. But now he saw a woman
whose long back reminded him of the sea near the Cliffs of Moher in
County Clare, the part of Ireland he'd seen when he'd visited, the sea
gently pushing against the mountainous shore. She looked beautiful.

The three chair haulers at the side door saw him first and quickly
moved inside, unstacking the chairs one by one and marching them
down the basement stairs without a word. Potts parked the squad car,
emerged, and walked past the side door to Sister Gee, standing in the
weeded field out back.

She saw him coming, the harbor water sparkling behind him, and
stopped swinging, leaning on the weed cutter with her hand on her hip
as he came. She was clad in a spring dress covered with azaleas, not or-
dinary garden clothing, he thought as he approached. Then again she'd
said she was a country woman, and country women, as he knew from
his mother and grandmother, didn't dress for success. They dressed up
and worked in the clothing they had. He walked straight into the weeds
to her. When he reached her she smiled, a small one that bore, he hoped,

just a hint of eagerness, then nodded at his patrol car, where his young partner, Mitch, sat in the passenger seat. "Why don't he come?" she asked.

"You scared him off," he said.

"We don't bite here."

"Tell him that. You scared the Jesus out of him last time."

She laughed. "We supposed to run Jesus *into* souls here, not out."

"Come to think of it, he was an angel till you laid boots on him and sent him the other direction."

The sight of her lovely brown face breaking into laughter and focusing tightly on him, as she stood in the dress of azaleas in the sunlit yard of weeds, made him feel light again. In that moment he realized that all the experience of thirty-two years on the NYPD and all the formal police training in the world was useless when the smile of someone you suddenly care about finds the bow that wraps your heart and undoes it. He wondered when he'd last had that feeling—indeed if he'd ever had it at all. For the life of him, he couldn't remember. Standing there in knee-high weeds behind an old black church that he'd passed by a hundred times over the last two decades without so much as a glance, he wondered if he had ever actually been in love or if love was, as his grandmother used to say, a kind of discovery of magic. He loved the stories she read to him when he was a boy, of kings and seafaring maidens and sailors gone awry and monsters slain, all for the sake of love. *"Who is it who throws the light into the meeting on the mountain?"* It was a poem she loved. He tried to recall the poet's name. Was it Yeats maybe?

He saw her staring at him and realized she was waiting for him to say something.

"I think Mitch has lost interest in this case," he managed to say.

"Who?"

"Mitch. The other officer. My partner."

"Good. So have I," she said. She shifted the weed cutter to the other

side and leaned on it again, one smooth hip thrust outward. "Or I'm trying to. We truck on here despite it all. Look at all these weeds."

"You do this often?"

She smiled. "Not enough. You cut 'em down. They come right back.
You cut 'em again. They come back again. That's their purpose. To keep
coming. Everything under God's sun got a purpose in this world. Everything wants to live. Everything deserves life, really."

"If everything deserves to live, why kill a weed?"

She chuckled. She loved this kind of talk. How was it that he could
draw this foolish chatter out of her? Her discourse with her husband,
what little conversation they had, was made up of stunted, dry, matter-
of-fact grunts about bills paid, church business, the affairs of their three
grown children, who were, thankfully, living away from the Cause Houses.
At forty-eight, most days she awakened feeling like there was nothing
left to live for other than her church and her children. She had been seventeen when she wed a man twelve years older than her. He had seemed
to have purpose but turned out to have none, other than an affinity for
football games and the ability to pretend to be what he was not, to pretend to feel things that he did not feel, to make jokes out of things that
did not work for him, and like too many men she knew, daydream about
meeting some lovely young thing from the choir, preferably at three a.m.,
in the choir pew. She didn't hate her husband. She just didn't know him.

"Well, I could let the weeds grow," she said. "But I'm not a person
who knows enough about what should or should not be to leave things
as they are when they got no purpose that I can understand. My purpose
is to keep this church open long enough to save somebody. That's all I
know. If I was a book-learned person, somebody who could use thirty-
four words instead of three words to say what I mean, I might know the
full answer to your question. But I'm a simple woman, Officer. These
weeds is a blight to this house of worship, so I goes at 'em. The truth is,

they do me no harm. They're unsightly to me but sightly to God. And still I cuts at 'em. I reckon I'm like most folks. Most times I don't know what I'm doing. Sometimes I feel like I don't hardly know enough to tie my own shoes."

"I can tie your shoes for you," he said, his eyes twinkling, "if you can't manage."

The comment, offered in the lilt of his Irish brogue, brought her to a blush, and she noticed Miss Izi standing by the church door, staring in their direction. "What brings you around?" she said quickly. She glanced at Miss Izi again, who thankfully was called away by Dominic at the basement door. "Better hurry and tell it. My friend Izi there," she said, nodding at Miss Izi's back, "is what they call the walking news."

"Gossip?"

"I wouldn't call it gossip. Everybody knows everybody's business in these projects, so why put a name to it? It's news one way or the other."

Potts nodded and sighed. "That's why I come. I have some."

"Do you now?"

"We arrested a young fella. Fella named Earl. We know you know him."

Her smile disappeared. "How's that?"

"We saw you. We . . . one of our guys . . . followed you. After the little ruckus over in the plaza last week."

"You mean Soup's party?"

"Whatever it was, they—uh, without my knowledge—had somebody roll behind you. He saw you and a big, giant fella carry Earl out of the projects to the Silver Street subway station. They saw the little deal there, where you closed the turnstiles and you two had a little talk with Earl and sent him on his way. That's a Transit Authority violation, I'm sorry to say. A pretty big one, to close down a subway station."

Sister Gee, thinking of Calvin in the tollbooth, felt the blood rising in her face. "It was my idea. I made Calvin do it. It wasn't but ten minutes. Till the train came. I don't want him fired from his job on account of my foolishness."

"What were you planning on doing?"

"I wasn't gonna have the man thrown on the tracks, if that's what you mean."

"What did you want?"

"I wanted him out of the Cause and I got him out. You can take that back to the precinct or tell it to the judge. Or I'll tell it to the judge myself. That fella was hunting somebody. Sportcoat, most likely. That's why he come there. I'm told that wasn't his first time in the Cause neither. We wanted him gone."

"Why didn't you call the police?"

She chortled. "It wasn't a crime for him to come to the plaza party. Somebody threw a bottle and he got struck over the head by accident. I'm telling you what God's pleased with. The truth. That's exactly what happened. He was in a fog when he come to. As God would have it, the darned thing didn't kill him, just knocked him out. I reckoned he'd come out of it swinging. So I had Soup carry him to the subway and told Calvin to shut the turnstiles down till the first train come. I didn't want nobody to get hurt. That's all there is to it."

"That's called taking matters into your own hands."

"Call it what you will or may. It's done now."

"You should've called us."

"Why we got to have the police around every time we has a simple party? Y'all don't watch out for us. Y'all watch *over* us. I don't see y'all out there standing over the white folks in Park Slope when they has their block parties. We was just having a celebration for poor old Soup, who went to jail a boy and come out a man. Much of a man, I'd say. Where's a man like him gonna get a job, big as he is? Soup wouldn't hurt a fly. Do you know when he was a tiny boy, he was scared to come out the house?

Used to stay inside and watch television all day. *Captain Kangaroo* and *Mister Rogers* and them type shows."

"The kiddie shows?"

"Been doing it since he was a child. He's a Muslim now. Can you believe it? All that work we put into him here." She nodded at the church, then shrugged. "Well . . . as long as he's got God in his life some kind of way." She shifted her weight off the weed cutter and absently swiped at a few weeds near her feet on the cracked, dry dirt.

"So you and kiddie-show guy and the token-booth guy shut down the station," Potts said.

Sister Gee stopped swiping at the weeds and looked at him, her face melted into the slightly angry expression she had worn when they first met. She saw his eyes slice away from hers and cut to the ground. Was that shame she saw in his eyes? She wasn't sure.

"*I* shut the station down. Me alone."

Potts removed his cap, wiped his brow with his sleeve, and replaced it on his head. She watched him closely. Every movement, she observed, was that of a man trying to maintain emotional control of himself. He didn't seem angry. Or even disappointed. Rather he seemed resolved to a kind of silent sadness that made her, despite herself, feel drawn to him, for she knew the feeling well. She found the whole business a little worrying, that common ground, but also wildly and almost terrifically exciting. She'd forgotten what that felt like. After thirty-one years of being married, the last five of which had been a trial of silent suffering, of infrequent bursts of small, almost minuscule, useless affection, she felt a part of herself she thought long dead shaking loose and awakening.

"Shutting down the station? I don't want to know about it," he said. "Neither does the precinct. Neither does Transit. I made sure of that. But we arrested that fella Earl—*I* arrested him—and that's something *you* ought to know about."

"Why?"

"He's . . . a suspect."

"So's a lot of people."

"Okay. He's more than a suspect. He's no junkie. He's what you call a strong-arm guy. A smart one. He knocks out teeth here and there. But he's not a concern now. No worries there. We got the goods on him. We're working with him—or he's working with us. That's all I can tell you. That's between you and me. So you don't have to worry about him coming around again. But the guy he works for. We don't have him and he *is* somebody to worry about."

"What's that got to do with Sportcoat?"

"How many times do I have to say it? Your guy kicked off something big. I don't know that he meant to. In fact, I'm sure he didn't. But he's got the wrong end of things. There's a drug war brewing. You don't want your guy or your church in the middle of it. These drug lords are a different breed. They don't play by the rules like the old crooks did. There's no handshake or silent agreements, no looking the other way. Nobody's safe. Nothing's sacred. There's too much money involved."

"What's that got to do with us?"

"I told you before. Turn your guy in and back out of it. Stay out of the way. We can protect him."

Sister Gee felt hot. She looked up into the sky, squinting, then raised a long, lovely brown arm to shade her eyes as she peered at him. "I'm burning up out here. Can we get in the shade?"

It was as if she'd asked him to go to the beach, or swimming, or to lounge in a cool air-conditioned library someplace, to sit and read Irish poems, the kind he liked, the simple ones, "Symbols of Erie" and "The Diaries of Humphrey," the ones his grandmother loved and taught him.

She walked past him, wading through the weeds to the back of the church building, out of view of the side door where Dominic, Bum-Bum, and Miss Izi were loading chairs. He followed behind, noting the shapely figure beneath the dress. When she reached the shade of the old building, a cinder-block structure built on a foundation of solid red bricks, she placed her back to the wall just underneath the faded painting of Jesus with his arms spread and leaned against it, propping her foot on the wall, showing a golden-brown knee. He faced her, standing just inside the shade, his hands clasped in front of him, rubbing his thumbs, trying not to stare. Everything she did, Potts realized, every move—the gentle arcs of her neck and mouth, the way she held herself erect along the wall and stretched a long arm out to wipe her forehead with gentle silklike smoothness—made something inside him want to kneel down.

"Sportcoat ain't hard to find," she said. "He's around. You wanna go get him, go ahead. It's not gonna change nothing. Deems is still out there slinging poison like clockwork every day at the flagpole at noon. He hasn't moved a peep toward bothering old Sportcoat, far as I know. Fact is, he's more polite now than before. They say he's changed a little. He don't sell to grandmothers or little kids now. Of course that don't matter, since they ain't got to do but walk five blocks to the Watch Houses and get what they want. Some folks send their children to buy drugs for 'em. Imagine that? Sending a little child nine, ten years old out to buy drugs. This projects was never that way. What are we doing wrong?"

She seemed so sad as she said it, it was all Potts could do to stop himself from placing an arm around her right there, right behind the church in the shade under Jesus's sad painted gaze, and saying, "It's all right. I got you."

Instead he said, "I'm speaking as a friend, miss. You—all of you—need to step back and let us do our job here."

"Arrest Deems then. That'll make it easier."

"We arrest him today, ten guys will be in his place tomorrow. You arrest ten guys, ten more guys will come. You know why? They're being bailed out. By the same man who sent that kid Earl to your little party. It's a whole organization we're talking about. This guy looking for your Sportcoat is part of a syndicate. You know what that means? Organized crime. That's why they call it organized. Guys like him have legitimate businesses mixed with illegitimate ones. He's not just one guy. He's an operator. He's got employees working for him. He runs a factory. The drugs they sell at your flagpole, they don't come packaged. They come to this country raw. They need to be prepared, prepped, and packaged, just like you'd package aspirin or soda pop to sell in a store. This guy's operation runs all the way from Queens to Georgia. It's something you can't get in the way of."

"Are you interested in doing that?"

"The police? Us? Yes."

"Well, you got us wrong," she said tersely. "All's we want is our Christmas Club money."

He laughed. "What are you talking about? You step in the middle of a major Brooklyn drug operation and send the drug king's muscle man home by subway with a lump on his head the size of Philadelphia. You threaten the same muscle man by saying you know his dead minister father. All for your church club money?"

"He came here courting trouble," she said angrily. "And them's hard dollars in our church club money. Nobody knows how much is in there."

"Whatever it is, it's not enough to risk your skin. You have no idea what you're dealing with!" Potts said.

"You don't live here," she said bitterly. "I know Deems's whole family. His grandfather, Mr. Louis, was a hard man. But it's a hard life out here. He came to New York from Kentucky with ten cents in his pocket. He swept and mopped an office for forty years till he died. And then his wife passed. His daughter prayed in this church every Sunday for years. Between you and me, she drinks like a fish and ain't worth a nickel. It was her son, Mr. Louis's grandson Deems, he was the gem of that family. He was the one with all the promise. That boy could throw a ball better'n anybody around here. He had the chance to get out on account of just that one thing. Now he's gonna die or go to jail, which amounts to the same thing. Once Deems comes outta prison, if he lives long enough to go in, he'll be worse than he was when first he gone in. Back and forth he'll go. None of that fits in your little reports and warrants does it? When the newspaper writes their little stories about coloreds and Spanish swinging around Brooklyn like a bunch of monkeys in trees, none of that gets in there, now does it?"

"You don't have to eat my head off about it. The Irish got kicked and booted the same way."

"We ain't talking about them."

"No we're not. You were talking about the church money. It's got nothing to do with this trouble," Potts said.

"It's got everything to do with it. That Christmas Club money is all we can control. We can't stop these drug dealers from selling poison in front our houses. Or make the city stop sending our kids to lousy schools. We can't stop folks from blaming us for everything gone wrong in New York, or stop the army from calling our sons to Vietnam after them Vietcong done cut the white soldiers' toenails too short to walk. But the little nickels and dimes we saved up so we can give our kids ten minutes of love at Christmastime, that's ours to control. What's wrong with that?"

She waved at the weeded lot, the projects nearby, the Elephant's old boxcar on the next block, and behind it the harbor and the Statue of Liberty, shimmering in the afternoon sunlight. "Look around you. What's normal about all this? This look normal to you?"

Potts sighed through clenched teeth. He wondered how someone who lived in this mess could be so naïve.

"Nothing in the world is normal," he said. "I can't understand why you'd even hope for that."

His comment sent the anger hissing out of her like a balloon, and her features softened. She eyed him with curiosity, then wiped the edge of her eye with the back of her hand and shifted her weight.

"Why are you here?" she asked.

"About this case."

"No. Right here. The preaching's inside. On Sundays. Not out here behind the church. The inside's what you need."

He shrugged. "Your sermons are enough," he said. "That last one was good. I like seeing you stirred up."

Now she frowned. "Is it funny to you, what I said?"

"Not at all," he said. "If you'd been on the job as long as I have, you'd feel the same way. We're the same, you and I. We have the same job, remember? We clean the things no one wants to clean. Dirt. That's our job. We clean up after people."

She smiled bitterly, and once again the mask she wore so well, the firm lady of strong, impatient indifference whom he'd met when he first walked into the church a week before, broke apart, revealing the vulnerable, lonely soul underneath. *She's just like me*, he thought in wonder. *She's as lost as I am.*

He managed to wing himself back under control and blurted, "You asked why I'm really here. I'll tell you. First of all, I know your deacon is around. He's good at making himself scarce. But we're gonna get him."

"Get him then."

"Thing is, we're stepping soft, trying not to rattle folks. But the people here are not making it easy. When we ask they say, 'He was just here,' or 'He just left his building,' or 'I think he's in the Bronx.' They're covering for him. But you ought to know something. And you can spread this around . . ."

He leaned in close. She noticed the lines in his face were etched with concern, and alarm.

"The man who wants your Sportcoat sent for somebody from out of town. A very dangerous guy. I got no information on him other than a name. Harold or Dean. Last name unknown. Might be a Harold. Or a Dean. Not sure. Whatever his name, he's rough business. He's in a different class than the knucklehead you sent off."

"Harold Dean."

"That's right. Harold Dean."

"Should I warn folks?"

"I'd stay out of that flagpole area if I were you."

"That's our place! Must be thirty people float by there every morning. Even Deems don't fool with us there."

"Gather someplace else."

"There is no place else. We surrender the flagpole, that's it. We're prisoners in our own homes then."

"You don't understand. Your deacon is not the only guy around here who's in danger now. I read the report. This Harold Dean is . . ."

She stared at him in silence and he halted.

He wanted to say, "He's a killer and I don't want him near you." But he had no idea what her reaction would be. He didn't even know what Harold Dean looked like. He had no information other than an FBI report with no photo, only the vaguest description that he was a Negro who was "armed and extremely dangerous." He wanted to say, "I'm worried about *you*," but he had no idea how to say it. It wouldn't do now anyway, because she was angry again, the dark eyes glowing, the pretty nostrils flaring. So he said simply, "He's dangerous."

"Nothing in this world is dangerous unless white folks says it is," she said flatly. "Danger here. Danger there. We don't need you to tell us about danger in these projects. We don't need you to say what the world is to us."

He offered a thin, sad smile and shook his head. So there it was. "Us?" he said.

He took a step back, away from the shade of the church, and turned for the squad car. Another dream spent. He'd had many of them. He supposed he was glad, really. He was off the hook. The responsibility, the magic that his grandmother had talked about was a weight he was not built to bear. Love, real love, was not for everyone.

He slowly walked along the back of the church, his right hand skimming the wall, moving with the slow, unsteady gait of a man who had just witnessed a building collapse.

Sister Gee watched him drift slowly down the back of the building and felt her heart pirouette toward her feet. She felt an ache. She couldn't help herself.

"I'm not saying *you* personally," she called after him.

He stopped but didn't turn around. "I was hoping to bring you better news," he said. "About the case."

Her eyes dropped to the ground and she swiped at a stray weed with her foot. She was afraid to look up. She wanted him to leave. It was too much. She wanted him to stay. It was not enough. Her emotions felt like two big waves crashing against one another. She could not ever remember being in this place before.

Finally she glanced up. He had moved to the edge of the building and was about to turn the corner toward his squad car and the side of the chuch where his partner, Miss Izi, Bum-Bum, and Dominic awaited, all of them part of the foolish world who'd never see him clearly. He was a man they were blind to, the man beyond the uniform, beyond the skin. Why she saw the man inside and others could not, she was not sure. She had thought about it after he left the church and decided that she and this officer were not the same, no matter what she'd said to him when they first met. She cleaned dirt. He chased bad people. She was a cleaning woman. He was a cop. They were both spoken for in matters of love. But that indefinable spirit, that special thing, that special song had not been heard by either of them. She was sure of that. As she watched his back slowly drift away, she saw her future and his, and knew she'd blame herself for not at least attempting to open the envelope to read whatever news the letter inside might contain. How many times had she done that, swallowed the gunk for the sake of a car, a home, a marriage, a school for her children, for her mother, for her church? For what? *What about my own heart, Lord? How many years do I have left?*

He had reached the corner of the church when she called out, "When you get some more news, come on back."

He stopped. He didn't turn but rather spoke over his shoulder. "It's only going to be bad news."

She saw his profile, and it was beautiful, framed by the Statue of Liberty and the harbor, with several gulls flying overhead and beyond. And because he hadn't uttered a desire to not return, her heart grew tiny wings again.

"Even if it's bad news," she said, "there's good news bound up in it— if you're the one bringing it."

She saw his hunched shoulders relax a little. He leaned on the church wall and gave his heart a moment to catch itself. He was afraid if he turned around, his face would give him away and he'd cause more trouble for both of them than the moment was worth. But more than that, for the first time in his fifty-nine years, despite all the poetry he read, and the wonderful Irish stories he could spin off at the drop of a hat, stories full of lyric and rhyme and hope and laughter and joy and pain, all wrapped like Christmas presents, he was suddenly, inexplicably unable to find the words to express himself.

"I'll be happy," he said, more to the ground than to her, "to come back and bring what news I can."

"I'll be waiting," Sister Gee said.

But she might as well have been speaking to the wind. He had slipped around the corner of the church toward his squad car and was gone.

16

MAY GOD HOLD YOU . . .

NINE DAYS AFTER SOUP LOPEZ'S HOMECOMING PARTY AND
two weeks after he blasted Deems in the face, Sportcoat, still very
much alive, arrived bright and early for work at the old Italian lady's
brownstone. He had to work in her garden. It was just another normal
Wednesday.

She was waiting for him and came right outside the gate when he
walked up, moving in a hurry. She was wearing a man's jacket over her
housedress, her kitchen apron still tied around her waist, and men's
oversized concrete walking boots on her feet.

"Deacon," she said, "we've got to find pokeweed."

"What for? It's poisonous."

"No it's not."

"Well alrighty then," he said.

They set off, moving down the block toward the empty lots that
stretched toward the harbor. He walked behind her as she stomped forward. When they reached the first weeded lot, just two blocks away, she
waded in and he followed. They both searched with their heads down.

They passed several fine specimens. "There's sandspur, beggar's-lice, partridge weed," Sportcoat said, "but no pokeweed."

"It's here," Mrs. Elefante said. She fanned through the weeds, several feet ahead of him, swatting the plants with her hands. "My doctor would hate for me to find a bunch of it. That would put him out of business."

"Yes, ma'am." Sportcoat chuckled. He felt good this morning. In fact, he felt good every morning he wandered the lots of the Cause looking for plants with the old lady whose name he could never remember. It was the only job he had that he didn't need to take a drink for. Normally, ever since Hettie died, he needed a booster in the mornings. But Wednesdays working with the old lady always left him feeling goosed. She was eighteen years older than him—close to eighty-nine, she said, but one of the few old folks in the Cause who preferred to be outdoors all day. Four months into the job and he'd never managed to remember her name, but she was a good white person, and that's what counted. He had always been terrible with names, and that was a problem, especially after he got soused. Most folks he called "Hey, brother man," or "ma'am," and if they had a name of any type, they'd simply respond. But after four months it didn't seem appropriate for him to ask her name again, so he'd taken to calling her Miss Four Pie, which she didn't mind, a point that amused Hot Sausage to no end when he told him.

"Don't she got a real name?" Sausage asked.

"Of course she do. In fact the lady from the senior center who recommended me for the job wrote her name down for me once. But I lost the paper."

"Whyn't you just ask the lady her name again?"

"She don't care what I call her!" Sportcoat declared. "She likes it when I calls her Miss Four Pie!"

"Why you call her that?"

"Sausage, she had four hot blueberry pies in her oven first day I come on the job. That whole house was stinking of blueberries," Sportcoat said. "I said, 'By God, miss, it do smell good in here.' She told me her name then."

"You don't remember it at all?"

"What difference do it make?" he said. "She pays in cash." He pondered it a moment. "I do believe she got an Italian name. Like Illy-at-ee or Ella-rant-ee or some such thing." He scratched his head. "I remembered it the first day, but I drunk a bottle of essence after I come home and forgot it. It just runned right outta me."

"Did she give you one that first day?" Hot Sausage asked.

"Give *me* a name? I got my own name."

"No. A pie! She had four of 'em."

"Do a buzzard fly? Course she did!" Sportcoat declared. "Miss Four Pie don't play around! She knows I'm a plant man. She's good people, Sausage." He thought a moment. "Now that I thinks on it, to be legal and proper, I reckon I ought to call her Miss *Three Pie* instead of Miss Four Pie, being she didn't have but three pies when I left that first day. She deducted herself one whole pie for old Sportcoat." He laughed. "I'm killing 'em, Sausage! They love me out here. She's crazy about me."

"That's because you probably got more teeth than her."

"Don't get jealous, son. She's a salty lady. Full of sand, as they say. Why, if she was colored and bowlegged, I'd run her down to Silky's and buy her a sip of some top-shelf brandy."

"Why she got to be bowlegged?"

"I do got standards."

Sausage laughed, but Sportcoat felt embarrassed about the wisecrack, which he felt was in poor taste. "Fact is, Sausage," he said soberly, "I miss my Hettie. She don't spare me talking this kind of devilment, and if she hears of it, she might not show around no more. I can't have that." To make up for his insult, he said: "Miss Four Pie's a spicy soul. She moves her tongue however she pleases. She ain't afraid to speak out. Fact is, I'm scared of her a little. Her husband's long dead, and I reckon she might've talked him into the ground, her being so strong-minded. That lady knows more about plants than anybody around here. The hours just whiles away when I'm working under her hand, for I favors plants myself. I hardly has a need to get a glow going on the days I works for her—well, I need a little protective custody, but not much. It don't compare to the rest of the week when I ain't got no garden to fool around in. Then I gets parched and goes from a toot to a tear to a wallbanger, especially if Hettie don't show, for then I get ever more bleary and swim on ahead, getting overserved, thinking about Hettie and whatever wrong I done to her and all. It ain't good."

Sausage was amused, but as usual, Sportcoat's long-winded talks about his adventures in plant life bored him, so he changed the subject. But it occurred to Sportcoat that talking with Miss Four Pie about plants, as they thrust about the weeds in the lot, was one of the few things he looked forward to every week, even if she was the one doing all the talking.

They were an odd sight, an elderly white woman in housedress, apron, and oversized men's construction boots, followed by an elderly black man in porkpie hat and plaid sports jacket, moving past the railroad boxcar, the abandoned docks and railroad tracks, and into the high weeds of discarded junk surrounding the abandoned factories that sat near the water's edge, the glistening Lower Manhattan just across the water.

That Wednesday, as he walked behind her, Sportcoat noticed she moved unsteadily. Over the past month or so, she'd seemed tired and unsteady on her feet. When they got back to her house, she'd occasionally ask him to step into the kitchen to clean and cut up some of the plants they'd found, but not very frequently. It was an unwritten rule he'd followed as a black man who grew up in the South that he always stay outside. That suited him fine, for he was afraid to step into any of their houses. Miss Four Pie had advised him early on that her son, who lived in the house with her—a son he had never met (or maybe he had met but could not recall)—was strict and did not want any strangers in their home. That was fine with Sportcoat, who worked under the assumption that if anything went wrong in any white person's house in any part of the world and he happened to be near it, why, there was no doubt on whose head the hammer of justice would fall. But over the months he'd worked for her she'd come to trust him. Once in her kitchen, after he did her bidding, he'd move back into the yard as quickly as possible. He was, after all, just an outdoor man. Miss Four Pie seemed to understand that.

They wandered into a lot filled with high weeds just south of the harbor and spread out from one another. He saw her disappear down an embankment out of sight momentarily. He went over to check on her and found her sitting on a discarded sink, scanning the swamp before her.

"I know pokeweed's here somewhere," she said. "The wetter the ground, the better the chance it's around."

"Maybe we ought not burn too much gas looking for it," Sportcoat said. "I had a cousin who got sick from eating it."

"It depends on what part you eat," she said. "What did he eat? The root, the stem, or the leaves?"

"Lord, I don't know. It was a long time ago."

"Well there it is," she said. "Me, I got numbness in my legs. Plus cataracts. I can't see a thing. The pokeweed cleans my blood. I can see better. My legs don't hurt so much. I can eat almost any part of it, anytime."

Sportcoat was impressed by her certainty. She stood up and ventured into the swamp, and he followed her. The two moved deeper into it, their feet sinking into the wet grass, which became marshier as they drew closer to the water. They searched for several minutes and came upon several treasures they liked: skunk cabbage, spring beauty, and fiddleheads. But no pokeweed. They spent another twenty minutes searching westward parallel to the water. Finally, they struck gold in a swampy lot next to an old paint factory that faced the water. In the lot behind the factory was a wealth of good things: wild mustard, wild garlic, huge geraniums, and—at last—pokeweed, some of it four feet high.

They gathered as much as they could carry and slowly made their way through the weeded lots to Miss Four Pie's house.

She was happy with their haul. "These things are big," she said of the pokeweed. "You couldn't find them this big in a store. Of course you can't buy good vegetables in the store anymore anyway. Tomatoes you buy now, they look so nice and shiny and red. When you get them home and slice them, they're all red mush inside. They taste like nothing. How can you make spaghetti sauce with that?"

"Don't reckon I could," Sportcoat said.

"Nothing's the way it was," she complained. "You ever see a son as good as his father? The son might be taller. Or stronger. Or thicker about the shoulders. But is he better? My son is stronger than his father. On the outside. But on the inside? Hmph."

"I don't reckon I've met your son, Miss Four Pie."

"Oh, you've seen him running around here," she said with a wave of her hand. "Trying to make fast money like the rest of these young people. Bigger. Better. Faster. More. That's all they want. Always in a hurry. Never takes time for things. He needs to meet a good Italian girl."

The thought seemed to distract her. As they made their way back through the lots to Silver Street, they bypassed some real treasures Sportcoat knew she liked: milkweed, knotweed, wild garlic, and beggar's-lice. But she was too busy chatting happily. "I tell my son, there's no such thing as fast money. Money's not everything, Deacon. If you have enough to live, that's enough."

"You're by golly right about that."

They walked on and she glanced back at him. "How long you been a deacon?"

"If I had to count the years, I'd lose track. But I'd say it's now going on twenty years over at Five Ends. My wife was a trustee, y'know."

"Is that right?"

"I had a good wife," he said wistfully.

"They don't make them like they used to, Deacon," she said.

"Surely don't."

By the time they arrived back at her brownstone, the old lady was tired and she took the unusual step of inviting him inside. She announced she was so tired she had to go upstairs to lie down and instructed him: "Put the plants in tubs and wash them in the sink. Then leave them on the counter and you're all done, Deacon. I left your money on the counter. Pull the back door when you leave."

"Okay, Miss Four Pie."

"Thank you, Deacon."

"You're welcome, ma'am."

She went upstairs, and he finished the job as instructed and left out the back door, which led to a tiny yard. He walked down the stairs and turned to the left to the alley that separated her brownstone from the one next door.

As he stepped into the alley he walked dead into the Elephant.

He didn't recognize him, of course. Few people from the Cause Houses knew which of the several Italians that moved in and out of the boxcar was the Elephant. But everyone knew the name, and the reputation and the dread associated with it.

Elefante had been home from the Bronx for a week, but the visit was still fresh in his mind. He was deep in thought about the whole business of it when he walked into the old colored man in his backyard. "Who are you?" he demanded.

"I'm the gardener."

"What you doing here?" Elefante asked.

Sportcoat smiled uneasily. "Well, the garden is where gardeners work, mister." He watched the Elephant's quick glance about the yard. "I reckon you must be the son, for you favors Miss Four Pie. She spoke of you all day long."

"Miss who?"

Sportcoat realized his mistake and puffed out his cheeks quickly, blowing the air through his mouth. "The lady inside . . . the plant lady. I take it that's your momma? I works for her. I forgot her name."

"Is she all right?"

"Oh yeah. She just went to lay down. She had me out there . . . uh . . . we was seeking pokeweed near the harbor."

Elefante relaxed a little, frowning. "Did you find it?"

"Do a buzzard fly? Your ma can find any plant around here, mister."

Elefante chuckled softly and relaxed. He stared at Sportcoat. "Don't I know you?"

"I reckon . . ." Sportcoat stared back, and then he realized it. "Lord . . . are you the fella there when my Hettie died?"

Elefante held out his hand. "Tom Elefante," he said.

"Yes, sir, I . . ." Sportcoat found himself sweating. He felt a thank-you coming, but for what? For pulling Hettie out of the bay? It was too much to think about. This was the Elephant. The real thing. A real gangster. "Well . . . I got to be going, mister."

"Wait a minute."

Elefante reached in his pocket, pulled out a wad of bills, counted off one hundred dollars, and held it out to Sportcoat. "For my mother."

Sportcoat looked down at the bills. "You ain't got to do that," he said. "Your momma paid me already."

"It's all right."

"I been paid, mister. Your ma treats me right," Sportcoat said. "I reckon she could run a learning school on plants, she knows so much about 'em. More'n me, that's for sure. And I knows quite a bit from my young days. She had her mind on that pokeweed and we walked quite a bit seeking it out. She was a little shaky walking toward the end, but she done all right. We found it and she says it's gonna make her feel better. I do hope it works."

"Take a little extra, mister." Elefante held out the money.

"If it's all the same to you, sir, you already done me a world of good when your fellers pulled my Hettie out the water."

Elefante stared a moment. He wanted to say, "I don't know how she got there," but the truth was, to admit that was to confess knowledge of something in which he had no part, which made it sound like a denial. One denial led to another and to another, and no gangster worth his salt went down that road. Better to say nothing.

The old man seemed to understand. "Oh, my Hettie was tired, is all. She was following God's light. Looking for a moonflower, is what it was. It was a beautiful day when she died. Best funeral the church ever had."

Elefante shrugged, pocketed his money, and leaned against the wall of his house. "I used to see her come and go from church," he said. "She'd say good morning. People don't do that no more."

"No they don't."

"She seemed like a nice lady. She always minded her business. Did she work?"

"Oh, she did day's work and this and that. Mostly she just lived a life like most of us. She lived for going to heaven, mister."

"Don't we all?"

"Are you a religious man?" Sportcoat asked.

"Not really. Maybe a little."

Sportcoat nodded. He couldn't wait to tell Sausage. He'd actually had a conversation with the Elephant. An honest-to-goodness gangster! And he wasn't so bad! He was religious! A little, maybe?

"Well, I got to mosey on," Sportcoat said. "I'll see your momma next Wednesday."

"All right, old-timer. What's your name, by the way?"

"Folks call me Deacon Cuffy. Some calls me Sportcoat, but mostly in these parts they calls me Deacon."

Elefante smiled. The old dud had a style about him. "Okay, Deacon. By the way, what does a deacon do?"

Sportcoat grinned. "Well now, that's a good question. We do all sorts of things. We helps the church. We throws out the garbage. We buys the furniture sometimes. We shop for the food for the deaconesses to make for the repast and such. We even preaches from time to time if we is called upon. We does whatever needs to be done. We're your holy handyman."

"I see."

"But mostly, truth be told, it's women that runs most of your colored churches out here. Like my late wife, and Sister Gee and Bum-Bum."

"Are they nuns?"

"No, I reckon not. They're just sisters."

"Real sisters?"

"No."

Elefante's brow furrowed in confusion. "Why call them sisters?"

"'Cause we all brothers and sisters in Christ, mister. Come visit our church sometime. Bring your momma. You'll see. We likes visitors at Five Ends."

"I might."

"Well, I'll leave you," Sportcoat said. "And until we meet again, I hope God holds you in the palm of His hand."

Elefante, who was about to head into the house, froze.

"Say that again," he said.

"Oh, that's a blessing my Hettie used to say to everybody she met. We say that in our church all the time to visitors. In fact, if you come visit us, you'll hear it yourself. It's our church motto, since before I come, and that's been twenty years. In fact, there's a picture of Jesus with that motto right over the top of his head outside on the back wall of the church. They got them words painted over his head in fancy gold letters. You can't miss it."

Elefante stared at him oddly, with a surprised expression that Sportcoat read as innocence, and it made Sportcoat feel right proud. He'd given the white man something to think about. And a gangster too! Maybe he was converting this feller to the word. *Wouldn't that be something! Your first convert! An honest-to-goodness gangster!* Feeling the moment, he said it again: "May God hold you in the palm of His hand. It's a pretty picture in your mind."

"Where's the picture?"

"The one in your mind?"

"No. The one in the church."

"Oh, that old thing? It's a big old circle with Jesus in the middle and them words over top of his head. Right out back behind the church."

"How long has it been there?"

"Lord . . . it's been there, oh, I don't know how long. Don't nobody quite know who drawed that thing. My Hettie said a man drawed it up there when they first built the church. She said, 'I don't know how those fools paid him, for our treasury ain't never had more than fifty-four dollars in it. They didn't use my Christmas Club money to pay him, that's for sure!'" Sportcoat chuckled, then added, "My Hettie kept the Christmas Club money, too, see. Kept it in a box . . . someplace."

"I see . . . you say the painting's . . . along the back wall outside?"

"Why yes it is. Big ol' pretty picture of Jesus in a circle with his hands just about touching the edge of that circle. Painted right on the cinder block. Folks used to come from miles to see that picture. It got covered over some, but if you stand back in the weeds you can still see the circle and the whole thing as it was. I heard tell once that there was something special about that picture."

"Is it a picture or a painting? Covered over? Is the picture covered over?"

Elefante stared at him so thoughtfully, curiosity etched in his face, yet for some reason Sportcoat felt, at that moment, that the spiritual part of his message was slipping. "No, it's not covered over. Well, the church kinda painted over it a little over the years, fixed it up. Colored it up some. But you can still see him, plain as day. It's not the words so much that's wrote there that's important, though," he added, going back to making his spiritual pitch. "It's the spirit of what Jesus wants, see. To hold you in the palm of His hand."

"Can you see his hands too?"

"Surely can."

Sportcoat carefully neglected to mention, "He was once white till we made him colored." Unbeknownst to Sportcoat, the church's version was actually a local artist's rendering of Jesus as depicted in the centerpiece of Italian artist Giotto di Bondone's *Last Judgment*, the original of which lived in the Scrovegni Chapel in Padua, which portrayed Jesus as a white man in a beard. Someone in the congregation some years back had insisted that Jesus be colored black, and Pastor Gee, anxious to please the congregation as always, had cheerfully hired Sister Bibb's son Zeke, a housepainter, to brown up Jesus some. With the help of Hot Sausage and Sportcoat, the three did just that, coloring Jesus's face and hands with dark brown house paint. The result was horrible, of course, with the facial features, so carefully detailed by the original copyist, so badly distorted and the hands so badly mangled, the face and hands looked like near blobs. But Jesus, Pastor Gee noted cheerfully at the time, had emerged a Negro, and a great spirit as always, and that was the point.

Sportcoat wisely didn't breathe a word of this, but Elefante stared at him with such an odd look that Sportcoat felt he was pattering on too much, which could, as usual, spell trouble with white folks. "Well alrighty then!" he said, and shuffled down the alley.

Elefante watched as Sportcoat walked down the alley and turned onto the sidewalk and out of sight. He felt slightly dazed, his heart still light with the thought of fresh, new love, the Governor's mesmerizing daughter, and now this. A Negro from the colored church two hundred yards from his boxcar? Negroes? And his father? He'd never seen his father with a Negro, ever. Was he losing his mind?

He climbed the narrow stairs to the back door, opened it to the kitchen, and stepped inside, feeling dizzy, the words still in his head.

May God hold you in the palm of His hand.

17

HAROLD

TWO HOURS LATER, WITH HIS PAY FROM MISS FOUR PIE IN his pocket and two bottles of booze standing atop a cinder block like crowns on a king's head, Sportcoat and Hot Sausage considered Sportcoat's encounter with the Elephant.

"Did the Elephant have a gun?" Sausage asked.

"Nar gun!" Sportcoat said triumphantly. The two were lounging in Sausage's basement lair, seated on overturned crates, sipping from the first bottle Sportcoat cracked open, peppermint bourbon, saving the second, a bottle of King Kong, for dessert later.

"What's he like?"

"He's all right, partner! A good man. He was fighting to give me that smooth hundred dollars."

"You shoulda taken it. But then, why would you do that? That would be the smart thing to do, which you is allergic to."

"Sausage, his momma already paid me. Plus he helped my Hettie."

"For all you know, he coulda been the one that throwed her in the harbor."

"Sausage, if ignorance is bliss, you is happy. A big man like the Elephant wouldn't bother my Hettie. He liked her. He said he seen her wave all the time as she come and go from church."

"When you get tired of thinking, Sport, call me. Maybe she seen something he done. Maybe she knew something. Maybe he robbed her!"

"You watch too many movies," Sportcoat said. "He wasn't hauling not a bit of trouble at her, not one bit. She was following God's light is all. And she found it."

"So you say."

"She's in a good place. She's turned loose, a free angel now, by God. I talks to her most every day."

"If you don't watch your points, you'll get your wings too. Deems is busy these days."

"I ain't studying him."

Sausage considered this. "I see him every day, out there selling that poison hand over fist, the devil keeping score. He knows we're partners. He ain't asked a lick about you. Not a mumbling word. That makes me nervous. He got a trick to play, Sport. When you ain't looking, he's gonna chop cotton and pull fodder. You got to get outta these projects."

Sportcoat ignored that. He stood up and stretched, took another sip of peppermint bourbon, then passed the bottle to Sausage. "You don't never get tired of thinking, do ya? Where's my umpire costume?"

Sausage nodded at a black plastic bag in the corner.

"I'mma take this home tonight. Tomorrow, I'mma go out there and see Deems again. I won't be drunk this time, for I wants to remember what he says. After I speaks to him, I'mma tell you all about it."

"Don't be a drag-behind fool."

"I'm going right out there and I'mma say, 'Deems, I'm getting the team together, and I just want you to pitch one game for us. One game. And if you don't wanna play no more baseball after that, why, you can quit. I won't bother you never no more. One game only.' He'll be begging me to get the team back together again after that."

Sausage sighed. "Well, I reckon to really understand the world, you got to die at least once."

"Stop talking crazy," Sportcoat said. "That boy loves baseball. He got the same ways old Josh Gibson had. You know Josh Gibson? Greatest catcher to ever play the game?"

Sausage rolled his eyes as Sportcoat extolled the virtues of Josh Gibson, the greatest Negro catcher ever, how he met Gibson after the war in 1945, and on he went, until Sausage finally said, "Sport, I don't know that you seen even half the people you calls out."

"Seen 'em all," Sportcoat said proudly. "Even barnstormed a little myself, but I had to make money. That ain't gonna be Deems's problem. He'll make plenty money in the bigs. He got the fire and the talent. You can't take the love of ball out of a ballplayer, Sausage. Can't be done. There's a baseball player in that boy."

"There's a killer in that boy, Sport."

"Well, I'll give him a crack at one or the other."

"No you won't! I'll fetch the police first."

"Ain't you forgot that warrant that's on you?"

"I'll let Sister Gee fetch 'em then."

"Sister Gee ain't studying no police. She's hard on me about that Christmas Club money. She'll be wanting that money first, Sausage. Folks is losing faith in me on account of it 'round these parts. Even you. Betting against my life for a cigar with Joaquin."

Sausage blanched, then took a quick snort of the peppermint. "That wasn't about you," he said. "That was about Joaquin. I been playing numbers with him for sixteen years. Only hit once. I think he's got it out for me. I wanted some of my money back."

"Sausage, you done found the secret of youth, 'cause you lying like a child."

"I figured it this way, Sport. Since you didn't wanna run off and was gonna be ki— gonna go out by Deems's hand, however the cut come or go, I figured you wouldn't mind if I made a few chips on account of it. I been a good friend, ain't I?"

"Very good friend, Sausage. I don't mind you making a few chips on my account. In fact I've got a proposition for you. Help me make peace with Deems. Tell him I wanna see him, and I'll forget the insult you done to me by betting against my life."

"You losing your marbles, son. I ain't going near him."

"Deems ain't mad at me. Do you know Deems bought me this very umpire uniform?"

"No."

"Yes he did. Brung it to me brand-new just after Hettie died. Come right to my house two days after we buried her. Knocked on the door and handed it to me saying, 'Don't tell nobody.' Now, would somebody like that shoot a friend in cold blood?"

Sausage listened in silence, then said, "If it was Deems, yes."

"Hogwash. I needs you to go out there and tell him I wants to speak privately. I'll meet him in private and clear this all up."

"I can't do it, Sport. I'm too chickenhearted, okay?"

"It's me he's pining for, Sausage. You ain't got to worry about your skin."

"I do worries about my skin. It covers my body."

"I'd go to the flagpole myself. But I don't wanna embarrass him in front of his friends. If I speak to him in private, he won't be shamed."

"You shamed him by shooting him. In fact, him giving you that umpire outfit makes things worse," Sausage said, "being that you shot him for his kindnesses."

"That boy got plenty goodness left in him," Sportcoat said, taking the bourbon from Sausage and sipping. "His grandfather Louis was all right, wasn't he?"

"Get shot on your own, Sport. I think I'll set here and strangle this bottle of bourbon."

"A true friend would do it. Otherwise, he would not be no true friend."

"Okay."

"Okay what?"

"I ain't your friend."

"I'll get Rufus then. He's from my home country. You can count on a South Carolina man. He always said Alabamans gets torn up when they got to stand up for something."

"Why should I hitch my mule to you, Sport? You the one that got drunk and shot him."

"You got a can tied to your tail, too, Sausage. Deems knows we is partners. You taught him in Sunday school too. But you go on. I'll get Rufus to do it."

Sausage frowned and poked at the ground with his boot, pursing his lips, his nostrils flaring angrily. He rose off the crate, turned away from Sportcoat, and with his back to him, held his arm out parallel to the ground, straight, fingers stretched.

"Bourbon."

Sportcoat, from behind, placed the bottle in Sausage's hand. Sausage took a long, deep sip, set the bottle down on the cinder block, and with his back to Sportcoat, stood a long moment, swaying as he got drunker. Finally, he shrugged and turned around. "All right, dammit. I'll be a fool with you. You don't give me no goddamned choice anyway. I'll set it up. I'll see Deems and ask him to come down here and talk to us—talk to you. I ain't got no pony in that race."

"Sausage, you never gets tired of thinking, do you. Why's he gonna come down here and talk to me? We got to go see him."

"*We* ain't gotta do nothing. It's you. But *I'll* go see him, man to man, and explain that you want to see him in private, in person, and that he got to come by hisself, so you can apologize to him in person and explain everything. That way, if he's gonna kill you he can do it in privacy some-place so I don't see it and he don't go to jail right off. I reckon he won't air me out for asking him, being that I wasn't the one who shot him."

"Don't you ever tire of bringing that up? I told you I don't recall not one bit of it."

"That's funny. 'Cause Deems damn well do remember it."

Sportcoat thought a moment, then said, "You go fetch him. You watch. I ain't gonna have to beg that youngster for nothing. I'd just as soon put him over my knee and paddle him for wasting what God gave him."

"I don't know that you could lift his hand, Sport. You seen him with his shirt off?"

"Seen more than that. I warmed his two little toasters in Sunday school many a day."

"That was ten years ago."

"Same difference," Sportcoat said. "You get to know a man after you seen his straight and narrow."

It was nearly dark when Deems and Phyllis, the new fly girl in the neighborhood, had settled onto the edge of Vitali Pier. They dangled their feet over the water, staring at Manhattan and the Statue of Liberty in the distance.

"Can you swim?" Deems asked, pretending to shove her from behind, as if pushing her off the dock.

"Stop it, boy," she said. She elbowed him playfully.

He'd seen her the very first day she came to the flagpole as a customer, then a couple of days later when she came for a second go-round. She'd bought two bags of smack, then another bag two days later. She was a light user, he guessed, and a hottie, a redbone, a killer looker: a light-skinned black girl with long limbs and a gaunt, tight jaw and high cheekbones. He noted she wore long sleeves on hot days like junkies did, to cover her arm tracks, but her skin was smooth and her hair was long. She seemed awfully nervous, but that didn't bother him. They all were when they were fucking up. He'd noticed her the first day she came out. He watched her disappear into Building 34 and sent Beanie into the building to find out who she was. He reported her name was Phyllis. A visitor. From Atlanta, niece of Fuller Richardson, a regular dope fiend who'd gotten busted and whose apartment was full of his wife, his cousins, his kids, and everybody he owed money to, which apparently included this girl's mother, who was his sister. "She says he owes her mom a bunch of dough, so she can stay in his bedroom till he gets back," Beanie reported. "She might be around awhile."

Deems wasn't taking any chances. He decided to move in quick before someone else popped game. He took a close look at Phyllis the second time she came through, just to make sure she was worth it, before he made a move. He happily concluded she had too much weight to be a full-blown junkie. She still owned a purse. Her shoes, coat, and clothing were clean. And she had some kind of temp job. She wasn't a dopehead yet. Just another light-skinned chick on her way to skankdom who maybe got herself skinned by some bad motherfucker in Georgia probably. Come to New York to ease her broken heart and play big. Telling all her friends in Georgia she was dating the Temptations or some shit, no doubt. But Phyllis was fly, and she was new. And he had money. And it was all good.

The third time she showed, he let Beanie and Dome handle sales, posted Stick, his main lookout, on the roof above with three other kids on roofs nearby, and broke from his bench to follow her back toward 34 as she left. Business was slow that day anyway.

She saw him coming. "Why you following me?"

"You want an extra bag of Big H?"

She looked at him and smirked.

"I don't need no extra," she said. "I'm doing too much now."

Deems liked that. He thought later, much later, that this very first exchange told him more than it should have. It was the body language more than anything. She didn't seem nervous when she copped her dope. Up close there was a directness, a tautness to her that was unusual. She was tight, almost stiff, and alert. He attributed that to an attempt to hide her nervousness, being a small-town girl from the South who confessed to him the very first day he'd asked her to meet him at the dock that she was, that she had once been, and still was, a church girl. He liked that. That meant she was a wild girl inside, all bunched up like him. He had a few church regulars, working junkies. He'd been a church boy himself. He knew that bunched-up feeling. He needed someone all coiled up like him. Everybody in the Cause knew him now. His rep had grown since he'd been shot by Sportcoat. He was bigger and better than ever. Everybody knew he was gonna rock old Sportcoat. Deems knew it too. It was just a matter of time. Why hurry? He was in no hurry. Hurry got you busted. He would deal with Sportcoat at the right time. Sportcoat wasn't a problem. But Earl? Now that was a problem.

There was a distance now, between him and Earl. He felt it. Earl, after his initial rage and displeasure with the whole Sportcoat business, now suddenly seemed to shrug the whole thing off. He insisted Mr. Bunch was pleased with his work. "The Cause is your area. You handle it like you want. Just keep moving the dope."

That wasn't like Earl. Everybody knew Earl got his head bonked in by a baseball at the Watch Houses after trying to bust down on Sportcoat. And then that doofus Soup Lopez was seen carrying Earl to the subway station after Earl tried to bust up Soup's homecoming party—with Sister Gee walking behind them like a damn schoolteacher. He'd also heard Earl got dragged out of Building 17 by Sportcoat and Sausage—after the two old fuckers supposedly tried to electrocute him in the basement of Building 17 but screwed up and put out the building lights for two hours instead. Earl was getting punked. There was something wrong with that.

If Mr. Bunch was so cool about his screwup with Sportcoat, why was he letting his main man, Earl, get his ass kicked up and down the Cause District? And why was Earl so cool about it? It felt like a trap. He'd copped heroin from Earl twice a week for four years. He'd watched him work. He'd seen Earl stick a fork in a guy's eye just for looking at him wrong. He'd once watched Earl pistol-whip a rival drug dealer to unconsciousness over a ten-dollar short. Earl did not fuck around. Something was wrong.

He couldn't get it out his head. There was a play involved. It was just a matter of time before it showed itself. But what was it?

The waiting didn't bother Deems, but the uncertainty of strategy did. Everything to him was about strategy. That's how he'd survived. He heard that other big-time dealers called him a boy genius. He liked that. It pleased him that his crew, his rivals, and even at times Mr. Bunch marveled at how someone so young managed to figure things out on his own and keep ahead of older men, some of whom were vicious and clawing to get his business. He liked that they wondered how he could stay ahead of the competition, knew when to attack rival drug dealers and when to back away, what to sell and when and for how much, what button to push and who to push against. Mr. Bunch once told him that the drug game is like war. Deems disagreed. He watched people, observed how they moved. He saw drug dealing as a kind of baseball game, a game involving strategy.

Deems loved baseball. He'd pitched all the way through high school and could have gone further had not his cousin Rooster lured him into the fast money of the heroin game. He still kept track of the game, the teams, the squads, the statistics, the hitters, the Miracle Mets, who, miraculously, might be in the World Series that year, and most of all, the strategy. Baseball was a pitcher's game. Your basic batter knew the pitcher had to throw the ball over the plate in order to get him out of the game. When you did, the batter would try to clobber it. So you had to keep him

guessing. Was the batter looking for a curve? A fastball? A curve outside? Or a fastball inside? Hitters, like most people, were guessers. The
good hitters studied pitchers, watched their moves, anything that might
give them a hint of what pitch was coming. But the good pitchers were
smarter than that. They kept the hitters guessing. Throw inside? Outside? Curveball? Splitter? Fastball up and away? Guess wrong and the
hitter knocks your pitch out of the yard. Guess right and the guy's out
and you're a baseball millionaire.

Drug selling was the same. Keep 'em guessing. Is that dealer coming
at me this way? Or that way? At night? Or during the day? Is he selling
smack now cheaper than me? Or the Big H? The Asian stuff? Or the
stuff from Turkey? Why was he giving away the brown smoking shit out
in Jamaica, Queens, for practically nothing and then selling it at triple
cost to buyers in Wyandanch, Long Island?

That kind of thinking had vaulted him to the top of the game in South
Brooklyn, and it allowed him to push into Queens and even parts of
Manhattan and Long Island. He felt good about that. He had a tight
crew and, most important, a baseball mind. He'd been trained by the
best. A man who knew the game.

Fucking Sportcoat.

Sportcoat was, Deems thought bitterly, a fucking idiot and a sticky
issue to be dealt with later. He had to focus on Earl now, and Mr. Bunch.
Had to.

But the going was difficult. He was so bent on trying to figure out
Mr. Bunch's strategy behind Earl's getting punked that he was losing
sleep. He woke up in the mornings feeling achy and with bumps on his
arms from rolling against the wall. His ear, what was left of it, still hurt
all the time. He needed sleep. And rest. And this fly girl Phyllis, seated
with him at Vitali Pier, was the perfect distraction. He needed this break.
Otherwise, he was an explosion waiting to happen. He'd seen in his own
housing project what happened to the dealers who didn't ease up and

figure things out. Mr. Bunch and Earl had a plan. What was it? He wasn't sure. But if he busted hard on Earl now, or even defended himself against Earl should he attack, his plan to get with Joe Peck could come crashing down before it even got started.

Peck, Deems knew, was the World Series. He was the man with the means. Deems couldn't toss a pitch for Peck till he got his own team together; he was still working on that, adding muscle to his crew, figuring the costs, the risks, the allies in the Watch Houses, in Far Rockaway, and the two trusted guys in Bed-Stuy from his days in Spofford, all of whom he needed to be in tight shape before he could approach Joe Peck. He'd sent Beanie, his most trusted crew member, out to Queens to sound out some fellow dealers in Jamaica, to ask if they'd buy from him if he sold to them at 20 percent less than Mr. Bunch. The answer was a quiet yes. He just needed to tighten things a little more before he approached Peck. Just be cool a few more weeks, then make his move.

But the stress was difficult to handle. There were so few people to trust. More and more, Deems found himself leaning on Beanie, who was more mature than the others and could keep his lips closed and not say dumb things. Outside of that, everything had gotten complicated. His mother was drinking more. His sister had disappeared someplace and hadn't been seen in months. Deems found himself unable to get out of bed in the morning. He'd lie in place, pining for the old days, hearing the crack of a baseball bat on a warm summer day, watching Beanie, Lightbulb, Dome, and his main ace boon coon Sugar shag balls in the outfield while Sportcoat hollered at them, sitting them down in the rancid dugout and telling them stupid stories of the old men in the Negro leagues with funny names. He'd recall the days he and his friends used to lie on the roof of Building 9 waiting for the ants in fall. They were innocent boys then. Not now. Deems at nineteen felt like fifty. He got out of bed each morning feeling like he'd slept on the edge of a dark abyss. He actually toyed with the idea of running away to Alabama, where Sugar had moved to, and cooling out at Sugar's house, just giving up the whole business altogether and finding a college down south that had a baseball team. He still had his stuff. He could still throw ninety miles per hour. He was sure he could still make a good college team as a walk-on. Mr. Bill Boyle, the baseball coach at St. John's, had said so. Deems had known Mr. Boyle for years. Mr. Boyle used to come around every summer asking about him, watching him throw. He kept scorecards, and ratings, and notes on him. Deems liked that. All the way through his days at John Jay High School, where his pitching took the team to the state championship, Mr. Boyle said, "You got a future if you don't screw up." But Deems screwed up. The summer after he graduated from high school, already enrolled in St. John's, Mr. Boyle came to visit, and by then his dope business was booming. He saw Mr. Boyle coming and scattered his dealers and pretended nothing was going on. He walked Mr. Boyle to the old ball field in the Cause and showed him he could still toss at ninety miles per hour and even faster. The old coach was excited. He called Deems when the fall semester began, and Deems said, "I'll be there," but something came up in his business— he couldn't even remember what it was, looking back, just some bullshit. And that was it. Mr. Boyle hadn't heard from him so he showed up in the Cause, unannounced, and spotted Deems at the flagpole, surrounded by dopers, moving heroin. "You're a waste of talent," he said to Deems, and was gone. Deems wanted to call him again, but he was too embarrassed.

Then again, he told himself, *Mr. Boyle drove an old Dodge Dart. My Firebird,* he told himself, *is nicer than his car.* Besides, Mr. Boyle didn't live out here in the Cause, where life was hard.

Sitting at the edge of the dock with the flyest girl he'd ever had a chance to put his arm around, with his feet clad in brand-new Converse sneakers with the star on the side, $3,200 cash in one pocket and a .32 caliber in the other, Beanie serving as his bodyguard because now he never went anywhere without crew, Deems dismissed the baseball idea and forced his mind back into the other game. The real one. He had to keep focused. He had gotten a call that afternoon from one of his boys in Bed-Stuy who'd served time with him in Spofford. His hunch was right. Bunch was about to make a play.

Bunch was on to him, the guy said. Bunch somehow learned that Deems wanted to cut a deal with Joe Peck to take over Bunch's distribution. Earl was just a feint to lull him to sleep. "Earl ain't the guy to look out for. Bunch sent for somebody else."

"Who?" Deems had asked.

"Some motherfucker named Harold Dean. Don't know nothing about him. But he's a shooter. Watch your back with him."

So that was it. Okay. Curveball. Harold Dean. He sent out an alert and got his crew ready, moving them into every building. Any strange dude not from the Cause, who walked through Buildings 9, 34, 17, all his strongholds, any man or kid who lagged through the flagpole plaza looking suspicious, watch him. It could be Harold Dean. Don't do nothing. Just report to him. That was the word. He'd made it clear. He spent some money and sent out a few extra bodies. There wasn't a corner of the Cause he hadn't considered. Every roof. Every building. Every alley had someone in his crew watching it, including his own Building 9, where he placed Stick on the roof, along with a second kid named Rick working the hallways, along with Lightbulb.

Lightbulb.

There was something about Lightbulb Deems didn't like. Lightbulb hadn't been feeling it. Ever since Deems had been shot, and Lightbulb and Beanie came to visit him two weeks ago, and Lightbulb got scared, talking about "you" instead of "we" when Deems said he planned to approach Peck, Deems had gotten suspicious. Lightbulb didn't like that plan. In fact, when Deems really thought about it, Lightbulb never had the heart for the game. Bunch was on to him because somebody had dimed on him. He'd gone through the list of possible double-crossers, and if he had to bet on the outcome . . .

He felt a burning in his throat as anger fought to take hold.

The cooing of the honeyed girl next to him, sighing and dangling her feet over the water, cooled the burning and brought him back to the moment. She was speaking to him but he didn't hear. His mind couldn't stop moving. It circled the Harold Dean problem again, then settled back on Lightbulb.

Fucking Lightbulb.

He couldn't believe it, but he had to. Lightbulb had tipped his hand when they were in the apartment two weeks ago. He hadn't been around much. He was also using, which meant that when Lightbulb made deliveries, he might be cutting the stuff with baking soda or whatever he could get his hands on. Diluting the goods to keep the good stuff for himself.

Rage climbed into Deems's clear thinking. It was a mistake, he knew. But he couldn't help it.

"He tipped his hand right then and there in the apartment." He spit out the words.

"Say what?" Phyllis was talking. She was so sweet. Her voice, lovely and lilting with that Southern accent, was a turn-on. She was almost like a real woman, like the black chicks he'd seen in the movies and on TV, Diahann Carroll and Cicely Tyson, sitting there looking fully grown with her fine self. He felt like a movie star and a grown man all at once, too, sitting next to her. He was embarrassed that he didn't have much experience with girls. She was twenty-four, five years older than him. Most of the girls he knew were younger and worked for him; the older ones occasionally screwed him for dope, or simply became whores for their own habit, which made them untouchable. This little honey was so fine and smart, it seemed a waste to let her get all fucked up on heroin before he got his dibs. Plus she was a little cold and distant, which made her irresistible.

She'd agreed to walk with him to the dock, where there were plenty of empty corners, perfect places for a guy to get his nuts dipped. It was better than risking his life using an apartment of some dopehead in the Cause who might set him up for the price of a ten-dollar bag of brown scag.

She looked at him oddly, waiting for his response. He shrugged and said, "It ain't nothing," then gazed out over the water at the twinkling lights, which began to appear one by one, as the sun made its last descent over the western skyline. He said, "Look at them lights."

"Nice."

"The very next thing I'm gonna get me is an apartment. In Manhattan."

"That's cool," she said.

He placed his arm around her shoulder. She removed it.

"I ain't that type of girl," she said.

He snickered, slightly embarrassed, aware that Beanie was fifteen feet off packing a Davis .380-caliber handgun, watching their backs. "What type of girl are you?"

"Well, not that type. Not yet. I don't know you that good."

"That's why we're here, baby."

She laughed. "How old are you?" she asked.

"Girl, we ain't gonna bang skins out here like teenagers, if that's what you asking. Not with him standing right there." He nodded to Beanie. "We come out here to just see the water and cool out and talk."

"Okay. But I need a little bit of something, y'know. I'm just feeling it . . . y'know. You ain't gonna ask me to do a little extra here for it, are you?"

He was disappointed. "Girl, I don't want no extra. Not right now. You need a hit, I'll give you a hit."

"Forget it," she said. She tilted her head side to side as if she were thinking about something, then said, "Well . . . I probably could use a little taste," she said.

He glared at her.

"I thought you said you wasn't hooked."

"I ain't talking about doing no works. I'm talking about tasting you, boy!" She tapped his pants near his zipper.

He chuckled. Once again, he had a fleeting feeling of sudden alert and would have driven into that feeling further had he not been interrupted by the sound of Beanie behind him bursting into laughter and saying, "Deems, oh shit, check this out!"

He turned around. Beanie, a good ten feet off, was standing next to old Hot Sausage, of all people, who was stone drunk and without his stupid porkpie cap. He was dressed instead in the garb of an umpire, complete with jacket, cap, and chest protector, and holding the face mask in his hand. He swayed unsteadily, completely blitzed.

Deems scrambled to his feet and stepped over to them. "What you doing here, Sausage?" he said, snickering. "You drunk? It ain't Halloween yet." He could smell the booze. Sausage was totaled and looked so ready to collapse that Deems almost felt sorry for him.

Sausage was bombed. "It wasn't my idea," he slurred. "But being that as you . . . well . . . I was told if you seen this here umpire outfit, it would be a message."

"What you talking about?" Deems said. An idea was forming in his head. He glanced at Beanie, who was still laughing, and at Phyllis, who had wandered over. He pointed in the direction of the park, several blocks away. "Baseball field's that way, Sausage," he said.

"Can I speak to you private a minute?" Sausage asked.

Now Deems smelled a rat. He glanced around. The dock was empty save Beanie, the new girl Phyllis, and Sausage. Behind them, the empty paint factory lay dark. Sausage, despite his inebriation, seemed nervous and was breathing hard.

"Come see me tomorrow. When you ain't drunk. I'm busy here."

"It won't take long, Mr. Deems."

"Don't Mr. Deems me, motherfucker. I hear you talking about me at the flagpole. You think I'm sitting around sucking eggs while you sneaking Sportcoat about? If it wasn't for my granddaddy, I'da knocked your teeth out two weeks ago. You and Sport. You two old-bag motherfuckers, starting up shit . . ."

"Gimme a minute, son. I gotta tell you something. It's important."

"Open your talking hole then. Go 'head."

Sausage seemed terrified. He glanced at Phyllis, then at Beanie, then back at Deems.

"It's private, Deems, I'm telling you. Man to man. It's about Sportcoat . . ."

"Fuck Sportcoat," Deems said.

"He wants to tell you something important!" Sausage insisted. "In private."

"Fuck him! Get the fuck outta here!"

"Show some respect for an old man, would ya? What have I ever done to you?"

Deems thought it through quickly, checking off boxes in his mind. His crew was at the flagpole. Chink was in place. Rags was in place. Stick had a crew of kids on the roofs. Beanie was there with him, packing heat. He was packing heat himself. Lightbulb was . . . well, in place, and far distant and no threat and was a problem that would be dealt with soon. He glanced at Phyllis, who was dusting off her pretty rear end. She took a step back toward the empty paint factory.

"I'll go away for a minute," she said. "You can talk."

"Naw, girl, stay here."

Hot Sausage said to Phyllis, "I think it's best you go."

"Git off her, Sausage!"

"It's just a minute, Deems. Please. Gimme a minute in privacy, will ya? For God's sake, boy! Just a minute!"

Deems lowered his voice, enraged now. "State your business right now, or I'll knock every Chiclet outta your mouth."

"All right," Sausage slurred. He glanced at Phyllis, then said, "Sister Gee . . . you remember her?"

"Out with it, motherfucker!"

"Okay then!" Sausage cleared his throat, swaying drunk, trying to control himself. "Sister Gee come by the boiler room today when me and Sport was there having a . . . taste, y'know. She said the cops been asking lots of questions. She come upon some information from one of them cops that she gived to Sportcoat. He wanted you to have it."

"What kind of information?"

"Somebody's coming to get you, Deems. Someone bad."

"Tell me what I don't know, old man."

"Somebody named Harold Dean."

Deems sucked his teeth and turned to Beanie. "Beanie, get him the fuck outta here." He turned away and suddenly noticed, out of the corner of his eye, a movement to his right.

The girl.

She had stepped away from him, and in one smooth motion she slid her arm into her leather jacket, pulled a .38 short-nose Smith & Wesson, aimed it at Beanie, and pulled the hammer on it. Beanie saw her and tried to reach, but he wasn't fast enough. She dropped him, pivoted to Hot Sausage, who was backing away, and popped him once in the chest, which sent the old man reeling to the deck. Then she turned the gun on Deems.

Deems, standing at the dock edge, leapt backward into the harbor when he saw the light wink from the eye of the Smith & Wesson. When he struck the water he felt his ear, still healing from Sportcoat's blast, burning, then the cool waters of the East River surrounding him, then an explosion of pain bursting out of his left arm, the pain seeming to paint his whole body, which felt as if it were ripping apart. He was sure his left arm was gone.

Like most kids who grew up in the Cause Houses, Deems had never learned to swim. He'd avoided the filthy harbor and the projects pool, which was used mostly by the white residents from the surrounding neighborhood and was policed by cops who discouraged the projects kids. Now, in the river, he flapped his hands uselessly and reached out desperately with his right hand. As he did, he swallowed a gulp of river and heard a splash of someone landing in the water near him and thought, *Oh shit, that bitch jumped in.* Then he went down again, and for the first time since he was a child, in the darkness of the water, he found himself calling on God, asking for help, pleading, *Please help me,* swallowing more water and panicking as he flailed. *Help me now, God, and if I don't drown . . . God, help me please.* Every lesson he'd learned in Sunday school, every prayer he'd uttered, every pain he'd felt in his young life, every sorrow he'd caused that stuck in his craw and nagged his conscience, like the gum he stuck under the pews of Five Ends Baptist Church as a kid, felt like they had risen up in a swirl to create a necklace around his neck that choked. He felt the current grab his legs, toss him to the surface, where he took a desperate gulp of air before it snatched his legs and pulled him down again—for good this time. He couldn't resist. He felt himself being gently sucked away by the current and was suddenly exhausted and could no longer fight back. He felt urgency seeping from his feet, and felt blackness coming.

Then something grabbed him by the jacket and pulled him up into air. He was yanked backward, slung against one of the deck pilings, and pinned there, held fast by a single strong forearm. Whoever was holding him was out of breath. Then he heard a harsh whisper: "Shhh."

He couldn't see a thing in the pitch black. Deems's left shoulder burned so badly it felt like it had been dipped in acid. He was dizzy and felt warm blood oozing down his left arm. Then the grip that held him loosed for a moment to get a better grip and pulled him farther back under the wooden dock and closer to the shore. He felt his feet touch rocky ground. The water was neck high now. Whoever held him was standing. Deems tried to stand himself but he couldn't move his legs.

"Jesus," he gurgled. A hand quickly slammed over his mouth and a face moved close to his, speaking just over his shoulder.

"Shush now," the voice said.

Even in the water, with the stench of the dock and the fish and the funk of the East River everywhere, Deems could smell the booze. And the smell of the man. The personal body funk of the old Sunday school teacher who had once held him in his lap by the warm woodstove at Five Ends Baptist when he was a howling boy of nine with wet pants, because his mother got too drunk to go to church on Sundays and sent him alone in piss-smelling church clothes, knowing that the old drunk Sunday school teacher and his kind wife, Hettie, would put shoes and clean pants, shirt, and underwear on him, clothes once worn by their blind son, Pudgy Fingers, knowing that Hettie, each and every Sunday, would discreetly carry Deems's soiled clothes back to her apartment in a bag she carried to church expressly for that purpose, along with a Christmas Club money box in which the two faithfully dropped fifty cents each week—twenty-five cents for Deems and twenty-five cents for their own son, Pudgy Fingers. Then she'd wash Deems's clothes and send them back to his mother's apartment in a paper bag with a piece of cake, or a piece of pie, or some fried fish for the children. True Christian kindness. Real Christian love. A hard woman showing hard love in a hard world. Her and her husband, a straight-up-and-down drunk, who years later would show the boy how to throw a pitch at ninety miles per hour and kiss the outside part of home plate with it, which was something no eighteen-year-old kid in Brooklyn could do.

Sportcoat held Deems against the piling, his old head cast upward, his old eyes peering through the slats in the pier walkway. He listened intently until the sound of the girl's running feet passed overhead, rang along the dock, and disappeared toward the paint factory and the street beyond.

When all was silent, save for the sound of the water lapping up against the pilings, Sportcoat's grip on Deems loosened and he spun Deems backward and yanked him toward the shore, pulling him like a rag doll till they reached the rocks. He laid him on his back on a sandy stretch near the rocks and sat next to him, exhausted. Then he called out to the docks directly above where they sat. "Sausage, you living?"

There was a gurgled response on the deck.

"Shit," Sportcoat said.

Deems had never heard the old man curse before. It felt sacrilegious. Sportcoat moved toward the edge of the dock to climb onto it, then dropped to one knee, his spent face illuminated by the lights of Manhattan just across the river. "I got to catch my breath, Sausage," Sportcoat called out. "I can't move quite yet. Just a minute. I'm coming."

Sausage gurgled again. Sportcoat glanced at Deems, who still lay on the sand, and shook his head. "I don't know what got into you," he panted. "You don't listen to nobody."

"That bitch shot me," Deems gasped.

"Oh shush. Your good arm ain't hurt."

"I didn't know she was packing."

"That's the problem with you young'uns. If you'da growed up down south, you'd knowed something. This city don't teach y'all nothing. I told Sausage to tell you. Sister Gee passed the word about Harold Dean coming to kill you."

"I was on the lookout."

"Yeah? Whyn't you look past your little wee wee then, which I expect was stout and hard as bone? Harold Dean was holding your hand, son, purring like a kitten and stinking of trouble. Harol-deen, boy. Harol-*deen* is a girl's name."

The old man stood up and climbed onto the dock where Sausage was. Deems watched him, then felt sweet blackness coming. It came right on time.

18

INVESTIGATION

THE FIGHT OVER THE FREE CHEESE IN HOT SAUSAGE'S BASE-ment boiler room that Saturday morning would have broken out into a full-scale riot if Soup Lopez hadn't been there. Sister Gee was glad she'd made him come. It wasn't so much that Hot Sausage wasn't there to dole out the free cheese, Sister Gee thought, but rather the fact that Sausage was dead—shot and killed the previous Wednesday, along with his dear friend Sportcoat. Apparently both had been shot and dumped in the harbor by Deems, who also shot himself dead. That's what the early word was. They were just bad rumors. The Cause was used to those, Sister Gee knew. Even so, the whole business hit everyone pretty hard.

"Damned Deems," Bum-Bum said. "He got the order wrong. He shoulda shot hisself first." She was usually the first in line at the basement ramp door, rising at five a.m. to arrive by six. It was part of a quest she'd begun in recent months to find out who the secret cheese giver was. She hadn't found out yet, but her early arrival confirmed three points: One, that Hot Sausage wasn't the cheese giver. Two, that her place at the front of the line was always assured, since most of her friends were there early too. And three, she'd have first dibs on the gossip, since all the early cheese grabbers were friends from the flagpole she'd known for years.

That morning she got there ten minutes later than normal, to find Miss Izi first in line, having arrived early as usual, chatting with Sister Gee, who stood behind the cheese distribution table, having been appointed to the sad duty of distributing the cheese in Sausage's absence. Not far behind her were the Cousins, Joaquin the numbers runner, and Bum-Bum's secret delight, Dominic the Haitian Sensation, whose face, she noted, looked freshly washed and whose fingernails looked clipped— always a sign of good sanitation in a man. Behind him were the two other members of the Puerto Rican Statehood Society of the Cause Houses. All the heavy hitters of news, views, and gossip were there in perfect formation. Today had all the makings of good conversation and excellent hot gossip.

She sidled into her honorary place at the front of the line just behind Miss Izi, who had saved her a spot, and slipped in just in time to hear Miss Izi give her views on the matter.

"Sportcoat had been drinking himself to the quit line for twenty years," she said. "But I didn't think Sausage drank that much. Maybe they got into a fight and shot each other."

"Sausage didn't shoot nobody," Bum-Bum said.

Standing in line behind her, Dominic—who just *happened* to rise up at five a.m. and just *happened* to arrive at the basement door at six a.m., and by golly just *happened* to find himself lined up behind Bum-Bum after trading places with several people in line so that he could move up—agreed. "Sausage was a good friend," he said.

Joaquin, several spots behind them, looked strangely sad. "I borrowed twelve dollars from Sausage," he said. "I'm glad I didn't pay it back."

"God, you are cheap," Miss Izi said. She was standing a good five people ahead of her ex-husband and stepped out of line to address him. "You're so tight with money your ass squeaks when you walk."

"At least I have an ass," he said.

"Yeah. Three. One's on your face."

"Pig!"

"*Gilipollas!*"

"*Perro!*"

A man at the back of the line yelled at Miss Izi to get her fat ass back in line.

"Mind your business!" Joaquin snapped.

"Make me, Joaquin!" he hollered.

Joaquin stepped out of line and a general ruckus was about to get out of hand but was quelled by Soup the giant, who stepped in, looking somber in his Nation of Islam suit. Sister Gee quickly intervened, moving from behind the long table piled high with cheese and gently coaxing Soup aside.

"Can y'all keep your heads, please?" she said. "We don't know what happened. We'll know more later."

Later came right away, as there was a bit of shuffling at the entranceway. Sister Gee watched as the cheese line that snaked out the door suddenly shifted. Several people stepped aside, and Sergeant Potts stepped into the boiler room.

He was followed by his young partner and two plainclothes detectives, all business, who squeezed past the line that jammed the doorway and into the middle of the suddenly crowded boiler room, which fell silent.

Potts looked at the table where Sister Gee stood, then at the nervous residents waiting in line. He noticed movement out of the corner of his eye and saw three people, one woman and two men, step out of line and slip toward the exit without a word. He guessed they were either parolees or had outstanding arrest warrants. A fourth, a huge, young, well-dressed Puerto Rican nearly seven feet tall, moved to follow. The young man looked vaguely familiar to Potts, and as the big figure moved toward the door, Potts's partner Mitch tapped him and nodded at Soup. "You want me to question him?"

"You kidding? You see the size of that guy?"

Soup slipped out, along with the others.

Potts turned his attention to Sister Gee. Even on an early, bleak Saturday in that dank, crowded basement, she looked lovely as an Irish spring morning. She wore jeans and a blouse that she tied at the waist and her hair tied in a bun with a colorful sash, which set off her lovely features.

"Morning," he said to her.

She smiled thinly. She didn't seem happy to see him. "Seems like you brought the whole force today," she said.

He glanced at the people in line, noticed Bum-Bum, Dominic, and Miss Izi staring at him, nodded toward the three officers, and said, "Could you speak to these officers a minute? Just routine. Nothing to worry about. I saw you three at the church, is all. We just wanna learn about the victims." To Sister Gee he said, "Can I speak to you outside?"

Sister Gee didn't bother to tell him that only Sister Bum-Bum was actually a member of Five Ends Baptist. Instead, she turned to one of the Cousins, Nanette, and said simply, "Nanette. Take over."

She followed Potts up the ramp and outside. When they were in the plaza he turned to her, placed his hands in his pockets, and frowned at the ground. She noticed he was wearing a double-breasted sergeant's jacket. He looked quite sharp, she thought, and also bothered. Finally he looked at her.

"I will not say I told you so."

"Good."

"But as you know, there's been an incident."

"I heard."

"All of it?"

"No. Just rumors. I don't believe in rumors."

"Well, we think Ralph Odum . . . Mr. Odum. Um, Hot Sausage, the boiler man, drowned in the harbor."

She heard herself gasp without really feeling it. She had no plan to howl and lose her face in front of him. She felt foolish suddenly. He was a wonderful stranger, a lovely dream, and now he was just like any other cop. Bringing bad news. And probably reports. And more warrants. And more questions. Always questions from these types. Never answers.

"I didn't believe it when I heard it," she said somberly. "I thought maybe Sportcoat was the one that drowned."

"No. Sausage drowned. Our guy—your guy—Sportcoat is alive. I saw him this morning."

"Is he okay?"

"Shot in the chest. He's alive, though. He'll make it."

"Where is he?"

"Maimonides hospital in Borough Park."

"Why'd they brung him all the way out there?"

Potts shrugged. "Also, Deems Clemens was shot in the left shoulder. He'll live too."

"Lord. They shot each other?"

"Unknown. Also there was a third person shot. Randall Collins. He was killed."

"I don't know him."

"Apparently he had a nickname."

"Everybody does out here."

"Beanie."

"I know him." She said it curtly, to cut off the choking sound of her own weeping. Once it started she knew it wouldn't stop. She was not going to cry in front of him. Then the first surge of shock and sorrow passed and he was still silent, so she spoke again, just to keep her composure. "What do you need from me?"

"Any reason your man Sportcoat would want to shoot those two?"

"You know the reason behind it much as I do," she said.

Potts's glance moved to the rooftop of the plaza building in front of him. He noticed a kid peek over the edge of the roof and disappear. A cop watcher, he thought.

"Actually, I don't," he said. "I saw your Sportcoat in the hospital this morning. He'd been shot close to the heart. They operated and took out the bullet, but he's okay. He was groggy. Sedated. He was kind of confused. We spoke only a few minutes. He said he didn't shoot Deems."

"That sounds like Sportcoat. He was drunk when he did it—that first time anyway. Says he don't remember a thing. Which he probably don't."

"Your Sportcoat, he says a woman shot them all."

"Well, I reckon a soul will say anything to stay outta jail."

"I told him that his buddy Hot Sausage drowned. That hit him hard."

Potts was silent a moment as she bit her lip and blinked back tears.

"You sure he's drowned?" she asked.

"I'm sure we can't find him. We found your Sportcoat in an umpire's outfit. Randall, the dead kid. And Deems, who was wounded. No Hot Sausage."

She was silent.

"I told you this was serious business, didn't I?" Potts said.

She looked away and said nothing.

"Were they close friends, those two, Thelonius Ellis, your Sportcoat, and Mr. Odum?" Potts asked.

"Very close." Sister Gee thought a moment about telling Potts that there was no Ralph Odum. That Ralph Odum was really Hot Sausage's phony name. That his real name was Thelonius Ellis. And that Sportcoat's real name was Cuffy Lambkin. And that those two traded off the driver's license from week to week. Yet Potts hadn't said a word about Cuffy Lambkin. Something was wrong.

"Sportcoat did seem concerned about his buddy drowning. He was woozy, but he kept talking about his buddy. I told him we weren't sure his pal Mr. Odum drowned, but the fact is we are. It's pretty clear. We got a witness from the old paint factory who heard the shots and saw Deems fall in. The witness saw Deems crawl out. Not the old man. Some of Hot Sausage's effects were in the water as well. Housing Authority hat. Housing Authority jacket. The current was going out by the time the divers got there. The current at this time of year moves out fast. The water's cold. Bodies sink in cold water, they don't float. Divers will go in later today and retrieve the body."

"Did you ask Deems what happened?"

"He's not talking."

"I'da thunk it'd be the other way around," Sister Gee said. "That Deems shot Sportcoat. Or shot them both. Sausage couldn't stand Deems. But Sausage wouldn't shoot nobody. Neither would Sportcoat. Not in his right mind. Sportcoat liked Deems—he loved Deems. Even though he shot him, he still loved him. He was Deems's Sunday school teacher for years. He coached him in baseball. That means something, don't it?"

Potts shrugged. "Just 'cause you toast marshmallows with a kid on a camping trip doesn't mean he'll become a Boy Scout."

"It's funny," she said. "Sport dodged death so many times . . . Sausage, he never got in no trouble with anyone. You sure it ain't some mistake? They look a little alike, you know."

"It's Sportcoat all right. We checked his wallet. His driver's license with a photo ID."

"His driver's license ID?"

She felt a spark go off in her mind, thinking back to Soup's party, when Sausage said that Sport had gone to the motor vehicle bureau and got a driver's license bearing Hot Sausage's real name: Thelonius Ellis. Which Sausage had retrieved from Sportcoat at Soup's party.

"He was even wearing an umpire's costume," Potts added, "which I'm told he wears sometimes."

"That's him." She nodded, but then she thought it through. Even though she saw Sportcoat hand that ID over to Sausage with her own eyes, it would likely take the cops weeks to figure out that the real Thelonius was Hot Sausage and not Sportcoat. Is it possible, she thought, that the two switched the ID again after Soup's party, on the chance that if the cops arrested Sausage, it would give Sportcoat a chance to run? She decided against it. *No. Sportcoat wouldn't do that. He'd be too drunk. He's too lazy to think that far ahead.* Still, her hopes glimmered a bit. If Hot Sausage was still too woozy to tell them what had happened and who was who, there was a chance.

"That umpire's vest saved Mr. Ellis's life," Potts said. "The bullet hit from the side and the chest protector slowed it. Otherwise, he would have been cooked. Thing is, he was kinda woozy and garbled in his talk. He wasn't all there. So we'll go back in a day or two and check with him again, when he's feeling better."

"Okay."

"Oh yeah, and he was talking about a woman. What'd you say his wife's name was?"

"Hettie."

"No, it wasn't Hettie. Something about a Denise Bibb."

"Sister Bibb?" Sister Gee felt another spark go off in her mind. She stared at the ground, working hard to keep her face blank. "She's the organ player at our church. Minister of music is her real title."

"Your Sportcoat said a woman was the shooter, and he mentioned this woman several times. Denise Bibb. Why would he do that? I thought his wife was dead."

Sister Gee bit her lip. "I reckon he had to be out of his head. You said he was woozy, right?"

"Very much so. Pretty gone, actually. He said some strange things about Mrs. Bibb. Something about her being a killer. A grinder. Strong as a man. A machine gunner. That kind of stuff. Did she have anything against him? You think she might have been involved in some way?"

Sister Gee felt the spark in her head turn to fireworks. *I knew it!* she thought. *Sausage and Sister Bibb had a thing going!* She kept staring, willing her face to stay emotionless, before she tried to speak.

"Sister Bibb wouldn't hurt a fly," she managed to croak.

"It's called evidence. I have to ask."

"It's called, 'when you get old, all's you got is your imagination,'" Sister Gee said. She tried to make her face take on a grim smile but was having trouble. The smile now was real.

Potts stared at her. *That smile*, he thought, *is like a rainbow*. He tried to keep his voice even, official. "No other reason to think that this Sister Bibb of yours might have had a grudge against Sportcoat? Lovers' quarrel maybe?"

Sister Gee shrugged. "There's plenty tipping going on in church, just like in anyplace in this world. People got feelings, y'know? They get lonesome, even when they're married. There's love in this world, mister. It don't stop for nothing or nobody. You ain't never seen that?"

She looked at him with such desire that he had to stifle an urge to raise his hand like a third grader in a classroom waiting to be called on—and reach for her hand. She had unmasked him. She didn't even know she'd done it.

"Of course," he managed to say.

"But I don't think there's nothing between them," she said. "Whyn't you ask Sister Bibb herself?"

"Where is she?"

"She's in Building Thirty-Four. But today being Saturday, she mostly works Saturdays at her job. She cooks in a cafeteria in Manhattan."

"Did you see her last night?"

"No." That was the truth. She'd seen her three minutes ago. In the cheese line. But he didn't ask that. Sister Gee felt a little better. At least she wasn't "wholesale lying," as her mother would say. Besides, would he ever know? She found herself hoping he would. It meant he'd likely have to come back and she'd see him again, and again and again. *I'll keep lying,* she thought, *just to fold into that big shoulder and see him smile and tell a joke in that heavy, pretty voice he got, the way he did that first day in church.* Then she felt acid creeping into her throat. *Ain't I a dreamer,* she thought bitterly. *He'll be gone when this is all done. Maybe I'll see him sometime outside Rattigan's joking with his buddies while I'm sweeping their bottles off the curb.* Thinking of it made her miserable.

Potts saw her face fall and was not sure why. "We'll come back later and check with her," he said.

She smiled, a sad, genuine one this time, and felt her heart fall to earth as she said the words that brought light to his heart every time he heard them. "Come on back then. Hurry back, if you wanna."

Potts forced himself to check his emotions. He would have slammed the door on them if he could. He was at work. People were dead. There were families to notify. Detectives to check up on. Paperwork to fill out. They'd rattle this case around the Seventy-Sixth Precinct till somebody got tired of it. The best he could get out of it was standing right in front of him, as gorgeous and kind a woman as he'd ever seen. He sighed deeply, offered a small smile, then glanced at the line at the basement door as his fellow officers waited.

"We better go back down lest they think we're out here ordering Chinese."

He turned to head down the ramp until she touched his arm, stopping him.

"Are you sure that Sausage fell in the harbor?" she asked.

"Not really," he admitted. "You can never be sure till you've seen the body."

She followed him down the ramp. He gathered the other three officers and the four officers filed out in silence.

When the cops were gone, Sister Gee turned to the relieved cheese gatherers, who stood in groups, the line now disbanded. They ignored the cheese, which lay in neat stacks on the table, Nanette guarding them. They gathered around Sister Gee instead.

"I thought I said take over," she said to Nanette.

"Forget that," Nanette snapped. "What'd the cop say?"

Sister Gee looked at the people staring at her: Dominic, Bum-Bum, Miss Izi, Joaquin, Nanette, and the rest, at least fifteen people in all. She'd known most of them her whole life. They stared at her with that look, that *projects* look: the sadness, the suspicion, the weariness, the knowledge that came from living a special misery in a world of misery. Four of their number were down—gone, changed forever, dead or not, it didn't matter. And there would be more. The drugs, big drugs, heroin, were here. Nothing could stop it. They knew that now. Someone else had already taken over Deems's bench at the flagpole. Nothing here would change. Life in the Cause would lurch forward as it always did. You worked, slaved, fought off the rats, the mice, the roaches, the ants, the Housing Authority, the cops, the muggers, and now the drug dealers. You lived a life of disappointment and suffering, of too-hot summers and too-cold winters, surviving in apartments with crummy stoves that didn't work and windows that didn't open and toilets that didn't flush and lead paint that flecked off the walls and poisoned your children, living in awful, dreary apartments built to house Italians who came to America to work the docks, which had emptied of boats, ships, tankers, dreams, money, and opportunity the moment the colored and the Latinos arrived. And still New York blamed you for all its problems. And who can you blame? You were the one who chose to live here, in this hard town with its hard people, the financial capital of the world, land of opportunity for the white man and a tundra of spent dreams and empty promises for anyone else stupid enough to believe the hype. Sister Gee stared at her neighbors as they surrounded her, and at that moment she saw them as she had never seen them before: they were crumbs, thimbles, flecks of sugar powder on a cookie, invisible, sporadic dots on the grid of promise, occasionally appearing on Broadway stages or on baseball teams with slogans like "You gotta believe," when in fact there was nothing to believe but that one colored in the room is fine, two is twenty, and three means close up shop and everybody go home; all living the New York dream in the Cause Houses, within sight of the Statue of Liberty, a gigantic copper reminder that this city was a grinding factory that diced the poor man's dreams worse than any cotton gin or sugar-cane field from the old country. And now heroin was here to make their children slaves again, to a useless white powder.

She looked them over, the friends of her life, staring at her. They saw what she saw, she realized. She read it in their faces. They would never win. The game was fixed. The villains would succeed. The heroes would die. The sight of Beanie's mother howling at her son's coffin would haunt them all in the next few days. Next week, or next month some time, some other mother would take her place, howling her grief. And another after that. They saw the future, too, she could tell. It would continue forever. It was all so very grim.

But then, she thought, every once in a while there's a glimmer of hope. Just a blip on the horizon, a whack on the nose of the giant that set him back on his heels or to the canvas, something that said, "Guess what, you so-and-so, I am God's child. And I. Am. Still. Here." She felt God's blessing at that moment, thanked Him in her heart, for right then she could see that glimmer in their faces, too, could see that they would understand what she was about to tell them, about the man who had wandered among them for most of his adult life, whose lymph nodes grew to the size of marbles when he was eighteen, who staggered around with scarlet fever, hematoid illness, acute viral infection, pulmonary embolism, lupus, a broken eye socket, two bouts of full-blown adult measles, and several flus, and whose one-hundred-proof body had survived more operations in one year than most of them would have in a lifetime, and she felt grateful that the Good Lord had given her the opportunity and presence of mind to share it with them, because in her heart it was proof that God was forever generous with His gifts: hope, love, truth, and the belief in the indestructability of the good in all people. If she could have, she would have stood on top of Building 17 with a bullhorn and shouted that truth for the whole projects to hear.

But telling it to this small group, she knew, was enough. She knew it would go far.

"Sausage ain't dead," she said. "He was shot but he's still living. He's in the hospital."

"And Sportcoat?" Bum-Bum asked.

A blanket of silence covered the room.

Sister Gee smiled. "Well now, that's a story . . ."

Potts and the three officers trooped grimly across the plaza to their squad car. They hadn't gone five steps when an unexpected sound from the basement boiler room caused them to stop. They stood in place and listened for a moment. The noise quickly dimmed, and after a moment the cops started walking again, this time more slowly.

One of the detectives fell in step with Potts, who was at the back of the group. "Potts, I don't understand these people. They're barbarians."

Potts shrugged and kept walking. He knew there would be strategy meetings, and calls from the mayor's office, and memos from the new drug task force down at the narcotics bureau in Manhattan. All a waste of time. And at the end of it, there would still be people who argued that housing projects cases weren't worth spending any more money and manpower on. And now there were three other cops who'd just heard what he'd heard, which would only make his argument that they should pursue this case that much more difficult and inexplicable to the higher-ups, because what the three officers had heard from the boiler room was outrageous—impossible to anyone who hadn't worked in the Cause Houses for twenty years like he had.

It was the sound of laughing.

19

DOUBLE-CROSSED

IT WAS TWO A.M. WHEN JOE PECK SWUNG THE BIG GTO RIGHT onto the dock of Elefante's boxcar with his headlights on bright. As usual, Peck came at the wrong time. The Elephant was in the middle of an operation, standing near the doorway of his boxcar carefully counting the last of thirty-four brand-new Panasonic television sets that four of his men were hastily transferring from a small docked boat to the back of a *Daily News* delivery truck. The truck had been "borrowed" from the newspaper printing plant on Atlantic Avenue at eleven that night by one of his men, a newspaper truck driver. It was due back at four, when the morning papers rolled out.

Peck's headlights swept across the dock and surprised two of Elefante's crew who were holding a crate. The two men, struggling with the crate, hurriedly scampered into the shadows. Their frenzied movement caught the attention of the nervous boat captain, who had kept his diesel engine running. Before Elefante could say a word, the captain motioned to a deckhand, who yanked the slipknot tying the boat to the dock, and the boat motored quickly into the harbor without lights, disappearing into the night, the last two Panasonics still on board.

Peck emerged from the car mad, stomping over to Elefante, who stood at the door of the boxcar. "I've never seen that before," Elefante said coolly. It would not do to get in a dustup with Joe right here, not while the truck was loading and had to go. There was still money to be made.

"Seen what?" Peck demanded.

"Seen somebody untie a boat that fast. He did it with one pull."

"So?"

"He still got the last two TV sets on there," he said. "I paid him for thirty-four. I only got thirty-two."

"I'll buy the last two," Peck said. "I gotta talk to you."

Elefante looked at the truck. The last TV was loaded and the cargo door closed. He motioned to his men to get the truck moving, then walked inside the boxcar to his desk and sat down. Peck followed and sat in the chair next to it, lighting a Winston cigarette.

"So what now?" Elefante said. He could see Peck was still angry. "I already told you I wasn't doing that Lebanon thing."

"I'm not here about that. Why you gotta monkey with my shipment?"

"What are you talking about?"

"You want me to shit eggs standing up, Tommy? I can't move one hairy ball now. The cops are all over me."

"What for?"

"For the thing over at the fishing harbor, at Vitali Pier."

"What thing?"

"Stop bullshitting me, Tommy."

"If you wanna talk in circles, Joe, join the circus. I don't know what you're talking about."

"Your guy . . . the old guy, he cut loose over at Enzo Vitali's pier last night. Shot three people."

Elefante carefully considered his response. Years of practice feigning ignorance helped him to keep a tight, straight face when he needed it. In his world, where rigor mortis was a job hazard, it was always better to pretend you didn't know even if you did. But in this case he had no idea what Joe was talking about.

"What old guy, Joe?"

"Stop fucking with me, Tommy!"

Elefante closed the door to the boxcar, then undid his tie, tossed it on the table, and reached into his drawer and drew out a bottle of Johnnie Walker scotch and two glasses.

"Have a drink, Joe. Tell me about it."

"Don't play bartender with me, Tommy. You think I'm a fuckin' mind reader? What's going on in your head? You losing your marbles?"

Elefante could feel his patience fading fast. Joe had a way of pushing his buttons. As he looked at Peck his face took on a calm grimness.

Peck saw the expression change and cooled quickly. When Elefante was mad, he was spookier than voodoo. "Easy, Tommy. I got a problem."

"Once again, for mother Mary, what is it, Joe?" Elefante asked.

"The Lebanon shipment is nine days off, and I been screwed. I had to get Ray at Coney Island to make the picku—"

"I don't wanna know about it."

"Tommy, would you let me finish? You know the old paint factory, where we used to swim? Enzo Vitali's old pier? Your old guy, your shooter, plugged three people down there yesterday."

"I don't have no old guy shooting for me," Elefante said.

"Tell that to the dead guy taking a nap with bullet holes in his face. Now the cops are all over me."

"Would you come up to street level, Joe? I didn't have nobody down at Vitali's last night. We spent the night getting ready for this haul. Thirty-four TV sets from Japan—till you came. Now it's thirty-two. The other two are at the bottom of the harbor by now."

"I told you I'd pay for 'em."

"Keep your dough and use it to go dancing next time I got an operation going. It'll make my life easier. I'm glad you came, though. Showed me what I already knew: that boat captain is just the lizard I thought he was."

"So you didn't have those guys shot?"

"What do I look like, Joe? You think I'm stupid enough to set fire to money in my own pocket? Why would I have the cops rattling the docks when I had a shipment to move the next day? I had something going."

Peck's anger eased a little. He reached for a glass and poured himself a shot of the Johnnie Walker. He sipped deeply, then said, "You remember that kid? The little whiz kid who worked for me in the Cause Houses? The one who got himself shot by that old bird? Well, last night, the old bird came back with a second old bird to finish the job. The two of 'em shot the kid again—didn't kill him, if you can believe it. This kid'll give a gunman blisters before he keels over. But they killed one of the kid's crew. One of the old guys got plugged. The old guy, your guy I think, he's dead too, I hear. Floating in the harbor someplace. The cops are dragging for him tomorrow."

"Why do you keep calling him my guy? I don't know him."

"You should. He's your gardener."

Elefante blinked hard and sat straight up. "Run that by me again."

"The old guy. The one who shot the kid and got tossed in the harbor without instructions. He's your gardener. He worked in your house. For your mother."

Elefante was silent a moment. He stared at the desk, then glanced around the room, as if the answer to this new problem were hiding in the nooks and crannies of the dank old boxcar.

"That can't be right."

"It is. I got it from a bird in the Seven-Six."

Elefante bit his bottom lip, thinking. How many times had he told his mother to be careful who she let in the house? Finally he said, "That old drunk can't shoot nobody."

"Well, he did."

"That old man drinks so much you can hear his stomach slosh. The fucker can't stand up straight. He uses a Mason jar for a jigger."

"Well, he's drinking all he wants now. Harbor water."

Elefante rubbed his forehead. He poured another drink and gulped it down. He blew out his cheeks, then swore softly, "Shit."

"Well?"

"I'm telling you, Joe. I didn't know a thing about it."

"Sure. And I'm a butterfly with a Jag."

"I swear on my father's grave, I don't know nothing about it."

Peck poured another shot of Johnnie Walker for himself. That was a pretty heavy denial: he'd never heard the Elephant mention his dead father. Everybody knew the Elephant and his old man had been close.

"It still screws me up," Peck said. "There's cops all over Vitali Pier now. And guess where Ray was gonna make my pickup?"

Elefante nodded. Vitali Pier would've been good. Unused. Vacant. Deep water. Dock still half-usable. This was a screwup, to be sure.

"When are the things from Lebanon coming?"

"Nine days."

Elefante thought quickly. Now he saw the problem, or the beginning of it. *Once again*, he thought, *Joe's dropping a bomb on me.* The shooting would bring—had brought—the cops. He realized that the only reason the heat hadn't descended on him tonight was because the night-duty captain at the Seven-Six, whom he regularly paid off, was a good Irishman who kept his word. Elefante had tried to reach the captain today and couldn't. Now he knew why. The poor cluck must've twisted like an octopus to keep squad cars and homicide detectives from trolling through his dock and was likely afraid to pick up the phone, thinking Internal Affairs was on to him. This kind of heat—three shootings, for

Christ's sake—brought the papers and full-blown attention from headquarters down on Centre Street. No precinct lieutenant or captain could
hold off that kind of heat for long. Elefante made a mental note to send
the captain an extra tip for his diligence.

"Things will cool down by then, Joe."

"Sure. And the Bed-Stuy bastard gunning for my territory is at a
peace conference right now," Joe fumed.

"Maybe he's the guy behind all of it."

"That's what I come to ask. You think your old guy worked for him?
Was he that type?"

"I don't know him," Elefante said. "I spoke to him once. But he
couldn't pull this kind of stunt. He's old, Joe. The guy's so drunk he gets
spirit messages from his dead wife. He's a . . ." He paused. He wanted to
say, "a deacon at his church," but he wasn't quite sure what that meant.
The old bird had told him, but in the thrust of the moment he forgot.

Peck's raspy voice cut into his thoughts. "He's a what?"

"A lush, Joe. A drunk, dammit. The guy couldn't see straight enough
to shoot an elephant in a bathtub. Not to mention somebody on Vitali
Pier in the middle of the night. How's an old geezer gonna hit two young
guys who are likely scrambling and shooting back in the dark? The guy
can barely stand up. He's a gardener, Joe. Works with plants. That's
why my mother got him. You know how crazy she is about plants."

Peck considered this. "Well, she's gonna need a new gardener."

"I didn't know he had anything to do with this kid. What's his name?
The kid that started it all?"

"Clemens. Deems Clemens. Honest kid. Didn't start nothing."

Elefante listened, aware of the irony. Honest kid. A dope seller. Didn't
start nothing.

"And the old guy?" he said. "What's his name?"

"I was gonna ask you that. You got so much money, you don't know
who you're paying?"

"My mother paid him! I can't remember his name. He's at the church there." He nodded over his shoulder toward the next block, where Five Ends sat. Then he said it: "He's a deacon."

Peck looked puzzled. "What do deacons do?" he asked.

"Carry eggs around, pay bar bills, quilt spaghetti—I don't know," Elefante said. "That ain't the question to be asking. The question is who's behind it. If I was you, that's what I'd be asking."

"I know who's behind it. Goddamn nigger bastard in Bed-Stuy, Bunch Moon's been tryi—"

"I don't wanna hear no names, Joe. And I don't wanna hear no more about any shipments. That's your business. My business is this dock. That's all I'm concerned with. I can work with you on anything involving my dock. That's it. As it stands, that thing at Vitali's is gonna make me radioactive for a while."

"What do you expect?" Joe said.

"You got a couple of birds down at the Seven-Six. I got one or two ants in that colony too. Let's find out what happened."

"We know what happened."

"No we don't. That guy was so old he sips his booze through a straw. He can't shoot two young dope slingers. Even with a second old guy he couldn't do it. Those young dope guys, they're fast and strong. Whoever fed you that story is wrong."

"A cop told me."

"Some of those goons at the Seven-Six couldn't fill in the return address on an envelope. Those kids were moving around unless they were tied up. Those boys from the Cause selling that crap are big, strong kids, Joe. I used to see 'em playing baseball against the Watch Houses. You ever see one of 'em with their shirt off? They're gonna let an old man— or two old men, if it was two—tie 'em up and bang away at 'em? The only way they coulda aired those kids out was if those boys were necking like girl and boy." He paused to consider. "I could see that. If it was two teenagers kissing or something, yeah, I could see it."

"Well, he did say something about a girl."

"Who did?"

"My bird in the Seven-Six. He read the report. He said the report didn't say anything about a girl. But somebody mentioned a girl."

"Who mentioned a girl?"

"Well, that's the other thing I forgot to tell you. Potts Mullen is back in the Seven-Six."

Elefante was silent a moment, then he sighed. "Gotta hand it to ya, Joe. When you bring trouble, you always bring it in threes. I thought Potts was gone."

"What you blaming me for?" Joe said. "Potts *was* gone. My guy told me Potts got sent to One-Oh-Three in Queens, then crossed a captain out there by trying to be a supercop and got busted from detective back to blues. He's a sergeant, or close to it. They say Potts was telling some of the guys in squad cars to look out for a girl shooter. Said he'd heard there'd been a girl at the dock."

"How'd he find that out?"

"Potts told my guy he went into the old paint factory behind Vitali Pier and found a drunk back there who saw it all. The guy told Potts there was a girl."

"You talked to Potts?"

Peck looked scornful. "Right. Me and Potts gonna sit down and sip ales and sing Irish ditties. I can't stand that holy-rolling mick bastard."

Elefante considered a moment. "Me and Potts go back a ways. I'll talk to him."

"You'd be dumb to try to grease him," Peck said as a warning.

"I ain't that stupid. I said I'll talk to him. I'll go to him before he comes to me."

"Why you gonna ask for trouble? He's not gonna tell you nothing."

"You forget, Joe. I run a legitimate business here. I rent boats. I got a construction company. I run a storage place. My mother walks around the neighborhood looking for plants. I can ask him about a dead guy in the harbor around here, especially since the guy worked for me—for Ma, really."

Peck shook his head slowly. "This area used to be safe. Before the coloreds came."

Elefante frowned. "Before the *drugs* came, Joe. It's not the coloreds. It's the drugs."

Peck shrugged and sipped his drink.

"We'll work this one together," Elefante said. "But you keep me outta that other business. And spread the word to those so-called honest kids of yours that my mother had nothing to do with that shooting at Vitali's. Because if something happens to her while she's walking around here picking daffodils and ferns and whatever the fuck else she feels a need to gather up, if she so much as falls down and scrapes a knee, they'll be outta business. And so will you."

"What you making something out of nothing for? Your mom's walked these lots for years. Nobody bothers her."

"That's just it. The old coloreds know her. The kids don't."

"I can't do anything about that, Tommy."

Elefante rose, downed his drink, put the bottle of Johnnie Walker back inside his desk drawer, and closed it. "You been told," he said.

20

PLANT MAN

SPORTCOAT LAY ON A BATTERED COUCH IN RUFUS'S BASE-
ment. He had been there by his count for three days, drinking, sleeping,
drinking, eating a little, sleeping, and mostly, Rufus acknowledged
curtly to him, drinking. Rufus came and went, delivering news that was
not so good, not so bad. Sausage and Deems were alive and in the hospital in Borough Park. The cops were looking for him. So was everyone at
his various jobs: Mr. Itkin; the ladies from Five Ends, including Sister
Gee; Miss Four Pie; and assorted customers he did odd work for. So
were some unusual-looking white men who had come over to the Cause
before.

Sportcoat didn't care. He was consumed with the events around fishing Deems out the water, the feel of being in the harbor water at night.
He had never done that. Once many years ago when he first came to
New York, when he and Hettie were young, they'd agreed they would
try that one day—just jump into the harbor at night to see the shore
from the water, to feel the water and what New York felt like from there.
It was one of the many promises they'd made to each other when they

were young. There were others. See the giant redwood trees in Northern California. Visit Hettie's brother in Oklahoma. Visit the Bronx botanical garden to see the hundreds of plants there. So many resolutions, none of them ever fulfilled—except that one. In the end, though, she had done it alone. She had felt that water at night.

That day, the third day, in the afternoon, he fell asleep and dreamed of her.

For the first time since her death, she appeared young. Her brown skin was shiny, moist, and clear. Her eyes were wide and sparkled with enthusiasm. Her hair was braided and parted neatly. She wore the brown dress that he remembered. She'd made it herself with her mother's sewing machine. It was adorned with a yellow flower stitched onto the left side, just above her breast.

She appeared in Rufus's basement boiler room looking as if she'd just breezed in from a Sunday church picnic back home in Possum Point. She sat on an old kitchen sink that lay on its side. She perched on it lightly, easily, the picture of grace, as if she were seated on an armchair and could float away from it if it fell over. Her pretty legs were crossed. Her brown arms rested on her lap. Sportcoat stared at her. With her brown dress and its yellow flower and her hair parted, her brown skin shimmering from some secret source of light in the dank, dark basement, she looked achingly beautiful.

"I remember that dress," he said.

She offered a sad, bashful smile. "Oh hush," she said.

"I do recollects it," he said. It was his awkward way of making up for previous arguments they'd had, tossing off a compliment at once.

She looked at him sadly. "You look like you been living rough and wrong, Cuffy. What's the matter?"

Cuffy. She hadn't called him that in years. Not since they were young. She called him "daddy," or "honey," or "fool," or sometimes even "Sportcoat," a name she despised. But rarely Cuffy. That was something from long ago. A different time.

"Everything's right as rain," he said cheerfully.

"Yet so much has gone wrong," she said.

"Not a bit," he said. "Everything is skippy now. It's all fixed. 'Cept that Christmas Club money. You can fix that."

She smiled and gave him the look. He'd forgotten Hettie's "look": her smile of understanding and acceptance that said, "All intangibles are forgiven, I accept them and more—your faults, your dips and turns, everything, because our love is a hammer forged at the anvil of God and not even your most foolish, irrational act can break it." That look. Sportcoat found it unsettling.

"I been thinking about back home," she said.

"Oh, that's old-time stuff," he said, waving his hand.

She ignored that. "I was thinking about them moonflowers. Remember how I used to go through the woods and gather up moonflowers? The ones that blossom at night? I was crazy about them things. I loved the way they smell! I've forgotten those things!"

"Oh, that ain't nothing," he said.

"Oh, c'mon! The way them things smell. How could you forget?"

She stood, clasping her hands near her chest, emboldened with the enthusiasm of love and youth, a way of being he'd long forgotten. That attachment was so long ago it seemed like it had never happened. The newness of love, the absolute freshness of youth. He was startled but tried to hide it by making a "pfffft" noise with his lips. He wanted to turn away, but he couldn't. She was so pretty. So young.

She sat back down onto the sink and, noticing his expression, leaned forward and touched his forearm playfully. He didn't move, but frowned: he was afraid to give in to the moment.

She sat up straight again, serious now, all playfulness gone. "Back home when I was little, I used to walk through the woods gathering up moonflowers," she said. "My daddy warned me off it. You know how he was. A colored girl's life wasn't worth two cents. And he wanted me to go to college and all. But I liked adventure. I was about seven or eight years old, jumping around the woods like a rabbit, having my fun, doing what I was told not to do. I had to search out quite a distance to find them flowers. I was deep out there one day and heard some yelling and hollering and jumped out of sight. The yelling was so loud and I got curious, so I crept up on it and who do I see but you and your daddy lumbering. Y'all was sawing a big old maple tree with a crosscut saw."

She paused, remembering. "Well, *he* was sawing it. He was drunk and you was a little bitty thing. And he was swinging you back and forth like a rag doll, working that crosscut saw to death, sawing at that tree."

She chuckled at the memory.

"You done your best, but you got tired. Back and forth you went and finally you dropped off. And your daddy was so drunk he loosed his end of the saw and stepped to you hard. He picked you up with one hand and hollered at you in a way that I never forgot. He didn't say but two words."

"'Saw on,'" Sportcoat said sadly.

Hettie sat thoughtfully a moment.

"Saw on," she said. "Imagine that. Talking to a child that way. There is nothing on this earth so low as a mother or father who treats their child cruel."

She scratched her jaw thoughtfully. "The world was just becoming clear to me then. Seeing how we lived under the white folks, how they treated us, how they treated each other, their cruelty and their phoniness, the lies they told each other, and the lies we learned to tell. The South was hard."

She sat and pondered a minute, and scratched her long, lovely shin. "'Saw on,' he said. Hollering at a little bitty boy. A boy doing a man's job. And he was a drunk his own self."

Staring at him, she said softly, "And despite all that, you had so much talent."

"Oh, them old-time days is good and gone," he said.

She sighed and gave him that look again, one of patience and understanding, one he'd known since they were both children. For a moment, the smell of fresh red earth seemed to float into his nostrils, and the aroma of spring flowers, evergreen pine, cucumber tree, sweetgum, spicebush, goldenrod, foamflowers, cinnamon ferns, asters, and then the overwhelming smell of moonflower drifted into the air. He shook his head, thinking he was drunk, because at that moment, lying amidst the junk of a basement boiler room of the battered Watch Houses in South Brooklyn, he felt as if he had drifted back to South Carolina, and he saw Hettie sitting atop her father's pony in her backyard, patting its neck, the pony standing near her daddy's garden, the tomatoes, the squash and collard greens. Hettie looking so tall and young and pretty, gazing out over her daddy's beautiful yard full of plants.

Hettie closed her eyes and raised her head, sniffing the air. She said, "Now you can smell it, can't you?"

Sportcoat remained silent, afraid to admit that he could.

"You used to love the smell of plants," she said. "Any plant. You could tell every plant, one from the other, just by its smells. I loved that about you. My Plant Man."

Sportcoat waved his hand in the air. "Oh, you talk of old things, woman."

"Yes I do," she said wistfully, staring out over his head. She seemed to be looking at something far away. "Remember Mrs. Ellard? The old white lady I used to work for? I ever tell you about why I left her?"

"'Cause you gone to New York."

She smiled sadly. "You're just like the white man. You change every story to suit your purpose. Listen to me for a change."

She rubbed her knee as she began her story.

"I was fourteen years old when I started looking after Mrs. Ellard. I cared for her for three years. There wasn't nobody she trusted more than me. I made her food, did her little exercises and things with her, gave her all her medicines the doctor gived her. She was very sick when I come on, but I had nursed white folks since I was twelve, so I knowed my business. Mrs. Ellard wouldn't go to the doctor unless I went with her. She wouldn't move till I come in the house in the morning. She wouldn't go to bed at night unless I tucked her in. I knew all her little ins and outs. She had a good heart. But her daughter was something. And her daughter's husband, he was the devil.

"That husband come to me one day saying some things was missing from the house. I asked what these things was and he got mad and said I was backtalking him and owed him eleven dollars. He had a fit about that eleven dollars. He said, 'I'm gonna take it out your next pay.'

"Well, I knew what that meant. The old woman was dying, see, and they wanted me out. I had just got paid when he accused me of stealing that eleven dollars and I only made fourteen dollars a week, so I gave two weeks' notice. But the daughter said, 'Don't tell my mother. She'll be upset about you leaving and she's dying and it'll make her feel worse.' She promised me my pay and a little extra to keep quiet on it. So I agreed.

"Well, I seen what they was doing. They didn't know more about caring for poor Mrs. Ellard than a dog knows a holiday. They complained about her, throwed things into her food which she wasn't supposed to eat, let her lay in her own filth, and forgot to give her medicine and all them things. I was just a teenager, but I knowed it was trouble. However the knife fell, I knew where the sharp end was gonna land, so I made ready to leave.

"About three days before my time was up, I come into the room to feed Mrs. Ellard and she started crying. She said, 'Hettie, why you leaving me?' I knew then that the daughter had spit out a lie. The doorknob hadn't bumped me in the back when that worthless daughter was up in my face pretending to be mad with me for telling her mother I was leaving. I knew that meant I had just worked two weeks for nothing. I knew right then whatever little pay I was supposed to get, well . . . that was gone, see."

She shrugged. "I reckon the daughter's husband put her up to all the devilment. He was as smart as his wife was simple. I could have never thought up such a rotten business myself. I would be ashamed to even think of it. Firing me over eleven dollars. The truth is, he could've said I stole one dollar or a thousand dollars. It didn't matter. He was white, so his word was the gospel. Nothing in this world happens unless white folks says it happens. The lies they tell each other sound better to them than the truth does when it comes out of our mouths.

"That's why I come to New York," she said. "And if you recall, you didn't want me to go. You was so drunk in them times you didn't know whether you was coming or going. Nor what I gone through from day to day. We had to leave the South or I was gonna kill somebody. So I come here. I worked day's work up here three years, waiting for you to get the courage to come. And you finally did."

"I did keep my promise," he said feebly. "I did come."

Her smile disappeared, and a familiar misery climbed into her face.

"Back home you gave life to things nobody paid the slightest attention to: flowers and trees and bushes and plants. These was things that most men stepped out on. But you . . . all the plants and flowers and miracles of God's heart—you had a touch for them things, even when you was drinking. That's who you was back home. But here . . ."

She sighed.

"The man who come here to New York wasn't the man I knowed in South Carolina. In all the years we been here, ain't been a plant in that house of ours. Not a green thing hung from the ceiling nor the wall, other than what I brung in from time to time."

"I got sick when I first come here," Sportcoat said. "My body broke down."

"Course it did."

"That's right. I had operations and all, don't you remember?"

"Course I do," she said.

"And my stepmomma—"

"I know all about your stepmother. I know everything: how she showed out to Jesus every Sunday and lived like a devil the rest of the week . . . doing improper things to you when you was but a wee child. Everything she ever done to you was wrong. The habits you acquired was put on you by the very folks who should have helped you be a better person. That's why you like Deems so much. He come down that same road. That boy was beat up bad, grinded down from the day he was slapped to life."

Sportcoat listened in stunned silence. There was a hammering sound in his ears and he glanced around the room but saw nothing move. Could that hammering be his own insides? The sound of his own heart beating? He felt as if part of him were splitting apart, and within his old self, the person he once was, the young man of physical strength with a wide-eyed thirst for wisdom and knowledge, had suddenly sat up, opened his eyes, and gazed around the room.

His head ached. He reached down toward the side of the couch, groping for the jug bottle, but it wasn't there.

"Isn't it something," Hettie said softly, "what ol' New York really is? We come here to be free and find life's worse here than back home. The white folks here just color it different. They don't mind you sitting next to 'em on the subway, or riding the bus in the front seat, but if you asks for the same pay, or wants to live next door, or get so beat down you don't wanna stand up and sing about how great America is, they'll bust down on you so hard pus'll come out your ears."

She thought a moment.

"'The Star-Spangled Banner,'" she scoffed. "I never did like that old lying, lollygagging, hypocritical, warring-ass drinking song. With the bombs bursting in air and so forth."

"My Hettie wouldn't talk this way," Sportcoat sputtered. "You ain't my Hettie. You's a ghost."

"Stop wasting what's left of your sorry-ass life with your shameful fear of the dead!" she snapped. "I ain't no ghost. I'm *you*. And stop goin' 'round telling people I would have loved my funeral. I hated it!"

"It was a beautiful funeral!"

"Our cheap death shows make me sick," she said calmly. "Why don't folks in church talk about life? They hardly ever talk about the birth of Jesus Christ in church. But they never get tired of singing and reveling in Jesus's death. Death is just one part of life. Jesus, Jesus, Jesus, all day long, the death of Jesus."

"You the one that's always hollering about Jesus! And how he gave you his cheese!"

"I holler about Jesus's cheese because Jesus could baptize shit into sugar! Because if I didn't have Jesus and his cheese, I'd kill somebody. That's what Jesus did for me for sixty-seven years. He kept me sane, and on the right side of the law. But he run out of gas, sweetheart. He got tired of me. I don't blame Him, for the hate in my heart done me in. I couldn't see the man I loved so much, my Plant Man, stand by the window in our apartment sucking on crab legs and looking at the Statue of Liberty outside our window chatting about nothing, when I knowed all he wanted was for me to go back to bed so he could let a liquor bottle suck his guts out the minute I gone to sleep again. The evil I felt at that moment was enough to kill us both. So instead, I walked into the harbor. And I left myself in God's hands."

For the first time in his life, Sportcoat felt something inside him breaking up.

"Is you happy now? Where you live now, Hettie? Is you happy there?"

"Oh, stop whimpering like a dog and be a man."

"You ain't got to insult me. I know who I am."

"Just 'cause you dragged Deems outta the water don't mean nothing. He was led to ruination by them that raised him, not you."

"I ain't frettin' about him. I'm worried about that Christmas Club money. The church wants their money. I can't pay them back. I ain't got nothing to live on myself."

"There you go again. Blaming somebody else for your troubles. The police wouldn't be circling around the church now if you hadn't got drunk!"

"It wasn't my fault Deems started selling poison!"

"At least he ain't destroying hisself by drinking hisself to death!"

"G'wan, woman! Leave me be. G'wan. Get along now!"

"I can't," she said softly. "I'd like to. That's the thing. You got to let me."

"Tell me how."

"I don't know how. I ain't that smart. All's I know is, you got to be right. To let me go, you got to be right."

A half hour later, Rufus walked into the room carrying a bologna sandwich, a can of Coke, and two aspirins. He found Sportcoat sitting up on the battered basement couch, the quart of King Kong moonshine in his lap.

"You ought to eat some food before you hit that Kong, Sport."

Sportcoat glanced at him, looked down at the quart bottle, then back at Rufus.

"I ain't hungry."

"Eat some, Sport. You'll feel better. You can't lay around and talk to yourself like you is two-headed for the rest of your life. Never seen a man lay on a couch and go back and forth like you done. You drunk already?"

"Rufus, can I ask you something?" Sportcoat asked, ignoring the question.

"Surely."

"Back home, where did your folks live?"

"Back home in Possum Point?"

"Yeah."

"We lived where you lived. Down the road."

"And what did your people do?"

"Worked shares. Same as yours. Working for the Calder family."

"And Hettie's people?"

"Well, you know more than me."

"I can't remember."

"Well, they was working shares with the Calders, too, for a while. Then Hettie's daddy moved off from working shares and he bought that little piece of land back there near Thomson Creek. Hettie's family was forward-thinking folks."

"Are they still living?"

"I don't know, Sport. She was your wife. You wasn't in touch with them?"

"Not after we moved up here. They never liked me much."

"They're long gone, Sport. Forget 'em. Hettie was the youngest, to my recollection. The parents died out long ago. Most of the rest likely left out Possum Point. Gone to Chicago or Detroit maybe. They didn't come here, I know that. Hettie might have some kin left down there some-place. Some cousins, maybe."

Sportcoat sat in silence a moment. Finally he said, "I miss the old country."

"Me too, Sport. You wanna eat? You don't want that Kong in your tummy without no food."

Sportcoat unscrewed the top of the quart bottle of liquor, raised it, then paused, the bottle poised in the air, and asked, "Tell me, Rufus. When you come up here, how old was you?"

"What's this, Sport? Sixty-four questions? I was forty-six."

"I was fifty-one," Sportcoat said thoughtfully.

"I come up three years before you," Rufus said. "In fact, I was the third member of Five Ends to come up here from down south. The first was my brother Irving. Then Sister Paul, her daughter Edie, and her husband. Then me and my late wife, Clemy. Then Hettie come up. Sister Paul was already here when me and Clemy and Hettie come. You was last."

"Lemme ask you. When y'all started building Five Ends, what did Hettie do?"

"Other than setting around pining for you? Well, she did day's work for white folks during the week. On weekends, she dug out the church's foundation. It was mostly me and Hettie and Edie, them two women at first. Sister Paul and her husband, they done a little. Sister Paul did. Reverend Chicksaw, her husband, he weren't too fond of digging. Then the Eye-talian came with his men. And some other folks showed up later. Sister Gee's folks. And the Cousins' parents. But it was the Eye-talian that got it going good. After he come, that freed us up. That's when Hettie made that big yard out behind the church that's all weeds now. She wanted a big garden back there. She said you was gonna come up and fill it with all sorts of collards and yams and even some special kind of flower, something you can see in the dark, I forget what's it called now . . ."

Sportcoat felt shame climb into his face. "Moonflowers," he said.

"That's right. Moonflowers. Course you didn't come up for three years. And you was sick when you come up. Plus who got time to make a garden? You can't grow nothing in New York."

Rufus stood above Sportcoat, still holding the sandwich. "This thing's gonna grow ears, Sport. You want it or not?"

Sportcoat shook his head. The sound of hammers banging in his brain had returned. He wished it would stop. With a sigh, he stared at the jug of King Kong in his lap. *Booze*, he thought. *I chose booze over my Moonflower.*

He reached over the armrest and picked up the bottle cap. He gently put it on the bottle, screwed it closed slowly, then lifted the bottle off his lap and placed it carefully on the floor.

"Where'd you say Sister Paul was?" he asked.

"Out in Bensonhurst. Near the hospital where Sausage and Deems is."

Rufus eyed the bottle of King Kong. "If you ain't sipping, I'll do the dipping," he said. He reached down and picked up the bottle, took a deep sip, then turned to hand the bottle to Sportcoat.

But the old man was already out the door and gone.

21

NEW DIRT

POTTS DROVE PAST THE ELEPHANT'S BOXCAR THREE TIMES, checking the empty alleys and the nearby streets. He did it both as a precaution and to telegraph his arrival. It was early evening, and at this hour pedestrians at the edge of the Cause Houses were sparse. There was little need to worry about lookouts. In the old days, even kids playing stickball on the docks would interrupt their game to send one of their number dashing off, and the news of a cop's arrival traveled to the mobsters running card games and loan sharks faster than any telephone.

Today there were no kids playing near the beaten, deserted docks, he noticed, and from the look of things there hadn't been for a while. Still, it was never a good idea to surprise the Elephant, so he did the exercise anyway, circling the block three times before turning onto the dock where the boxcar lived. He let the cruiser drift slowly onto the dock, then stopped at the door of the boxcar and let the car idle. He sat behind the wheel several minutes, waiting.

He had come alone. He had to. His suspicions about his young partner, Mitch, the lieutenant at the Seven-Six, and the captain above him were just too great. He didn't blame them for being on the take. If they wanted to climb up the greasy payoff pole, nipping a bit here and there from the family, looking the other way while the crooked bums ran their rackets, that was their business. But three months short of retirement, Potts saw no reason to risk his own pension. He was glad he'd stayed clean in his career, especially now, because a shooting like the one at Vitali Pier three days ago could touch off a drug war or a department political fight. Both were traps that no cop near retirement wanted to be in the vicinity of. You stick your foot in it and before you know it you're on your own, in the wilderness all by your lonesome, broke self, wondering where your pension went, all boiled up on Benzedrine and coffee, waiting for the political hacks at PBA to come cut you loose, which was like waiting for a herd of crocodiles.

Dirt, he thought bitterly, staring through the windshield. Like the beautiful cleaning woman, Sister Gee, from the church said. *"You and I got the same job. We clean dirt."* And dirt it was, he thought. And not just any dirt. New dirt surfacing. He could smell it, feel it coming, and it was big, whatever it was. The Cause was changing, he could see the transformation everywhere. It was 1969; the New York Mets, once the laughingstock of Major League Baseball, would win the World Series in a week. America had landed a man on the moon in July, and the Cause was falling apart. *1969. I'm gonna call it*, he thought bitterly. *This is the year the Cause falls to bits.* He could see the disintegration: old black tenants who had come to New York from the South decades ago were retiring or moving out to Queens; the lovable old drunks, bums, shoplifters, prostitutes, low-level harmless habitual criminals who had once brought him laughs and even solace in his long days as a patrolman and detective, were going, going, and soon to be gone, moving away, dying, disappearing, locked up. Young girls who had once waved at him had matured into unwed drug-addict mothers. A few had fallen into prostitution. Kids who used to joke with him on the way home from school as he patrolled in his car, pulling out trombones from instrument cases and blasting horrible music at his cruiser as it rolled past while he laughed, had vanished—the city was cutting music from the schools, someone said. Kids who had once bragged about their baseball games had become sullen and silent, the baseball fields empty. Just about every young kid who had once waved now walked the other way when his cruiser appeared. Even his old friend Dub Washington, the hobo he had peeled off curbs around the neighborhood on countless cold nights, was worn by the change. He'd seen Dub two days ago and the old wino bore awful news. He'd picked up Dub the day after the Vitali Pier shooting, just routine, his usual once-a-month task of hauling him to nearby Sisters of Mercy on Willoughby Avenue, where the kind Catholic nuns fed him and let him shower and sent him on his way. Dub was harmless and always fun, a wonderful aficionado of city news: he claimed to be the only one in the Cause Houses who read the *New York Times* every day. But that day Potts found the old man grim and shaken.

"I seen something bad," Dub said.

"Where?" Potts asked.

"Down at Vitali Pier. Two old fellers walked into a hot mess."

Dub explained what he'd seen. Young kids. A girl shooter. Two old men. Two young men. Two of them dropped. A third, maybe a fourth, fell into the harbor.

"Who were they?" Potts asked.

"Sportcoat was one," Dub said. "Hot Sausage the other."

That did it, Potts thought. That would wrap it up. He'd spent two weeks seeking information about the old man. Nobody knew anything, of course. They all deflected. Leave it to good old Dub to come up with some answers. It was old-time police work: an old source, developed over the years, paying off. There were puzzles here, of course, but as it worked out, Sportcoat apparently got the back end of what he'd delivered on the front. Of course he did. Don't these stories always end up that way? He'd tried to warn Sister Gee.

Still, there were questions. Was this a drug war? Or just payback to even things out with the old man and that was the end of it? He was just not sure.

He'd taken Dub to the sisters and then sought a follow-up with the two shooting victims out at Maimonides Medical Center in Borough Park. For some reason, his request had been delayed several days. By then, the fourth person present at the shooting was assumed to be dead in the harbor, the body yet to appear. The girl hit man, if that's what she was, had long fled.

This borough and this goddamned department, he thought bitterly, *are changing too fast for me. They're both worse than they ever were.*

The new normal in the old Brooklyn, he decided, was heroin. There was so much money in it. It was unstoppable. How long would it take before the drugs plaguing the Negro in the Cause Houses would spread past the district to the rest of Brooklyn? Today it was the Negroes in the Cause and a few Italians from the surrounding blocks. Tomorrow, he thought . . .

He was irritated and felt the need to move. He opened the cruiser's door and got out, leaving the engine running. He leaned one arm on the roof of the car and the other on the top of the open car door. From that position, he could see the boxcar in front of him, its dock, and Five Ends Baptist Church just a block away, easily seen above the high weeds of the bare lot next door. It had never occurred to him that the boxcar and the church, both located at the barren edges of the Cause Houses, were within sight of each other. One could go directly from one building to the next, they were so near each other. Yet they were from two worlds. The boxcar of the proud Elefante family—old Guido, who staggered around with a gimpy arm and leg after his stroke, suffered while doing twelve years in Sing Sing for keeping his mouth shut, along with his slick, closed-mouthed kid, Tommy, and the strange wife who wandered the lots looking for junk plants. And then the proud Negroes in their dilapidated old church with the gorgeous woman leader who loved dirt. He couldn't get her out of his mind. Sister Gee. Veronica Gee. Even the name sounded wonderful. Veronica. Sister Veronica. Like the Veronica in the Bible who offered Jesus her veil to wipe his face with as he bore the cross to Calvary. Glorious. She could wipe his face with her cloth anytime. He sighed. He imagined she was at work right now, her dark, regal face bent in concentration, dusting the halls of the handsome brownstone across the street from Rattigan's, or maybe cleaning some snot-nosed kid's toilet or dusting off a chandelier and thinking about all the things that dirt represented. *"You and I got the same job,"* she'd said to him. *"We clean dirt."*

I need cleaning myself, he thought. *If I let her clean me the rest of my life, maybe I'd have a chance at happiness.* But why would she bother?

He slammed the door of the cruiser and headed toward the boxcar just as Tommy Elefante emerged, hands in his pockets. He knew Elefante had spotted him on his first pass.

"What brings you to my dock, Potts?" Elefante said.

"Loneliness."

"Yours or mine?"

"Stop complaining, Tommy. At least you're rich."

Elefante laughed. "That brings a lump to my throat, Potts."

Now it was Potts's turn to laugh.

There were three makeshift stairs to the doorway where Elefante stood, a normal-sized door cut into the frame of the railroad car. Elefante took a seat on the top step, above him. Potts noted that Elefante had carefully closed the door behind him. Clearly, Potts thought, he wasn't invited inside.

Elefante seemed to read that thought. "I got a Ferrari inside," he said, nodding at the door behind him. "I only let my closest friends see it."

"How'd you get it in there?"

"Prayer. And insurance. The only two things a good Catholic ever needs."

Potts smiled. He'd always liked Tommy Elefante. Tommy was like the father—but with words. Silent as old Guido was, there was a grim good-ness to the old man, an honesty and sense of humor that Potts, despite himself, always appreciated. Both men—the cop at the bottom, the mobster at the top—looked out toward the harbor, watching the gulls skimming the water and gliding toward the Statue of Liberty shining in the dusky distance.

"I haven't parked my duff on this step in twenty years," Potts said.

"I didn't know you ever did."

"I talked to your father a lot in the old days."

"Got any more lies?"

"I broke his six-words-a-day limit a couple of times. I ever tell you the story about how I met him?"

"If there's a story," Elefante said, "it's one-sided."

"I'd walked a beat for six years, and finally they gave me my first squad car," Potts chuckled. "It must have been, oh, 1948. There was a tip that old Guido Elefante, our local smuggler, just got out of jail, had a ship-ment of illegal cigarettes coming through his boxcar. On a certain night, at a certain time. You know the drill: Buy the cigarettes cheap in North Carolina. Pull the tags. Add new ones. Sell 'em at fifty percent profit."

"Is that how they did it?"

Potts ignored the remark and continued. "They sent a squad down to bust the operation wide open. They were tired of him, I guess. Or maybe he hadn't greased somebody. Whatever the case, we had three squad cars and a sergeant. It must have been three or four in the morning. We swooped in here all piss and vinegar, lights flashing, making noise, the works. I was young and bothered in those days. Gung ho. Still feeling my oats from the war. Finally had my own squad car. A cherry top, they called it. I was just so hot.

"We kicked in the door and got nothing. The place was dark. Guido was obviously home sleeping. So we left. The other two cars pulled out first. I was the last to leave.

"We often rode solo in those days. So I got in my car, and as I do, I see this guy running off the dock. Where he was hiding, I don't know. I don't even know why he was running, but I figured he was running from me. So I cranked the squad car to get him, and damn if the car wouldn't start. No kidding. That's the first thing they tell you: 'Don't shut the car off.' So now I'm cooked, being a rookie. So I didn't radio ahead to the other two cars there was a suspect on foot. Instead I took off on foot after the guy.

"He was moving, but I was young then. I almost had him at Van Marl and Linder, but then he got an extra gear somewhere and pulled away and got a few yards on me. At the corner of Slag and Van Marl, I was gaining on him. Then in the middle of the intersection, the gobshit turned around and pulled a gun on me. Pulled it outta nowhere. He had me dead to rights.

"And then this truck comes outta nowhere about forty miles an hour. Boom—ran him down in the intersection. Killed him on the spot.

"The truck driver said, 'I never saw the guy. Never saw him.'

"He was right. It was dark. The guy jumped into the intersection outta nowhere. No way the driver could've seen him. It was an accident. It happened fast.

"The truck driver kept apologizing. I said it's okay. Hell, I was grateful. Anyway, I ran to a police phone around the corner to get help. When I came back, the truck was gone. All we could do was scrape the guy up off the ground and call the morgue.

"Well, about six months later, they sent me over here again, saying they'd got this guy Guido for transporting some tractors, or some such thing. So I drove over here in a rush again, this time alone. But instead of transporting crap, I see a big front-end loader over there where your storage place is now. It's a big tractor that scoops up the dirt and there's a guy in there working the thing. He's got only one good hand and one good leg. I get in close and look in the cab. It was the guy who was driving that truck.

"I said, 'You're the truck driver!'

"He didn't miss a beat. He said, 'I never saw the guy. If you hadn't shut your motor off, the whole thing would've never happened.'"

Potts chuckled. "I think that was one of the two or three things Guido ever said to me."

Elefante tried to stifle a grin, but he couldn't help himself. "A lot of saints don't start out well, but they end that way."

"You saying he was a saint?"

"Not at all. But he never forgot a face. And he was loyal. Aren't saints loyal?"

"Speaking of saints," Potts said. He pointed to Five Ends church. "Know anybody there?"

"I see 'em from time to time. Nice people. Never bother anybody."

"I seem to recall a lady from there died in the harbor a couple of years ago."

"Nice lady. Took a swim. Can't blame her, really."

"That happened after I got transferred to the One-Oh-Three in Queens," Potts said.

"I never did hear how that movie ended," Elefante said.

"It didn't end well."

"Why's that?"

Potts was silent a moment. "I'm retiring in three months, Tommy. I'll be outta your hair."

"Me too."

"How's that?"

"Doesn't matter. I'm gone in about that time. Less if I can. I'm selling this place."

"You in trouble?"

"Not at all. I'm retiring."

Potts ate that one for a long minute. He looked over his shoulder at Elefante. He was tempted to say "Retiring from what?" He'd heard criminals declare they would retire all the time. But Elefante was different. A smuggler, yes. Effective, yes. But a bad criminal? Potts wasn't sure what that was anymore. Elefante was surly, clever, unpredictable. Never moved the same thing twice in a short time period. Never seemed to get too greedy. Never moved drugs. He kept his storage place and normal shipments from his boxcar to cover his tracks. He greased the cops like the rest, but with an instinct for survival, and—Potts had to admit it— decency. He could smell a young, hungry cop, and could sniff out a clean one too. He never framed cops or cornered those on payola. He rarely asked for favors. It was just business to him. He was smart enough never to try to grease Potts or any of the few square cops Potts knew at the Seven-Six. That said a lot about Elefante.

Still, Elefante was part of the family, and they did some terrible things. Potts tried to ferret out the difference between an unfair world and a terrible one. Thinking about it confused him. What difference did it make if a guy stole a dozen refrigerators and sold them for five thousand bucks as opposed to a guy who sold fifty thousand bucks' worth of re- frigerators and changed the tax code to help him make eighty thousand? Or a dope-dealing bum whose heroin destroyed entire families? Which one to turn a blind eye to? If any? *I ought to be an ostrich*, he thought bitterly. *'Cause I don't give a damn. I'm in love with a dirt woman. And she doesn't know my heart.*

Through the blisters of thought, he saw Elefante watching him. "I hear guys say they'll retire all the time," he said finally.

"You never heard it here."

"Is it hard on you out here?" Potts asked. "With all the changes?"

There was the slightest twitch on Elefante's eyebrow. "A little. How about you?"

"Same here. But guys in my business retire."

"They do in mine too."

"How? Rigor mortis?"

Elefante smirked. "What do you want from me, Potts? You waiting on me to get sore eyelids from blinking too much? I want out. I'm tired. I been working all my life. You know an oak tree doesn't produce acorns until they're over fifty years old?"

"So you wanna be an oak tree?"

"I wanna be a guy that every cop in the Seven-Six doesn't come see twice a year like the dentist."

"I came because I heard you want to see me."

"Who told you? I didn't call."

"You're not the only one who's got birds crowing in the Seven-Six, Tommy. But if you're Tarzan, I'm Jane. I'm hearing things I don't understand about a case. I'm hoping you'll clear them up."

"Is it really about a case?"

"Goddammit, just because everyone in this precinct wants to skim his neighbor for a piece of bread doesn't mean I'm the same as them. Yes, it's really about a case. My last case, if I'm lucky. I come down here to talk to you square. Maybe you can clear some things up for me. Maybe I can do the same for you. Does that sound good? Then we can retire together."

"We got competing interests, Potts. How exactly I'm getting out is none of your affair. But I'm getting out. I already told you too much."

"Don't get smart. I already know too much."

"I'm not getting smart. In my business, trouble creeps up on you like an old charge account. So you work it out with the guys who won't knife you in the back and hope the rest that you owe have amnesia. That's how it works. But where our interests connect, I'm interested in doing business."

"Fair enough."

"So what you got?"

"I got a dead kid at Vitali Pier. And two wounded. And an old man on the lam."

"Who's the guy?"

Potts looked at Elefante. "C'mon, Tommy."

"You ever think about it? That I might not know him?"

"He works for your mother, for Chrissake."

Elefante sighed. "Come up to street level, would ya? You know how she is. She's the same as she was when you first started kicking tail around here. She wanders around these empty lots looking for anything that doesn't smell like shit on a stick so she can stick it in my yard."

"What's wrong with that?"

"You see the neighborhood. It's not safe around here no more."

"Not even for her?"

"I don't know these new people, Potts. And I don't know that guy."

"He was in your house!"

"He wasn't. He was in the yard. For a few months. Maybe three months. Once a week. Sticking plants in the ground. Old guy. Called himself the Deacon. They call him Sport Jacket or something. He's good with plants. Can grow anything. Lots of families on my street used him."

"So what's he sticking a burner in Deems's chest for?"

"I don't know, Potts. I was gonna ask you."

"You sound like some guy at a peace conference, Tommy," Potts said, exasperated. "You're full of questions with no answers."

"And I'm telling you I don't know the guy. I said a few words to the guy in three months. He worked in the yard. He grew whatever weeds my mother told him to grow. She paid him a little cash and he cut out. He's a drunk. One of those guys who dies at twenty and is buried at eighty. He's a church guy. A deacon over at the church there."

"What does a deacon do?" Potts asked.

"You're the second person that's asked me that this week. How the fuck do I know? They sing songs, maybe, or give homilies to donkeys, or sleep like snails, or slobber while they collect church money and give out the hymnals."

"So he drinks and grows plants and goes to church," Potts said. "So far, he sounds Catholic."

Elefante laughed. "I always liked you, Potts. Even though you were a headache."

"Were?" Potts said.

"You said you're getting out."

"I am."

"Maybe you can do me a favor then. 'Cause I'm getting out too."

"Are you lying, exaggerating, or just thinking big?"

"I'm telling you, I really am."

"If you're trying to use that as an excuse to burn yourself out of whatever hole you've dug, it ain't gonna work, Tommy. I hear that all the time."

"But not from me."

Potts was silent. Elefante, he thought, sounded serious.

"Honest to God, Potts. I am getting out. My mother, she's getting up there. And I'm working on . . . I'm . . . can you keep a secret? It'll brighten your day. I'm moving to the Bronx."

"What for? Their baseball team stinks."

"That's my business. But I don't wanna leave no debts behind. I want out clean. You know the people I work with. You know how they are."

"If you're worried about that, you should've picked better friends. Your buddy Joe Peck's in trouble, by the way."

Elefante was quiet a moment. "You wired?" he asked.

Potts snorted. "The only wire I wear is the one the captain uses to run up my ass. They hate me at the Seven-Six. Here's the truth, Tommy, take it or leave it: If you're a cop, be a cop. If not, then be a square like me. Or be a bum like Peck. Or one of these dope runners selling crap to these kids. There's no in between. The Gorvinos are so busy selling dope to the Negroes with one hand and saluting the flag with the other they can't see what's coming. Their kids are gonna be dope addicts. You'll see. You think the Negroes around here are stupid? They got guns and like money too. It's not the good old days, Tommy. It's not like it was."

Potts felt his anger surging and tried to control it. "I'm not going out like the old guys before me," he said. "Mad and pissed and screwed." He glanced at the church and again he thought of Sister Gee. At the moment she seemed distant. A far-off dream. Then he said it.

"I think it's a woman," he said. "Not your gardener. If it was me, I'd move to the Bronx for a woman."

Elefante didn't reply.

Potts changed the subject. "The shooting at the pier. You know anything about that girl?"

Elefante shook his head.

Potts sighed. "There's an old bum I know who stays around the paint factory at Vitali Pier," he said. "He more or less lives there. You know him. Dub, they call him."

"I seen him around."

"Old Dub was sleeping off a binge that night, right beneath the first-floor window, fighting it out with the rats. He woke up to some talking on the dock. Peeked out the window and saw what happened. Saw the whole thing. I picked him up for vagrancy and a shower the next day. For a four-dollar bottle of wine, he spilled everything he saw."

"Was it good wine?"

"It was my four dollars. Damn good wine."

"Then it was money well spent."

Potts sighed. "Now I've shared my song, you got one to share?"

"I can't do that, Potts. I don't mind kicking around a few scruples to make a living, but talking to the cops can make a guy keel over. And not from old age."

"I understand. But let me ask you this. There's a colored fella out in Bed-Stuy. Smart fella. Name of Moon. Bunch Moon. That name sound familiar?"

"It might."

"Do the Gorvinos know that name?"

"They oughta," Elefante said.

Potts nodded. That was enough. He placed his hat on his head. "If you're gonna retire, this would be a good time. Because when things get rolling, it won't be pretty."

"They're already rolling," Elefante said.

"See? I told you it won't be pretty. But the girl is."

"What girl?"

"Don't play dumb, Tommy. I'm giving you some skin here. It's a girl. A Negro girl. A shooter. A good one. For hire. From out of town. That's all I know. She's a looker. And she's got a name like a man. Shoots like a man too. Your buddy Peck oughta watch himself. Bunch Moon is ambitious."

"What's her name?"

"If I told you, I'd hate myself in the morning. Especially if I have to drag her out of the harbor."

"I got no bone to pick with any girl. What's in a name anyway?"

Potts stood up. This interview was finished. "When you retire to the Bronx, Tommy, would you send me a card?"

"I might. What you gonna do when you retire?"

"I'm going fishing. What about you?" Potts asked.

"I'm gonna make bagels."

Potts stifled a smile. "You're Italian, in case you forgot."

"*Grazie*, but since when did that monkey stop the show?" Elefante said. "I'll take what I can get. That's the thing when you get out and you're still breathing. Every day is a new world."

Potts glanced at Five Ends Baptist Church down the street. The lights were on. In the distance, he heard singing. Choir practice. He thought of a lovely woman sitting at the front of the choir pew, dangling her house keys in her hand as she sang. He sighed.

"I understand," he said.

22

281 DELPHI

THE BROWNSTONE AT 281 DELPHI STREET NEAR THE CORner of Cunningham Avenue sat hunched and alone, with weeded lots on both sides. It was the perfect defensive spot. Inside, on the second floor, Bunch Moon sat near a window, staring at the street below. From his position, he could see anyone who turned the corner and approached. Children played in the hulks of the cars on the street. It was an unusually warm October day, and the kids had opened the fire hydrant again. He made a note to pull his dilapidated pickup truck up to the hydrant later to let the kids make a few quarters washing it. There were a couple he had noticed, and they were almost ready for employment.

He opened the window and peered out, looking to the right, then left, then right again. The right was not a problem. He could see several blocks, clear down to Bedford Avenue. To the left was trickier. Delphi Street came to a T at the corner. He had wanted a house on a dead-end street. But when he first came to look for a secret meeting place on that deserted block, there were so many boarded-up, empty brownstones, he'd had his choice of several along that street, and he'd decided the block would work fine. He'd chosen 281 because it had a better view of approaching traffic than any other house. To the right he could see anyone coming down from Bedford for blocks. To the left, the T formed at an empty weeded lot, with several dilapidated houses to the left of the intersection that he could not see. To the right of that, within view, was an abandoned warehouse that he could only see part of. Whoever came down that side street from the right, if they came in a car, would be in sight for about ten feet before they turned onto Delphi Street and could make a rush up his steps. It wasn't ideal, but the spot worked. It was as close to a lookout spot as he could get without attracting attention from the cops. He rarely drove there; he usually took the subway. He always wore an MTA uniform, so the neighbors believed he was a transit worker as he moved in and out. Few of his crew or his employees who processed his raw heroin shipments knew about 281. It was safe. Still, he could never be too careful. Standing at the window, he took one long look in both directions.

When he was satisfied, he ducked his head back inside and closed the window. He sat down at his dining room table, glanced at the headlines of the *New York Times*, the *Daily News,* and the *Amsterdam News* that lay before him, then at the pretty young woman across the table. She was regarding her nails.

Haroldeen the Death Queen was in the same spot where Earl, that lowdown grizzle-faced stupid son-of-a-bitch snitch, had sat. She was working at her nails with a nail file. He stifled an impulse to curse at her and then said, "How'd you get here?"

"The bus."

"You ain't got a car?"

"I don't drive."

"How do you get around in Virginia?"

"That's my business."

"You fucked up bad. You know that, right?"

"I did my best. What happened was unavoidable."

"I ain't paying for that."

"I'll fix it. I need the money. I'm going to college."

Bunch snorted. "Why you wasting your talent?"

Haroldeen took that in silence as she continued to work on her nails. He neglected to mention that he'd taken advantage of her other "talents" when she was fourteen, living on a street just like this one with her mother, hauling everything they owned in shopping carts from place to place.

He continued. "The basement door leads to the backyard. At the end of the fence there, if you push on it, it's a gate. Leave here that way."

"All right," Haroldeen said.

"Where you staying?"

"With my mother in Queens."

"That ain't smart. For a college girl."

Haroldeen worked her nails in silence. He neglected to mention, she noted, that her mother was busy cooking heroin with baking soda, flour, and water in one of his processing houses out in Jamaica. He thought she didn't know. He also thought she didn't know that he'd taken advantage of her mother's "talents," too, back in the day, when her mother was young. But that, she thought bitterly, was how she'd survived. Pretending not to know. Pretending to be dumb. A dumb cutie. Fuck being dumb. She was done with it.

"I'm gonna study accounting," she said.

Bunch laughed. "You'd be better off learning to milk a camel. There's no money in that."

Haroldeen said nothing. She pulled a bottle of nail polish from her purse and started to paint her nails. She hadn't been comfortable with the hit on those two boys. They weren't grown-up hardened men like Bunch, men who knew the game and who had done so much to her when she was young and pretty beyond her years, with her long hair and milky brown skin and thick legs, wandering around with her shy, gentle mother who pushed their things about in a shopping cart after her father died, the guys squeezing her mother's tits for a quarter and letting dope dealers use Haroldeen as a whore and a lure to set up drug robberies. "Bunch saved us," her mother liked to say. But that was her mother's way of processing pain. It was the daughter who saved them, they both knew. The social worker who helped them said it best. Haroldeen had read the social worker's report after she left New York. "The daughter raised the mother," the lady wrote, "not the other way around."

Her saving came with a price. Every bit of hair on Haroldeen's pretty head, care of her handsome Dominican father and pretty African-American mother, had vanished. At twenty, she had been bald. Her hair just fell out one day. A result, she assumed, of the difficult life she had lived. She wore a wig now, and long sleeves to cover her back, shoulders, and upper arms, which were burned, care of a job that had gone horribly wrong two years ago. Nothing was certain now, except for her lovely apartment in Richmond and the medicine she occasionally ate at night to keep the howls of the men she killed out of her dreams. They were horrible sons of bitches—men who set upon one another with welding torches, scorched each other with hot irons, and poured Clorox into one another's eyes for the sake of dope; men who made their girlfriends do horrible things, servicing four or five or eight men a night, who made their women do push-ups over piles of dogshit for a hit of heroin until, exhausted, the girls dropped into the shit so the men could get a laugh. These were the men her mother allowed in her life. Her stay with her mother was more out of a sense of duty than anything else. She bought her mom some food, gave her a little money. But the two hardly spoke anymore.

"I'll make enough money in accounting. I'm a saver."

"How's your ma doing these days?" Bunch asked.

As if he didn't know, Haroldeen thought. She shrugged. "What's that got to do with the price of tea in China?"

"You sound like a college kid already. Can you count your fingers and toes too?"

Haroldeen considered this thoughtfully for a moment, then said, "I have to leave in two days. I'll finish by then. After that I'm heading home."

"What's the hurry?"

"I got another job in Richmond."

"What kind of job?"

"I don't ask your business," she said.

"I'm the one paying."

"I ain't seen a dime yet," she said. "Not even train fare."

Bunch pushed back from the table. "You're awful loose around the mouth for someone who fucked up bad."

Haroldeen bit her lower lip. "Those two old guys came outta no-where."

"I'm paying you to work through them kind of problems."

"I said I'll take care of it. I mean it."

Bunch sighed. How to keep this whole thing from toppling down—or worse, blowing up in his face? He'd tipped his hand to Peck now for sure.

"You sure there was nobody else down there at the pier?"

"Nobody I saw. Just the two young guys and the two old drunks."

"How about the people in the plaza? At the flagpole. They saw you, right? You were there for a week getting a line on Deems."

"I'm not going back there anyway. I'll take care of Deems and the old guy somewhere else."

"What are you, Agent 007? You gonna put on a fuckin' disguise? Deems is in the hospital. The old drunk, he's disappeared I heard."

"I told you I'd take care of it somewhere else."

"Where would that be? And how can I be sure?"

Haroldeen sat in silence, her face a mask. He had to admit, she was the most beautiful stone wall he'd ever seen. A cold fucking beauty. You never knew what you were looking at. She could play petulant beauty one moment and bright innocent teenager the next. She was his greatest discovery. He'd heard a rumor that when she had sex she barked like a dog. He remembered her faintly from his years of running wild, working his way up, but it was so long ago and she was so young. Maybe fourteen or fifteen? She didn't bark like a dog then. He would've remembered it. She said nothing. She didn't whimper, groan, or lose a breath. Even as a child, that pretty girl with the soft features was hard as a rock inside. Now, at twenty-nine, she could still pass for twenty, but if somebody looked close, the wrinkles at the corners of her eyes and around her ears suggested that maybe she was twenty-three, or even twenty-five. Was it that long ago that he had at her? Fourteen years? He couldn't remember.

She nodded at the newspapers on the table before him. "When I finish, you'll read about it. But I need my money."

"You ain't finished."

She glanced at him, and the lines of her face that had twisted into petulance when she talked about college were gone. Rather there was a grim coldness to the look, and he was glad, at that moment, that he'd insisted they meet at a place he suggested. She had certainly checked out his safe house and likely assumed that he, not she, was safe with backup, surrounded by his people, all of whom were close but none of whom she could see. The emptiness of the room was a warning to her that there was danger nearby, because death meant eyewitnesses, and the fewer witnesses the better. He sure she understood that the emptiness of this room in this old brownstone deep in Bed-Stuy, his country, meant her life was in danger, not his, though the truth was, there was no backup. No men surrounding 281 Delphi, not working the street, not in cars, not pretending to be neighbors, not driving past. Two eighty-one Delphi was safe because it was a secret. He wasn't sure she sensed that, but he decided it didn't matter. She wanted to collect her gold dust and split town on the first thing smoking, which is what he'd have wanted if he were in her shoes. Anyway, he had a revolver on the seat of the chair next to him. He needed no more eyeballs putting him and Haroldeen the Death Queen in the same place, not after Earl had fucked up so bad.

Discovering that Earl was a squealer had been a stroke of luck, a chance encounter with a black cop from the Seven-Six who told him, "You better tighten down." The knowledge had nearly dropped him. He trusted Earl more than anyone. What had made Earl, who once had balls, so squeamish? Was it the thought of killing off Joe Peck's distribution network and maybe taking down Peck himself and making their own that did it? Because Joe Peck was white? Or was it that church shit that Earl was always so weird about? *Why is the Negro,* he thought bitterly, *so scared of the white man? What's in their souls that makes them that way?* It had to be that church shit.

"Did you grow up in church, believing in Jesus?" he asked Haroldeen.

Haroldeen snorted. "Please."

He eyed her a moment, the grim stare, the gleaming eyes, the face that could soften into tenderness at the snap of a finger, inviting trust, then harden to ice. "I could use ten of you," he said.

"How about paying this one of me."

"I'll give you half now. Plus train fare. The other half when you're finished."

"How I'm gonna get the other half?"

"Pony express. Overnight mail. However you want it."

"I look that stupid?"

"I'll bring it myself. I'll drive it down."

"No thanks."

"Why not? Virginia ain't far. Unless you live in one of those places where the welcome mat's printed in Old English and they don't like niggers. If that's the case, I'll pretend I'm the milkman. Or the gardener. You oughta be familiar with gardeners."

She frowned. "I thought you said you didn't know much about what happened."

"Fuckups carry far, sister."

"All right. Gimme half now. I'll tell you where to send the rest after I'm done."

"I got a junkpile of shit now 'cause of you. I got Joe Peck on my ass. He'll be gunning for all my people. He'll try to switch out my people with his Uncle Tom niggers."

"I'll clean up my end," she said. "That's all I can tell you."

Bunch rose. He moved to the window, speaking with his back to her. "This is the last time you and I do business," he said. He glanced out the window and noticed a motorcycle puttering down the street, followed by a car, a GTO. But they were coming from the right, the safe side, in full view. Not down the side street, so they weren't dangerous. Still, he wondered: had he seen them before? He decided to watch to see if they circled the block, then saw the motorcycle throw on a turn signal before reaching the corner, and the girl was talking again, so he turned away.

"Where's my money?" she asked.

He nodded toward the dining room door. "Downstairs. At the back door, there's a cabinet there."

"Where's the back door?"

"Do they call it a back door because it's in the front?"

"Is it the basement back door, or the first-floor back door?"

That drew him from the front window. He marched to the dining room door and pointed down the stairs. They were on the second-floor landing. "Go all the way to the basement. Use the back basement door. Don't go out the front basement door. Don't go out the ground-floor front door. Go to the basement back door. Near that back door is a cabinet. Open the top drawer. There's an envelope in there. It's got half. And train fare."

"All right."

"We clear on who's who?"

"Deems and the Deacon. And the other guy."

"What other guy?"

"The old guy with the Deacon."

"I didn't say nothing about a third guy. I ain't paying you for no third guy."

"I don't care," she said. "He saw me."

She slipped down the stairs quickly and deftly. Bunch found himself watching her back, feeling a little regretful. Those stairs were creaky and she slipped down like a ghost, silent and fast, barely making a sound. That girl, he thought, had skills. He decided to watch her out the back window to make sure no neighbors spotted her exiting the yard—he didn't want her near him anymore. Then he remembered the car he'd seen through the front window and quickly stepped to it to check on the GTO. It was gone. It was safe.

At the basement back door, Haroldeen found the cabinet and removed the envelope. It was dark down there, so she held it to the sliver of light from a nearby small ground-level window to check its contents, then hastily stuck it in her jeans. From there, she removed her shoes, took the stairs two at a time up to the ground floor, unlocked the front door, then sprinted back to the basement, put on her shoes, exited through the back door, and stepped outside.

The yard was piled high with junk and trash and was full of weeds. She picked her way through it slowly, as if she weren't certain where she was going, then looked up.

Sure enough, Bunch was watching her through the open second-floor window, glaring.

That was all she needed to see. She turned and ran toward the back gate, as fast as she could, leaping over the piles of junk that lay in the way, making toward the gate at top speed.

Up on the second floor, Bunch saw her sprinting for the gate and heard the thunder of footsteps on his stairwell at the same time, and a sudden dread seized his insides. He glanced in panic to the seat of the chair next to his, several long feet away, where his gun lay. He was still looking when the door burst open and Joe Peck charged in bearing a revolver, followed by two other men, one of them with a shotgun.

Just before she reached the gate and heard the boom of gunshots, Haroldeen heard yelling and thought she heard someone scream, "You fucking black bitch!"

But she wasn't sure. She was out the back gate and gone.

23

LAST OCTOBERS

ON HIS THIRD DAY IN THE HOSPITAL, DEEMS AWOKE WITH
his arm in a cast and the familiar painful buzzing in his ears that made
his blood tingle and rush to his head. His hospital bed was tilted at a
slight angle, which prevented him from rolling onto his left shoulder and
further aggravating the injury. Not that he would. Every time he leaned
in that direction the pain across his back and down his spine was so
powerful he felt like throwing up, so lying on his right side was obliga-
tory. But it meant he couldn't turn away from any visitors that came.
Not that many did other than the cops and Sister Gee and a couple of
assorted "sisters" from Five Ends. He'd said nothing to them. Even Potts,
the old-time cop he remembered who used to come by to watch him
pitch baseball games from his squad car. He'd said nothing to Potts.
Potts was okay, but at the end of the day, Potts was just a cop. Deems's
problem was bigger than cops and stupid Five Ends people. He'd been
betrayed by somebody—probably Lightbulb, he guessed—and Beanie
was dead.

He shifted slightly to lie on his back, moving slowly, then reached for the cup of water that the nurses kept beside his bed.

Instead of a cup, a hand caught his, and he glanced up and saw the wrinkled face of Sportcoat standing above him.

He almost didn't recognize him for a moment. The old fool wasn't wearing his usual ragged, ugly sport coat from some era gone past. The plaid green-and-white one—the one that the old drunk wore for special occasions and church—used to bring howls of laughter from Deems and his friends every time they saw Sportcoat proudly strut out of Building 9 wearing it. The plaid sport coat looked like a walking flag draped around the old fart. Instead, the old man wore the blue pants and blue shirt of a Housing Authority worker and a porkpie hat. Clutched in his right hand was a homemade doll of some kind, a hideous-looking thing the size of a small pillow, brown with knitting material for hair and buttons stitched across the fabric to create a face. In his other hand was a small paper bag.

Deems nodded at the doll. "What's that for?"

"It's for you," Sportcoat said proudly. "Remember Dominic, the Haitian Sensation? He lives in our building. Old Dominic makes these. He says they're magic. They bring good luck. Or bad luck. Or whatever he wants 'em to. This here's a get-well one. He made it special for you. And this here"—he reached into the paper bag, squirming his hand inside the bag, and produced a pink ball—"I got for you myself." He held the ball out. "It's an exercise ball. Squeeze that," he said. "It'll make your pitching hand stronger."

Deems frowned. "What the fuck you doing here, man?"

"Son, you ain't got to use that filthy language. I come a long way to see you."

"You seen me. Now git."

"That ain't no way to talk to a friend."

"You want me to say thank you, Sport? Okay, thank you. Now get lost."

"I ain't come here for that."

"Well don't ask me my business. The cops been doing that for two days."

Sportcoat smiled, then placed the doll pillow at the edge of the bed. "I don't care none about your business," he said. "I care about mine."

Deems rolled his eyes. What was it about this old man that made him tolerant of his stupid bullshit? "What kind of business you got in this hospital, Sport? They make your grape here? Your King Kong? You and your drink. Deacon King Kong," he snickered. "That's what they call you."

Sportcoat ignored the insult. "Them names can't hurt me. I got friends in this world," he said proudly. "Two of 'em's in this hospital. They put Hot Sausage in here, too, you know that? Right on the same floor. Can you believe it? I don't know why they done that. I just come from him. He was digging at me the minute I walked in his room. Saying, 'If you wasn't chunking at me so bad, Sport, I'da never gone out there dressed like an umpire to bother Deems about that dumb ball game.' I said, 'Sausage, you can't deny the boy got a future in base—'"

"What the fuck are you talking about?" Deems said.

"Huh?"

"Shut your talking hole, you stupid motherfucker!"

"What?"

"Who wants to hear about you, you drunk bastard? You's a fuckup, man. You fucked up everything. Don't you ever get tired of hearing yourself talk? Deacon King Kong!"

Sportcoat blinked, feeling slightly cowed. "I already told you, your words can't hurt me, boy, for I ain't never done nothing wrong to ya. Other than care for you, a little bit."

"You shot me, ya dumb nigger."

"I don't recall none of it, son."

"Don't 'son' me, you shitface bitch! You fucked around and shot me. The only reason I didn't smoke your ass was because of my grandfather. That was my first mistake. Now Beanie's dead because of you—and Sausage, that lazy, stupid chickenshit plumber's-helper bitch. Two dumb-ass, old-time, donkey-ass idiots."

Sportcoat was silent. He looked down at his hands, holding the pink Spaldeen ball. "Ain't no cause for you to use them kind of words 'round me, son."

"Don't call me 'son,' you cockeyed, hundred-proof bitch bastard!"

Sportcoat looked at him oddly. Deems noted that the old drunk's face was unusually clear. Sportcoat's eyes, normally bloodshot, his eyelids, normally drooping and half-closed, were wide open. He was sweating, and his hands were shaking slightly. Deems also noticed, for the first time, that beneath the old drunk's Housing Authority shirt, Sportcoat, even as an old man, was thickly built around the chest and arms. He had never noticed that before.

"Has I wronged you, son?" Sportcoat said softly. "In all them times we played baseball and all. Me giving encouragement and all . . . in Sunday school, teaching you the good word."

"Get the fuck outta here, man. Get gone!"

Sportcoat puffed out his cheeks and released a long, drawn-out sigh. "All right," he said. "Just one more thing. Then I'll leave."

The old man shuffled to the door, stuck his head into the hallway, looked both ways, then closed the door tightly. He shuffled back to Deems's bed and leaned over him, to whisper something in his ear.

Deems snapped, "Get the fuck away—"

And then Sportcoat was on him. The old man lifted his knee quickly, pinned Deems's usable right arm to his body with it, and with his right hand, picked up the doll pillow on Deems's bed and rammed it onto Deems's upturned face.

Deems, pinned, couldn't move. He felt his air supply suddenly choke off. His head was pressed as in a vise. Sportcoat held firm, pressing down as Deems struggled, frantically gasping for air. Sportcoat spoke, slowly and calmly:

"When I was but a wee boy, my daddy did this to me. Said this would make me grow big and tough. He was an ignorant man, my daddy was. Mean as the devil. But he was chickenhearted when it come to the white man. He bought a mule once from a white man. That mule was sick when my daddy bought him. But the white told him that the mule couldn't die because he, a white man, had ordered it to live. Know what happened?"

Deems struggled, panicked, straining for air. There was none.

"My daddy believed him. He took that mule home. And sure as we setting here, that mule died. I told him not to do it, but he didn't listen to me."

Sportcoat felt Deems's struggles strengthen for a moment, then pressed the pillow down harder and continued speaking, his voice quiet, insistent, and frighteningly calm.

"See, my daddy thought I was too smart. He believed my mind was my enemy. So he pushed that pillow on my head to crush my mind. He wanted to make sure he was in control of my mind and my body. He was just like every white man I ever knowed who wanted power."

He tightened the pillow against Deems's face and felt Deems's strains grow desperate now; he arched his back off the bed, struggling to live. But Sportcoat didn't let up, pressing the pillow down even harder than ever; he continued talking:

"But then again, I can't rightly say that if a colored man was in a position of power, he wouldn't be the same."

He felt Deems's struggles grow wildly desperate now, the murmurs from beneath the doll pillow sounding like cat mewing, long ga-ga sounds, like the muffled bleating of a goat, then Deems's frantic antics slowed and the sounds grew weaker, but Sportcoat kept pressing down and continued speaking calmly:

"See, Deems, in them days, everything had been decided for you. You had to go along. You didn't even know that you were going along. You didn't know there was anything else to do. You never wondered about anything else. You was locked into a kind of thinking. It never occurred to you to do anything but what you was told. I never asked why I was doing something or why I wasn't doing something. I just did whatever I was told. So when my daddy did this to me, I didn't feel no wrong in it. It was just another natural thing in the world."

Deems's struggles ceased now. He'd quit fighting.

Sportcoat released the pillow, and the suction of Deems pulling air into his lungs sounded like the starting of a car, a long, loud whirring noise, followed by several choking gasps. Barely conscious, Deems tried to turn away but could not, as Sportcoat still had his head pinned under one powerful hand, the other hand still holding the pillow doll high.

Then the spell was released, and Sportcoat casually tossed the doll pillow onto the floor and, rising, removed his knee from Deems's right arm. "You understand?" he said.

But Deems didn't understand. He was still gasping for breath and struggling to stay conscious. He wanted to reach for the nurse call button, but his good arm, his right one, felt frozen from where Sportcoat had smashed it. His broken left arm was roaring in pain. The noise in his ears sounded like a screeching buzz. With a great effort, he reached with his right hand for the nurse call button, but Sportcoat slapped the hand away and suddenly grabbed Deems by the hospital gown with hands that were firm and veined from seven decades of pulling weeds, digging trenches, planting trees, opening bottles, yanking out toilets, tightening pliers, hauling steel beams, and driving mules. The hands wrenched him to a nearly sitting position with a firm, tight snatch that felt like steel claws, yanking Deems so hard that the force of the pulling caused Deems to squeal, and Deems saw Sportcoat inches away from his face. And from there, so close, he saw in the old man's face what he had felt down in the darkness of the harbor when the old man had yanked him to safety: the strength, the love, the resilience, the peace, the patience, and this time, something new, something he'd never seen in all the years he'd known old Sportcoat, the happy-go-lucky drunk of the Cause Houses: absolute, indestructible rage.

"Now I know why I tried to kill you," Sportcoat said. "For the life of goodness is not one that your people has chosen for you. I don't want that you should end up like me, or my Hettie, dead of sorrow in the harbor. I'm in the last Octobers of life, boy. I ain't got many more Aprils left. It's a right end for an old drunk like me, and a right end for you too that you die as a good boy, strong and handsome and smart, like I remembers you. Best pitcher in the world. Boy who could pitch his way outta the shithole we all has to live in. Better to remember you that way than as the sewer you has become. That's a good dream. That's a dream an old drunk like me deserves at the end of his days. For I done wasted every penny I had in the ways of goodness so long ago, I can't remember 'em no more."

He released Deems and flung him back against the bed so hard Deems's head hit the headboard and he nearly passed out again.

"Don't ever come near me again," Sportcoat said. "If you do, I'll deaden you where you stand."

24

SISTER PAUL

MARJORIE DELANY, THE YOUNG IRISH-AMERICAN RECEP-
tionist working at the Brewster Memorial Home for the Aged in Bensonhurst, was accustomed to the wide range of strange visitors strolling in
asking stupid questions. The amalgam of parents, kids, relatives, and
old friends who wandered into the lobby angling to get into the rooms,
and sometimes the pockets, of the home's permanent residents—the
aged, the dying, and the near dead—ran the gamut from gangsters to
lowdown bums to homeless children. She had a keen sense of humor
about the whole business and a large streak of compassion, despite having seen it all. But after three years on the job, even Marjorie was unpre-
pared for the unsightly elderly black man who ambled in wearing the
blue uniform of the New York City Housing Authority that afternoon.

His face was seized in a crooked smile. He seemed to have trouble
walking. He was sweating profusely. He looked, she thought, mad as a
hatter. If he weren't wearing the uniform, she would have had Mel, the
security guard, who sat near the door and spent his afternoons reading
the *Daily News* and nodding off, toss him. But she had an uncle who

worked for Housing, and he had several colored friends, so she let him amble to the desk. He took his time about it, peering around the lobby, seemingly impressed.

"Looking for Sister Paul," the old man mumbled.

"What's the name?"

"Paul," Sportcoat said. He leaned on the desk for support. He had a blasting headache, which was unusual. He was also exhausted, which was also unusual. He hadn't had a drink since he spoke to Hettie fourteen hours ago—though it felt like years ago. The effect of not drinking was enormous. He felt weak and agitated, sick to his stomach and trembling, as if he were in a nightmare falling off a cliff and stuck in the air, spinning 'round and 'round as he fell, no bottom, topsy-turvy, just falling. He had just come from seeing Deems and Sausage at the hospital and couldn't seem to remember what he'd said to either of them or even how he got here. The nursing home was fifteen blocks from the hospital in nearby Borough Park. Normally, Sportcoat could make that kind of walk in a cinch. But now he'd had to stop several times, both to rest and to ask for directions. The last time he'd asked, he was actually standing right in front of the place when he stopped and asked a white man, who simply pointed over Sportcoat's shoulder, swore under his breath, and walked away. Now he was standing in front of a young white woman behind a desk who had a look on her face just like the folks did back in the Social Security office in downtown Brooklyn when he went to see about his late wife's benefits. The same look, the irritated questions, the impatience, the demand for documents that had odd names he'd never heard of, pushing forms through the window at him with titles he couldn't even pronounce or understand; forms that demanded lists and birth dates and more papers, and even some forms that demanded names of other forms, all of which were so complicated that they might as well have been in Greek, the whole conglomeration of document names vanishing into thin air the moment the clerks uttered them. He could not remember what a "Lifetime Sheet for Pro Forma Work Information Record" was from the moment the words came out of a clerk's mouth, or what it was supposed to be or do, which meant by the time he walked out of the Social Security office, tossing the form in the garbage as he left, he was so addled by the experience that he worked to forget about it, which meant it was as if he hadn't been there at all.

Now felt like one of those times.

"Is that the first or last name?" Marjorie the receptionist asked.

"Sister Paul? That's her name."

"Isn't that a man's name?"

"It ain't a he. It's a she."

Marjorie smirked. "A woman named Paul."

"Well, that's all the name I knowed of her in my time."

Marjorie quickly flipped through a list of names on a sheet of paper at her desk. "There's no woman named Paul here."

"I'm sure she's here. Paul. Sister Paul."

"First of all, sir, like I said, that's a man's name."

Sportcoat, sweating, felt irritable and weak. He glanced over his shoulder and noticed the white-haired elderly security guard stationed near the front door. The guard folded his newspaper. For the second time that day, Sportcoat felt an unusual feeling: anger, which was overcome again by fear, and the usual feeling of utter confusion and helplessness. He didn't like being this far from the Cause Houses. Anything could happen out here in New York.

He turned back to Marjorie. "Miss, there's women that do got men's names in this world."

"Do they now," she said, her smirk widening.

"I seen a woman with a man's name throw a pistol on three fellas last Wednesday. Killed one of 'em dead, blessed God. Now, *she* was a

Haroldeen, that one. Evil as any man. Pretty as a peacock, too, with feathers and all. That was a whole evil person altogether, man and woman combined. A name ain't nuthing."

Marjorie looked up to see Mel, the security guard, approach them. "Anything wrong?" he said.

Sportcoat saw the security guard coming and realized his mistake. Now the white folks was getting ready to start counting fingers and toes. His head was pounding so hard he could only see spots in front of his face. He addressed the security guard. "I'm here for Sister Paul," he said. "She's a church lady."

"From where?"

"I don't know where her home country is."

"Home country? She American?"

"Course she is!"

"How do you know her?"

"How do anybody know anybody? They meets 'em someplace. She come from church."

"Which church?"

"Five Ends is the church. I'm a deacon there."

"Is that so?"

Sportcoat grew frustrated. "She sends money in letters every week! Who sends letters every week? Even the electric company don't send letters every week!"

The security guard looked at him thoughtfully.

"How much money?" he asked.

Sportcoat felt his anger growing new, raw, ice-hard edges, ones he'd never felt before. He spoke to the white man in a manner in which he had never spoken to a white person in his entire life. "Mister, I am seventy-one years old. And unless I am Ray Charles, you is close to my age. Now, this young lady here"—he pointed to the receptionist—"don't believe nothing I say. She got an excuse, being privileged and young, for young folks believes they has the mojo and say-so, and she has most likely lived her life hearing folks talking up and down and in and out, saying what they think she would like to hear rather than what she ought be hearing. I ain't against it. If somebody's hearing a song and don't know but that one song alone, well, nothing can be done. But you is old like me. And you ought to see clear that a man my age who hasn't had a drink in a whole day ought to get a little credit for still being able to hear his own heartbeat—and maybe even deserves a lollipop or two— for not speaking in tongues about the whole bit, being that I am so thirsty for some rotgut at the moment I'd milk a camel for a drop of Everclear or even vodka, which I can't stand. It's four dollars and thirteen cents, by the way, that she sends to church every week, if you have to know. And I'm not supposed to know, for it *is* a church. And I'm *only* a deacon. I *ain't* the treasurer."

To his surprise, the white security guard nodded sympathetically and said, "How long you been dry?"

"'Bout a day, more or less."

The security guard offered a low whistle. "Her room's that way," he said, pointing down a long hallway behind the desk. "Room one fifty-three."

Sportcoat started down the hallway, then turned around, irritated, and grunted, "What's it your business how much she gives to God?"

The old security guard looked sheepish. "I'm the one who goes to the post office and gets the money order," he said.

"Every week?"

The elderly man shrugged. "Gotta keep moving. If I sit around here too long, they might give me a room."

Sportcoat tipped his hat, still grumbling, and made his way past the desk to the hallway, the young receptionist and Mel the security guard watching as he went.

"What was that all about?" Marjorie asked.

Mel watched Sportcoat's back as he tottered down the hallway, stopped, straightened out his clothing, dusted off his sleeves, and plodded farther on.

"The only difference between me and him," Mel said, "is two hundred forty-three days."

Sportcoat, sweating now, feeling delirious, dizzy, and weak, marched into room 153 and found no living human being there. Instead, he encountered a turkey buzzard sitting in the corner, facing the wall, in a wheelchair, holding what appeared to be a bowl of yarn. The bird heard him enter, and with its back to him, spoke.

"Where's my cheese?"

Then the bird spun the wheelchair around to face him.

It took Sportcoat a full minute to realize that the creature he was staring at was a human being who was 104 years old. The woman was almost completely bald. Her face muscles had drooped, giving the impression that a powerful magnetic force was pulling her jaws, lips, and eye sockets toward the earth. Her mouth sagged nearly into her chin and it was turned down at the corners, giving her a look of perpetual frowning. What hair she had looked like scrambled eggs in string form, in wild clumps and in single strands, giving her the appearance of a wired, harried, ancient, terrified professor. The edge of a nightgown could be seen under the blanket covering her, and her bare feet were shoved into a pair of bed slippers two sizes too big. She was so tiny she covered only a third of the wheelchair seat and sat hunched over, curled, in the form of a question mark.

He had no clear memory of Sister Paul. He had been drunk a lot during the years she was active in the church, before she moved to the nursing home. She left before he got sanctified and saved. As it was, he hadn't seen her in nearly two decades, and even if he had, he realized she was probably nearly unrecognizable to anyone who didn't know her well.

Sportcoat swayed for a moment, feeling dizzy and hoping he wouldn't pass out. A sudden burst of thirst nearly overwhelmed him. He saw a pitcher of water on the nightstand on the other side of her bed. He pointed at it and said, "Can I?" Without waiting for an answer, he staggered to it, picked it up, and took a short sip straight from the pitcher, then realized he was parched and gulped the whole thing down. When he was finished he slammed it back to the table, panted heavily, then burped loudly. He felt better.

He glanced at her again, trying not to stare.

"You is some kind of dish," she said.

"Huh?"

"Son, you looks like a character witness for a nightmare. You ugly enough to have your face capped."

"We can't all be pretty," he grumbled.

"Well, you ain't no gemstone, son. You got a face for swim trunk ads."

"I'm seventy-one, Sister Paul. I'm a spring chicken compared to you. I don't see no mens doing backflips at the door over you. At least I ain't got enough wrinkles in my face to hold ten days of rain."

She glared at him intently, her dark eyes like coals, and for a moment Sportcoat had the dreadful thought that the old nag might turn into a witch and throw a mojo at him, a horrible spell. Instead, she threw her head back and laughed, displaying a mouth full of gums and one sole yellow tooth, which stood out like a clump of butter on a plate. Her howls and cackles sounded like the bleating of a goat.

"No wonder Hettie put up with you!" she guffawed.

"You knew my Hettie?"

It took a moment before she regained herself, moving her empty jaws in a chewing motion and chortling, "Course I did, son."

"She never told me about you."

"Why should she? You was a drunk and not listening no way. You don't hardly remember nothing. I bet you don't remember me."

"A little . . ."

"Uh-huh. Men used to ask me to bed in eight languages. Not no more. You drinking now?"

"Not since I saw . . . no, not right now."

"You look like you could use one. I bet you could."

"Could indeed. But I'm trying to . . . uh . . . naw. I don't want one."

"Well, you set tight, mister, and I'mma tell you a few things that'll drive anybody to drink. And after I'm done, you go ahead and do whatever it is you got to do. But first, where's my cheese?"

"What?"

"My cheese."

"I ain't got no cheese."

"Then that's the thing I'll tell you first," she said, "for it is all connected. I'll tell it this once. But don't darken my doorway again if you ain't got my cheese."

Sportcoat sat calmly in a chair near the window, rubbing his jaw, taking deep breaths, after Sister Paul had motioned him to push her closer to the window where they could both see the sunshine. Once he had locked her chair as she requested and pulled a chair up to the window she started in:

"We all knowed each other," she said. "Hettie, me, my husband, my daughter Edie, Sister Gee's parents—they was the aunt and uncle of the Cousins, by the way. Nanette and Sweet Corn. And of course your friend Rufus. We all come up from various parts of the South around 'bout the same time. Hettie and Rufus was the youngest. Me and my husband was the oldest. We come up following Edie, who brung us out the South. Me and my husband started the church in my living room. Then we got the congregation, and after a while we got enough money together to buy us a piece of dirt just outside the Cause Houses. The land was cheap then. That's the beginning of Five Ends. That's how it got started.

"See, the Cause was all Italians in the forties when we come. They built them projects for the Italians to unload the boats at the harbor. That business was dead when we come. The boats left. The docks closed, and them Italians didn't want us. Fact is, you couldn't walk down Silver Street to go downtown. You had to take the bus or the subway, or get a ride—nobody had no car—so you'd just run past if you had to. You didn't walk down Silver Street unless you wanted to lose your teeth, or if it was very late or you didn't have no bus money.

"Well, we didn't mind too much. The South was worse. Myself, I paid them Italians no more mind than I would watching a bird snatch crumbs off the ground.

"I did day's work for a white lady lived up in Cobble Hill. One night she had a party and I worked late. Well, it was cold and the buses was running slow, so I walked home. I done that from time to time when it was late. I didn't walk down Silver Street. I skirted the outside. I come all the way down Van Marl, and when I got to Slag Street, I turned and come that way, skirting along the harbor where the factories were. That's how the colored walked home late at night.

"I was walking down Van Marl that night—I reckon maybe it was just three in the morning or so, and I seen two, maybe three blocks coming at me two men running to beat the band. White men. Hauling tail. Coming right at me. One right behind the other.

"Well, I'm a colored woman and it was dark and I know however that cobweb spins out, I'd likely be blamed for whatever wrong happened. So I hid in a doorway and let 'em come. They run right past me. The first fella zipped past, and right behind him come the second. That second feller was a cop.

"When they got to the corner of Van Marl and Slag, the first fella running stopped in the intersection and turned around and pulled a pistol on the second feller, the policeman. Caught that cop by surprise. He looked to blow that cop's head off.

"And don't you know, outta nowhere come this truck and boom! Hit that feller standing in the intersection. Cleaned him up good. Deadened 'em right there. Then the truck stopped and it got quiet.

"The cop ran into the street and checked out the man with the gun. He was deader than yesterday's spaghetti. Then he went to the driver. I heard the driver say, 'I never saw him.' Then the cop said to the driver, 'Don't move. I'm going to a call box.' He ran off to one of them police call boxes to get help. Ran clear around the corner and out of sight.

"Well, that was my time to go. I come outta the doorway and walked fast down the sidewalk past the truck. As I was scooting past, the feller driving the truck, he hollered, 'Help me, please.'

"I wanted to keep walking. I was scared. That wasn't none of my business. So I kept going a few more steps. But the feller driving the truck begged me. He said please, please, help me, begging me to help him.

"Well, I reckon the Lord said to me, 'Go 'head on and help. Maybe he's hurt or injured.' So I goes to the driver's side where he's setting and I says, 'Is you hurt?'

"He was an Italian man. He spoke with such a hard accent it was the devil understanding him. But the gist of it was he said this: 'I'm in trouble.'

"I said, 'You ain't done nothing wrong. The man jumped in front of you. I seen it.'

"He says, 'That ain't the problem. I got to get this truck home. *I'll give you one hundred dollars to drive this truck.*'"

Here Sister Paul paused and shrugged, as if apologizing for the ridiculous problem she'd stumbled into. Then her age took over and she yawned, then continued.

"I was just an old country woman. I hadn't been in the city that long, see. But I knowed trouble. So I said, 'Drive on, mister. I ain't gonna meddle in your affairs. I ain't seen nothing. I'm going home to the Cause Houses, where I live. Goodbye.'

"Well, I turned to leave and he begged me to stay. He wouldn't let me go. He popped open the truck door and said, 'Look at my foot. It's broken.'

"I look in there. Seems like he hit the pedal so hard he broke his right foot some kind of way. His right foot was twisted cockeyed. And then he lifted his left leg with his arm and showed me his other foot. His left one, the clutch pedal foot, he had to hold *that* leg up with his hand. That foot was lame. He said, 'I had a stroke. I only got one good side. I ain't got no feet to drive.'

"I said, 'I can't give you my feet to drive, mister. That's God's work, giving a man feet.'

"He said, 'Please. I got a wife and son. I'll give you a hundred dollars. Can't you use a hundred dollars?'

"'I surely could,' I said. 'But I likes being free out here. Plus I'm old. I can't drive nothing but a mule, mister. I ain't never driven a car or truck in my life.'

"He got to begging and pleading so much, Lord, I didn't know what to do. He was an Italian man and he seemed sincere, even though I couldn't hardly understand every word that man was talking. But he kept saying, 'I'll give you one hundred dollars. We'll drive the truck together. Please. I'm gonna go to jail for twenty-five years this time. I got a son. I already messed up on raising him.'

"Well, my daddy went to jail when I was but a little wee girl. He gone to prison for trying to start a sharecroppers' union back in my home country in Alabama. I knows the feeling of not having your daddy there when you need him. Still, I didn't want to do it. I had already put one foot in it anyway by standing there talking to him at three in the morning. But I turned to God and I heard His voice say, 'I will hold you in the palm of My hand.'

"I said, 'All right, mister. I will help you. But I ain't taking no money. If I'm going to jail, I'm going for what the Lord told me to do.'

"Well as God would have it, I moved that truck some kind of way. My husband the Reverend Chicksaw was a truck driver, and I seen him drive a truck many a day back home in Alabama, so I done the pedals and turned the steering this way and that like the man told me to, and he shifted the gears, and we got that thing a-roaring and jerking along for a few blocks, and not too far up the road at Silver Street, he shut off the motor by turning the key and I helped him into his house. There was another Italian man waiting who come out saying, 'Where you been?' and runned to the truck, and then a second man ran out the house to the truck and they drove that thing off and I never seen it again. Meanwhile, I helped that cripple get in his house. His good leg was all cock-eyed. He was messed up bad.

"His wife come downstairs and he said to her, 'Give that lady one hundred dollars.'

"I said, 'I don't want your money, mister. I'm going home. I ain't seen nothing.'

"He said, 'What can I do for you? I have to do something for you.'

"I said, 'You ain't got to do a thing. I done what God has told me to do. I prayed before I done what you asked and God said He would hold me in the palm of His hand. I hope He holds you the same. And your wife too. Just please don't tell nobody what I has done—not even my husband if you is to meet him, for I lives over in the Cause Houses and you might see him about, preaching in the streets.' And I left out. His wife did not say a mumbling word to me. Not a word. If she did say a word, I can't call it. I was gone.

"Well, I didn't see him no more till we was building the church. See, we couldn't find nobody wanted to sell us the land. We had saved up our money, the church did, but them Italians didn't want us out there. Every time we'd offer to buy a building someplace, we'd look here or there in the paper, we'd call and they'd say it's for sale and soon as they'd see us they'd say, 'No, we changed our mind. We ain't selling.' And the thing is, whoever was running them docks was closing them down and them Italians was moving out fast as they could. But they still wouldn't sell to us. Every one of 'em was selling what they could, the devil keeping score. But our money was no good. Well, we kept asking around, asking around, and finally somebody said, 'There's a fella over yonder on Silver Street who's selling some land. He's over there on the dock in that old railroad car.' So me and my husband went over there and knocked. And who should answer the door but this fella.

"That just knocked me out. I didn't say a mumbling word. I acted like I never seen him before. He done the same. He didn't make no fuss about it. He said to my husband, 'I'll sell you that lot over yonder. I'm building a storage house on one side of the lot. You can build your church on the other.'

"And that's how Five Ends got there."

Sportcoat listened, his eye squinting in concentration. "You reckon you still remember that fella's name?" he asked.

Sister Paul drew a shallow breath and leaned her head back in the wheelchair. "I remember his name rightly. One of the finest men I ever knowed. Old Guido Elefante."

"The Elephant?"

"No. The Elephant's daddy."

Sportcoat felt thirsty again. He rose from his chair at the window, picked up the empty water pitcher, and went to the bathroom, where he filled it up again, drank it down, then returned and sat by the window.

"Honest to my savior, if it wasn't you telling it, I'd say you was stretching my blanket. That's the strangest thing I ever heard," he said.

"It's the God's truth. And that ain't all of it. Not only did old man Guido let us have our lot for six thousand dollars. No bank would loan us nothing. We took out a mortgage with him. We stepped on that lot without spending a penny to nobody's bank. We gave him four hundred dollars and got to digging: me and my husband done a little, but it was mostly my Edie, Rufus, and Hettie. Sister Gee's parents, and the Cousins' parents, they come along later. In the beginning it was mostly us. We didn't get far. We didn't have no machines nor money for none. We dug by shovel. We done what we could.

"One afternoon Mr. Guido seen us digging and came by with one of them big tractor things and dug out the entire foundation, including the basement. He done it in three days. Didn't say a mumbling word. He never did talk much. Never said much to nobody but me, and he didn't waste too many words on me neither. But we was grateful for him.

"After we started bricking up the walls with cinder block, he stopped by again and pulled me aside and said, 'I wants to repay you for what you done.'

"I says, 'You done it. We building a church.'

"He says, 'You got a mortgage on that church with me. I will *give* you the land if you let me set a gift inside the church.'

"I said, 'You don't have to do nothing. We gonna buy the land over time.'

"He said, 'You don't have to. I will give it to you. Take the note and burn it if you want.'

"I said, 'Well, I don't know nothing about burning no notes, Mr. Guido. We owes you fifty-six hundred dollars on a straight mortgage to you. We'll pay you free and clear in a few years.'

"He says, 'I ain't got a few years. I will tear the mortgage up right now if you let me put something beautiful on the back wall of the church.'

"I said, 'Is you saved to Jesus?'

"That tied him up. He said, 'I can't lie. I am not. But I got a friend who is. I got to save something for him. I made a promise to him to keep something for him. I plan to keep that promise. I wanna get somebody to draw a picture on the back wall of the church where he can see it, so that when he comes by this church someday, or his children, or his children's children come by, they'll look at it and know it's there on account of me and that I kept my word.' He said wouldn't nobody know about it but us—me and him.

"Well, I talked about it with my husband, for he was the pastor of the church. He tried to talk to old Guido hisself, but the old Italian wouldn't say a word to him. Not a mumbling word did he say to my husband or nobody else at Five Ends. I seen him talk to the building inspector from the city who came around saying you have to do thus and so when we was getting ready to build. I don't know what was said there, but that inspector needed talking to 'cause you just can't build nothing in New York by saying it, not even back in them days. You had to go through the city. Well, Mr. Guido talked to him. But not a word did he waste on nobody colored but me, to my knowing. So my husband finally said, 'If it's okay by you, it's okay by me, since you is the only one he talks to.'

"So I went to Mr. Elefante and said, 'Okay, do what you want.'

"A couple of days later he come by with three of his Italian men and them fellas got to work bricking that cinder block. They knowed their business, so we left them to it and worked the inside. We put down the floor and finished the roof. That's how it went. They worked the outside. We worked the inside. Colored and white working together.

"After Mr. Elefante's men built the walls about waist high, he come to me at lunch—" She paused and then corrected herself. "Well, that ain't right. I came to *him* at lunch. See, those days when we broke for lunch, the Italians went one way to eat at home and the colored went the other. But I always made Mr. Guido a little something for lunch 'cause he didn't eat much, and I'd bring it back to him a few minutes early because he hardly didn't go to lunch. I come back early one afternoon and found him working as usual, bricking up that back wall. When I walked up on him, he says, 'Is you alone?'

"I said, 'I just brought you some vittles 'cause I know you don't eat.'

"He looked around to make sure nobody was about, then said, 'I got something to show you. It's a good-luck charm.'

"He brung this little metal box and opened it. He said, 'This is the thing that bought your church land.'"

"What was it?" Sportcoat asked.

"It wasn't nothing," Sister Paul said. "It looked like a piece of soap shaped like a fat girl. 'Bout the color of an old trumpet. A little colored lady, is what it looked like. He closed that soap thing in the metal box, set that box inside the hollow part of a cinder block, put his concrete and mortar on it, done something to the bottom so it could set in there good, and set another cinder block over it. You couldn't tell one from the other.

"Then he says to me, 'You the only one that knows. Even my wife don't know.'

"I said, 'Why you trust me?'

"He said, 'A person who trusts can be trusted.'

"I said, 'Well, I ain't got nothing to do with where you puts your soap, Mr. Guido. I keeps my soap in the bathroom. But you a grown man, and it's your soap. It ain't gonna do you no good where it's at, but I reckon you got more soap at home.'

"I do believe that's one of the few times I seen that man laugh. He was a serious man, see.

"When his men come back, they built that wall up before the day was done. The next day he had another Italian feller came by with a black-and-white picture of a painting. He called it a Jell-O or some kind of painting. That feller copied that painting exactly as it was, right to the back wall of the church. It took him two days. The first day he drawed a big circle and colored it in some. Framed it out some, I guess. The second day he drawed Jesus in his robes right in the middle circle—with Jesus's hands outspread. Them hands touch the outside of that circle he drawed. One of them hands, Jesus's left hand, is right on the cinder block where that soap is. Right on top of it."

She paused and nodded.

"And that thing is in there yet today."

"You sure?" Sportcoat asked.

"Sure as I'm sitting here. Unless the building fell down to dust. Then they finished bricking the other walls, helped us finish the inside, do the floors and such. And at the end, that same painter came back and put up the lettering on the back wall over Jesus's head that says 'May God Hold You in the Palm of His Hand.' It was the prettiest thing."

She yawned, her story finished.

"That's how the church come to have that motto."

Sportcoat scratched his jaw, perplexed. "But you didn't tell me about the cheese," he said.

"What about it? I done told you," she said.

"No you didn't."

"I told you about the truck, didn't I?"

"What do a truck got to do with it?"

She shook her old head. "Son, you so old your mind has shrunk to the size of a full-grown pea. What do a truck carry? The truck I drove for Mr. Guido was full of cheese. Stolen cheese, I reckon. Old Guido started sending me that cheese five minutes after we opened the church doors. After I let him stick that good-luck soap box with the colored doll in it or whatever it was in that wall, I could do no wrong for him. I asked him many a day to stop sending that cheese, for it was good cheese. Expensive cheese. Too much for our little church. But he said, 'I wanna send it. People need food.' So after a while I told him to send it to Building Seventeen in the Cause, for Hot Sausage come to run that building after a time, and Sausage is honest, and I knowed he'd give it out in the Cause to them who could use it. Mr. Guido sent that cheese for years and years. After he died, it still come. When I come here to this old folks' home, it was yet coming. It comes to this day."

"So who's sending it now?"

"Jesus," she said.

"Oh hush!" Sportcoat hissed. "You sound like Hettie. That cheese got to come from someplace!"

Sister Paul shrugged. "Genesis twenty-seven twenty-eight says, 'May God give you heaven's dew and earth's richness—an abundance of grain and new wine.'"

"This is cheese."

"Son, a blessing favors them that needs it. Don't matter how it comes. It just matters that it does."

25

DO

IT WAS A DREAM SO ALIVE—AND SO MANY OF THEM SEEMED
dead before they started—that at times Elefante felt he had to keep himself from levitating when he thought about it. He gripped the steering
wheel of his Lincoln tightly as he considered it. Melissa, the Governor's
daughter, rode beside him in silence. It was four a.m. He was happy.
It wasn't so much that Melissa had accepted his invitation to "look into
her father's affairs," but rather the way she handled her own affairs—
and his.

He'd never met anyone like her before. She was, as they say in Italian,
a *stellina*, a star, a most beautiful one. From the first, she was shy and
reticent, as he'd seen. But beneath the reserve was a sureness of manner,
a certainty that belied deep confidence and engendered trust. Over the
weeks as they courted, he saw how she was with her employees at her
bagel shop and factory, the way she figured out important problems for
them without making them feel stupid, the politeness she showed them,
her respect and deference for older people in general, including the old

deacon, the rummy who'd worked for his mother, whom she'd finally met just a month ago. She didn't refer to him as "colored," or "Negro." She called him "Mister" and referred to him as "Afro-American," which, to Elefante, sounded dangerous, odd, and foreign. That was hippie talk. It reminded him of Bunch Moon, the colored bastard. He'd heard through the grapevine that Peck had dispatched Bunch—badly. There was danger everywhere now, full-out shooting coming because of the whites, the blacks, the Spanish, the Irish cops, the Italian families, the drug wars. It wouldn't stop. Yet despite the dark days ahead he felt himself moving into a light of a different kind. The wonderful, bursting, gorgeous, eye-opening panorama of light that love can bring into a lonely man's life.

The romance was new territory for them both. A couple of lunches and a quick dinner at a Bronx diner had dissolved into long, peaceful dinners at the Peter Luger Steak House in Williamsburg, then lovely walks along the Brooklyn Esplanade as the cocoon of affection and lust blossomed into the kaleidoscope of bursting, passionate, gorgeous love.

Even so, he thought, as he steered the car down the FDR Drive, the Chrysler Building at Forty-Second Street receding in the distance, to love a man by the light of day when the sun is shining and there is a promise of love is one thing. But to rumble into the housing projects of Brooklyn in his Lincoln to pick up the old deacon in the dead of night was quite another.

He pondered it as he spun the Lincoln into the Battery Tunnel, the fluorescent lights along its ceiling glinting across Melissa's face as she sat next to him. Until then he'd always believed a partner brought worry, fear, and weakness to a man, especially one in his business. But Melissa brought courage and humility and humor to places he'd never known existed. He'd never partnered with a woman before, if you didn't include his mother, but Melissa's quiet sincerity was a weapon of a new kind. It drew people in, disarmed them. It made them friends—and that was a weapon too. He'd seen that happen with the old colored woman in the Bensonhurst nursing home who called herself Sister Paul.

He thanked God he'd brought Melissa to the old folks' home the week before. He almost didn't do it. He took her along as an afterthought, to show his sincerity and openness. She'd turned matters in his favor.

The old deacon had assured him that he'd told Sister Paul all about him. But when he walked into the room, the old biddy, wrinkled and covered in a gray blanket, gave him the *malocchio*, the evil eye. She ignored his greeting and, without a word, extended an old claw, pointing at an old tin coffee can near her bed. He reached for it and handed it to her. She spat in it.

"You look like your daddy but fatter," she said.

He placed a chair close to her wheelchair and sat in it facing her, trying to smile. Melissa sat on the bed behind him. "I ate more peanuts than he did." He said it as a joke, to loosen things.

She waved that off with an ancient, wrinkled hand. "Your daddy didn't eat no peanuts to my recollection. And he didn't say but four or five words a day. Which means you is not only fatter, but you uses your talking hole more."

He felt the color moving into his face. "Didn't the deacon talk to you?"

"Don't be coming in here sassifying and frying up air castles 'bout some old deacon! Do you do?"

"Huh?"

"Do you *do*?"

"Do what?"

"I asked you a question, mister. Do you *do*?"

"Listen, miss—"

"Don't sass me," she barked. "I'm asking you a question. Yes or no. Do you do?"

He raised his finger to make a point, to try to slow her down. "I'm only here bec—"

"Put that finger in your pocket and listen, sonny! You walk in here without a can of sardines, nor gift, nor bowl of beans, not even a glass of water to offer somebody who is aiming to give you a free hand to the thing you come for. And you don't even know if you gonna hit the bull's-eye on that or not. You is like most white men. You believes you is enti-tled to something you ain't got no hand in. Everything in the world got a price, mister. Well now, the bottom rail's on top, sir, for I has been walked on all my life, and I don't know you from Adam. You could be Italian, being that the old suit you wearing has got wine stains all over it. On the other hand, you could be some fancy-figuring devil-may-care wino *pretending* to be Mr. Guido's son. I don't know why you is here in the first place, mister. I don't know the deacon that good. He didn't ex-plain nothing to me about you. Like most mens, he don't feel he got to explain nothing to a woman, including his own wife, who did all the frying and cooking and hair straightening while he rumbled 'round throwing joy juice down his throat for all them long years he done it. I been around the sun one hundred four whole times and nobody's ex-plained nothing to me. I read the book on not being explained to. That's called being an old colored woman, sir. Now I ask it again. For the last time—and if you don't show your points here, then you can slip your corns inside them little Hush Puppy shoes of yours with the little quar-ters inside 'em and git on down the road. *Do you do?*"

He blinked, exasperated, and glanced at Melissa, who—thank God—said softly, "Mrs. Paul, he *does* do."

The old lady's shriveled face, a mass of wrinkled, angry rivers, loos-ened as she turned her ancient head to look at Melissa. "Is you his wife, miss?"

"Fiancée. We're gonna be married."

The old biddy's anger loosened a bit more. "Hmph. What kind of feller is he?"

"He doesn't talk much."

"His daddy didn't talk much neither. Talked a lot less than him, that's for sure. Why you wanna marry this loser? He comes tumbling in here rough and wrong, asking questions like he's the police or some God-sent minister. His daddy never asked me but one single question. Never asked me na'ar question after. Is he that type of man, this feller of yours? Is he the type that's good for his word? Is he the type who *do* stuff and don't talk about it to nobody later? Do he *talk* or do he *do*? Which is it?"

"I hope so. I think so. I'm gonna see. I think he does . . . do."

"All right then." The old lady seemed satisfied. She turned to stare at Elefante, but still spoke to Melissa, as if Elefante were not in the room. "I hope you is right, miss, for your sake. If you is, you got something. For his daddy listened. His daddy didn't set around spouting questions and blasting air and making pronouncements and pointing his claw like he was top dog. His daddy didn't point his finger at nobody. He gived us that church free and clear."

"I wish somebody would give me a church," Melissa said.

The old lady seemed suddenly outraged. She grew furious. She arched her head back, glaring, staring at Melissa, enraged, then suddenly threw back her head and burst into laughter, her mouth wide, showing one stained, rancid old tooth. "Haw! You something, girl!" And then Melissa went in, smoothing things out, talking it over, chatting easily with the old crocodile for the next two hours, until the salt in the old lady dissolved, vanishing completely, revealing the kind, odd soul who lived beneath, sharing her life and past, pouring out the soul music of an old black woman's suffering, sorrow, and joy: her late husband, her beloved daughter who spent her young life building Five Ends church and died fourteen years before. With Melissa's coaxing, Sister Paul worked through her beginnings at a sharecropping farm in Valley Creek, Alabama, north to Kentucky, where she met her husband, and their move to New York following their daughter. Then he got the calling to teach Christ's wisdom, and by the time she reached the point in her narrative

about the birth of Five Ends Baptist Church and old Mr. Guido's role in
building it, and of course the box that he'd hidden there, she was talking
to them both. But she didn't stop there, for as she spoke she revealed an
even greater treasure, the old Cause neighborhood of Elefante's youth,
the one that he'd forgotten in his years of hardship and hustle, rolling
back the neighborhood he remembered as a boy, the Italian kids playing
Johnny-on-the-pony and ring-a-levio in the street on Sunday afternoons;
the Irish kids over on Thirteenth Street hammering pink stickballs for
the length of two sewers; the Jewish kids on Dikeman guffawing as they
tossed water balloons on passersby out the upstairs windows of the tene-
ment building where their dad ran the grocery store on the first floor;
the old dockworkers, Italian, colored, and Spanish, arguing about the
Brooklyn Dodgers in three languages while they rolled dice; and of
course the Negroes from the Cause Houses, hurrying past in their Sunday best toward downtown Brooklyn, chuckling nervously as he acted
like an idiot in front of them in his teenage years, drunk, angry, threatening, pissing behind a parked car as the Negroes passed, even chasing
their children down Silver Street at night. How could he be so dumb?
He saw himself then as his mother had referred to him in rage when she
learned of his behavior: a dumb *paisan*, worrying that the colored, the
Irish, the Jews, the outsiders were invading our block. We got no block,
she said. The Italians don't own the block. Nobody owns the block. Nobody was king of nothing in New York. It's *life*. Survival. *How could he
have been so stupid?* he thought. Is this what love does? It changes you
this way? It allows you to see the past this clearly?

When the old lady was done, he felt as if he'd been blessed and had
communion, his sins washed clean by confession. It was evening, and
she'd nearly talked herself to sleep. He had stood to thank her and to
leave when she asked, "Your mother still living?"

"She is," he said.

"You ought to honor her, son. For whatever good your daddy has wrought, it's she who held him up to it. She does what these days?"

"She works her garden."

"That's nice. Maybe you ought not tell her you and I spoke."

"Who said I was gonna do that?"

Sister Paul eyed him thoughtfully a moment, then said, "I'm one hundred four, son. I knows every trick. You'll be wanting to check on me, hoping she'll remember that hundred dollars your daddy offered me for driving that truck. She'll recollect it surely, for that was big money in them days, and I reckon them was tight minutes for her, setting in her living room in the wee hours with her husband's right foot pointing one way while his ankle was pointing the other, and that truck full of trouble in front of her house, and you laying upstairs snoring with a smeller full of snot and a life full of headaches ahead, for I bet raising you wasn't no bed of roses. A wife knows everything, son. If she wanted you to know what happened that night, I reckon she'd a spilled the beans long past. Why worry an old mother's heart? If some harm was to come to you on account of what I just told you, then I got her sorrow to carry too. I'm old, son. I got no reason to lie."

Elefante considered this a moment, then said, "All right." He paused. "Thank you . . . for everything. Is there something I can do for you?"

"If you's a praying man, pray that the Lord sends me a hunk of my cheese."

"Your what?"

"Your daddy liked my vittles, see . . ."

"Vittles?"

"My food. He liked my cooking. He put a hurting on my fried chicken. I gived him some one afternoon when we was building the church. He gived me a piece of his cheese in return. Italian cheese. Don't know the name of it. But that cheese was something! I told him that! After we got the church built up, he sent that cheese to us for years. Now he's long dead and I hear tell the cheese keeps coming. Like magic. From Jesus, I reckon."

That was Elefante's opening, and he cleared his throat, the big man again. "I can find out who sends i—"

"Did I ask you that, son?"

"Maybe my moth—"

"Son, why you keep wanting to get your momma all gooked up in this mess? You asked me what I wanted and I said it. I said just pray for Jesus to send me a hunk of that cheese. I told old Sportcoat to do it, but he's scarce these days. Jesus sends that cheese, son. Nobody else. It comes from Jesus. I'm asking you to ask Jesus to send me some. Just a piece. I ain't had it in years."

"Um . . . okay." Elefante stood and moved to the door. Melissa followed. "Anything else?" he asked.

"Well, if you want, you can tip Mr. Mel before you leave."

"Who's Mr. Mel?"

"He's that old white feller by the front door who makes sure none of us old folks escape."

Elefante looked at Melissa, who nodded down the hall at the building entrance, where an old security guard could be seen, nodding off into the *Daily News*.

"I been sending my tithes to Five Ends every week for twelve years," Sister Paul said. "Four dollars and thirteen cents, from my Social Security. He walks it to the post office every week. He gets a money order and puts it in an envelope and mails it. Unless the post office is paying him in beers and liquor, I owes him twelve years' worth of stamps and envelopes. Plus the cost of making that four dollars and thirteen cents into a money order. Now Mel's donated that whiskey down his little red lane free as the rivers run for as long as I been here, till he quit a year or so past. But, honest to my savior, he's a good man. I'd like to pay him what I owes him before I gets my wings. You think you can spare a little something for him? He won't take money. He says he's too old."

"Does he like anything else other than booze?"

"He favors them Mars candy bars."

"I'll give 'im enough to last the rest of his life."

They made the move into the wall that night at 4:20 a.m. Elefante and Sportcoat. Melissa remained in the car at the curb, the lights out and motor running. No need for her to risk getting busted. She had done the work, and the research too. After hearing the description of the object, reading a few newspapers from the period, then calling the man in Europe to make arrangements for transfer and sale, she knew what it was. Apparently "the soap" her uncle Macy—the Governor's brother—had hidden and brought back to America among his "collection" stolen from the Vienna cave in 1945 was not soap at all. It was the oldest three-dimensional object in the world. The Venus of Willendorf, the goddess of fertility. A tiny piece of limestone, carved in the shape of a pregnant woman, said to be thousands of years old. And it was sitting in the palm of Jesus's hand, a colored hand, painted on the cinder-block back wall of Five Ends Baptist Church of the Cause Houses in Brooklyn, New York, by Sister Bibb's son Zeke with Sportcoat and Sausage's help, at the direction of Pastor Gee, who some years before felt that Jesus should be transformed from a white Jesus into a colored man. What hand was there looked like a blob. But it was a hand nonetheless.

There was no moon out as Elefante and Sportcoat made their way along the side of the building to the pitch-black yard of the church, hidden by high weeds, the twinkling lights of a few Manhattan skyscrapers seen in the distance. Elefante had a flashlight, covered with a black cloth, and a hammer and stone chisel. Sportcoat glanced at Elefante's tools and said, "I don't need no light." But when he led Elefante to the back wall, he took the light and flashed it a moment, revealing the portrait of Jesus, now badly discolored, a white man painted brown, his arms outstretched, the two hands roughly eight feet apart. Then he handed the flashlight back to Elefante.

"Did Sister Paul say the right hand or the left hand?" Elefante asked.

"Can't recollect. Ain't but two hands there," Sportcoat said pointedly. They started on the left hand, carefully tapping around the brick. They chinked the mortar away until the brick was nearly free. "Wait," Sportcoat said. "Gimme a minute to get inside, then just chink that brick in toward me. There ain't nothing on the inside wall. Tap it. Don't hit it too hard now. It's hollow. That hammer'll bust a hole in it."

With the head of his hammer, Elefante carefully tapped at the edges of the cinder block softly. The block gave way with a few taps and the cinder block tumbled inside.

It occurred to him as it fell in, *What if the thing falls?*

He heard the old man on the other side grunt as he grabbed it. Elefante spoke through the wall: "Anything there?"

"In where?"

"In that cinder block. Something like a bar of soap in there?"

"Naw. No soap."

That caught Elefante off guard. He could see the old man's face in the hole left by the cinder block. He stuck his head in the blank space where the cinder block had been removed and looked, at an angle, shining his flashlight at the cinder block below and the one above. Nothing. He could see inside the church, and saw the old man's eye peering out at him.

"There's nothing here," he said. "These blocks are staggered. That thing could've fell off the edge of these blocks and bounced all the way to the bottom and broken to pieces. We'll have to take the whole wall of the church down to see the bottom. Let's try the other hand."

He moved to the other side and had begun chinking away at the cinder block of Jesus's right hand when the sound of the church door opening and the old man's feet shuffling across the pavement stopped him.

"You gotta get inside to catch this cinder block when it falls in," he said.

"I do?" Sportcoat said.

"Yeah. We're looking for a box of soap. It can't break. It's valuable."

"Well this ain't soap," Sportcoat said. He held up a dusty metal box.

"Why you trying to bust my *cojones*!" Elefante said, snatching it.

"Your what?"

"My balls."

"I ain't got nothing to do with them things."

"I thought you said nothing was in there."

"You said soap. This don't look like no soap. It's a box. It was mortared to the side of the brick."

"Side of what?"

"The cinder block. Somebody put a metal plate on the side and fixed this to it."

"I thought you said there was nothing in there."

"You said soap, mister."

"Stop calling me mister!" Elefante squealed in excitement, and dropped to his knees and thrust the flashlight at Sportcoat. "Shine it."

Sportcoat complied. Elefante opened the box and pulled out a plump stone figurine, about four inches high, with large breasts.

"What do you know," Sportcoat said. He resisted saying "a little colored lady." Instead he muttered, "It's a doll."

"Just like he said. No bigger than a bar of Palmolive soap," Elefante muttered, turning it back and forth.

"I seen country mice that was bigger," Sportcoat said. "Can I touch it?"

Elefante handed it to him. "It do feel heavy," Sportcoat said, handing it back. "She's a hefty little woman. I seen a few of them in my time."

"Like this thing?"

"Hefty women with big love knobs? Sure. This church is full of 'em."

Elefante ignored that, glancing around instinctively. The yard was dark. There wasn't a soul about. The Lincoln sat at the curb, motor idling. He had it. He was free. Time to move.

"I'll drop you off. Then call you later. I'll take care of you, buddy."

Sportcoat didn't move. "Wait a minute. You think, on account of me and Sister Paul helping you here, you could help me find the Christmas box too?"

"The what?"

"The Christmas box. All the Christmas money. Money saved up by people in the church to buy gifts for their children. My Hettie collected it every year and hid it in the church someplace. Christmas ain't but a month away now."

"Where is it?"

"If I'd known, I wouldn't be asking you to help."

"How much was saved in it?"

"Well, when you add it all up, and figure out the liars who claim they had this or that in there, I reckon it's probably about three or four thousand dollars. Cash."

"I think I can handle that, Mr. Sportcoat."

"Come again? Mister?"

"Mr. Sportcoat."

Sportcoat pawed at his forehead with a wrinkled hand. There was a clarity to the world now that felt new, not uncomfortable, but at times the newness of it felt odd, like the feeling of breaking in a new suit of clothing. The constant headaches and nausea that had been his companions after leaving the swigfest for decades had lifted. He felt like a radio tuning in to a new channel, one that was beginning to fuzz into range, slowly coming in clear, proper, the way his Hettie had always wanted him to be. The new feeling humbled him. It made him feel religious, it made him feel closer to God, and to man, God's honored child. "I ain't never been called Mr. Sportcoat by nobody."

"Well what do you want to be called?"

Sportcoat thought for a moment. "Maybe a child of God."

"All right. Child of God. I can handle it. I'll get you a new Christmas box."

Elefante moved to the car.

"Wait!"

"What now?"

"How we gonna explain this brick missing from the wall?"

But Elefante had already moved to the car. "I'll have it fixed tomorrow. Just tell the church not to say a word. Tell 'em to ask Sister Paul. I'll handle everything else."

"What about Jesus's hand? They gonna be mad about that. It's gotta be fixed back."

"Tell 'em Jesus is gonna get a new wall. And a new hand. And a new building if they want. You got my word."

26

BEAUTIFUL

SPORTCOAT'S FUNERAL TWENTY-TWO MONTHS AFTER THE
Deems Clemens shooting was, without a doubt, the greatest funeral in
Cause Houses history. It was the usual Five Ends Baptist Church catas-
trophe, of course. Reverend Gee was twenty minutes late because his
new Chevy—six-years-old new—didn't start. One of the flower delivery
guys fell in front of the church and broke his arm, having tripped over a
wayward brick left out in front that was part of the new renovation that
seemed to be ongoing—money coming from God knows where. He fell
through the open rectory door, sending moonflowers everywhere. The
Cousins, Nanette and Sweet Corn, got into a hissing match in the choir
pew over the ownership of a hat. The hearse carrying the body from the
funeral home was late as usual, this time because old Morris Hurly, affectionately known as Hurly Girly, claimed he got in a fender bender on
the BQE with an oil truck, which prompted him to do some quick rear-
ranging of Sportcoat's body as it lay in the casket inside the hearse,
which was hurriedly parked smack in the middle of the church's brand-
new garden out back, for lack of a parking space in front. Several angry

attendees, glaring out the church back door—including Bum-Bum, Sister Bibb, and several members of the now-bulked-up Puerto Rican Statehood Society of the Cause Houses, thanks to its new president, Miss Izi—watched in disgust, noting there were no bent or dented fenders on the shiny limo, and guessed correctly that when Hurly Girly saw the line of people standing outside the church stretching around the corner and into the projects courtyard, he panicked and decided to tidy up Sportcoat.

"Morris wants to impress new customers," Bum-Bum fumed, watching as two men in black suits from the Hurly home stood guard over the limo's open tailgate, while the rear end of the aged Morris, a grim-looking soul with a completely white Afro, dangled out the back, his shiny shoes getting muddied from the black soil of the new garden. Back and forth his shoes went, in and out of the limousine, as he made last-minute adjustments to Sportcoat.

"Look at him," Bum-Bum said in disgust. "Morris looks like a ferret."

Still, it was a homecoming that beat all, a celebration of celebrations. All of the Cause Houses came. Folks from Mount Tabernacle, St. Augustine, and even Mr. Itkin and two members of the Jewish temple on Van Marl Street showed. The line stretched past the Elephant's boxcar, up Ingrid Avenue, down Slag Avenue, and all the way back into the plaza of Cause Houses, nearly all the way to the flagpole. The free distribution of cheese at the funeral might have helped, some said, and where it came from still no one knew, but it arrived the night before in bulk, weight, and volume never before seen, crates of it, neatly stacked in the basement of the church, waiting, when Sister Gee came to open the building at five a.m.

The viewing lasted nine hours.

Five Ends only held 150 people—that was what the fire code allowed. Twice that many actually squeezed in for the service. There were so many people that someone called local Fire Engine Company Station 131, which sent a truck over. The firemen took one look at the crowd and left, radioing for the cops, who sent over two squad cars from the Seventy-Sixth Precinct. The officers took one look at the crowd and the line of double-parked cars that required onerous traffic-ticket writing and announced they'd been called away for an emergency accident in Bay Ridge that would hold them up for approximately three hours, exactly long enough for Reverend Gee to shout his sermon to all about what a great man Sportcoat had been, and for the Cousins to lead the Five Ends choir in some of the most saintly and heavenly rousing and hollering that anyone had ever heard, joined in the end by Joaquin and Los Soñadores, who were, praise Jesus, drowned out by the hollering of the Cousins, who, as usual, stole the show.

It was a death extravaganza, only this time the usual suspects—Sister Gee, Sister Bibb, Hot Sausage, Pudgy Fingers, now legally in the care of the Cousins, who fought over him with the same tenacity with which they fought over everything else—were amended by Sister Paul, who now, at 106, enjoyed a special seat on the dais, accompanied by none other than former deacon Rufus Harley, janitor of the Watch Houses, who had sworn up and down that he would never, ever darken the doorway of that hotbed of hypocrisy and holy impotence known as Five Ends Baptist Church as long as he drew air. Also there was Miss Izi, flanked by all seventeen of the newly sworn-in members of the Puerto Rican Statehood Society of the Cause Houses. The gentle giant Soup Lopez was there as well, along with Joaquin's cousin Elena from the Bronx and Calvin the subway tollbooth operator—those two talked trains. Bum-Bum, accompanied by her new husband, Dominic the Haitian Sensation, along with his best friend, Mingo the witch doctor, were in attendance, as were several members of Sportcoat's All-Cause Boys Baseball Team, now grown and retired from baseball, save one. And an unusual conglomerate of outsiders: Potts Mullen, the retired cop, and his former rookie partner, Jet Hardman, who was currently working for the

New York City Harbor Patrol, the first black ever, having broken that color barrier at the NYPD Bomb Squad, the Department of Internal Affairs, the accounting department, the traffic division, and the mechanic transportation division, which fixed squad cars—all of which broke down five minutes after Jet finished working on them.

And finally two of the most interesting parties: Thomas G. Elefante, formerly known as the Elephant, resplendent in a gray suit, along with his mother and his new wife, a hefty, shy Irish woman said to be from the Bronx; and Deems Clemens himself, the former drug-dealing terror of the Cause—now a twenty-one-year-old rookie pitcher for the Iowa Cubs, a minor-league affiliate for the hapless major-league Chicago Cubs, accompanied by baseball coach Bill Boyle from St. John's University, with whom he lived for a year while pitching St. John's to the NCAA finals in his only college season. The wound that the right-handed-pitching Clemens had received in the shooting twenty-two months earlier was, thankfully, in his left shoulder, and had healed nicely, along with his mental state, which had improved dramatically when he vacated the Cause Houses to live in Coach Boyle's home.

Deems's appearance—he arrived twenty minutes late—and the news of his good fortune in professional baseball blitzed through the church mourners like a cyclone. "It's just our luck," Joaquin mumbled. "The only guy from the Cause who goes to the bigs gets drafted by the lousy Cubs. That team hasn't won a World Series in sixty-three years. Who's gonna bet on them? I won't make a dime on him."

"Who cares?" said Miss Izi. "Did you see his car?"

She had a point. Clemens, who had owned a used Pontiac Firebird during his drug-selling days, had arrived driving a brand-new Volkswagen Beetle.

After the service and burial, a large group of about forty neighborhood residents gathered in the basement of Five Ends and talked late into the night, in part because there was so much food to eat, and in part because there was so much cheese left to distribute they had no idea what to do with it all. The arguing about the cheese distribution took hours. It was later determined, from an eyewitness account of Bum-Bum, that ever-vigilant cheese cop, and old Dub Washington, who had fallen asleep in the old factory at Vitali Pier and had wandered outside in the middle of the night to forage through the garbage on Silver Street, that the cheese had arrived the night before in a refrigerated eighteen-foot box truck containing forty-one cases, each bearing twenty-eight five-pound hunks of delicious, delectable, delightful white man's cheese. It had been distributed because it could not be stored, but despite the crowd at the viewing, the church ran out of takers, so it was hurriedly decided after Sportcoat's service that they would spread the love into the wider Cause Houses district. They shoved eight hunks into the trunk of the two squad cars of the cops from the Seven-Six who had returned from their Bay Ridge "traffic emergency." The cops protested that it was too much, so they were instructed by Sister Gee to carry half of the cheese out to Ladder Company 131 over on Van Marl Street and share it with their fellow city workers. The cops agreed but didn't give the firemen a single curd, since the cops and firemen in the Cause District hated each other just like they did all over New York. Word was spread also to the Watch Houses. A line formed outside the church, residents from both housing projects came back in droves, and still there were not enough takers. Many of the people who did show up were forced to carry home more than they could handle. They hauled blocks of it in shopping carts, sacks, shopping bags, wagons, purses, baby carriages, and mail carrier carts swiped from the nearby post office. There had never been so much cheese in the Cause District. And sadly, there never would be cheese there again.

It's hard to say if the cheese, or Clemens and his Volkswagen, or Elefante's presence caused more of a dustup in the church core group that

stayed into the night, discussing matters, arguing and joking and regal-
ing into the wee hours, accusing one another of the treachery of knowing
Sportcoat's whereabouts and the circumstances of his mysterious death.
No one seemed to know. No one had ever seen anything like it before in
the Cause. But at seven p.m., after the tables had been cleared, the dishes
washed and the last of the cheese distributed, the church swept clean,
and the remaining leftover moonflowers given away because there were
so many, the outside neighbors peeled away, leaving only the hard-core
souls of Five Ends Baptist: Sister Gee, Hot Sausage, Sister Bibb, and
Bum-Bum, along with two visitors, Miss Izi and Soup. The last two were
not church members but were allowed special attendance as representatives of their various institutions: Miss Izi as the newly elected president
of the Puerto Rican Statehood Society, and Soup, who no longer went by
the name Soup but rather carried the moniker Rick X, a proud member
of the Nation of Islam and also the top seller in the Brooklyn Mosque
#34 sales division, having sold the most bean pies and newspapers in
that mosque's storied history. He was also wanted in Kansas for false
imprisonment related to a domestic squabble and robbery, but that, he
assured the group, was a long story.

The six talked late into the night.

The conversation danced up and down, draping the walls with con-
jecture as they pushed various theories into play, then oblivion, and then
back again. Where did Sportcoat go for the last fourteen months? Did
Sportcoat drink at the end? How did he die? Why did the Elephant show
up? And where did all that cheese come from?

The cheese business burned them most of all. "After all these years,"
Miss Izi said. "Nobody still knows. That's just stupid."

"I grabbed the driver of the truck," Bum-Bum said proudly. "I saw the
truck coming around three thirty and ran out and caught him before
he pulled off. There were two of them. One had just got in the truck.

The other one, the driver, was coming out of the church. I grabbed him by the arm before he could get in his truck. I asked him, 'Who are you?' He didn't say much. He had an Italian accent. I think he was a gangster."

"Why you say that?" Miss Izi asked.

"He had a lot of pockmarks on his face."

"That's nothing," Miss Izi said. "That could be from learning to use a fork."

That caused a flurry of laughter and comment.

No one seemed to know much more than that.

Then they turned the heat on Hot Sausage. For the better part of an hour, they grilled Sportcoat's best friend. Hot Sausage pleaded ignorance. "The man went to jail," he said. "It was in the paper."

"It was *not* in the paper," Miss Izi said. "The man was supposed to go to jail. He was supposed to go to trial. *That* was in the paper. Sportcoat didn't *go* no place."

"Well, he wasn't here!" Sausage said.

"Where was he then?"

"What am I, a Ouija board? I don't know," Hot Sausage said. "The man is dead. He did a lot of good in his life. What you worried about?"

The argument sallied forth until midnight. Where did Sportcoat go? When was he sighted? No one seemed to know.

At last, around one a.m. they got up to leave, more dissatisfied than ever.

"After twenty years of guessing how the old coot would depart this world, this is too much," Bum-Bum said, glaring at Sausage as she left. "I can't stand it when somebody who got a reputation for blasting hot air suddenly grows cold when they know something you don't."

Hot Sausage paid her no mind. He was busy keeping an eye on Sister Bibb, his secret lover, who was making ready to leave. He had watched glumly for the last hour, waiting for the wink, the nod, the head shake, some sign that all was okay and that the coast would be clear to follow her home for a bit of humpty dumpty in Sportcoat's honor. But Sister Bibb offered no sign. Instead, as the clock struck the hour, she grabbed her purse and made for the door. Then as she reached the door and silently turned the door handle, she nodded at him. Hot Sausage leaped to his feet, but Sister Gee put a hand on his arm.

"Sausage, can you stay a minute? I need a private word."

Sausage glanced at Sister Bibb, who was halfway out the door. "Do it have to be now?" he asked.

"Just a minute. It won't take long."

Sister Bibb, standing at the open door, moved her eyebrows up and down twice in a quick motion, which sent Sausage's heart soaring, then he watched as she slipped out. He sank dejectedly into a folding chair.

Sister Gee stood before him, hands on her hips. Sausage looked up at her like a guilty puppy.

"All right. Out with it," she said.

"Out with what?"

Sister Gee pulled another folding chair and sat backward on it facing him, her forearms pressed against the chair, her legs straddling it, her dress pushed down to cover her upper thighs. Her long brown face stared at his, and her bottom lip pressed against her lower teeth. She thought a moment, nodded slowly, then rocked back and forth calmly.

"Man is a curious creature, don't you think?" she said casually.

Sausage looked at her suspiciously. "I reckon."

She stopped rocking and leaned forward, smiling. Her smile was disarming, and Hot Sausage felt nervous.

"I don't know why I have the desire to mind other folks' business," she said. "That's the child in me, I reckon. But then again, life takes ahold of you as soon as you leave your mother. I don't know what it is. But the older I get, the more I become what I really am. Do you find that, Sausage?" she asked.

Hot Sausage frowned. "Sister Gee, I'm all tuckered out. If you's in the mood to start chunking away about dirt and the ways of man and things that happened in Chattanooga back in 1929 that you read about in a book someplace, we can go at this tomorrow."

"The truth will be the same tomorrow," she said. "It just won't take as long to tell it."

Hot Sausage spread his hands. "What's there to know? The man is dead. He drunk hisself to death."

"Then the booze got him? It's really true?" she said.

"It is."

It was as if an anvil had dropped on her. Her shoulders sagged, and Sausage saw, for the first time that day—after hours of handling the funeral ceremony, playing the puppeteer for her inept husband, arranging the flowers, calming the Cousins, comforting the bereaved, distributing the programs, arranging the manner of service, greeting the people, dealing with the cops, the firemen, the parking, essentially doing her husband's job in a dying church, a church that, like many around them, was held up more and more by women like her—her deep, heartfelt sorrow. She bowed her head and covered her face with open palms, and as she did so her own pain unsealed his, and he swallowed, clearing his throat.

They sat in silence a long moment, her face covered with her hands. When she took her hands away, he saw that her face was wet where the tears had smudged her makeup.

"I thought he licked it," she said.

Sausage beat back his own sorrow and considered the situation. He thought it through quickly. His chance for a night frolic with Sister Bibb, he realized, was ruined. He was too tired for some action anyway. Sister Bibb would wear him down to a nub. He might as well tell what he knew. When it came down to it, he saw no harm in it. Sister Gee had done a lot for him. And the church. For all of them. She deserved better. He spoke up.

"Well, it *is* true," he said. "And it isn't."

Sister Gee looked startled. "What?"

"All of it. And none of it."

"What are you talking about? Did he drink himself to death or not?"

Sausage scratched his head slowly. "No. He did not."

"How did he land in the harbor? That's where somebody said they found him. Did he jump in there?"

"No he did not! I did not see him jump in no harbor!"

Sister Gee demanded, "What the hell happened then?"

Sausage frowned and said, "I can only tell you what happened after I come outta the hospital, for that's when I seen him in his right mind."

"Well?"

Sausage continued: "After I got out, I found Sportcoat. He was at his place. He wasn't arrested. He wasn't in jail. Cops hadn't talked to him, not even your friend the sergeant who come to the service today. Sport was walking around free. First thing he told me when I seen him was, 'Sausage, I quit drinking.' Well, I didn't believe him. Then I didn't see him no more for a few days. That's when the Elephant come around. Now from there, you know more'n I do, Sister Gee. For you was the one that the Elephant spoke to. You and Sport. I don't know what you all three talked about, for the building of Five Ends Baptist come before my time. But Sport was talking crazy at the end. I thought it was on account of him stopping drinking."

"It wasn't that," Sister Gee said. "He wanted to rebuild the garden behind the church, make a garden full of moonflowers back there. That's where the idea to build the garden in the church come from. It wasn't my idea or Mr. Elefante's. That came from Sportcoat."

"Why's that?"

Sister Gee nodded at the back wall of the church, newly repaired and painted. "Mr. Elefante had something in that wall that belonged to his father. That old painting on the back wall that you all mucked up by trying to make Jesus colored wasn't just some old painting. It's a copy of something famous. Mr. Elefante wrote it down on a piece of paper. He showed it to me. It was something called *Last Judgment*. By an Italian man named Giotto."

"Giotto? Like Jell-O?"

"I'm serious, Sausage. He's a famous painter and that's a famous painting and right there on the back of our church was a copy of it. For twenty-two years."

"Well, if Mr. Gelato got famous out of it and he's long dead, I ought to be famous too. Fact is, me and Sport painted that thing nice for your husband some years back, when he wanted to make Jesus colored."

"I remember that ruination," Sister Gee said. "There was something inside the painting that Mr. Elefante wanted. It was hidden in the cinder block right behind Jesus's hand."

"What was it?"

"I didn't see it. From what Sister Paul said, it was a fancy box with a bar of soap in it."

"Wasn't no gold, or cash, or rocks?" Hot Sausage said.

"Rocks?"

"Jewels."

"Nope. Well, the box had a doll in it. A little statue. Shaped like a fat lady. The color of brown soap, Sister Paul said. They call her the Venus of something or other."

"Hmm. Nothing somebody doing day's work would find on her job, I reckon."

"Very funny."

He thought for a minute. "That do seem strange," he admitted. "What else did Sister Paul say?"

"She said she was there when old Guido Elefante stuck it in the wall and was glad to live long enough to know the son got hold of it. I didn't ask the son no questions. You seen what Mr. Elefante done for the church, didn't ya? He asked me how much was in Hettie's missing Christmas money box. I told him what I thought it was—four thousand dollars. I told him that figure includes some liars who *said* they put money in there and likely didn't. He said it don't matter and gived me that much anyway. Plus he redid the pulpit. Rebuilt the whole back wall after he tore it open. Put a whole new garden in. Got someone to fix that foolish painting y'all did and make it a regular black Jesus. And redid the slogan about man being in the palm of God's hand. Never did figure out why that slogan was there. But it's a good one, and we're keeping it."

"What about the cheese?" Sausage asked.

"That was the Elephant's daddy who did that."

"His daddy's been dead longer than Moses. It's been twenty years, at least."

"Honest to God, Sausage, I don't know where it came from," Sister Gee said. "Sportcoat knew. When I asked him where the cheese was from, all he said was, 'Jesus sent it,' and not a word more."

Sausage nodded thoughtfully, and Sister Gee continued. "The only other time he ever referred to it was when the Elephant drove me and Sportcoat to visit Sister Paul out in the old folks' home in Bensonhurst that time. Turns out Sister Paul and the Elephant's daddy was old friends, was all I could make of it. How that happened, I don't know. What the Elephant and Sister Paul spoke about, well, that too was private. I wasn't in the room. I did overhear Sister Paul say something to the Elephant about a hundred dollars and driving a truck. I overheard 'em laughing about it. But I didn't see no money change hands. And I seen them shake hands. Sportcoat and the Elephant."

"Bless me! The Elephant and Sportcoat shook hands?" Hot Sausage said.

"Hand to God," Sister Gee said. "They shook hands. And when the Elephant was digging out the back of the church in the dead of the night without our permission—though you and I know he had plenty

permission, in fact he had all the permission he wanted—Sportcoat was
the only one from our congregation he'd let help him. I seen it, too, of
course. Wasn't supposed to. But Deacon told me they was coming, so I
hid behind the choir pew and saw the whole thing. They was together on
it, them two. But after they lifted that little doll thing from the wall, I
never saw 'em together again."

"Then what?"

"Then Sportcoat dropped clean out of sight. And I didn't see him no
more. Ever more. Now you tell me the rest, Sausage, for I done told you
everything I know."

Sausage nodded. "Okay."

And then he told it. Told what he knew and what he'd seen. And when
he was done, Sister Gee stared at him in awe, then reached over her chair
and hugged him where he sat.

"Hot Sausage," she said softly. "You're a man and a half."

The Staten Island Ferry docked lazily into Whitehall Terminal at
South Ferry and the riders clambered aboard. Among them was a dark,
handsome woman in a bowknot bowler cloche hat tied with a ribbon
atop her neatly combed hair who stood at the railing, her hand covering
half her face. Not that Sister Gee thought that she'd be recognized. Who
from the Cause Houses ever took the Staten Island Ferry? Nobody she
knew. But you never know. Half the people in the Cause, she remembered, seemed to work for Transit. If anybody saw her, she'd have a hard
time explaining why she was on the boat. You can't be too careful.

She was dressed for summer pleasure, clad in a cool blue dress, with
azaleas stitched across the side and hips and with a casual open back,
revealing brown, slender arms. She had turned fifty the day before. She

had lived in New York for thirty-three of her fifty years, yet had not once ridden the Staten Island Ferry.

As the ferry pulled away from the dock and arced into New York Harbor, heading due southwest, it offered her a clear view of the redbrick Cause housing projects on one side, and the Statue of Liberty and Staten Island on the other. One side represented the certainty of the past. The other side the uncertainty of the future. She felt suddenly nervous. All she had was an address. And a letter. And a promise. From a newly retired, newly divorced sixty-one-year-old white man who had spent most of his life, like her, cleaning up the mess of others and doing for everyone but himself. *I don't even have a phone number for him*, she thought anxiously. It was just as well, she decided. If she wanted to back out, it would be easy.

As the weather-beaten boat eased across the harbor, she stood on the deck, glancing at the Cause Houses disappearing in the distance, and at the Statue of Liberty floating by on the right, then mused as a seagull rode the wind near her, skimming the water at eye height, gliding effortlessly alongside the deck before pulling away and rising. She watched it pump its wings and move higher into the air, then turn back toward the Cause Houses. Only then did her mind click back over the past week to Sportcoat, and the conversation she'd had with Hot Sausage. As Sausage recounted it in the basement that night, it was as if her own future were being revealed, unrolling itself before her like a carpet, one whose design and weave changed as it stretched out ahead. She recalled every word he said clearly:

When they was building the garden in back of the church, Sport come to me. He said, "Sausage, there's something you ought to know about that Jesus picture out yonder in the back of the church. I got to tell somebody."

I said, "What is it?"

Sport said, "I don't quite know what to call that thing. And I don't wanna know. But whatever it was, it belonged to the Elephant. He found it in that wall and paid the church a whole truckload of money to reclaim it—more money than any Christmas box could hold. So you don't have to worry about Deems no more. Or none of his people. Or the Christmas money. The Elephant done took care of it."

I said, "What about the policeman?"

"What the Elephant got to do with the police? That's his business."

I said, "Sport, I ain't studying the Elephant. I'm talking about the police. They still looking for you."

He said, "Let 'em look. I been talking to Hettie."

I said, "You been drinking?" 'Cause he was always mostly drunk when he talked to Hettie. He said, "No. I don't need to drink to see her, Sausage. I see her clear as day now. We gets along like when we was young. I was a better man back then. I miss drinking. But I like being a man with my wife now. We don't fight now. We talks like the old days."

"What y'all talk about now?"

"Mostly Five Ends. She loves that old church, Sausage. She wants it to grow. She wanted me to fix that garden behind the church and grow moonflowers for the longest time. I married a good woman, Sausage. But I made some bad choices."

"Well, that's all behind you," I said. "You done cleaned up."

"Naw," he said. "I ain't cleaned up. The Lord might not give me redemption, Sausage. I can't stop drinking. I ain't drunk a drop yet, but I wanna drink again. I'm gonna drink again."

And here he pulled a bottle of King Kong out his pocket. The good stuff. Rufus's homemade.

I said, "You don't wanna do that, Sport."

"Yes I do. And I'm gonna. But I'mma tell you this, Sausage. Hettie was so happy when I got to do the garden over behind the church. That was something she always dreamed about. Not for herself. She wanted *them moonflowers and the big garden with all them plants and things behind the church not for herself—but for me. And when I got the church to agree on it, I told her, 'Hettie, them moonflowers is coming soon.'*

"But instead of being happy, she growed sad and said, 'I'mma tell you something, darling, that I shouldn't tell you. When you finish that garden, you won't see me no more.'

"I said, 'What you mean?'

"She said, 'Once it's done. Once them moonflowers is in, I'm gone to glory.' Then before I could kick at it, she said, 'What's gonna become of Pudgy Fingers?'

"I told her, 'Well, Hettie, it approaches my mind like this. What is a woman but her labor and her children? God put us all here to work. You was a Christian gal when I married you. And all the forty years I carried on drinking and making a fool of myself, there wasn't a lazy bone in your body. You raised Pudgy Fingers good. You was strict to yourself and true to me and to Pudgy Fingers, and he will be strong in his life for it.'

"Truth be told, Sausage, Hettie couldn't bear no children. Pudgy Fingers wasn't hers. He come to her before I come to New York. I was still back home in South Carolina. She was in New York by herself waiting for me in Building Nine. She opened the apartment door one morning and seen Pudgy Fingers roaming the hallway. He wasn't but five or six, wandering around, trying to get downstairs to the blind children's bus. She knocked on the lady's door where he lived and the lady said, 'Can you keep him till Monday? I got to go to my brother's in the Bronx.' She ain't seen hide nor hair of that woman since.

"When I come here, Hettie already had herself a child. I never made no bones about it. I loved Pudgy Fingers. I didn't know how he come. For all I know, Pudgy Fingers could've been Hettie's blood from some other man. But I trusted her, and she knowed my heart. So I said to her, 'The Cousins is gonna take Pudgy Fingers. I can't care for him.'

"*She said, 'All right.'*

"*I said, 'Is you worried about him? Is that why you hung about?'*

"*She said, 'I ain't worried about him. I'm worried about you. Because I was born again unto the Word, and that gives me strength. Has you got that?'*

"*I says, 'I has got it. Been born again to the Word for a whole year and then some. I said I was before, but I wasn't. But I am now.'*

"*'Then I'm finished here. I loves you for God's sake, Cuffy Lambkin. Not for my sake. Not for your sake. But for God's sake.' And then she was gone. And I ain't seen her since.*"

He was still holding that bottle of Kong when he told me this, and here he uncorked it. Didn't sip it. Just unscrewed the cap and said, "I wanna drink this whole thing down." Then he said to me, "Walk with me, Sausage."

He was acting funny, so I went on, and we walked down to Vitali Pier, the same spot where he pulled Deems out the harbor. We walked down to the water, and standing on the sand there, I gave him the news on Deems. I said, "Sport, Deems called me. He's doing good in triple-A ball. Said he's gonna make it to the big leagues in about a month or so."

Sportcoat said, "I told you he can still pitch with one ear."

Then he patted me on the back and said, "Look after them moonflowers behind the church for my Hettie." Then he walked into the water. Walked right into the harbor holding that bottle of King Kong. I said, "Wait a minute, Sport, that water's cold." But he went on ahead.

First it come up to his hips, then to his waist, then to the top of his arms, then to his neck. When it got to his neck he turned around to me and said, "Sausage, the water is so warm! It's beautiful."

ACKNOWLEDGMENTS

Thanks to the humble Redeemer who gives us the rain, the snow, and all the things in between.